FALLEN WOMEN

Sue Welfare is the author of *A Few Little Lies*, *Just Desserts*, *Off the Record*, *Moving On Up*, *Guilty Creatures* and many erotic novels. Born on the edge of the Fens, she is perfectly placed to write about the vagaries of life in East Anglia. She was the runner-up in the *Mail on Sunday* novel competition in 1995, and winner of the Wyrd Short Story prize in the same year. She is also a scriptwriter and her comedy 'Write Back Home' was part of the 1999 Channel 4 Sitcom Festival. *Fallen Women* is her sixth mainstream novel.

By the same author

A FEW LITTLE LIES
JUST DESSERTS
OFF THE RECORD
MOVING ON UP
GUILTY CREATURES

SUE WELFARE

Fallen Women

HarperCollins*Publishers*

This novel is entirely a work of fiction.
The names, characters and incidents portrayed in it are the work of the author's imagination. Any resemblance to actual persons, living or dead, events or localities is entirely coincidental.

HarperCollins*Publishers*
77–85 Fulham Palace Road,
Hammersmith, London W6 8JB

www.fireandwater.com

A Paperback Original 2002
1 3 5 7 9 8 6 4 2

Copyright © Sue Welfare 2002

Sue Welfare asserts the moral right to be identified as the author of this work

A catalogue record for this book is available from the British Library

ISBN 0 00 710658 0

Typeset in Sabon by Palimpsest Book Production Limited,
Polmont, Stirlingshire

Printed and bound in Great Britain by
Clays Ltd, St Ives plc

All rights reserved. No part of this publication may be reproduced, stored in a retrieval system, or transmitted, in any form or by any means, electronic, mechanical, photocopying, recording or otherwise, without the prior permission of the publishers.

This book is sold subject to the condition that it shall not, by way of trade or otherwise, be lent, re-sold, hired out or otherwise circulated without the publisher's prior consent in any form of binding or cover other than that in which it in published and without a similar condition including this condition being imposed on the subsequent purchaser.

This book is dedicated with love to all the usual suspects, in particular Susan Opie at HarperCollins, Maggie Phillips at Ed Victor, and Mike Bell in Oakington, but most of all to my mum, who – with her impeccable sense of timing – managed to break her ankle three months after I began writing this book . . . although as yet there are no signs of her trading my father in for a toy boy.

'May you live in interesting times . . .'

An ancient Chinese curse

Chapter 1

'So, how tall do you want this dream man to be then, Chrissie?' Kate scanned down the form on the computer screen, her face blank with concentration.

'You can specify height as well? Jesus,' said Bill, who'd been helping fill in Chrissie's profile. He popped the top on another can of Bud. 'And there's you girls always telling us that size doesn't matter.'

He said it in a sly, sarky way, which made Chrissie and Kate both turn round to give him a withering look. Grinning, he held up his hands in surrender, while Kate's attention moved back to the screen.

'Okay, so what have we got here? *5′ to 5′5″*,

5′6 to 5′8″, 5′9″ to 6′00″,' Kate read, 'small, medium or large. Mr Right comes in several handy sizes apparently.'

'Not in my experience he doesn't,' said Chrissie bitterly. She was half way through her second large glass of Archers and orange juice, the glow from the screen picking out cheekbones that only appeared when she was seriously depressed. Leaning over Kate's shoulder, she peered myopically at the what are you looking for wish list. 'Or over 6′4″? Good God no, I'd have to take a stepladder out with me every time I wanted a snog.'

'Up to about 6′?' suggested Kate.

Chrissie nodded.

'How about hair?'

'I'm getting bored with this,' whined Bill. 'It's Friday, end of the week. I want to – to . . .'

They all looked at him.

'What?' snapped Chrissie. 'Cut loose? Get lucky? Get laid? What did happen to What's-her-name anyway?'

'Oh, meow. Did you ever get that job in personnel?' Bill growled right back.

'No, I'm still flogging frocks; they decided I wasn't fit to be let loose on real people.'

'Hair,' Kate said, attempting to whip them in.

'Is that a straight choice between without or without?' asked Joe, Kate's husband, who had been watching the three of them. He ran his hand back over a crew cut that couldn't quite disguise the fact he hadn't got an awful lot of hair left.

Joe had been idly picking out a riff on the guitar in his lap, making out he wasn't at all interested in what was going on. Since Kate first knew him Joe had constantly doodled with music; living with Joe was like having your very own incidental music, a soundtrack to all life's little ups and downs.

'What is that?' said Bill, taking a pull on the beer. 'Fleetwood?'

Joe shook his head. 'Unfortunately not. It's a jingle for a margarine commercial that I've been working on for one of Kate's clients.' He picked at the strings again, with more determination this time, transforming something sensual and bluesy into a hayseed cartoon sound. 'Why don' all you good folks rush down to y'local convenience store and buy our delicious yella spreadable fat,' he mugged in a southern-style deep-fried accent.

'Yes, very nice. Now about hair,' Kate said impatiently, dragging everyone's attention back to the task in hand.

'Well, I don't know, do I?' Joe snapped peevishly. 'I'm not a bloody expert on cyberdating. What does it for you in the hair department, Chrissie? Bald, a mullet, football boy perm? Early Jon Bon Jovi?'

Kate glared at him, not that it did a lot of good.

It was Friday evening in early summer in a semi-detached off a little side street on the Muswell Hill Road. Kate's home was a mix of tasteful and cosy, cream walls hung with good prints, generous chairs and sofas upholstered in autumnal shades of orange and reds, the whole place dotted with plants. It was a house that encouraged you to lie back and linger

Tonight the whole place was full of the smell of tikka masala and Bombay potatoes. The supper party was a cheering up, new start, relaxing after a long rough week kind of an evening – or at least that was what Kate had in mind when she'd invited them round.

The four of them were sprawled around Kate's office while Kate and Joe's two boys were watching TV and creaming assorted life forms on the Playstation upstairs.

Working from home was a mixed blessing. Under normal circumstances the office was the holy of holies. Kate worked very hard to maintain a boundary where domestic life stopped and earning a living began, in case clients thought it implied a lack of professionalism, but tonight, for Chrissie, who was currently getting over some heartless bastard who had cut her up, made her cry and generally messed her around just three short months after being declared Mr Right, she was prepared to make an exception.

When she wasn't patching up her best friend's love life, Kate freelanced for a PR agency, which always sounded glamorous but these days mostly seemed to involve writing advertorials, press releases and recruitment stuff, helping to co-ordinate the odd trade show, and generally keeping her clients out there in the public eye. It paid well enough, though, and meant that Kate had been able to work from home since the boys were small. There were just about enough jollies, freebies and days out to make sure it was, if not exactly exciting, then at least never truly monotonous.

So, Friday night; Kate was on the computer while in one corner of the office Joe was lolling in her new incredibly uncomfortable ergonomically-designed swivel chair that had cost an arm, a leg and a kidney. Chrissie was grazing through the munchies on top of the filing cabinet, eyes firmly on the screen, while Bill was propped up alongside her drinking a beer.

Chrissie, still mulling over the hair question, scooped up another handful of Bombay mix. 'As long as they haven't got any on the palms of their hands. Oh and no rugs, toupees, knits, weaves, transplants or comb overs either. What's that?' She pointed to a box on the screen. She wasn't wearing her contacts because crying constantly and rubbing her eyes had made them unbearably sore and Chrissie was way too vain to wear her glasses out of the house, which was why Kate was doing the typing.

'It's a sample ad from the RomanticSouls.com web-site. A little taster of the delights on offer once you've signed up. "Adam X is 45, 6′, tanned, with his own business, he likes to work out, eat out, go sailing at weekends and enjoys the theatre. With his own holiday home in the south of France, he's looking for . . ."'

'Whoa,' said Chrissie, grabbing Kate's arm. 'That'll do very nicely, thank you. Can you just wrap him up, pop him in the trolley and lead me to the checkout? Is there a photo? What sizes does he come in?'

It was funny, or at least they all laughed – all except Joe.

Before Chrissie had shown up, and Kate was still fluffing the table and sorting the kids out, Joe had come through into the kitchen carrying the wine and a few more beers for the cooler.

'I wish you'd asked me before inviting people round for the evening,' he said, levering the fridge door open with his foot.

'Oh for God's sake, they're not people, they're Bill and Chrissie.'

'You know what I mean and you know how I feel about Chrissie, Kate. You ought to be doing this computer dating thing when I'm not about. She's, she's – Oh, Christ, I don't know.'

Kate lifted an eyebrow. 'What, Joe? A bad influence? Trouble? A nasty rough girl? Why don't you just spit it out and get it over with?'

'You know that isn't what I mean – she's always in debt, credit cards whacked up to the hilt, one man after another. She ought to get herself sorted out. Those boys of hers must wonder what the hell is going on half the time.'

Kate stared at him in astonishment. 'The boys are great, Joe, you can't say that. She's been through a tough time.'

'Most of which is her own bloody fault.'

Kate paused, about to leap to Chrissie's defence, and then considered for a few seconds before nodding. 'Okay, maybe you're right, sometimes she does weird stuff and makes bad choices – but it doesn't matter, she's still my best friend. Come on, we're really lucky to have friends living so close –'

'It's your country roots showing. Kate, getting on with the neighbours is not what Londoners do best,' Joe sniffed. 'So, you really think you ought to be doing this?' He picked up the sheet of paper where Kate had jotted down lonely hearts web-site addresses from an article she'd been reading in the *Mail*.

'I'm not doing it, Chrissie is.'

Joe pulled his world famous don't-prat-with-me face. 'You know what I'm saying here, Kate. This is like giving a psychopath a loaded gun.'

At which point the doorbell had rung. Kate went to answer it to get away from Joe, and met Bill and Chrissie standing on the door-step, each of them clutching a bottle of New World red.

'You're not trying to fix me up with Bill, are you?' asked Chrissie suspiciously, eyeing him up and down. He was looking particularly tasty in faded jeans and a black tee-shirt, a well-worn leather jacket hooked on one finger slung over his shoulder.

Kate grinned, kissing first one and then the other. 'Good God no, I like you both far too much to inflict you on each other. Come on in. Supper won't be very long. Joe'll get you a drink.' And once he had, they had all crocodiled off to Kate's office.

'Maybe I should order one as well, get something with a little more get up and go?' Kate said, throwing Joe a sideways glance. Since they'd arrived he'd been concentrating on playing his guitar, sulking, picking his nose and drinking his beer. Looking up, he grimaced in a way that implied Kate really shouldn't push her luck.

'Maybe I ought to have a look myself,' he replied.

'Maybe you should,' Kate snapped right back. 'If you think you could find some other mug who'd put up with you.'

Currently they were slap bang in the middle of one of Joe's moody tortured artist phases. It was always the same when he'd got a well-paid bread and butter job that he considered a piss-take of his musical talent. Maybe, Kate thought, staring him out, willing him to look away first, under the circumstances it ought to be bread and margarine. But whichever it was he'd given her the whole soulless artless world speech earlier in the day, the one about how great men have always been paid peanuts for artistry and magic and mega-bucks for popsy-pink cute commercial drek. How he was worth more than this creatively, far more. Not that he was planning to turn the margarine commercial down, obviously.

'Can you pair finish your row later?' snipped Chrissie, 'I'm famished.'

'Just a couple more questions,' said Kate

'Age?'

'Over thirty-five and under fifty, own teeth, and nothing that unscrews at night. I've only ever sent off for books and CDs, till now,' Chrissie paused for effect. 'Do these guys come with a no-quibble guarantee?'

'Only if you haven't tampered with the packaging,' said Kate.

Across the room, Joe snorted.

So they finished off the questions and Kate nipped out to check on the food, while Bill checked the form through.

Joe followed Kate into the kitchen. 'This is

totally and utterly crazy,' he hissed, pulling another beer out of the fridge.

'What is?'

'What do you mean *what is*? She's got crap taste in men. She'll end up picking some nutter and we'll be the ones sitting up till three in the morning listening to her going on and on about how bloody awful he is to her.'

'You mean, I will,' Kate said, pushing a thick tendril of dark red-brown hair back behind her ear. She kept it long even when it was fashionable to have a crop or a bob. Naturally wavy, her hair framed a gamine face and huge grey eyes. Handsome rather than pretty, Kate Harvey had a face that lingered in the mind like a tune. A sensual bluesy tune that is, not popsy-pink cute commercial drek.

'Well, don't say that I didn't warn you. You know what she's like.'

'And exactly what *am* I like, Joe?' Chrissie said, right on cue, as she stepped in to the kitchen behind him.

He spun round, reddening furiously. 'I was just saying you need to be careful with this dating stuff, meet somewhere public. We've all read things in the papers.' He was speaking fast, the words crisp, sharp and defensive. 'Don't give them your address or phone number. You don't know who they are, they could tell you anything. Anything at all.'

Nice recovery, Kate thought, stirring the curry.

Chrissie lifted her eyebrows. 'Oh right, and so real live men, talking face to face, always tell you truth, do they, Joe?' She poured herself another long shot of Archers.

'No. You've got to be careful, that's all I'm saying.'

Chrissie rolled her eyes heavenwards as if to say she didn't need nannying by anyone, least of all Joe. 'How long till we eat?'

'Few more minutes,' replied Kate.

Back in the office, at the computer, Bill was still reading through Chrissie's application form. 'Do they have women on here *as well*?' he asked, as Kate and Chrissie came back in.

'Uhuh, in fact just about anything your pretty little heart desires.' Kate slipped back into the seat as Bill vacated it and moved the cursor across to one of the menus.

'Here you are, darling, no need to go without, what are you looking for? Male, female, bisexual, gay, lesbian, transsexual, transvestite. If you can't find anything you fancy there, Bill, they've also got a category "Other, please specify".'

'Sweet Jesus.'

'You want to knock yourself up a profile while we're here?' Kate asked with a grin

'Not at this precise moment, no.'

'So did we miss anything out?' Kate enquired, glancing back at the screen.

'Do you only want to see profiles of members with photos?'

'Oh yes,' said Chrissie, who was on a roll now. 'I'd like to see who it is I'm going to spend the rest of my life with.'

Joe shot Kate another warning glance.

'I'd take a chance if I were you,' Bill was saying, 'looks aren't everything.'

'Presumably that's something you've learned from personal experience, is it, eh, Bill?' said Chrissie.

'Ouch,' Kate said. 'Saucer of milk, for this table please.'

The two of them enjoyed needling each other so much, although it always seemed to Kate that it wasn't so much a fancying thing, more that they were both desperate to out-clever each other.

When he first moved in to their street she and Chrissie had suspected Bill was gay, for no other good reason than he was tall and dark-haired, softly spoken, nicely preserved and kept himself in good shape. He was a photographer, which kind of fitted the profile.

Then one summer, when the kids were smaller, they had invited loads of friends over for a barbecue and Bill had been included somewhere along the line. Half a dozen drunken musos jamming away at the bottom of the garden, picking out Neil Young tunes under a starry sky, lots of very right-on conversation and barefoot women cradling sleeping babies and wine glasses, rocking buggies, sitting around putting the world to rights; it had been a good evening.

When the party was whittling down to the well-known, well-loved hardcore, Bill had had a huge row with some little blonde bird, who stood in the middle of their patio, hands on hips, letting off a great tirade of abuse.

Seconds later they'd all watched Bill leg it out of Kate's garden like a rat up a drainpipe, bolting back to his house, vaulting over the back fence, although unfortunately the little blonde had seen him go and hared down the alley to cut him off.

'You bastard, Bill, you think you can just screw me and throw me out, do you? I'm not like your other women. You bastard! Talk to me. Talk to me. Bill? Bill? Let me in. Let me in. I love you, I love you,' she had wailed, all bottle blonde hair, sun bed tan and white stilettos. So, definitely not gay then.

Everyone at the party was totally enthralled and shuffled out into the street with their drinks to watch the performance. By this time the little blonde was hammering on the front door and then began throwing handfuls of gravel up at the window. When that didn't work and Bill didn't come out, she'd thrown a milk bottle and then another one, followed by his precious red geraniums in their terracotta pots, until the front steps and the light well outside the basement window were totally covered in shards of glass and bits of pot plant. Then she had thrown something else, something bigger, that had smashed the main pane in the bay window at street level. Finally, exhausted and wild with frustration, she had burst into tears, jumped into her car and driven away, tyres screaming, horn blaring. When Bill came out a few minutes later, looking sheepish and scarlet with embarrassment, everyone had cheered furiously.

Kate glanced up at them; she and Joe and Bill and Chrissie went back a long way. Although

Bill's taste in women didn't appear to have improved significantly over the years.

'Play nicely, you two. Just because Bill's latest woman was gorgeous but – but . . .' Kate winced; it was too late to pull out of the dive where she was headed. 'Is there any way I can put this nicely?'

'No need to pull your punches, she was decorative but deeply, deeply dumb,' said Bill, taking another slurp of his beer. 'Which was a real shame, because she was a lovely girl, but what I'm really looking for is a good woman. No, make that a great woman. Someone you don't have to explain the punch line of every joke to. It was bloody terrifying being with someone so young, she treated me like this heroic super stud, someone who knew everything, in and out of bed, someone who had all the answers.'

'Oh right, that's it, rub it in, why don't you,' said Joe.

'No, I'm serious. It was flattering being picked up by someone like her but not once I realised she was looking for a father figure. It was bloody awful, I totally felt responsible for her,' and then he grinned, 'although actually I thought that Chrissie was talking about me, not my choice in women. Anything else we have to do before we send off Madam's application?'

Kate glanced back at the screen. 'Not really, we just need a pseudonym now.'

'Oh, this should be fun,' said Joe in a voice that suggested it would be anything but.

'How about Vulnerable Venus?' suggested Bill after they'd tried out a few rude ones and a few clever ones and a few downright daft ones.

'Oh please,' said Chrissie, pulling a face.

'It's got a ring to it,' said Joe.

'And you can always change it later,' said Bill. No one liked to say it but Chrissie's laughter was getting more brittle with every passing second, it was time to wrap this up and eat, and so that's what Kate typed in. 'Vulnerable Venus.'

'You don't think this is a bit sad?' Chrissie said, just as Kate was about to press 'send'.

Bill shook his head. It was a very definite gesture. 'It's only another way to meet people. But like Joe said, just be careful. Then again falling in love is about chemistry and attraction and all that stuff you can't possibly define on your shopping list.'

Kate looked at Bill and laughed, 'Ohhhhh, my God, you are such a soft touchy feely bunny, Bill.

It's such a terrible shame you pair don't fancy each other.'

And then Joe snorted, put his guitar down, and said. 'And let's face it, they can't be any worse than the prats and no hopers that's she's picked up before.' Before Chrissie could react, he continued, 'Come on, for Christ's sake, let's go and eat. I'm starving,' and so they did.

Later everyone was sitting around the kitchen table when they heard the phone ring. Nobody moved.

After three more rings it stopped and the hall door swung open.

'Mum, it's for you.'

'Can you take a message?' Kate said to Danny.

'They said it's really urgent.'

It was around nine o'clock, maybe half past. Half way through supper.

'Nothing is that urgent. I'm not planning to deliver anything anywhere for anybody tonight,' Kate said.

'So, you want me to tell them that then, do you?' snapped Danny. It was one of those family face-off moments. Danny looked a lot like Joe but with more hair. Same attitude.

They stared at each other for a few seconds, mother and son, and then Kate got to her feet. Clients really don't like to be told the truth. 'No' does not appear anywhere in the Client-English dictionary. 'Actually I'm working on it at the moment. I'm just waiting for agency to email more copy, more images, more bullshit,' are just fine. Acceptable. 'No' is strictly a no-no.

'Excuse me, folks, won't be a minute. Bloody clients,' Kate mumbled under her breath.

Except that it wasn't a client. It was her little sister, Liz.

'Kate? Is that you?' The words were strung as tight as piano wire.

'Yes, what on earth is the matter? Are you okay?'

'It's Mum. She's had an accident.'

Kate felt an odd nip in her throat and then a great lurch of pain and panic in her solar plexus. 'Oh God, what happened?'

'She's fallen over.'

Momentarily, the pain pulled back like a wave on a beach, replaced by relief, only to return an instant later, gentler but still raw. 'Fallen over?' Kate repeated.

'She was coming home from the shops, I think, and fell down the steps at the back of the house.

God alone knows how long she'd been lying there before they found her. It's terrible. Anything could have happened. I mean, at her age. She's getting frailer; when was the last time you saw her?'

There was a pause, well larded with guilt and any number of unspoken accusations. Kate leant back against the hallstand waiting for the next salvo.

The whole house smelt of curry. It hadn't been a bad evening so far, a couple of beers and half a bottle of wine, and even Joe was starting to thaw out a bit.

'Doesn't bear thinking about, lying there, all on her own,' Liz added, in case there was some possibility Kate might have missed the point. There was an even longer pause and then she said, 'You know what Mum's like, she won't ask for help and she certainly wouldn't ring up to let us know she had a fall. If it hadn't been for her lodger, I probably wouldn't have known at all. I told him that I'd ring you.' Heavy sigh. 'I wonder whether we ought to have a family conference. I've been looking at brochures for sheltered accommodation; if you can find the time to get up to Norfolk, obviously.'

The implication, of course, was that Kate

was so busy in the fast lane that she never spared her poor old widowed mother a second thought. Kate glanced across the hall into the kitchen. The door was ajar, framing the supper party. The fast lane looked remarkably like a coffee advert, all low lights and soft autumnal tones. Behind the low babble of voices someone had put Gabrielle's new CD on the hi-fi as a soundtrack.

'So where did you say Mum is now?'

Bill was busy uncorking another bottle of red. Joe was holding court. Chrissie was looking pale and interesting.

'The local hospital. They're keeping her in for observation overnight. I've been over to see her, obviously. Unfortunately, I couldn't stay because of the girls, but she's in plaster up to the knee and her face looks awful, dreadfully bruised, lots of stitches. It could have been very nasty. I thought you ought to know. I didn't want to say anything to Daniel, didn't want to upset him.'

Kate sighed. Presumably Liz had put on her best telephone voice so that he wouldn't recognise who it was. There was that silence again, the one into which Kate guessed she was meant to leap head first.

In the kitchen, in the lamplight, Joe was rolling a joint while at the same time going on about how bloody terrible the parking was getting. The terrible dichotomy of hippiedom finally meeting middle age.

She stood still for a few moments after hanging up the phone; from upstairs Kate could hear the boys playing – the bass beat of Danny's music overlaid with the ping-ping of a video game from Jake's room. Where would they be when they got phone calls like this? Never mind getting married, giving birth, or signing up for a mortgage, the realisation that your parents don't have the secret of everlasting life is the real ticket into adulthood.

Kate had been totally incredulous when her dad died. How the hell did that happen? How could it happen? He hadn't even been ill. Part of her was still outraged.

Even after five years, the first thought Kate had whenever she thought about her dad was that he couldn't possibly be dead, it had to be a trick of the light, he was there somewhere if only she knew where to look. He was just hiding, maybe in the next room, and along with a residual ache of loss was a terrible nagging frustration that he kept giving her the slip.

* * *

'Who was that then?' Joe asked, topping up his wine. 'Not one of your clients again? You need to get them to ring in office hours, Kate. I've told you before. You've got this cosy cottage industry attitude towards business – boundaries, that's what you need. I've always said that if you want people to consider you as a professional you have to –'

'Actually, it was Liz. My mum's had an accident. I'm just going to go and put a few things in a bag.' For some reason saying it out loud made Kate feel shaky and weepy. 'I ought to go and – well, just go and make sure she's all right. Keep an eye on her. You know.'

'You're not going to drive to Norfolk tonight surely?' Joe asked incredulously. 'Can't it wait until tomorrow?'

'No, I don't think it can, I'm not sure what sort of state she's in – and I've only had one glass of wine. I'll be fine. They're keeping her in overnight. I want to be there for her, sort the place out, pick her up tomorrow. She can hardly come home to an empty house and Liz's girls are still little –'

'Of course you've got to go,' said Chrissie, on

her feet, instantly sober, and instantly supportive. She was always calm in a crisis, or at least always calm in someone else's crisis. 'We can see to everything here, can't we, Joe?'

'Well, yes,' he began more hesitantly. 'But I've got stuff to do; there's some Yank flying in for a breakfast meeting tomorrow. I need to drop in to the office – I did tell you, Kate – it's important.' And then he looked at her. 'And you said you'd be able to pick my suit up from the cleaners –' He blew out his lips and shook his head as if all this had nothing to do with him. 'And what about the boys?'

Kate stared at him.

Joe had polished off several glasses of Merlot. He had a patch of high colour on each cheek, like a Punch and Judy rouge spot, a little flush that only ever appeared in two situations: when he was drunk or in the first throes of post-orgasmic bliss; not something there had been a lot of just recently.

She felt a flurry of annoyance; she needed him to help her and here he was busy passing the buck before it had even landed. Joe returned the stare, obviously expecting her to come up with something that didn't include him the equation.

Kate looked away first. In lots of ways Joe was a really good man. But recently they had been stumbling through the raw bickering no-man's-land of some itch or other.

Forty-two and Joe was only just coming to terms with the fact he was never going to be Sting, that writing the odd jingle and helping out with the sound and light systems for corporate dos was probably the closest he was going to get to the big time or the bright lights of Wembley Arena, and that he was unlikely to be asked to guest at an open air concert in Hyde Park because some roadie had spotted him mingling with the hoi polloi, trying to blend in.

It was Kate who found a lot of Joe's work – the radio jingles, anyway – and who'd introduced him to the guy who ran the light and sound company. They'd met when she was doing a trade show at the NEC in Birmingham and got talking. He had needed someone who knew something about sound, they had needed the money. How was it Kate could feel guilty about that? Because unfortunately somewhere down the line it had turned from a good thing into her fault; Kate felt as if she'd stolen something from Joe.

At the moment things between them were

tense for no particular reason that she could define. But they'd been there before and would probably be there again. Kate had no doubt they'd sort it out; on the whole they were good together.

'Danny is nearly fifteen, for God's sake, he should be able to get himself and Jake up and stay out of trouble till you get home,' Kate said coolly.

Joe didn't look convinced. 'I've got no idea what time I'll be back.'

Across the table, Chrissie shook her head. 'Oh please, Joe. This is an emergency. Jake and Danny can come round to mine. Robbie's at home tonight. They'll be fine. Now is there anything else you need?'

The question was aimed squarely at Kate but Joe was in like Flynn. 'Any chance you can pick my suit up from the cleaner's tomorrow?'

It didn't take very long or very much to unravel what remained of the evening. Within half an hour Kate had packed a bag and sorted out Joe and the kids.

Chrissie, arms crossed over her chest, gathered a cardigan up around her shoulders. She leant in through the driver's side window to say her goodbyes. 'Now don't you go talking to any strange men, and give me a ring as soon as you get to your mum's. And don't worry, there's nothing here that we can't handle between us.'

'Thanks, Chrissie. What on earth would I do without you?'

'Christ only knows. House train Joe maybe?'

Kate laughed. 'Give me a break. I haven't got that many years left.'

Chapter 2

M25, M11, A10: Kate's parents' house was in Denham, a small Norfolk market town a few miles inland from King's Lynn, set on a rise of land high above the black rolling Fens. She could make it home in around two and a half hours, always assuming there were no major hold ups.

Once she was away from familiar streets, Kate stretched and settled herself in for the long haul home. The night seemed unnaturally dark outside the tunnel of lights. It was hard not to yawn. Hard not to let her mind wander. Resisting the temptation to rub her eyes, Kate tried to relax her grip on the steering wheel and settled into the drive.

Less than an hour up the road and already her

neck ached with tension and tiredness and an odd nagging fear. Taillights like demon eyes headed away from her into the dark. Kate loathed driving on motorways, nervous of getting so caught up and so tangled in the system that she'd never be able to find her way out again. Which was one of the reasons she told herself, pulling up hard behind some moron with a death wish, why she didn't get home as often as she would like, why she hadn't been to see her mum in, in – in – was it months or was it closer to a year? Surely it couldn't be that long?

Kate pulled a face, trying to add up the time. Work had been crazy, which had been good, they could certainly use the money. The boys had both had flu at Christmas so they hadn't gone home then, they stayed in front of the TV, sniffing, sleeping and drinking Lemsips, but Kate and her mum had talked a lot on the phone. New Year's Eve, Kate and Joe had gone to a party in a flat overlooking the Thames with some of the guys Kate freelanced for while Chrissie had kept an eye on the boys. But they always rang each other once a week, most weeks, Kate's conscience protested. And besides Mum liked her independence; Kate always felt that Maggie – her mum – was busy making a new life for herself. That was it. Her own life. She'd raised her kids and moved on, got herself a part-time job, always sounded really chirpy on the phone. They loved each other but that was no reason to live in each other's pockets, no reason at all.

Kate squared she shoulders as her argument steadily backed itself up. Re-run over and over again in her head it still sounded like a series of pathetically weak excuses.

The traffic in front slowed to a bad-tempered unpredictable crawl and Kate forgot just how long it was since she had been to see Maggie and concentrated instead on trying to stay focused and not let sleep seduce her.

It wasn't that her mum ever complained, but Liz did. Frequently. Liz, who was married to Peter who did something incomprehensible in the City and who always did as he was told. Good old Liz, with her three perfect little girls, lived in Norwich, about an hour's drive away from Denham.

Kate peeled a mint out of the packet on the dashboard. The accusatory voice in her head, the one that berated her for not caring, not ringing or visiting often enough, was hardly the best travelling companion she could have wished for. It sounded an awful lot like her sister on a bad day.

Kate crunched the mint into gravel, tuned in to Radio 4, and let it haul her through the long dark miles while the voice in her head carried on moaning about the play, the book, the news and the price of fish.

Just over two hours later Kate indicated and pulled off the A10 and into Denham. Driving up towards Church Hill, slowing the car to a crawl, she looked out for the landmarks, etched deep on the retina of an older eye. The family house was up in the good end of town, up the long slow rise from the town centre, near the high school and the church. It was a big rambling Edwardian semi, faced with dark Norfolk carrstone and an over-abundance of Virginia creeper.

Kate vaguely remembered her parents struggling to make the move up there – it was a big step up in the world for them, marking some promotion that now, Kate realised, had changed their lives for ever, taking her dad off the shop floor and into management. She remembered the huge battered sofas in the big sitting room covered with Indian throws, and her dad out in the conservatory, rubbing down a table that her mother had found in an auction, remembered the whole make do and mend ethic of people trying to do better for themselves.

Glancing up at the handsome old house, Kate wondered whether Liz was right, whether the time had come to talk about selling up and getting something smaller. It was crazy keeping such a big house for just one person, particularly a person who couldn't manage. She shivered; had it come to that already? Surely it hadn't come to that yet?

Pulling into the drive, Kate struggled with the perpetual sense of *déjà vu* that inevitably preceded her arrival. Was she late? Would they still be waiting up for her? Had she forgotten to do or pick up something important? The sensation was fleeting but always left a peculiar bittersweet aftertaste.

Her car crunched over the gravel. Beyond the arc of the headlights the house was in total darkness. It wasn't that late, a little before midnight. Here and there in the borders the magnolias glowed creamy white in the moonlight. Kate parked up under the laburnums. Which were poisonous. How many times had Dad told Liz and Kate that? The whole tree, every leaf, every single bud, every last flower just waiting to strike you down dead.

Giving the laburnum a wide berth she locked the car and stretched, feeling the blood creeping back through her body. The night was warm and heavy with the perfume of honeysuckle and night scented stock. Kate drank it all in. On the surface it seemed that nothing had changed; the spare key was there, tucked under the stone cat by the conservatory door where it had been ever since she could remember.

Inside the air was cool and still and smelt of home.

Tick-tick-tick, the hall clock welcomed Kate in. She shut the door and finally felt the tension in her stomach easing. Home. Dropping her bag onto the chest by the hallstand, every sense was suffused by wave after wave of compassion and nostalgia. It seemed like a very long time since Kate had been there. Certainly a long time since she'd caught the house this unguarded, undefended by the bright voices of her mother or her sister and the kids. Pulling off her coat, Kate walked across the lobby and switched on the kitchen light.

'Who the fuck is that?' barked a male voice.

Stunned, Kate froze and looked up as the landing light snapped on. Peering over the handrail was a figure, a half-naked man, and behind him, leaning heavily against the doorframe and blinking down into the semi-darkness was her mother, Maggie.

'I've rung the police,' snapped Maggie, in a tough no-nonsense don't mess with me kind of voice. 'They're already on their way. Stay exactly where you are and don't do anything stupid.'

'Mum?'

There was a peculiar little silence, and then Maggie said, 'Kate, is that you? What the hell are you doing here?'

Which wasn't exactly the sort of welcome Kate had expected.

'Liz rang. She said you'd had an accident – she said . . .' The words curled up and died in Kate's throat. Her little sister, Liz, for whom every headache was a brain tumour, every chest pain a heart attack. It suddenly occurred to Kate that maybe it would have been a good idea to have rung the hospital and check on exactly how Maggie was and where she was before hurtling up to Norfolk.

Not that that explained everything.

As her eyes adjusted to the gloom, Kate could see the man on the landing more clearly. He was naked except for a small pair of very white pants. They were tight high-cut cotton pants that did very little to cover his nakedness – rather they enhanced it. Behind him Maggie was wearing a plaster cast to the knee, a dark silky chemise and not a lot else.

Her mother.

Kate took a deep breath and made every effort to rekindle her explanation. 'Liz said you'd fallen down and broken your ankle and that you were all on your own and had got stitches and – and that she couldn't stay here with you because of the girls. And . . .' Those weren't necessarily the things Kate really wanted to say, so she stopped. 'What exactly is going on, Mum, and who the hell is that?'

Maggie didn't miss a beat.

'Kate, I'd like you to meet Guy, Guy, this is my eldest daughter, Kate.'

Guy nodded. 'Hi, I've heard a lot about you,' he said, as if this was the most natural thing in the world, and as he spoke pulled a bath sheet off the banister and wrapped it tight around his waist. He had no hips to speak of; a belly like the underside of a turtle, broad shoulders, what could surely only be a sun bed tan, but no hips. Kate felt that the towel was more to cover her embarrassment than his.

'I'll go and put the kettle on, Mags-baby, go

and get yourself back into bed. Would you like some tea, Kate?'

'Er, yes, please,' she mumbled.

He had to pass Kate on the stairs. He loped. He smelt of something trendy and couldn't be more than thirty-five if he was a day. And he had been in bed with her mother. Her mother. Kate was very tempted to slap him.

'Come on up,' said Maggie, without a shred of the self consciousness or the shame Kate felt she surely ought to be feeling. 'Why didn't you ring to let me know you were coming?'

Making every effort to compose herself, Kate said, 'Because Liz told me that you were still in hospital. Did you really ring the police?'

Maggie laughed. 'No, no, of course not. You were making such a lot of noise that Guy thought if you were a burglar you were probably thick and might be taken in if we bluffed it out.' She eased herself back into the bedroom, wincing with every step, and then lowered herself down very gently onto the side of her big feather bed. 'There's no way I could have stayed in hospital, it would have driven me crazy, and Guy was here, so they let me come home.' As she spoke Maggie set about rolling a cigarette.

'I thought you told me you'd given up.'

Maggie looked up at her. 'Give me a break, Kate.'

Caught in the lamplight Kate could see that Liz hadn't been exaggerating about the damage; one side of Maggie's face was shiny, taut and navy blue with great claret and gold highlights, a row of stitches adding a macabre Frankensteinesque codicil to the fine skin above her eyebrow.

For the briefest of instants Kate caught a glimpse of the woman her mother really was. Maggie Sutherland was small framed and attractive in a handsome rather than pretty way; she had good bones and her hair, styled into a shaggy chin length *coupe savage* and coloured to a warm glossy chestnut, was thick and wavy and framed a strong jaw line. It was a face shaped by time rather than worn down by it. She watched Kate watching her, ran her tongue along the sticky edge of the cigarette paper and at the same time lifted one perfectly plucked eyebrow.

'Well?' she said, picking up the lighter from beside the bed.

'You shouldn't smoke.'

'I don't, at least not very much these days. And?'

'What happened – and who is that?' Kate

indicated the stairwell with a flick of the head, unsure what she wanted to ask first, unsure whether she really wanted to hear the answers.

'Oh, come on, Kate,' said Maggie, through a rolling boil of cigarette smoke. 'What do you call them when you're over fifteen? His name is Guy Morrison and he's my lover, my companion, and yes, before you ask, he is living here. He's letting his place while we see if this works out. Kind of a trial run.'

Kate felt her jaw dropping but was powerless to stop it.

'So that's who Guy is.' Maggie stopped talking and concentrated on flinching as she lifted her leg, trying to find a comfortable spot on the bed.

Kate felt her colour rising. 'Liz told me that you were seeing someone, but I thought – well, you know I was thinking more whist drives, grey hair and driving gloves. Days out in the country with a picnic and a corgi – but he's, he's –'

Kate was squirming now. What exactly was it she was trying to say and why was she trying to say it? That Guy was way too sexy? Too young, far, far too good-looking. God, she would have been pleased these days if someone like Guy gave her a second glance, let alone clambered into her bed. Kate glanced back over her shoulder thinking about the way Guy had looked on the stairs; she'd have to make love with the light off and perpetually hold her stomach in. Kate tried to shift the image, while making a sterling effort to nip that particular train of thought in the bud.

Side-stepping what Guy might or might not be, Maggie continued, 'You and I don't see much of each other, Kate. We've both got busy lives – it's not always easy to explain things over the phone.' In contrast to her earlier conversation with Liz it was a statement with not the barest hint of accusation in it. 'And anyway I assumed you knew. Liz met Guy when she was here at Christmas.'

Oh, Liz would have met him, thought Kate ruefully. How was it Liz knew all about her mother's fancy man and why hadn't she rung and told Kate? How could she have kept something like that to herself; Maggie was living with the man for God's sake.

But her mum was still talking and still looking at her. 'Who really knows how serious these things are going to be and, Kate,' she said, taking a long pull on the roll-up, 'when we get right down to it it isn't really any of your business who I'm sleeping with, is it?'

Kate flinched and then blushed. 'But you fell over,' she said, in a tone that implied that somehow the two events were quite obviously linked.

'Which was my own fault, which was why I didn't ring. Guy and I went out to lunch – it was Taz's birthday – I don't think you've met Taz. She works in the bookshop with me? Anyway, there's a great new brasserie opened in the high street. They do the most fantastic food and cocktails and we all got there about twelve and didn't leave until three and I –'

'Came back here, pissed as a whippet, tripped over her handbag and fell down the steps round the back. Don't be taken in by all this poor me stuff,' Guy said warmly. 'Besides nursing those bruises she's also got a stonking great hangover. Do you take sugar?'

Kate hadn't heard him coming back up the stairs. She looked up into his big brown eyes and wished she hadn't. Guy was truly gorgeous. Worse still, he loved her mother.

He grinned. 'Actually you look as if you could do with something a bit stronger. I know it must be a bit of a shock but she's going to be fine. Do you fancy a drop of brandy, there's some in the kitchen?'

'No, thank you. Tea, no sugar, will be fine,'

Kate managed in a clipped tone, realising that she sounded uncannily like Liz.

'Okay.' He vanished back downstairs and Kate turned her attention back to her mother.

'Embarrassing, isn't it?' laughed Maggie

She could say that again, thought Kate, except Kate was almost certain that she and Maggie weren't talking about the same thing.

'I lay there for God knows how long. Guy had gone back to work. When I finally managed to get my act together I rang him on my mobile.'

'Liz didn't say anything about you being drunk.'

Maggie snorted. 'Good God, you think Guy told her?'

Kate looked Maggie up and down, sitting there in her chemise, hair all mussed up, smoking a roll-up, and suddenly – amongst all the other emotions – was really proud of her.

'Liz told me she thought it was a very good idea your mum taking me in,' said Guy, returning with a tray. He sounded mischievous rather than cruel. 'Someone to keep an eye on her, it put Liz's mind at rest knowing that your mum wouldn't be on her own at nights.'

This time Maggie giggled.

It was not the kind of giggle you would naturally associate with your mother.

'It's a damned good thing it happened today and not next week,' Guy was saying. 'I was supposed to be going to Germany first thing Monday morning.'

'And you still will be. Stop worrying, I'll be perfectly all right, I've already told you,' Maggie said. 'I can manage.' She couldn't, it was quite obvious, but that didn't stop her sounding certain.

Guy looked at her. 'Sometimes I think that Liz is right, you are such a stubborn cow. I'm going to cancel and that's final.'

'Don't be silly. It's only for a few days. I can sleep downstairs if you help me make the bed up in the sitting room. It'll be fine. I can use the loo downstairs and the shower.'

Kate took the mug Guy offered her and tried not to concentrate on their bickering or ogle Guy's exquisite body as he clambered back into bed, very gently lifting Maggie's foot as he did so that she could settle back amongst a great heap of pillows. It occurred to Kate that he had probably carried her upstairs too. Damn him.

Guy pulled the duvet up around them both. He had a tattoo, a dark blue Celtic knot that wrapped itself around his suntanned biceps. Kate looked away because her mouth had started to water and because she knew she was staring.

This was not the natural order of things. Watching them in bed together, Kate had the same kind of feeling in her belly as she had had when she'd found a pile of girlie magazines under Danny's mattress. It had come as a shock to realise her son might be sexually active; to discover her mother was was totally beyond comprehension.

Maggie was still talking. 'There are clean sheets in the airing cupboard, sweetheart. You can have your old room. Sorry that I'm not more talkative, but I've had a lot of painkillers tonight and I feel really spacey.'

Really spacey? *Really spacey*? What sort of expression was that for your mother to use?

'It's all right, you really ought to try and get some sleep,' Kate said briskly, gathering her things and her thoughts together. 'I was planning to stay overnight and then come and collect you tomorrow from the hospital. Maybe hang around if you needed help –' the words were coming out a touch too jauntily. 'But I can see that you're in very good hands. No need for me to stay.'

'Do you want me to help you sort the bed out?' asked Guy. 'I've put your bag in your room.' He made as if to get up again.

'No, no. I'll be fine, really I – thanks,' she said waving him back down. 'I'll take my tea into the bedroom. Been a long drive –' Kate yawned theatrically. 'It was Liz. You know what she's like. I wouldn't have come if she hadn't . . . I mean, and there's Guy, I didn't know about – well, I just thought . . .' the words jammed up in her throat.

Maggie smiled. 'I'm really glad you did come, Kate.' Spacey or not, her voice was soft and full of love. 'Can you stay a day or two? It would be so good to catch up. It seems like ages since we've talked, I want to hear all your news. How are the boys? How's work going? And Joe? I've missed you, sweet pea.'

Kate looked from one face to the other and felt tears prickling up all hot and raw behind her eyes, which was all the more disturbing because it was the last thing she had expected. And then she nodded, 'Maybe, probably, possibly.' As she got to the door Kate realised she'd promised to ring Chrissie. The question was what the hell was she going to say to her?

Chapter 3

'Are you okay?' said Guy, kissing Maggie gently on the forehead, careful to avoid the bruises and stitches.

She sighed, welcoming his touch. 'Better now that Kate's here.'

He stroked her hair back off her face. 'Good. I'm sorry that she had to find out about us like this.'

Maggie jiggled to try and get herself comfortable. Despite the painkillers, she couldn't find an easy spot to settle. 'I'm not ashamed of you, Guy – I love you – and the last thing I want is to hide you away from my kids, but I needed to be sure before I told them.'

He grinned. 'And you're not?'

She snorted and shook her head. 'It's all academic now, isn't it? I suppose even though they're grown up, I'm still protecting them. But honestly, I'm glad Kate knows and I'm sure it'll be fine. Really. Just give it a bit of time.'

'Is there anything I can do to make it easier? I'd really like Kate to like me.'

Maggie grinned and settled her head down on his shoulder. 'I don't know – the usual stuff. Take her to the park, buy her a pony.'

Kate phoned home because she'd said she would. She rang Chrissie's house first and when no one answered, she hung up before the machine cut in and rang her house instead.

'Got there okay, then?' Joe asked. He had always had a natural talent for stating the obvious.

'Yep, I'm fine thanks, safely tucked up in bed with a nice mug of tea,' Kate said with a heartiness she most certainly didn't feel.

'Right. Chrissie's still here, we're just finishing off the last of the Baileys. Do you want to talk to her?'

'I'm packing the dishwasher,' Chrissie said, when Joe handed her the phone. Joe sounded pissed, Chrissie didn't, and God only knows where Bill had got to.

'Mum's okay,' Kate said. 'Bit bruised and battered.'

'You don't sound too good either.'

'It seemed to take hours to get up here and to be honest I was knackered before I left,' Kate hedged.

'So have you rung the hospital?'

'No need to. When I let myself in Mum was already here.'

'Bloody hell, that's awful. I didn't think they'd discharge her if she hadn't got anyone there to look after her.'

'They didn't – she has. His name's Guy.'

'A man? Her neighbour?'

'Her boyfriend.'

'Wow! You didn't tell me she was seeing someone.'

'Because I didn't know and no, it's not "wow",' snapped Kate. 'He's the same age as I am. Younger probably – with a tattoo.' And then Kate told Chrissie all about meeting Guy, very quietly and very quickly, because she wasn't sure if her voice would carry and if Mum and Guy could hear her from their room.

Curled up, warm and whispering in the gloom,

her clothes neatly folded on the ottoman at the foot of the bed, wrapped in a duvet, Kate felt like a kid all over again, wondering if Mum and Dad could hear the radio. It was a disturbing sensation, sitting there in her old bed, staring at the same four walls that had surrounded her for the best part of her childhood.

Although at least her parents had had the decency to decorate the room since the whole Adam Ant, Duran Duran, New Romantic phase, thought Kate ruefully. It was cream now with a navy blue picture rail, and curtains and bed-clothes to match, her shabby teenage skip-chic replaced by handsome reclaimed pine furniture. A large mirror hung on the wall where her giant poster of Spandau Ballet once was, although screwing her eyes up, Kate could just make out the heart shape on the back of the door, carved into the soft wood with a dead biro, where she'd pledged her undying love for Tony Hadley, Spandau's tall dark lead singer, the one with the floppy hair. It took her a moment or two to realise she'd stopped talking and at the far end of the ether Chrissie was still listening.

'So, I've decided to come home tomorrow.'

'Don't be ridiculous,' Chrissie snorted. 'You've only just got there. Bill, Joe and the boys are planning a pizza and video fest tomorrow night. Blood, gore and lashings of extra pepperoni. It'll be like the Mutiny on the Bounty here if you come back before Monday at the earliest. Besides you've already said your mum wants you to stay. I think you ought to – everything is going just fine here. What's she going to do next week when this guy Guy isn't around?'

It wasn't the question Kate particularly wanted to answer.

'I don't know, I haven't even thought about it. I wish you could've seen him. He's got a tan and works out. You don't get a six pack by accident, and he's in bed with my mother, a woman whose idea of exercise and a good time used to be throwing a stick for the family Labrador.'

Kate took a long pull on her tea.

'My mother is sleeping with a man whose body is in better shape than any man I've ever been out with. A Chippendale is screwing my mother. My mother is *having sex*, for God's sake.'

Wisely, Chrissie said nothing, so Kate continued in a hoarse whisper, 'He calls her "Mags-baby". There is just no way I can stay here with the pair of them, Chrissie. It's sickening. He was dotting about making tea in his knickers. I'm going to tell them that I've spoken to you and that you need me to get back for the boys, and besides that I've got work to do – clients that I can't possibly let down.'

'Right.' Chrissie didn't sound convinced.

'Chrissie, I've just driven up here, worried sick about what I'm going to find, all set to play Florence Nightingale, only to discover that when I wasn't looking my mother transmogrified into Mrs Robinson. And I can't believe that this guy Guy has moved in here with her without her saying so much as a word to either me or Liz.'

'I read somewhere that the original Mrs Robinson was only about thirty-seven or thirty-eight.'

'I'm thirty-eight,' Kate hissed, 'and I'll tell you now I am certainly not Mrs Robinson material. My mother is fifty-eight. She should be making jam and doing yoga, going to evening classes to expand her mind not be, not be –'

'In bed with some good-looking guy and his suntanned six pack?' said Chrissie.

'Exactly,' hissed Kate.

Chrissie sighed. 'Look. If it wasn't your mother and I wasn't meant to say how disgusted and horrified I am, which I obviously I am, I'd cheer and so would you. If you could just see beyond this whole mother daughter thing, you'd go out and buy a roll of bunting and a couple of bottles of fizzy pink plonk, celebrating the breaking down of sexual mores and God knows how many years of indoctrination and sexual repression.'

There was a long pause and then Kate said, 'You've been reading *Cosmo* again, haven't you?'

'What are you going to do?' asked Chrissie.

'Do? What do you mean, do?'

'While Guy is away in Germany?'

'He's already said he's going to cancel his trip.'

'And you think she'll let him?'

'All right, all right – but I do have work to sort out and I can hardly leave the boys there with you all week, it's not fair.'

'Don't worry, Joe and I will manage between us and Bill offered to lend a hand if the going gets tough. We'll be fine. Honest. I'd stay where you are, at least over the weekend until you see how they manage. Oh and Kate –'

'Yes?'

'Enjoy the view.'

Kate snorted and as she said her goodbyes made up her mind to go home the next morning, whatever Chrissie said and come back again on Monday, if and when Guy flew off to wherever it was he was going.

While it was true nobody was going to die if Kate took the week off, all the projects she was working on did have a deadline. Kate was justifiably proud of her reputation for delivering on time, even – in the long distant past – if it meant composing copy while breast-feeding. Her job had paid the lion's share of bills for years. If she really was going to be away for a few days, Kate ought to sort work out. All of which could have been done at her mum's if she'd had the nous to pack the laptop. Once she had sorted out the justification for going home Kate began to relax.

As she switched off the bedroom light and settled down, she heard the bed squeaking across the hallway, which very briefly conjured up an image which was just too horrible to contemplate.

'Are you certain that you have to go home? It seems such a pity.' Maggie was sitting up in bed, flanked by a set of crutches, drinking tea. In the daylight her bruises looked more painful, bright navy in contrast to her pallor and so violent that Kate couldn't look at them directly without wincing. It was around ten the next morning, not that it really mattered what time Kate left for home; the boys were staying with Chrissie, and Joe would be off schmoozing some Yank but it felt like the right time to leave.

'I'll try and get back next week. I need to sort my client list out and make arrangements for the kids.'

Maggie painted on what passed for a brave smile. 'Okay, if you're sure. Thanks for coming to the rescue, darling. It was so nice to see you. Ring me when you get back.'

Kate kissed her goodbye and then jogged down the stairs, fighting with her guilt, not protesting when Guy offered to carry her bag out to the car.

At the car, to her surprise, he gave her a hug. 'It's been great to meet you at last, Kate, I've heard a lot about you. It's a real shame you couldn't stay longer, but don't worry I'll take good care of your mum.' He kissed her on the cheek. 'Safe journey home.'

Kate nodded. It was sickening, Guy was so genuinely nice and pleasant that Kate was ashamed of herself for feeling so – so what? So jealous? So put out, so aggrieved? Angry? Disgusted, excluded? What on earth was it that was churning away in the bottom of her belly? Some odd out-of-the-cradle, pseudo-sibling rivalry? Was she jealous of Maggie or jealous of Guy? It was all far too Freudian to contemplate; she would glad to be safe in the car and on her way home.

Breakfast had been almost more than Kate could bear. Guy loping round in the kitchen wrapped up in a white towelling robe, all buffed and puffed and pink from the shower, making up a tray for Maggie, with *a bunch of daisies on it*. He was way too gentle and funny. Tender, warm. There had to be a catch, surely to God no one could be that good? What must it be like to be loved by someone who did all that sort of thing and really meant it?

'Don't beat yourself up if you can't make it next week,' he was saying, as she buckled up her seat belt. 'It'll be okay, we'll manage, don't worry.' He was standing alongside the car. 'Viv next door has already said she'll keep on eye on Maggie and help her out if I can't reschedule the Germany trip. I should know later today –'

Kate reversed out onto the road, managing to give Guy a smile and a perfunctory wave, wondering how her conscience would feel if she decided not to come back at all, ever. Her mind shuffled and reshuffled the possible permutations. Maybe Guy would be able to reorganise the trip. Maybe if she just went back for a day or two, arrive Monday and go home Wednesday morning. Maybe by the time she got home Kate would have worked out why she felt so bloody strange about the whole setup.

The drive home wasn't bad and as Kate turned off the main drag into Windsor Street it looked as though the houses had been waiting for her, all stretched out, basking in the summer sun, Bill's red geraniums glowing like a beacon on his windowsill. It felt really good to be back. It was hard to believe she had only been away overnight.

Joe's car was still parked in the road outside their house, wedged tightly between a VW and a dark purple Ka. Kate sighed; back to reality, she thought, with something less than a wry smile. Silly bugger had probably been so drunk the night before that he hadn't dared drive in to his meeting. Interesting combination, a raging hangover and the Underground.

Kate found a space to park a little way up the road and as she walked back a peculiar thought appeared in her head. It sprang from nowhere, was totally irrational, and Kate had absolutely no idea what triggered it, but as soon it did, she tried very hard to unthink it. It was ridiculous and yet some part of her was absolutely certain that when she got in Joe and Chrissie would be together in her house.

And the even more ridiculous thing was that she was right.

Kate pushed opened the back door and there was Chrissie, as bold as brass, sitting at the kitchen table, all wrapped up in Kate's favourite pale blue bathrobe, drinking coffee with Joe. Her best friend and her husband.

It was around about lunchtime; the boys were nowhere in sight. Joe was sitting at the other side of the table, cradling a mug. He was dressed in an old tee-shirt and boxer shorts and hadn't shaved. Kate knew, without a shadow of a doubt, that there was no innocent explanation for what she was looking at; Joe and Chrissie had slept together. More than that, she knew with the same degree of certainty, that they had done it before. Several times, lots and lots of times, enough times so they had stopped counting because they were in the kind of comfort zone that only comes with familiarity.

For an instant Kate felt as if she was the one on the outside, an intruder, a stranger, excluded, and felt almost guilty for barging in on the pair of them.

As fast as the thoughts bubbled up, Kate struggled to suppress them; it was crazy even though she knew she was right. In those few seconds which seemed to last forever it felt as if someone was squeezing every last breath of air out of her lungs and she was wading towards them through mud and treacle.

There had to be some other explanation, except of course that there wasn't. Instead there was a moment when Joe and Chrissie and Kate all looked at one another and everyone knew and everyone caught some glimpse of the enormity of what was going on and what had been discovered, and just as quickly all that knowing vanished beneath the waves. Chrissie papered a very convincing smile on over a look of complete surprise and shock, and said, 'Hi Kate, how was the drive? I've just made a cup of coffee, do you want one?'

Which was a preposterous thing to say but at least it was quick. Kate stared at her.

Joe peered across the table, looking for all the world as if someone had hit him over the head with a baseball bat. His mouth had dropped open, his eyes bulged wide.

'We weren't expecting you back today,' he said. She could always rely on Joe to state the obvious. And then he added, almost as an afterthought, 'It isn't what you think.'

At least Chrissie had the decency to blush.

'And what might that be?' Kate said, very slowly, looking first at one and then the other, while something inside her contracted so hard that Kate thought there was a good chance that she might be sick.

And then Joe laughed. It might have been embarrassment, or nerves or self-consciousness, Kate had no idea at all. But whatever it was the sound broke through into the stunned place where she was.

'I think you'd better go home now, Chrissie,' Kate said, mainly because she had no idea what else to say. For one awful moment Kate thought there was a chance that Chrissie might protest or say something smart, but she thought better of it, pulled Kate's bathrobe tighter around her chest and headed off into the hall.

Kate looked around the kitchen, her home, which now seemed and felt like an alien place, feeling slightly faint and longing to sit down.

Unfortunately the most obvious chair was the one Chrissie had just vacated. The others were either side of Joe and she had no desire whatsoever to sit next to him. So she stood in silence, one hand on the sink to keep her balance, and stared out into the garden while Chrissie went upstairs and got dressed. The clock ticked. The tap dripped and she could feel Joe looking at her with those big doleful eyes of his. It felt like months before Chrissie finally came tap-tap-tapping down the stairs in her supper party clothes, opened the front door and let herself out.

And then, as if the backdraft from the door closing ignited the fire that had been the smouldering inside her, Kate turned to Joe.

'So?' she said in voice that would have cut through sheet steel.

Part of her was tempted to let the fire inside her roar. Sweep the remains of his adulterous little brunch away with a single swipe of an angry arm, maybe throw the cups across the room, punch his stupid, stupid lights out, but Kate reined the feelings all in because even in the icy cold heart of her, Kate knew that if anyone was going to storm out indignantly it would most probably be Joe and she had no desire to be left with the chaos to clear up after the maelstrom had passed. And so she looked at him, long and hard, trying to see all those things she had missed before.

'I'm sorry, Kate,' he said. He spoke in a throwaway, bumped into someone on the pavement kind of voice. It was a ludicrous thing to say.

'Sorry for screwing my best friend or sorry that you got caught? Which is it?' she asked icily. 'How long has this been going on, Joe?'

Along with every other thought clamouring around inside Kate's head was this crazy fury that somehow Joe had managed to reduce their life to an excerpt from a daytime soap opera.

'Kate, please,' he said in a strangled tangled voice. 'Don't do this. I'm really sorry. Chrissie and I were just saying that we should never have let it happen.'

'Oh well, that's really big of you,' Kate snapped back, her voice dripping with sarcasm.

'We were drunk. It was an accident.'

'An accident? What do you mean, an accident? Accidents involve cars, and crockery and wet floors, Joe. What did she do, trip up and impale herself on you?'

He didn't say a word, but then again what was there to say?

'How many accidents have you and Chrissie had over the years, Joe? How many?' Inside Kate was churning. She was struggling not to lose it, not to sound too angry or hurt because she wanted to know the answers. Wanted to know before she dissolved into the raw emotions. There were just too many things going around inside her head to decide which one was driving, and so her voice came out flat and cold and cruel.

'Kate, please don't do this.'

'Don't do what? Ask for answers? Want to know how long my best friend and my husband have been getting it on behind my back. How long has it been, Joe? How long?' Kate could hear the fury rumble, developing in her ears and in her voice like a summer storm. She couldn't remember a time when she had felt so much, so fiercely.

'Look, Kate, I've already said I'm sorry; we didn't mean to.'

'What the fuck do you mean you didn't mean to? What did it do, jump up and take you both by surprise? It's not like you're magnetic or anything. How long, Joe?'

He looked at Kate, wide-eyed and speechless.

'Tell me,' Kate roared with a voice that seemed to erupt from somewhere deep beneath her feet.

'I can't,' he said, ashen now.

'A year, two years. Five, ten?'

'It isn't like that.'

'What is it like then, Joe? Or would you prefer me to ring Chrissie and ask her? You've gone on and on for years about what a fucking little tramp she is. How she neglects her kids, always getting herself into debt, going out with all sorts of misfits and morons. Christ, there were times when I was afraid to invite her round for a coffee in case we ended up rowing about it. And all that time you were screwing her?'

He said nothing.

Kate felt so sick that she thought she might die. 'Since she moved in?'

Nothing.

'Since she moved in?' Kate roared, waiting for Joe to protest, to deny it.

But he didn't. He didn't deny it, instead he just looked up at Kate with eyes full of tears, and then at last very slowly said, 'No, not all the time. When Chrissie first moved in you and I were going through a bad patch. The band was falling apart, things weren't right between us. I don't need to tell you this stuff, Kate, you already know it. I thought I was letting you and the boys down, that you didn't need me, that you'd be better off without me. I was up to my arse in debt, what with all the gear, and then getting the van repossessed. Chrissie thought I was special. She just needed someone to give her a hand with a few jobs, put some shelves up, she was down on her uppers too. Depressed. I don't know, I suppose we both needed a shoulder to cry on. What I'm saying is that it just happened. I don't know what else to say. It just happened –'

Kate felt her whole life shift a little to the left. Where had she been when all this was going on? How was it she hadn't known? Kate stared at him, remembering how she'd gone round to introduce herself to Chrissie, remembering how that first night she'd moved in Kate had invited her round to supper because Chrissie hadn't got any gas or maybe it was electricity.

Staring at Joe, Kate watched a quick fire slide show of memories and images rip through her mind like bullets in a machine gun belt. She would have to go back now and look again at every single frame trying to spot the things she had missed the first time round. How could she possibly have not known? Was her intuition so bad?

'And since then? How many times since you went to fix her shelves?'

Joe squirmed in the chair, a naughty boy caught with the stolen fruit in his jacket pocket.

'Well?'

'Look Kate, it's not like we're having a full-scale affair or anything.'

'So what is it then? A harmless meeting of minds?'

He shook his head. It wasn't so much a denial more a gesture of dismissal, of a desire to escape. Watching him, Kate wasn't sure which hurt the most, Chrissie's betrayal or Joe's, and then she realised with a gut wrenching certainty it was, without a doubt, Chrissie's.

Joe had never been privy to her thoughts and fears and dreams and giggling drunken confessions in the same unguarded way Chrissie had. Kate might have shared her body with Joe but it had been Chrissie Kate had told about her first snog, the first time she had ever seen a man naked and what she thought and felt and dreamed about almost everything else that had happened since then. Chrissie had been into those secret sacred places where only best friends go. And apparently, now it seemed, a few more besides.

Between them, they had betrayed Kate beyond words and it hurt so hard that she couldn't gauge just how big the pain was. It spread out all around her like a rolling fog with no edge and no relief. She was angry and then furious and then humiliated; between them they had made a total fool of her, and she felt so hurt and so raw that she wanted to hit Joe and wreak some terrible, terrible vengeance. For an instant Kate wanted the pair of them dead, worse than dead, and then with a great wave of grief thought maybe it would be better if she was dead. All this ebbed and flowed through Kate's mind in a handful of seconds.

'Would you like some tea?' Joe asked, getting up.

Kate finally slid down into the chair Chrissie had so recently vacated. 'Yes,' she said exhausted, head in hand. It was as if all those emotions had burnt off a huge amount of energy. But she wasn't too tired to fight. 'How could you do this to me?'

'Kate, I didn't mean to hurt you.'

'You should have thought about that before

you screwed Chrissie. I don't know where this leaves us, Joe. Where do we go from here?'

She looked up at him. His expression held but she could see the panic and pain flash behind his eyes.

Kate spoke very slowly. 'I've always been on your side, Joe, I thought we were a team. I know things haven't always gone the way you wanted but I've never given you a hard time about it. I've always believed in what you do, your talent, I never ever said give up the music, get real, get a proper job,' Kate paused. Maybe that was the problem, maybe he needed something to kick against, maybe she had killed him with kindness. 'Are you planning to leave? Do you want to be with her? Have you just been waiting for the right time to tell me?'

He looked completely horrified. 'God – no, of course not. I don't want Chrissie, Kate, I never wanted Chrissie. I want you.'

'It doesn't look much like that from where I'm sitting, Joe. And actually don't bother about the tea, either, it would most probably choke me.'

Feeling incredibly tired and world-weary Kate picked up her bags and headed upstairs.

Despite an odd sense of unreality, and a voice

in her head that said that this couldn't be happening, standing in the doorway to their bedroom Kate felt another great wave of nausea rising up in her stomach. There was no way she would ever be able to bring herself to wash the sheets. Ripping them off the bed Kate bundled everything, sheets, duvet cover, pillowcases into a big untidy roll and stuffed the whole lot into a black plastic rubbish bag.

When she was done, Kate pushed her hair back out of her eyes and – as she brushed her finger across her face – was amazed to find that she had been crying. While she worked Kate had no idea where Joe was or what he was doing. It was as if her consciousness edited him out. Who could she tell, who she could talk to about this, who was there who would put their arms around her and hold her tight until the tears boiled dry?

As she got clean sheets out of the airing cupboard Danny and Jake came jogging up the stairs.

'We saw your car,' said Danny, slumping down onto the bare mattress.

Jake grinned a hello. 'We weren't expecting you back until Monday.'

Kate didn't trust herself to speak.

'How's Gran? Is there any chance of a lift to –' but before Danny had chance to say anything more, the phone rang in the hall. 'Bugger,' he said.

It rang once, twice, 'I'll get it,' Kate said and hurried downstairs to pick it up.

'Hi,' said Maggie. 'I rang to see if you'd got back okay. It was lovely to see you. It was such a shame you couldn't have stayed longer.'

If only Maggie knew how big a shame.

'It would be great if you could come down next week, if you can spare the time obviously. You don't have to stay all week –'

It was the first time she remembered Maggie asking her for anything. Kate paused for a moment; on the drive home she had come up with all kinds of valid excuses for not going back, although that seemed like a long time ago now. On the edge of her hearing she heard the back door close. It had to be Joe going out. Kate swallowed hard. She longed to be away from this mess more than almost anything else, and so Kate said, as brightly as she could manage, 'Don't worry. I'll be down first thing Monday morning if that's okay. It'll give me chance to sort some work out –'

‘Oh, that’s wonderful,’ Maggie sounded surprised and relieved.

‘I’ve got to go now though, Mum, I’ve – I’ve –’ Kate paused again, unable to think of any plausible reason to hang up. The possibilities were too painful to contemplate. ‘I’ll ring you later.’

Kate was barely half way up the stairs before the phone rang again.

‘I’m pleased that you’ve been to see Mum,’ said Liz, before Kate could get more than a few words of greeting in.

‘Obviously she’s got my mobile number if she needs me,’ Liz continued. Her tone was emphatic, dry, businesslike and above all, defensive. ‘She’s never appreciated a lot of fuss.’ The inference was of course that haring up to Norfolk in the middle of the night most definitely constituted fuss.

‘I’ve told her that we’ll pop down next weekend. Toby and Gillian are having a barbecue this weekend. It’s a fundraiser for some orphanage in Rumania. We’d already RSVP’d and I don’t like to let people down.’

‘Obviously,’ Kate said, in a voice so heavy with sarcasm that she assumed even Liz wouldn’t be able to overlook it. ‘I’m going to stay with Mum next week,' Kate continued, not adding that she was also running away from the discovery that the man Liz had always thought was an arrogant, smug, second-rate musician, was also a lying, adulterous bastard.

'Oh right,' Liz couldn't quite keep the surprise out of her voice. 'Mum said that Guy will be there over the weekend, so we needn't worry too much I suppose, although it's not like family.'

We; we: Liz and Mr Peter Patently-Successful. Fleetingly Kate wondered if she had always been this cynical and nasty or whether she had turned that way and not noticed. Maybe that's why Joe had gone off with Chrissie. The words stung. Had he gone off with Chrissie? Is that where he was now? She started to tremble.

Odd how it was possible to behave and talk normally while all around you Rome burns. What had they been talking about? Guy. Oh yes. 'What do you think of Guy?'

Liz had to have an opinion on the whole Guy-mother thing. But instead of saying anything Liz made a noncommittal noise, so Kate pressed, 'Have you met him?'

'Well yes, very briefly, at Christmas,' said Liz vaguely. 'He seemed very pleasant.'

'Pleasant?'

'Well, you know, he's fine as lodgers go; we didn't have much chance to talk. He was off to see his ex-wife I think it was, or maybe it was his mother. I can't really remember now.'

So Liz didn't know about Guy and Maggie.

'You sound very tense. Are you all right? How's Joe?' asked Liz.

'What do you mean?' Kate snapped, aware of an excess of emotion in her voice.

'Nothing. I just wondered how things were. Not that I'm prying or anything but it must be a strain being freelance, never knowing how much you're going to earn each month or whether you'll have any work at all.' She made a noise that under other circumstances might have passed for a laugh. 'I've always said to Peter that you're both very brave, I don't know how you manage.'

For brave substitute stupid, thought Kate. This conversation was never far from Liz's lips as if Joe's and Kate's continued survival was an affront to Liz's neatly structured life. Sometimes she could head Liz off before it was too late but today she hadn't the energy or the inclination.

'We do worry about you, and I know Mum does too, you looked so tired last time we came up to see you, and Peter thought Joe was very off with everybody.'

Kate kept schtum, not wanting to point out that Liz and Peter's visit was the reason for everyone being so tense and grumpy. There was a silence as deep as the ocean.

Kate knew that anything she said would be taken down and used in evidence against her later. A previous conversation about Kate's marriage had hinged on the premise that most of the family thought Joe was an arrogant, overbearing waster who should grow up and get a proper job; although when pressed, Liz had been reluctant to name names.

'There's no need to get upset,' said Liz.

'Upset, what do you mean, upset? I'm not at all upset,' Kate growled. Damn, damn, damn, now Liz would think she really *was* upset.

'You know, if there's any way that Peter and I can ever help,' she said, in a viperous undertone, 'you know you only have to ask.'

Kate took a deep breath to let Liz have a piece of her mind, although which piece she wasn't altogether certain.

'Mum, can I have a fiver?'

That wasn't what Kate planned to say at all, with a mouth full of unspoken words as sharp as broken glass, she swung round. Danny was standing on the bottom of the stairs, grinning. By some terrible trick of genetics, time and protein, he stood more than head and shoulders above her and looked just like a younger version of Joe.

He shifted from foot to foot, moving in a way that implied he was extremely busy, and had very little time to wait for Kate to give him the money. Good God, he'd got all kinds of things to do. Important things. He was nearly fifteen, didn't she realise? Over the last few months it increasingly seemed as if Danny only spoke to Kate when she was on the phone or quite obviously busy doing something else. It was a tactic. He was hoping Kate would be so absorbed in whatever she was doing that she won't notice what he was asking for.

'No chance,' she snapped in a tone that let Danny know that the situation was not up for discussion. Unfortunately, she didn't cover the receiver.

'Well pardon me for asking,' said Liz, slightly cowed. 'I was only trying to help.'

'I'm not talking to you,' Kate replied almost as sharply. Which didn't help at all.

'Why?' Now Liz sounded upset. 'What on earth have I done?'

Kate slumped forward against the hallstand. 'Nothing, nothing at all, Liz. I was talking to Danny. He was asking me for money.' Which didn't sound good either.

Jake, who was almost eleven, squeezed past Kate on his way to the kitchen. He'd left his bedroom door open so the hall filled up with the sounds of laser blasts and engine roar from his TV.

'I'm really worried about you, Kate,' Liz said, and then as if sensing that it was perhaps not a good place to go, said, 'Why did you want to know about Guy?'

'Curiosity,' Kate growled.

'He's been giving Mum a hand with the garden at weekends apparently. Which is nice –'

That isn't the only thing he's been giving her a hand with, Kate thought.

'And he's given the conservatory a lick of paint,' Liz continued oblivious. While Kate's little sister might be as devious as bucket of adders she had never been very quick on the uptake.

'And what else do you know about Guy?'

Liz was away now. 'He's in computers, divorced, staying with Mum until he gets himself on his feet. I'd imagine it's quite nice for them both. Why?' There was a pause and then Liz laughed.

'Oh my God, you're not interested in Guy, are you? Things with Joe can't be that bad, surely?' She was laughing. 'Peter reckons Guy's used to having someone to wait on him and you know what Mum's like, she's always loved to have someone to cook for and make a fuss of.'

Kate wondered who on earth it was Liz saw when she looked at Maggie. She was just toying with the idea of explaining to Liz that their mum wasn't just making the boy cocoa, when Liz said, 'Oh and how's Chrissie? I keep meaning to ring her. Last time we met at yours she was telling me she'd found this gorgeous new man, he was married, I think, which made it all a bit messy –' and then Liz said, 'Mind you, I don't suppose it can be easy starting again at her age. She is quite nice-looking though, isn't she? In a common sort of way. I suppose there's a lot of men who find that sort of thing attractive.'

And at that moment Kate decided not to tell Liz anything at all. Ever again. It would be infinitely more satisfying when Liz found out about Guy for herself.

When she finally hung up Kate went into the kitchen made a mug of tea and dumped the bed linen alongside the swing bin. From the window she could see Joe in the garden, sitting on the wall. She watched him for a few minutes and then went outside.

'Joe?' She noticed that he flinched at the sound of her voice. Kate felt tears welling up inside, her anger momentarily displaced by a great wave of grief and sharp, pointed loss. Maybe it would be easier never to speak to Joe again, except of course that there were all those things she wanted to say, all those things that she needed to know, and things that had to be said if they stood any chance at all of putting things right.

Kate swallowed hard; did she really want to put it right? Wasn't this the chance she'd been waiting for for years, a get out of jail free card with all the fine views that came from having the moral high ground? She had as much leverage and power now as she could ever want. The idea made her shiver; surely she was more honourable than this?

Joe turned and looked up at her.

On Thursday, the night before the supper party, when Kate had gone to bed a couple of hours after Joe? When she crept in beside him, that moment when he had turned towards her half-awake and half-asleep? When he had snuggled up against her, encircling her body with his to share his warmth, who had he been thinking of then?

Kate had been so pleased, so bloody grateful that whatever had been firing his discontent had gone – even if only temporarily. Joe had held her in his arms and slowly, oh-so-slowly, begun nuzzling into her neck with a flurry of soft kisses, rekindling the fire, that long slow familiar dance that they had shared so many times. As it was, Joe had been deeper asleep than Kate had first thought and after a few moments he had slowed and stopped and slipped back to unconsciousness but now that image, that seduction, was frozen on an inner canvas.

Did Joe do the same dance with Chrissie, go through those same compelling steps? Join the same dots? Did he make those soft puppy noises of pleasure; did those little high spots of colour appear on his cheeks when he came? Did he nuzzle her neck, cup her breasts, purr into her hair in just the same way as he did with Kate? The thoughts piled in one on top of the other. Kate blinked hard, her whole body rigid. It was agony to swallow down the tears, each one as hot as molten lava.

'Hi,' Joe said.

He looked as if he'd been crying. He looked very pale. She knew that men, or at least Joe, didn't go hunting for the truth in the same way that women do. Men don't want to know, women do, and once they do know the truth they torture themselves with the things they find out.

But that wasn't what Kate said aloud, instead she said, 'Mum rang me. I've told her I'll go up and give her a hand next week.'

'So what's changed?' Joe said. Kate was certain that couldn't be what he had meant to say. She looked at him. What little colour Joe had left suddenly drained away and as if the words hadn't been spoken, he continued hastily, 'What – all week?'

'Probably.' Kate paused, wondering how best to describe Guy and then decided not to bother, she didn't want to share her thoughts or her secrets with Joe any more. 'There's no way Mum can manage on her own.'

'What, so you want me to have the boys all next week?'

Was it that hard to understand, or was it that he was protesting?

'Yes.'

Joe sucked his bottom lip thoughtfully. 'I'm really busy at the moment, Kate.'

He paused and looked up at her; Kate knew that the disappointment and pain had already registered on her face, and it struck her as typical that even now, when she needed him most, Joe couldn't help her. Even now when, if not logic then most certainly guilt, should have him making all kind of rash promises, he just couldn't do it.

'I'll try and reschedule some of the stuff but it's not going to be easy. I've got things booked. Rehearsals, studio time for the radio jingle –' He didn't add that he had already missed this morning's meeting, even Joe wouldn't sink that low. 'I'm pretty booked up one way and another.'

'I'm not a client, Joe. This is my mum and our kids I'm talking about; besides they're at school all day –'

'I know, I know – I'm just saying.' For an instant Joe sounded almost triumphant. He might be in the wrong, but at the moment Kate needed him to do what Joe – at some level – perceived as a favour and somehow that helped to redress the balance of power. And then, all of sudden, Joe leaned forward and smiled. A great big genuine smile. Kate could hardly believe it.

'Don't worry, we can sort this out, Kate,' he said, as if he was talking about the cupboard under the stairs, and then he held out his arm. 'Come on, it'll be okay. I'm really sorry, babe. Believe me this whole Chrissie thing was nothing. Just a storm in a teacup. Honest.'

He stood up, nodding his head and stepping closer as if to cuddle her.

Kate felt the hackles on the back of her neck rise. 'It's that simple is it, Joe? A few clichés and a promise to look into childcare arrangements and that's it, is it. Job done? Game over?'

He looked bemused. 'I don't know what the hell you're on about, Kate.'

Had the man got no shame? She backed away, not quite able to believe it.

'What? What *is* the matter with you?' he said, looking genuinely surprised, shocked even, as she took another step away from him. 'I've said I'll try and sort work and the kids out next week for you. Come on,' he waved her closer. 'We're bigger than this, Kate.'

'Bigger than this? Bigger than what? Infidelity, lying, cheating?' For an instant Kate saw Joe in a completely different light. How was it that they had ever stayed together for so long? Were all those years and the man she thought she was married to some clever trick of the light? 'You're always telling people you'll do anything, absolutely anything, for me and the kids. Anything at all as long as it didn't upset your plans, obviously.'

'Oh for Christ's sake, be reasonable.'

'Reasonable? Reasonable – how dare you?' Kate took a deep breath, struggling not to choke as a great roaring gust of betrayal blew like a hurricane wind through her memory. She stared at him, trying to fathom out which things between them were still true, which were false, which words of love, which promises, were real now?

'I've already said we can sort this out.'

'I don't know if there is anything left for us to sort out, Joe.'

He pulled a puzzled face as if she'd sprung some huge surprise on him.

'I need to get away from here – from you, I need time to think –'

'Think?' he repeated, and then laughed nervously 'What about?'

'What do you mean, what about? What do you think?' she said incredulously. He was about to say something, God alone knows what, when Danny appeared in the kitchen door looking seriously miffed, clutching a family-sized bag of blue Doritos in one paw and a jar of salsa dip in the other. He grinned at Kate. He'd obviously been on a search and destroy mission through the fridge, had a rather fetching milk moustache and was still, it seemed, waiting for the reply and the fiver he wanted.

He looked from face to face; like the dinosaur, the adolescent brain is situated a long way from the site of any meaningful activity, so it took Danny about a minute of glacier-grinding silence to work out that things weren't exactly going well in the back yard and to make a tactical withdrawal. As he did, Kate got up and followed him inside, her whole body trembling with a volatile cocktail of intense unnameable emotions.

Chapter 4

The rest of the weekend was horrible. Worse than horrible; it was so painful that it made every bone and muscle in Kate's body hurt, even her teeth ached. Nothing felt or sounded right or real. It felt as if her life didn't fit any more.

She didn't see Chrissie and could barely bring herself to talk to Joe, who walked around the house like some wounded misunderstood much put upon hero. Kate had to keep reminding herself it was him not her who was in the wrong. Or was he?

What had made him sleep with Chrissie in the first place? Was it her fault? Had she driven him to it? And if it was, what had she done? What *exactly* had been the thing that had driven him into her arms when other men just sulked or skulked or fought back?

And when? And how often? It was torturous. With Joe camped out in the spare room Kate had plenty of time to think. She lay staring up at the ceiling in their bedroom replaying the last few years over and over again in her mind, trying to spot the moment, the instant when it had all gone wrong.

And then there was Chrissie. The one person who she trusted with her kids, her secrets; she daren't go near those thoughts.

'Please just tell me why you did it, wasn't I good enough for you? What is it she does that I don't? Tell me why?' Kate demanded, when she could finally face speaking to Joe.

Joe stared up at her as if he had absolutely no idea what she was talking about and raised his hands in surrender. 'I don't know, Kate, I really don't know. I'm sorry. We've been over and over and over this. I don't know what else to say to you. I'm sorry.' And that was it.

'Look, I already told you it was going to be hard to reschedule this week.'

'Yes, but you told me that on Saturday. I

thought by now you would have worked something out. I'm about to go, Joe –'

It was first thing on Monday morning. Kate was on the point of leaving. She had her suitcase beside her on the doormat.

'I've had other things on my mind,' he said darkly.

'And you think that I haven't? What I am supposed to do? I told Mum I'd be there early.'

Joe sighed. 'And I've rung my mum, the boys can go and stay with her after school until I get home tonight, but I've got to be in Fulham this morning,' he glanced down at his watch. 'I'm going to be late as it is.'

Kate was almost past caring; family life, Joe, even the boys felt like part of some strange abstraction, as if she was walking around inside a dream and when she woke up she wouldn't be at all surprised to find that it – they – had all been a complex illusion.

'You knew I'd got a meeting this morning,' he whined.

Kate stared at him. Technically, he was right, she must have known at some time or other. It just seemed as if that was part of a different life.

'Don't look at me like that, Kate. All you have to do is sort the boys out and drop their stuff off at my mum's. It's not much to ask bearing in mind I've got them all week.'

He was unbelievable.

'And if I'm too late back they can stay there the night, it's the best I can do.' His tone had a take it or leave it edge.

'Why couldn't you have told me this last night?'

He shrugged. It was all Kate could do to keep her hands off him.

Which meant in a nutshell, that she had to get the boys up and ferry their gear over to Joe's mum and then drop them off at school before leaving for Norfolk. Or vice versa. Whichever way round she did it, given the state of the traffic at this time of the morning, it would probably mean another couple of hours on the road at least.

'Do we have to go?' said Danny, as Kate and the boys were loading up the car. 'Why can't me and Jake just stay here? I've already said I can look after him. I can get him to school. I can be responsible, you know. You just don't trust me, do you? And Chrissie could keep an eye on us until Dad gets home. You know she wouldn't mind. What do you think I'm going to do?'

'How long have you got, Danny?' Kate snapped,

slamming the back door of her car shut. She paused, trying very hard not to let rip and take all the things that had been brewing out on him. ‘Actually, it’s not that I don’t trust you, Danny, it’s just that I need to know you’re safe. You two staying with Granny is one less thing for me to worry about.’ Kate couldn’t bring herself to even mention Chrissie.

Danny groaned but, undaunted and apparently unable to read the weather forecast etched on Kate’s features, pressed on, ‘But her flat’s totally and utterly gross. It’s damp, and everywhere smells of fags and frying and cats.’

Now that everything was packed into the car it looked like they were fleeing the country.

‘And she cooks some seriously weird stuff.’

‘And Dad never helps me with my homework and you won’t be there, and we’ve got a test on Wednesday,’ said Jake, desperate to add his two penneth, sounding mortally wounded, swinging his rollerblades in alongside the holdall in the boot.

‘Oh right, and you see that as a real problem, do you?’ Kate was getting close to the crumbly edge of self-control. ‘I seem to remember last term that I had to pay you to get your science project in on time. You’ll live.’

Everyone had been grumbling on and off since Kate got them up and any remaining shreds of good humour were wearing very thin. 'It's only till the end of the week.'

'Oh my God,' sighed Danny. 'Five bloody days.'

'Just shut up and get in the sodding car, will you?' Kate slammed the boot shut. 'It can't be helped. It's not as if I'm off on a luxury cruise; Grandma Maggie can't cope on her own.' Because unfortunately Grandma's toy boy was away all week on business, said the treacherous little voice in her head.

The air in the car was thick with accusations both silent and otherwise. Every set of traffic lights was red, the stereo ate Jake's favourite tape, Kate had to double-park outside the flat and Joe's mum didn't bother coming to the door even when they rang the bell. Kate sent Danny in; there was no way she could face Joe's mum at this time of the morning. When he finally re-emerged, Danny said, 'Dad told Gran to make sure you leave us enough for dinner money this week because he hasn't got any cash and lost his card so can you get him fifty quid out before you go?'

They had to drive round to find a cash machine.

And things got worse. There were road works and an accident, and whole stretches of motorway that were full of Sunday afternoon drivers who hadn't been going fast enough to make it home before Monday morning.

By the time Kate got to Denham Market and drove up Church Hill she had a headache that filled her entire body, and her spine felt as if it had been plaited into a sheepshank and two half hitches. So, with a sense of relief, she swung into the drive without looking and nearly hit a black and silver jeep pulling out.

'Shit. What the –' Kate slammed on the anchors, spraying gravel and four-letter words as she whipped forward towards the windscreen, bringing the car to a dramatic halt. 'Bastard, bastard, bastard,' she spat, sitting very still, glaring through the windscreen at a set of chrome bull bars.

A tall, wiry, anxious-looking man clambered down from the driver's seat and round to her side of the car. The 4x4 was black and shiny and fashionably chunky, the kind of thing you'd drive across the open tundra stopping to winch the occasional reindeer to safety from an ice floe.

'You okay?' he asked. He was tall and sounded

genuinely concerned and looked as if he might be something medical, a country doctor maybe. He was wearing ginger-coloured cords and a matching open-necked blue and ginger checked shirt and as he spoke pushed a mop of greying red-blond hair back off his forehead.

Not that Kate really noticed. She just nodded, trying hard to disguise the fact that she'd been driving on autopilot.

'Sorry about that, I couldn't see through the wall,' he said. Which was a generous and conciliatory thing to say under the circumstances. He said it with a grin not a growl which was nice, or would have been, except that Kate wasn't feeling generous or conciliatory and most definitely not nice and could feel herself getting angry with him for being so bloody cheerful.

'Not many people can,' she snarled. 'Are you looking for my mother?'

'Is she small, grey, deaf, incontinent and in obvious distress?'

'Not when I left her last week.' A picture of Guy in his tight white underpants flashed briefly through her mind.

'Then no, probably not. I'm Andrew Taylor, the local vet.' He extended a hand.

Kate struggled with an inclination to decline

the introduction but couldn't quite bring herself to be that rude. His handshake was warm and businesslike. And then the grin widened out into something else. 'Kate? It is, it's Kate Sutherland, isn't it?'

Kate looked more closely at him. 'Do I know you?' she said icily.

'Yes, I think you probably do – Denham High? You're a couple of years younger than me – Andy Taylor, I used to be in the drama club with you?'

Kate looked again, trying hard to hold on to her annoyance, while shuffling through the memories and there he was, sixteen with a mass of floppy hair and no shoulders to speak of, the grin hadn't changed though. 'Andy Taylor. God you've grown. I thought you were in – in –' Kate fished around for the tail end of something she'd heard on the family grapevine. 'Somewhere hot and foreign.'

'Australia. Yeh, I was out there for eight years then came home to take over my dad's practice. I've been back three years now.'

Trying to stay outraged and angry Kate didn't ask him how he liked it or wait for him to ask how her life was going, instead she said, 'And what are you doing here?'

'Looking for the meaning of life and the heart of a good woman.' It was corny and daft but at least he did have the decency to say it with a big grin.

Kate laughed aloud, aware of how bitter it sounded. 'Then you're most definitely in the wrong place, Mister,' was what she wanted to say, but instead Kate raised her eyebrows and said, 'Really?' in what she hoped was a superior way.

His expression didn't falter. 'Actually I'm looking for a grey and white tabby called Tiddles and a woman called Mrs Hall, 84 Church Hill?'

'Viv. Next door.'

'Thanks.' He smiled. 'Home on a visit?'

'My mum's broken her ankle.'

'Damn, sorry to hear that.'

Kate waved the words away. 'She'll be okay. I've come to give her a hand for a few days.'

'Well, I hope she gets better soon. It was really nice to see you again. Have a good day. Maybe we'll catch up again some time.' He looked ruefully at the vehicles nose to nose on the gravel. 'And mind how you go.'

It didn't sound rude or churlish, which was annoying, and as Kate couldn't think of anything smart to say, she nodded in acknowledgement, wound up her window and reversed out into the road. This time she looked both ways. Twice.

Andrew eased out and Kate drove back in and parked up under the laburnums. It was barely lunchtime and already she felt in need of two paracetamol, a warm bed and a good night's sleep. Kate didn't notice whether Andrew waved goodbye or looked back as she unfolded herself from the car, she was too busy swearing.

'Hi Mum, it's only me.'

Kate let herself in, dropped her bag in the hall and tried very hard to paint on a happy face. Maggie was reclining on the sofa in the sitting room, crutches propped up within easy reach. She was wearing a long cream silk shirt, a single flat leather sandal and a pair of baggy black tracksuit bottoms, one leg of which was cut off and rolled up in a rakish pirate fashion just above her cast. Kate sniffed; she suspected Guy had done it before he left. It looked like a Guy thing. The French windows were open onto the garden and Maggie was looking pale but nevertheless radiant and not in a deathbed, verge-of-something-terminal way.

She smiled and put down her book. 'Hi love, how was the drive?'

Kate grimaced and stretched, trying hard to ease the nasty kinks out of her soul as she bent down to kiss her hello. 'Ask me something else.'

Maggie laughed. It was a good wholesome laugh, a laugh that made Kate feel quite envious.

'How's Joe?'

Bad choice.

Chapter 5

'For someone so small you weigh a bloody ton.' The words, hissed between gritted teeth, sounded far grumpier than Kate had intended but then again she was sweating and fighting for breath having struggled down Church Hill, steering Maggie in a wheelchair, trying very hard to avoid letting her mother roll off the kerb and under passing juggernauts. Controlling a wheelchair was a lot harder than Kate had anticipated; they'd been out of the house less than ten minutes and she was totally knackered. Maybe flat shoes would have been a better choice rather than the little kitten heels sandals that she was wearing.

Kate had been home about an hour. Once she

had recovered from her encounter with Andrew and finished the unpacking and bedmaking, Kate rapidly realised that if they didn't do something she would probably end up asking Maggie about Guy or alternatively telling her about Joe and Chrissie, and she didn't feel ready to do either.

A walk, that was what she decided they needed, get Maggie out in the air, must be awful to be cooped up in the house all day with just four walls to look at. Kate paused; who the hell was she trying to kid? It sounded like bliss to have a few days on the sofa with a pile of magazines, with nothing to do and no one to disturb you.

Watching Joe drive away that morning, before going back inside to wake the boys, Kate had wondered if he had arranged to meet Chrissie somewhere. Maybe they had met up for breakfast. Had he grinned and waved, hurried across some road somewhere to join her for croissants and coffee?

Chrissie would be hurting like hell, Kate thought, as she manoeuvred Maggie down the drop kerb and across the traffic lights. She and Chrissie had been friends for years, which made everything worse than impossible. How the hell could she be having an empathic response for the woman who had been sleeping with her husband? A woman who had betrayed all those sacred arcane laws about shagging your best friend's bloke?

Kate could guess exactly how Chrissie would be feeling and there was part of her, against all the odds, that felt really sorry for her. It was impossible not to think about all the things they'd done together, as families, as a couple, as friends; it seemed just so unlikely, so impossible and so bloody unfair that all that time Joe and Chrissie had been holding on to this huge secret thing. They knew and Kate didn't. It gave her the most awful sick feeling.

Did Joe and Chrissie look at each other while they were all together, while they were on holiday together, while the kids were playing cricket on the beach, or at a barbecue, and long to be alone? Did they brush past each other in the kitchen, and smile knowingly while Kate was outside turning the beefburgers; did they talk about her when they were in bed together? Had they got secret jokes and magic words that she had heard and yet never recognised?

She and Chrissie had often talked about sex, life, kids. Kate couldn't think of a single area of life where they hadn't been in conversation. Years before, over a coffee, or maybe a bottle of wine, Kate had told Chrissie, amongst a million other things, how Joe had once grabbed her in the kitchen, dragging her off for a quickie in the coal shed where they stored the bikes. How they'd screwed like rattlesnakes, giggling and half cut, trying so very hard not to make too much noise, while Kate's parents and the kids were sitting inside waiting for them to dish up Christmas dinner. What was it Chrissie had thought as Kate had been telling her? Had she been there too? Stolen moments while Kate had been somewhere else, patiently waiting? Had it been better for her or worse?

Kate felt cold fingers track up and down her spine; a person could easily drive herself mad thinking about this stuff. She was so deep in thought Kate had almost totally forgotten about Maggie.

'You were the one who suggested it would be nice to walk into town.' Maggie sounded tense. 'Guy thought it would be a good idea to borrow a wheelchair from the hospital. He took me down the pub for lunch yesterday.'

Kate snapped back to the present; good for bloody Guy. There was no way she could possibly compete with the bronzed boy wonder. Pushing the wheelchair was like trying to steer a human shopping trolley. Kate glanced over her shoulder wondering how the hell she was ever going to get Maggie back up the hill.

As if she could read her mind, Maggie said, 'Kate, instead of struggling like this why don't you park me over there under the trees and go back and fetch the car? I don't mind. We could have a sandwich at home if you like? I've got loads of food in. Guy felt so guilty about leaving me he's laid in enough for a siege.'

'No, it'll be fine. Don't worry.' Kate did her best to sound brisk and capable. 'Now where did you say you wanted to go?'

Which was a stupid thing to ask because up until a quarter of an hour ago Maggie had been happily reading on the sofa with no desire to go anywhere whatsoever.

There was a pause and then Maggie, in that same kind of oh well we're here now better get on with it way, said, 'We could drop into the bookshop if you like. You can meet everyone, and then we could find somewhere for a late lunch – the brasserie? I'm sure they would be pleased to see I'm still alive. My treat.'

'Sounds fine, although when we get back I really must get on with some work,' Kate said, implying that coming home to Maggie's had dragged her away from something vitally important.

Maggie nodded. 'Okay. Did I tell you I'm thinking about remodelling the garden later this year? We've drawn it up and measured it. I've promised myself that while Guy's away I'll go through all those gardening magazines and books I've got. It's really nice to have someone to plan things with again and he loves gardening –' Kate could hear the enthusiasm in her mother's voice and didn't know what to say, but it appeared that she wasn't expected to say anything, as Maggie continued, 'I thought I'd do some textural things – cobbles, gravel and water. I've seen this wonderful water feature that was built into the top of a brick wall; you end up with this thin, rather elegant stream, dropping over different levels and then being pumped back. And then –' Using her hands for emphasis Maggie started to wax lyrical about patios and pots and pools as Kate braced herself against the handles of the chair. 'Maybe we could go to the local garden centre some time while you're here? I've been thinking about building a pergola; Guy is very good with his hands.'

Kate decided not to comment.

In a funny way, Guy or no Guy, it was a relief to see Maggie so animated. This was the woman

Kate thought about when she visualised her mother, self-contained, joy-filled, always with some scheme or project on the boil. It was reassuring that things weren't so far out of kilter after all. Instead of playing nursemaid Kate could let go and give her mum some space. Part of her, she realised, felt that she was obligated to amuse and entertain and generally be with her mum all the time. For as long as she could remember Kate had never felt that way about Maggie.

Although, said the rogue voice in her head, wasn't that the main reason she had volunteered to come back home? While protesting she needed time and space to think, wasn't Kate really hoping that nursing Maggie would take her thoughts away from Joe and Chrissie, that somehow, in her absence, all those things that were broken would miraculously heal themselves?

While her mind was busy having an argument with itself, Kate steered the wheelchair in through the gates of the Memorial Playing Fields, a short cut into the town. After the rigours of Church Hill and the dash across the traffic lights before they changed, it was also blessedly flat and totally traffic-free.

The cricket pavilion was still there, where once upon a time, a long time ago, Kate had curled up against the peeling paintwork and smoked her very first cigarette. Head spinning, she had wondered why anyone in their right mind would ever want to smoke and then a few minutes later lit another one to see if she could pin it down.

It wasn't the only rite of passage marked there. On the boundary of the cricket pitch, under a stand of copper beech, was the bench where she had her first real snog. It was with a boy in the form above her. Kate fished around for his name and found it tucked away under a pile of other dusty, neglected memories: Alan Hart. They'd had several half-hearted attempts on the walk home from school, but because he was so much taller than she was, to make it work he'd had to stoop while she stood on tiptoes. It wasn't pretty. It most certainly wasn't sexy.

So, by mutual agreement, they had taken a detour through the park, and found a bench somewhere over there under the trees. He had put his arms around her and pulling Kate close had kissed her with closed, dry lips, pressing his face hard up against hers, furiously, hungrily, as if he might be burrowing for something.

Kate smiled. For an instant the memory was so vivid that she could almost smell him, remembering a boyish mix of sweat and Brut. It made her shiver, how could it be that she had forgotten Alan for all these years? Glancing across the grass Kate wouldn't have been in the least bit surprised to see a younger version of herself, entwined around Alan Hart, all arms and legs and inhibitions, despite having the waistband of her school skirt rolled over to show an extra couple of inches of leg. Kate tried hard to conjure up his face, but could only manage a long shot of him loping towards her across the playing field, hands stuffed in the pockets of his parka, shoulders slightly hunched against some long gone breeze.

By the end of the summer they had progressed to kissing with tongues and him alternately trying to undo her blouse and get his hand up her skirt. It was around then that Kate decided that whatever it was Alan was trying to do he wasn't the one she wanted to do it with and called it a day. With the robust survivalism of youth she'd gone on to have a crush on a boy in the sixth form, while Alan, she seemed to remember, had been very upset and bombarded her with notes and cards.

What had happened to him since then? Did he ever think about her? Did he think about them walking hand in hand on the way home? Did her blame her still? Kate stared at the benches wondering what it was they had talked about then? What did they know then?

Unexpectedly, her eyes filled up with tears. The wind that rippled her hair did the same to the canopy of the trees overhead so that the sunlight dappled the tarmac ahead of the wheelchair, making it look as if Maggie and Kate were walking through a babbling, bubbling brook.

'I'm so pleased you're home, love,' said Maggie, breaking into Kate's train of thought and through the wave of melancholy that threatened to engulf her. 'Seems a long time since you and I have had a chance to talk.'

Kate slowed down, wondering if they had ever really talked at all.

'I know you're busy,' Maggie was saying.

'But?'

'But nothing, I just wanted to say thank you for coming. I'd have had a hell of a job managing on my own if you weren't here.'

It was almost more than Kate could bear, she'd come to Denham under false pretences.

Without turning, Maggie continued, 'So do you want to talk about it?'

Kate swallowed hard; was she so transparent? What was she supposed to say?

'It?'

There was a small silence when Kate realised that she was fooling no one and made an effort to control the little tic under her eye and the other one that threatened to make her voice quiver and break. 'Not really, it's just one of those things. Joe and I are going through a bit of a rough patch at the moment. That's all.' Kate spoke slowly, holding tight to her emotions in case they caught her by surprise and spilt out. 'It'll be fine,' she added with a surety she most definitely didn't feel.

Maggie craned around in the chair and caught her gaze. Maggie didn't actually say that she didn't believe a word, but Kate thought she saw it in Maggie's expression.

'I'm not going to drag out it out of you, Kate. Every generation thinks that they invented sex, lies, all that stuff, that they're the only ones who have ever gone through anything, but it's not true. We all struggle sometimes and however unlikely it sounds somebody has always been that way before.'

'Should I be writing this down? Is that the good mother lecture?'

Maggie laughed, 'I wouldn't be that presumptuous. But I think you need to talk to someone about whatever it is that's eating you up. Your face is full of it, Kate.'

It was a deeply perceptive thing to say and made Kate's skin prickle. She just hoped Maggie didn't suggest she ring Chrissie. People always told her that Maggie was wise and funny and good company and although Kate had kind of known that, walking across the playing field was the first time she had truly felt it or appreciated the power of it in a long time.

'Knowing what's right and doing it are two very different things. Making choices, knowing what you want and what is worth saving and what it's better to let go of – even the best marriages can be bloody hard work at times,' Maggie continued.

Kate held her breath, wondering where the conversation was going to go next. It was one thing to get a glimpse of her mother as a real person – which was disturbing enough – but quite another to look with seeing eyes at her parents' marriage.

There was a pause and then Maggie said

thoughtfully, 'Although if I were you I wouldn't say anything to Liz, not that I suppose you would, but she always enjoyed high-octane dramatics. You must remember what she was like when she didn't want to go to school? Flinging herself on the sofa, wailing like a banshee,' Maggie laughed. 'I always thought Liz would end up on the stage rather than the civil service.'

There was a moment's silence; a moment of mutual remembering, and then Kate said, 'Liz told me that Guy was your lodger.'

This time they both laughed.

The people in the bookshop were delighted to see Maggie. They insisted Maggie and Kate stayed for coffee and then wrote risqué things on Maggie's cast while asking after Guy, how she was coping, everyone promising to drop by bearing gifts and gossip.

'I feel really guilty about this, I was the one who insisted we had another round of cocktails,' said Taz, handing Kate a mug of decaf. Taz had cropped hennaed hair, creamy white skin and a nose ring, and couldn't have been a day over twenty-five. She was also the bookshop manager.

Maggie laughed. 'Oh come on, Ginge, you didn't exactly force me to drink it, and one more round wasn't going to make any difference. I should have known better; it's that cocktail trick – they don't taste very alcoholic. But don't worry, we were short-staffed before this, so you'll have lots and lots of opportunities to work off any residual guilt.'

Taz laughed as Maggie wheeled herself over towards the gardening section.

'It's nice to meet you at long last,' said Taz warmly, turning her attention to Kate. 'Maggie is always talking about you and the boys. You look a lot like her. She's very proud of you, you know, successful businesswoman, kids, house and all that jazz. Must be nice to be self-employed, set your own schedule. How long are you staying in Denham?'

'Just till the end of the week, until Guy gets home,' said Kate, sipping her coffee

Taz smiled a broad predatory smile, 'Yum, yum, yum. Isn't he just the cutest little thing? It's such a shame he's into older women.' She glanced across at Maggie. 'I can't believe that your mum wouldn't marry him, she must be crazy to turn a man like that down. I mean, mad or what? If he'd asked me, Christ, I'd have snapped him up and dragged him off squealing to the back of the cave.'

Kate felt the breath catch in her throat but she smiled, turned away quickly, and took another sip of coffee as if her complete attention had just been grabbed by the pile of cut-price hardbacks featuring World War Two bombers, which were stacked up on the table beside them. It gave her just enough time to try and compose herself. When she looked back at Taz, Kate had fixed on what she hoped was a, 'well, of course Mum and I tell each other everything because we're very close and I support her decision wholeheartedly,' expression, while her mind struggled to work out what the hell was going on. It felt as if her whole life had transformed into one of those intricate domino games where the first one is pushed over and sets off a complex and confusing chain reaction.

She glanced round the shop; Maggie was still parked up in the gardening section and laughing with one of the other sales staff. She looked great when she laughed.

Taz was still talking, while Kate made every effort to keep a grip, looking for something, anything to hold on to. It seemed as if everything she had known and believed to be true for most of her adult life had suddenly all shifted and was still moving. Maggie breaking her ankle had been the spark that had lit a fuse on the bomb that had blown her world apart.

How long would the Chrissie and Joe thing have gone undiscovered if Maggie hadn't fallen down? How long before Maggie would have spilt the beans about Guy if Kate hadn't driven home? Struggling to pull her mind away from the flames that threatened to engulf it Kate had a fleeting vision of Maggie and Guy standing by a Christmas tree in the hall, arm in arm, elegant newlyweds, hosting some fictional family get-together. They were barely able to keep their hands off each other. Kate shivered – Maggie was wearing a wedding dress and veil. Guy was wrapped in a small white fluffy bath towel. Kate closed her eyes, trying to wipe the image off her retina only to find it was immediately replaced by an equally vivid picture of Joe and Chrissie sitting hand in hand at her kitchen table. Chrissie was wearing Kate's dressing gown and a bridal veil. 'It's not what you think, Kate,' Joe was saying.

Kate sighed. The storm clouds pressing down inside her head had been gathering there since finding them together. Everything else that was happening in her life seemed to be being played out against the sense of an even greater storm brewing.

Instinctively, Kate knew that that sensation would follow her and be with her and to some extent alter the way she behaved and thought and reacted until the situation with Joe was resolved – and somewhere in that resolution her life would change for ever. Which sounded a bit melodramatic but then again Kate thought ruefully, picking up one of the books on the display, her sister Liz didn't have the monopoly on high drama.

'Oh, do you like him? Have you read the new one?' Taz was busily waving another copy of the book in her direction. 'We had him in last week, this is a signed copy if you're interested.' It was only then that Kate realised with a start that she'd been holding a conversation without actually being aware of a single word.

Denham had barely changed in the years since Kate had left home. The main streets and market-place were mostly Georgian with a strong Dutch influence shaping the roof lines and plaster work; if you glanced up above the modern shop fronts and brightly painted facades it didn't take much to pick out the handsome symmetrical lines of an older time.

Walking along the High Street, Kate realised that even if she hadn't come to stay with Maggie, her mother had more than enough friends and people who loved and cared about her to ensure she didn't starve or die of neglect while Guy was away. It was heartwarming and at the same time a bit threatening to be greeted every hundred yards or so by all manner of faces, remembered, half remembered, known and unknown.

The sun shone, the people smiled and gossiped and asked solicitously after Maggie's health. It felt as if they were making some kind of royal progress. Kate had completely forgotten what it was like to live amongst people who knew you and your family and each other in a loose, overlapping web of emotional connections.

The people who had watched her grow up still ran and worked in a lot of the shops. Kate resisted the temptation to run through them on her internal check list, wondering whether too much sentiment was bad for the health.

The other thing that struck her was that people seemed to have the time to linger, that frantic metropolitan pulse that had her rushing across roads and hauling Maggie up kerbs was totally lost on the people they met on the pavement. Denham just didn't move that fast.

'Kate? Kate, is that you? Kate? Cooooeeeeee. Over here! Kate!'

They were on their way towards the restaurant Maggie had suggested for lunch. Kate looked around and scanned the people close enough to have called out and didn't recognise a single one of them, and then an extremely rotund woman in a lime-green floral sundress waved enthusiastically and scurried across the road towards them

'Well, hello. Fancy seeing you here, how are things going?' she asked warmly, looking Kate up and down. 'You so look well. God, it's so good to see you again.'

Kate smiled without committing herself, determined not to show herself up by admitting that she hadn't got a clue who the woman was. Meanwhile she could feel her face screwing itself up while her brain scurried off to find a mug shot and details that fitted the evidence. It had to have something stored somewhere surely, after all Andrew Taylor had been in there. The woman certainly didn't look like a loony and she most definitely knew Kate's name.

Kate knew she was staring and gurning and grimacing and then some far distant penny dropped and she felt her mouth fall open. 'Julie? Julie Hicks? Oh my God. It can't be.' She smiled with relief as much as recognition.

The last time she remembered seeing Julie had been on Leavers' Day in, in – God knows how long ago it was. Back in those days Julie had been a 4′ 10″ pocket sized Goth weighing in at about five stone with lots of eyeliner and buck teeth.

Kate was tempted to say that she'd grown but before she could speak Julie grinned; at least she still had the buckteeth.

'Took you long enough. I didn't realise I'd changed that much, you look just the same as ever.' Which was even more worrying as the last time they'd seen each other Kate was certain she'd had a brace, a very dodgy haircut, and a good crop of blackheads. Julie turned her attention to Maggie.

'Hello, Mrs Sutherland. What on earth have you been up to? Maybe you ought to take more water with it.'

They all laughed politely at what passed for a joke in Julie's neck of the woods and swapped where-are-they-now and why-we-were-there stories and then Julie said, 'Actually, I've just moved back to Denham. We've bought one of the houses up in Berbeck Road, you know, on the little estate up behind the churchyard, Church Pines? Near the doctor's? We've been in nearly a fortnight now, just long enough to let the dust settle.'

Maggie and Kate made approving noises as Kate was certain they were meant to. Berbeck Road was full of doctors and solicitors and men who did sensible things while wearing good suits.

'And how about you?' asked Julie pleasantly.

'Home for a few days to give Mum a hand.' Said that way it sounded almost saintly.

Julie nodded. 'Oh right. Actually I'm really glad that I've seen you both. We're having a house-warming party tomorrow evening. Why don't you come along? It's very informal, it won't be very late as it's a weeknight. It's really for the girls; you know what kids are like. There'll be loads of people there that you know.'

Kate was about to protest that there would be absolutely no one there that she knew when it occurred to her that Julie was talking to Maggie. She didn't even have the wit to ask who 'we' was – husband, lover, kids, a cat?

'Number 62, seven o'clock. It'll be lovely to

catch up.' She looked back at Kate. 'Is your husband staying here with you?'

Kate's face must have answered for her because Julie said, 'Job for them to get away, isn't it? I just thought that if he was around you might like to bring him along with you. Extra pair of hands on the barbecue always welcome. Although these days you never know whether to say husband or not do you?' she laughed conspiratorially. 'Remember Pippa Rose?'

Kate didn't have time to reply or even draw breath.

'Pretty? Went to work in the Nat West? Travelled a lot. Long ginger hair. You must remember her. Good at games. Got her colours in the cross-country.' Julie paused, waiting for Kate to catch up and then leaned forward and said conspiratorially, 'Lesbian.' And when they didn't immediately say anything, continued, 'I'd never have guessed. Nose ring, Doc Martens and everything.'

Kate would have laughed if Julie hadn't looked so serious. 'I was talking to her mother last week in the library.'

Which presumably assured the validity of the statement, thought Kate.

'Still not come to terms with it.'

Kate wondered whether Julie meant Pippa or her mother.

Walking through town with Maggie, who appeared to be on first name terms with practically everyone they met, had made Kate sentimental for small town life, but at that moment she remembered just how claustrophobic and judgmental it could be. Nodding in a way that she hoped conveyed something appropriate Kate silently thanked the stars that had guided her away.

'See you tomorrow night,' Julie said, as she marched off towards Boots. Kate nodded and waved and made agreeable noises; not that there was a cat's chance in hell that they were going to go.

Chapter 6

Joe supped the froth off a fresh pint; his eyes, if not his thoughts firmly fixed on the empty stage in the corner of the bar. He'd played at the Royal Oak quite a few times in the last few years, certainly enough to be on nodding terms with the management and his missus.

It felt familiar, not quite home but the sort of place Joe had hung out since he'd downed his first pint; a pub where the jukebox was full of classics – Clapton, Hendrix, Stones, The Who. Places like this were his natural habitat, this and battered church halls and dodgy clubs; he'd served his time. Joe squared his shoulders; he could walk the talk.

When they did the Joe Harvey special on

Channel 4, they'd shoot it in pubs like the Oak. There was a real gritty heart to the place. Melvyn Bragg would look great here leaning up against the bar supping a pint.

'I'm terribly sorry about this, Joe, but Lucy and I really do have to dash,' said the guy from Kate's agency. 'So, I'll ring you at the end of the month? Right? See what you've come up with. You've got the brief there, haven't you? And the art work?' He had a lisp that changed 'terribly' to 'tweribbly' and 'ring' to 'wing', 'brief' to 'bwief.' It was hard not to laugh.

Joe nodded; half a dozen shots of some wholesome toothy teenager in a pink gingham cowgirl outfit, cradling a tub of marg like it was a cross between the Holy Grail and Brad Pitt. At the bar, Lucy, What's-his-name's assistant, bent over to slide half a dozen pastel-coloured folders back into a rucksack. While Joe admired her arse, the man, who drank designer water and wore trendy specs, and looked about as happy in the public bar of the Oak as Joe would at a Baptist revival meeting, pulled out a Palm Pilot to add something vital.

He had wanted a slice of lime in his drink, in the Oak where you were lucky to get a clean glass. Lucy was a different kettle of fish altogether. She was wearing a white tee-shirt with pink arms that might once have fitted her kid sister, on the front the legend 'little princess,' the words snuggled up between large, high and very round breasts. Her outfit was finished off with tight shiny black flares and bleach blonde hair scrunched up into ridiculous little knots. Joe couldn't quite work out exactly what her role was. She had taken the odd note here and there but she spent most of the meeting drinking gin and tonic while watching him surreptitiously out of the corner of her eye as if he might be dangerous. Maybe she was on work experience.

Whatever, so much nervous interest gave Joe a real boost; he was pleased he hadn't shaved now: it made him look unkempt and dangerous. Lucy shuffled off her stool and smiled, blushing furiously as he shook her hand, lowering her eyes she scuttled after What's-his-name.

'Sure you don't want another drink before you go?' offered Joe jovially, toasting their retreating backs.

The man shook his head and mimed huge amounts of regret. Lucy shrugged; what could you do?

Life's hell, Joe thought, watching them scurry

out of the matt black door, and turned his attention back to the thoughts that had dogged him all morning.

Where there was a band, there were always girls. Girls not unlike Lucy; it was one of the constants of life. A given. Bands = Birds. Girls and women of all ages who got off on attracting their attention, girls who giggled and waved and got more brazen at the slightest encouragement, girls who longed to be touched by the magic that they believed performers had. Girls, who even in a dive like the Oak, would give almost anything to leave with the band. Almost anything – and very often everything. It was one of the reasons why Joe had learned to play guitar in the first place – the money, the fame and the chance to get laid. The stuff that drove teenage boys everywhere.

Not that Kate had ever been one of those girls. Oh no, Joe and Kate met during one of Joe's brief brushes with regular gainful employment. He'd been working in a music shop and she'd come in with a guy from work. Joe never did find out whether they were an item or had been or maybe planned to be.

Joe grinned; Kate had been standing there in the shop, bored out of her crust, staring into the middle distance while this geek she was with went off to play at being Hendrix on some seriously expensive guitars.

Joe had sidled over and flirted a bit because there was no one else about and the guy who ran the place, sniffing some real money, had made a beeline for Kate's mate. Joe was as bored as she was. Kate was moderately impressed that he was a guitarist but not in the same way as the girls in the pubs and clubs were.

She didn't have the same addiction, that same hungry need for bright glittery stuff that those girls had. While he was chatting her up Kate just saw a guy who worked in a music shop, someone who happened to play guitar, not someone likely to take the world by storm, not someone bright and glittery and made of white-hot stardust. Maybe that was it, maybe Kate had always seen through him.

Joe sighed and watched the other punters, perched like crows on stools around the bar. The Oak was a music pub so it didn't generally do much of a lunch-time trade in the week. In the daylight the interior, painted mostly black and red with a splash of gold here and there, looked cheap and tacky.

It needed the night, the darkness to make it

special. The night and the music. The Oak had showcased all kinds of bands, new bands, blues bands, young bands, bad bands. He and his best band had had their opening gig on that very stage. Joe made a mental note to tell Melvyn Bragg.

He couldn't remember if it was here that he'd first met Chrissie. If it wasn't this pub it was one very much like it. Not that he'd done anything about it, there was no need to, but he had noticed her, in the way that those sort of girls, women, want to be noticed. Joe smiled and then drained his glass down to the suds. Oh yes, he had most definitely noticed her.

'Would you like me to get out? You could have a little rest?'

'No, I'll be fine.'

Pushing the wheelchair back up Church Hill was hell, made all the worse by Maggie apologising to Kate every hundred yards or so for being so heavy.

'Wasn't it Julie's mum who ran off with some chap from the bank?'

Kate was too breathless to answer even if she wanted to; had these people got no shame?

It was a relief to be back home.

'I'm going to go up to my room and get on with some work,' Kate said once Maggie was back inside.

'Why don't you use the dining room? There's a power point near the table, a phone line. It'll be a lot more comfortable for you and you can leave your things out.'

So Maggie settled herself down on the sofa to look through the gardening books, after which she planned to have a little nap, while Kate unpacked her briefcase and papers and set out her work on the table.

Work was the one space Kate always felt able to retreat into. Today was no exception. She unpacked the folders and notes, mock-ups of ads and photos – a little bit of re-organising and it looked like home from home, she thought ruefully, plugging in her laptop and firing it up. The to-do list popped up on the screen followed by the job she was working on; Kate sighed and put on her glasses. Home from home with just as many deadlines and jobs.

'Four star-studded nights and five excitement-filled days exploring the magic of the Algarve . . . aboard our luxury air-conditioned coach.' There ought to be some photos for this somewhere Kate thought, glancing back at the file.

When she looked up again it was late afternoon. She yawned and got up for a stretch.

True to her word, Maggie was sound asleep on the sofa surrounded by piles of books, graph paper, felt tips and magazines. Kate made herself a cup of tea and then went back to email the afternoon's work to the office. She plugged the modem into the house phone and logged on, watched the little bundles of work fly off into the ether. It felt good to see them vanish, electronic homing pigeons weighed down with words. When that was done Kate settled down with her mug and picked up her email. The menu said she had six new messages.

Kate idly scanned down the list of incoming messages, work, work, a couple of things from the office – nothing that she couldn't sort out from Maggie's with a phone call – and then clicked on the next one down. It was a receipt from the on-line dating agency that they'd signed Chrissie up for on Friday evening. For a moment it made the breath catch in her throat; maybe they'd made a mistake, and then Kate looked at it more closely and re-read the profile. It was Chrissie's all right – all the right ticks in all the right boxes, but for some reason her email address was on the receipt instead of Chrissie's.

Maybe Bill had put it in by accident. Bad timing, but it shouldn't take much to put right. There were bound to be instructions somewhere on how to change the personal details. Or maybe she should just delete it – after all, Chrissie had a man now, Kate thought bitterly.

'Dear Vulnerable Venus, we are delighted to receive your personality profile and details and to tell you that you have passed our stringent vetting policy. Your profile will appear on our web-site as from today.

It had Saturday's date on it.

'To protect your anonymity, just like regular ads in the personal columns we at RomanticSouls.com give all our clients their own personal box number, yours is box number 2758. You'll need your password and your box number to access any replies, to edit your personal details or add a photo or additional text. To do any of these please go to our web-site at www.RomanticSouls.com.'

Kate glanced down the list at the remaining

unopened emails – they all began '2758, you have mail' – and were dated over the weekend.

She re-read the letter again then clicked the link which took her straight to the dating agency's pages. As their home page appeared, Kate took a deep breath and banged in Chrissie's box number. When she got to the Vulnerable Venus's ad, Kate picked up her mobile.

But who should she ring? Chrissie? Joe?

'Kate, hi, how are you?' Bill said, picking up after two rings. He worked from home too and at least she wouldn't have to explain to him who all the people involved were.

He didn't sound all that surprised to hear from her and for an instant Kate hesitated; did he know about Joe and Chrissie already? And if that was true how long had he known? Her stomach fluttered; maybe Bill had always known. Maybe he had been protecting her right from the start. Kate took a steadying breath; she was beginning to get more than a little paranoid about this whole thing.

'How's it going? How's your mum doing?' Bill asked cheerfully.

There was a pause as Kate struggled to find her voice, which Bill spotted. 'Are you okay?'

Did that mean he knew?

'Have you see Joe over the last couple of days?'

'No, I haven't. I've been working my arse off. Why?' Now he sounded surprised and a bit bemused. 'Should I have? Was I meant to come round or something? Joe cancelled the video thing with the boys because you came home early. I've missed something, haven't I?'

'I've run away from home, Bill.' He was the first person she had admitted it to.

He laughed. 'What do you mean, run away? What's the matter?'

Kate sighed; where did she begin? 'I feel as if my head is about to explode.'

'Too much red wine or is Joe off on one again? He was really uptight on Friday.'

'Joe and Chrissie are having an affair or have been having one, I don't know which tense to use.' Her voice quavered. 'When I got home on Saturday morning they were there.'

It sounded so stark, so clear cut, so very easy to understand when said out loud.

'Jesus, are you sure?' Bill sounded genuinely shocked. 'Joe and Chrissie?'

'You didn't know about them?'

'No – Jesus,' he repeated. Kate was relieved. 'Bloody hell. I'm stunned. I don't know what to say. Where are you now? Are you okay? Do you need anything?' The words tumbled out one after the other.

'I've come back to my mum's for a few days. She needs a hand but I need time to think, work out where we go from here.'

'Right,' said Bill. 'I don't know what to say.'

Kate sighed. 'There isn't anything much you can say. The thing is I've just logged on and there are loads of replies for that ad we worked up for Chrissie.'

There was a brief silence and then he said, 'Delete the bloody things – it isn't rocket science, Kate, for Christ's sake. Do you want me to drive up there?'

Kate laughed grimly and said, 'No, and anyway I've seen how you cope with women in distress and if I start crying I don't think I'll be able to stop. Maybe I ought to reply to one of these guys, after all Chrissie and I have obviously got very similar tastes in men.' She was thinking no such thing but Kate wanted to ease the tension.

There was no way Bill could miss the raw emotion in her voice. 'Don't be stupid,' he said. 'I'm good with women. I only had a go at Helena because I was wearing a cream silk shirt; I didn't want mascara all over it, that's all. What's so bad about that? I seem to remember you had tissues and brandy.'

Sniffing back the tears, Kate snorted. 'And Diana?'

'White foundation, pink mohair and a new black suit? You have got to be kidding.'

'Ellen?'

'If you're gonna make a meal of it,' Bill growled.

Kate laughed, 'No, you're okay. I just wanted a friend to talk to, I didn't expect you to come up here and rescue me but I'm touched that you offered.'

As she spoke, Kate clicked one of the symbols beside the ad, putting her glasses on so as not to overlook a single syllable, and opened the profile they had written for Chrissie. 'Maybe I should leave my email address on here, and start over?'

> 'Vulnerable Venus: Good woman seeks genuine man with a warm heart. Are you solvent, sexy, and looking for someone special to share your life with?'

To get any further Kate needed to type in

Chrissie's password, 'Desperate' – it had seemed funny when Chrissie had come up with it on Friday night. As Kate typed it in, the email appeared.

'For fuck's sake, Kate,' Bill was saying.

'It's all right, I'm fine.'

'You don't sound fine to me.'

Silence.

'Kate, talk to me.' He sounded annoyed.

'Would you like me to read them out?'

Silence.

'Dear Venus . . .'

'Stop it, Kate. They aren't for you, they're meant for Vulnerable Venus. They're meant for Chrissie. You aren't vulnerable, you just need a friend.'

Kate didn't like to point out that up until Saturday she had had a very good friend, or at least so she had thought, and it had done her no good whatsoever.

'Do you want me to go round and talk to Joe?'

'And say what, Bill?' Kate stared, blinking back the tears, at the RomanticSouls.com web page, all strewn with hearts and flowers and boxed testimonials from successfully mated and dated members, and then at the flashing envelope besides the words 'New mail for you.'

'Tell him what a moron he is,' said Bill.

'I don't think that'll help. How about this one?' Kate said, reading from the screen. 'Forty-five and fat, this frisky and friendly fella wants a wild woman to share his life. Likes Elvis, Abba and Showaddywaddy.' It was too horrible to contemplate. 'There's more.'

'Kate.' Bill sounded exasperated.

'I don't know what *else* to do, Bill. I'm in shreds. I daren't think about Joe and Chrissie. It hurts so much. I've woken up the last two mornings and for a few seconds I've thought it was a bad dream and then it all comes pouring in and I know that it's not and it's horrible. Terrible. How could he do this to me?' The words caught in her throat.

Kate stared at the next email and read the tag line, 'Long tall Larry seeks –' and clicked the little icon on the bottom left-hand corner that promised a picture and then stared at the photo that slowly appeared. It seemed that RomanticSouls.com stringent policy checks on the contents of its advertisements weren't quite so rigorous after all. She laughed through the knot of tears. 'You should see this one. Long tall Larry sent me a picture of his willie as a calling card – and trust me, it was nothing much to write home about before he added the little black velvet bow.'

Bill didn't sound amused. 'Delete them, Kate. Cancel the subscription and close the damned thing down.'

Kate opened the next one almost as an act of pure defiance. How much worse could it get?

> 'Genuinely nice guy, looking for a woman
> with a good heart and sense of humour
> for friendship and maybe, if it works out,
> even love.'

'Bugger,' Kate sighed, 'though of course, he would say that. He's hardly going to say axe-wielding psychopath seeks hapless woman for unpleasant encounter resulting in chargeable offences now, is he?' Kate scanned down the rest of the profile. Against the odds he actually sounded quite appealing. He would have been perfect for Chrissie. 'He likes music, the theatre and movies, eating out and cooking. Do you want me to email them to you so you can have a look too? Do you want me to send you the willie-man?'

Bill hesitated so long before speaking that Kate decided to send them all anyway.

‘Thanks for listening to me. It feels like I’ve woken up in the middle of someone else’s life. I needed to talk to someone.’

Bill groaned. ‘Don’t go now, Kate. Is there anything I can do? Kate –’

She had no idea and hung up without saying goodbye.

The house phone rang almost soon as Kate came off-line. It was Guy for Maggie. He’d arrived at the hotel, was all settled in, and was missing her already, apparently. He was also delighted that Kate had arrived.

Feeling like the spectre at the feast, Kate took the walkabout phone through to the sitting room and handed it to Maggie who had been woken by the sound of the ringing. Kate went back to work, trying hard to ignore the sounds of billing and cooing from the sitting room.

A few minutes later the house phone rang again.

‘Kate?’ Maggie called through ‘Are you there, love? It’s Liz. She wondered if we’d like to go over for supper this evening. Would you like to talk to her?’

‘What do you want to do?’ Kate asked in a whisper, covering the mouthpiece as she took the phone.

Maggie shrugged. 'I don't mind, you're the one who's got to drive over there.'

Kate considered for a few seconds; the natural alternative, if they didn't accept, would be for Maggie to invite Liz and family over later in the week, so that they could meet up, which would mean that Kate would have to cook. Liz would moan about the state of the roads. Peter probably wouldn't come anyway because he'd have been working in London all day and had to be up early the next morning or was late home, or had an acre of work to do in his study and the girls would expect Kate to entertain them while Liz monopolised Maggie. Or at least that was how Kate imagined it panning out in the split second before she put the phone to her ear. An active imagination can be a terrible thing.

Liz was permanently on some sort of low fat, no fat, nothing vaguely interesting diet, which she forced on Peter Perfect. Kate seemed to remember Peter as a man who used to like red meat, a decent curry and a bottle of red back in the good old days before Liz got her paws on him. One of the girls had a gluten allergy, one was a vegetarian, which left one normal one who, if Kate remembered correctly, lived entirely on breakfast cereals and bananas.

'So what time would you like us to get over there?' Kate asked cheerily.

Joe was in the kitchen cooking supper for the boys when Bill got round there.

'Hi, you want to stay and eat with us? I'm just making a lasagne. There's plenty. In fact you could do me a favour, keep an eye on it while I nip over to pick the kids up if you like.' He pulled a cloth off the table and wiped his hands. 'My mum's taking up the slack while Kate's away.' He glanced at his watch. 'I told her not to cook but they've probably been stuffing all kinds of crap down their throats since they got back from school. She used to be a complete bloody dragon when I was a kid, but those pair can get away with murder.'

Bill stuck his hands in his pockets. 'No thanks, mate. I can't stay long. Kate rang me a little while ago.'

Joe barely looked up from sprinkling a great wave of grated cheese over the pasta sheets. 'So you know all about it then, do you?' He sounded defensive and put out all at the same time.

Bill shook his head. 'Hardly. Do you want to talk?'

Joe sighed and his shoulders slumped forward. 'Those are the magic words, aren't they? I don't know what there is to say. It was a mistake. I wish I could make Kate understand that. We were drunk.' Joe seemed to have forgotten that Bill was at the supper party too. 'She told me that she needs time to think, but I mean what is there to think about? I made a mistake, one mistake. Surely to God we're all allowed to make a mistake once in a while?'

Bill just looked at him. It was no excuse and it wasn't as if any of them had had so much to drink that they didn't know what they were doing.

'Come on, Bill,' said Joe, in a man to man voice. 'You know what it's like. When Chrissie first moved in next door there was a thing between us – you know, that buzz, that little kick in the bottom of the belly when we saw each other. I never meant to do anything about it but it's just one of those things that you can't fight, eventually something has to give. It's been going on for years, or at least we've both been trying to resist it for years.'

Bill looked him up and down. 'What? Until Friday night you mean? Are you trying to tell me that the pair of you hung out till Friday, that you gambled your marriage on a one-night stand with your wife's best friend?'

For a moment their eyes met; they both knew Joe was lying. Joe looked away first.

'No, no that's not what I'm saying. It wasn't like that, but it isn't like it's a full on affair or anything. It was an on-off thing. The thing this weekend was just shit timing, that's all. Me and Chrissie got together when the band were splitting up – briefly, I mean, nothing heavy – I'd lost a lot of money one way and another and I was home a lot playing Mr Mom and next door there was this dizzy, ditsy good-looking, horny blonde who thought I was sexy, successful and the best thing since white sliced. You know how it is.'

'And what about Kate? Didn't she know how it was too?'

Joe sighed. 'That's the trouble, isn't it? She knows exactly how it was. She knows that all this singer-songwriter stuff is all wind and glitter and basically back then, I was flat on my arse, hadn't got two brass farthings to rub together and owed Christ knows how much. No illusions there, mate; Kate was working all the hours God sends to keep us from sinking without trace. She was brilliant, used to come back in from delivering stuff to the agency, looking totally bloody knackered, and she would never say anything, never get angry. Not a word, not a single sodding word.' He was getting louder and angrier. 'Mrs Utterly-Saintly, rubbing it in with all that silence, not complaining, never moaning. I keep thinking it would have been so much better if she'd come in and tore me off a strip once in a while.'

Bill's expression didn't change. 'What? So that you could have screwed Chrissie with a clear conscience? Persuade yourself that Kate drove you to it?'

Joe winced. 'No, no, but at the time it felt like some kind of martyr treatment. She just got on with it.'

Bill snorted. 'Heartless bitch.'

Joe waved the sarcasm away. 'Look, Bill, the Chrissie thing didn't mean anything. I don't see why Kate can't understand.'

'You really want me to answer that?'

Joe sighed. 'Bloody women. Are you sure you don't want to stay for supper? There's plenty.'

Bill shook his head. 'Thanks but no thanks.'

In Norwich Peter Perfect was just finishing off preparing their aperitifs.

'So how's business going then?' he asked, handing Kate a glass of chilled Aqua Libra with a slice of lime floating in it.

Maggie was sipping a glass of wine while sitting on the sofa surrounded by a whole squadron of very serious-looking little girls. It was early evening in Peter and Liz's neat executive house. Liz's children always struck Kate as scary en masse and were fairly unnerving individually. They were blonde and plump and when not shrieking or giggling maniacally looked like bad-tempered frogs.

Maggie's foot was up on a stool, stuck out in front of her like the gun barrel of a tank, crutches alongside her to trip the unwary, and no one was allowed to sit on her lap, because Mummy had said so, twice, just in case there was any doubt about it. This didn't stop the three of them elbowing each other out of the way for pole position, which was tucked up under Granny Maggie's non-page turning arm.

The little girls were all wearing long pink cotton nighties and bunny rabbit slippers. The youngest one was wading her way through a bowl of Rice Krispies while Maggie read them a story about kittens.

Liz had installed everyone in the sitting room,

having insisted that she didn't want anyone to help her in the kitchen, except for the au pair and the lady who came in to do the cleaning, obviously.

Peter smiled and Kate nodded, 'Fine, thanks.'

'Good.'

'And you?'

'Good.'

Kate sipped her drink. On balance natural childbirth was preferable to these cosy conversations with Peter. They usually only did this at Christmas and at family weddings, which was more than enough. Kate always suspected that there was more to Peter than met the eye, there just had to be, but somewhere down the line Liz had discouraged him from having a personality because they were terribly difficult to house-train and might cause a mess.

'How are the boys faring?' he said, sipping the sherry Liz had suggested he might enjoy.

'Fine, thanks.'

As the girls were in the room and the picture of health she and Peter were denied the next scintillating round of conversation. Kate glanced towards the kitchen, wondering how much longer it would be before they ate and then glanced surreptitiously down at her watch.

At least, as the chauffeur to an invalid, she could say – however much Maggie protested – that she needed to get her home, get some rest, what with her broken ankle and all that, and obviously Peter and Liz needed to get up early so they couldn't stay too long. Please God.

Peter smiled. 'Awfully nice weather we've been having, although we could do with some rain for the garden.'

Peter was around 5′ 10, nice-looking in a homely way, with sandy gold hair, thinning on top, and the beginnings of a paunch. Whenever Kate saw him he was always dressed in smart casuals. Tonight this consisted of a crisp cranberry-coloured shirt, folded back to the elbows – the folds had been carefully ironed in – and a pair of cream chinos with a crease you could have shaved your legs on and penny loafers, although Kate's guess was that Peter wouldn't have chosen those clothes in a million years if left to his own devices.

Before Liz got hold of him, Kate and Peter had met half a dozen times at various young farmers dos and rugby club barbecues that she gate-crashed with . . . Kate beetled around for the name of her fellow conspirator and realised with a start that it had to have been Julie Hicks;

God look what happens when you grow up. Kate seemed to remember that up until he and Liz got engaged Peter was more of a jeans and tour tee-shirt man.

He used to live in a flat above a record shop in Kings Lynn and liked to cook and party and had on this occasion arranged for them all to go and see some band he was mad about. Kate paused and surreptitiously looked Peter up and down – it was hard to believe this was the same man. Although all of Liz's men had been very similar in looks and outlook. White collar or gentleman farmer types, successful in a stolid non-high-flying, non-boat rocking sort of way, and mostly blonde or at least fair, red-faced, serious or potentially serious, with strong family values and easily led without appearing too weak. They were boys and then men who wouldn't look out of place on the cricket pitch, at the rugby club or later, on the golf course, and who all looked as if they might end up bald and have heart trouble in later life. The kind of men who looked good in a Landrover with a springer spaniel at their side.

Thinking about attraction and marriage Kate's mind scuttled right past Peter back towards Joe and betrayal. She was just having a sudden death/insurance policy moment that would have been infinitely better than the best friend in bed with her husband moment, when Peter, waving a bottle in her direction, said, 'Would you like a little top up? Rather nice, isn't it? I often have it when I'm driving. Liz gets it from Tesco's, they've just opened a new store in Denham, haven't they. Amazing, isn't it?'

Hardly, thought Kate, although she didn't plan to point out that a new supermarket wasn't exactly on a par with alien landings, so instead she smiled while Peter continued, 'Supermarkets everywhere now, quite remarkable – you know, I remember when I was a boy . . .'

Kate grimaced. Oh God, they were already on his 'when I was a boy' speech. Peter was a couple of years older than Kate, four at the most, and here he was already playing the grand old patriarch card. He caught hold of his shirt where the lapel would have been if he had one and puffed out his chest.

Kate took a pull on her Aqua Libra wishing for all the world that it was a long tall Jack Daniels. There were times over the years when Kate considered the possibility that Liz and Peter had had their personalities expunged, surgically removed, wiped clean at some stage of their life. Liz probably rang up one of the classier Sunday magazines, sent off for a case of wine or two of New World wines, a full set of ecologically sound patio furniture, and the painless removal of any shred of individuality. Peter presumably paid for it all with his platinum credit card.

Kate sighed into the top of her glass, clearly remembering long distant days when she had been a nice well-brought-up sort of girl and not a cynical bitter old bat.

'So, planning to go anywhere nice for your holidays, are you?' Peter said cheerfully, once his world famous monologue on how incredibly hard it was to get your hands on a red pepper in 1976 in rural Norfolk had run its course.

'No, how about you?'

But before Peter had a chance to surprise them all with tales of backpacking from Yurt to Yurt living entirely on yak's milk in Outer Mongolia, Liz appeared in the doorway. She was wearing an apron. It had frills.

'Say good night to Grandma, girls, and Kate and Daddy. It's time for bed now.' And then to Kate, Maggie and Peter in the same no nonsense tone, 'If you'd like to come through, dinner's ready. I've cooked my speciality: Thai. Not too spicy obviously because we don't like spicy food, do we, Peter? Particularly not at this time of night, sets Peter's heartburn off, so I've adapted something I got out of the *Mail on Sunday*. I've always thought it's a sign of a good cook to be able to adapt a recipe without losing the basic character.'

As she waved them all through into the dining room, the au pair rounded up the girls, muttering something incomprehensible in Spanish, and Peter grabbed hold of Maggie's crutches and helped her to her feet.

'Steady as she goes,' he said, as they made their way into the hall. 'There we are, easy does it. Easy does it.'

He was speaking to Maggie in a tone slightly louder than necessary and enunciated every syllable as if his, or possibly her, life depended on it.

'Mum hasn't gone deaf, Peter,' Kate snapped, before she could stop herself.

Maggie said nothing. Peter gave them both a pitying glance. Drunk or not, one fall and you're senile apparently.

'Right,' said Liz, whipping the lid off a tureen once they were all settled, 'who's for wild rice?'

Kate smiled wanly. There was a peculiar floral smell in the room which was intensified as she took the lid off the dish next to her.

'It's green curry,' said Liz pleasantly. 'Just help yourself. Tuck in.'

Gamely, Kate picked up a ladle; the curry slithered onto her plate with an obscene glooping sound.

Liz's specially adapted curry recipe tasted like wallpaper paste and lemon washing-up liquid with spring onions sliced into it; it was the colour of new peas.

'Go on,' said Liz to Kate. 'Have a bit more than that. I've made plenty. It's low fat.'

Peter, fork poised above the puddle on his plate, smiled manfully, '*Bon appetit.*'

Kate looked down wondering how much she could realistically hide under the cutlery, while Liz embarked on a rundown of the girls' most recent achievements.

Dessert was something sweet, pink and pale yellow that Liz had defrosted from the freezer which, although it didn't taste of anything in particular, went very well with the raspberry sorbet and sage green-coloured dining room.

'I thought we'd go into the sitting room for coffee. Marie already made it – it'll give her chance to clear the table and pack the dishwasher,' suggested Liz, pressing a napkin to her lips as she got to the end of yet another ballet class anecdote.

The coffee was so strong it made Kate's eyes water. Liz, who was drinking jasmine tea, came in smiling, 'I was just saying to Mum that now we've had the new extension done you and Joe ought to come down and stay for a few days. I'm sure Chrissie would have the boys for you, you could have a romantic little weekend break away. Now does anyone want some cheese and biscuits?'

Kate eyeballed Maggie, who shrugged. Liz was more than capable of having a whole conversation on her own.

Maggie had barely yawned before Kate suggested they were on their way.

As soon as they were in the car Kate switched on her mobile in case the boys had rung. They hadn't, but there were three messages for her: one from Chrissie, one from Joe and one from Bill.

Chapter 7

In Windsor Street the door bell rang once, tentatively. Chrissie, who'd been stretched out on the sofa watching a detective thing with some old scrote in a mac on ITV, yawned, scratched and then glanced up at the clock. It was late for a social call on a weeknight, not that she was expecting anybody. Although, of course, there was a chance it might be Joe.

Both her boys were out. The eldest, Simon, wasn't likely to come home at all. His girlfriend had moved into a new flat and he was spending most of his time over there helping to decorate – or at least that was the excuse everyone was agreed on. Chrissie was just waiting for him to announce that he wasn't coming back at all.

Robbie, the youngest, had a summer job working behind the bar in a trendy new place in Highgate. Chrissie wasn't expecting him home until the wrong side of late, and he'd already said that he might stay overnight with friends. It seemed as if the kids were hardly in at all these days, and they certainly weren't likely to ring the bell as they both had their own keys.

Chrissie eased herself up off the sofa, stiffly, feeling tired and achy and for an instant terribly old.

Since Kate had walked in and found her in the kitchen with Joe, Chrissie had treated herself gently, as if she was suffering from a bad case of flu, as if she was delicate and poorly and much in need of kind treatment and a lot of TLC.

The worst thing – and the craziest thing – was that without Kate to confide in there was no one Chrissie could really talk to about what was going on. If you said anything to anybody at work it had done the rounds before your back was turned. Chrissie sighed; without Kate there was no one to lean on, no one to talk it right with. If it had been someone else's husband – and Joe certainly wasn't the first and she doubted that he would be the last – Kate would have made them both a mug of coffee in her kitchen, shaking her head incredulously, and somewhere in amongst all the giggling, and the squeals and the, 'Oh my God, no, you didn't, did you, and then what did he say?' somewhere in the act of making it into a story, the pain and the indignity, the sting would have gradually faded away.

Chrissie glanced into the mirror in the hall and plumped her hair up, wondering if it might be Joe at the door. She had been half expecting him although he might have rung before dropping in, that way she would have at least had chance to put a bit of a face on, had a shower, changed her clothes.

Feeling distinctly grubby, Chrissie sucked at her teeth and the inside of her mouth, and then rubbed a blob of make-up out of the corner of one eye. Bloody man. She'd got in from work, kicked off her shoes, made a mug of tea while nuking a curry in the microwave and eaten it straight out of the plastic tray in front of the telly with a fork, both of which were still on the floor by the sofa.

And why was Joe calling round so late? He knew that she'd got work in the morning. Maybe he had been waiting for the boys to settle down, although it didn't strike her as likely. Mind you, she thought, leaning forward to rub some colour into her cheeks, it was typical Joe to turn up unannounced and at a bad time.

Several times over the weekend Chrissie had thought that he might have at least had the decency to ring up and see if she was all right. She had watched him from behind the net curtains drive away in the car twice and both times had waited in, stood by the phone. Just in case he called on his mobile. But no, since Chrissie had walked down the stairs and out of Kate and Joe's house, nothing, not so much as a peep out of him. It hurt, really stung, although she wasn't altogether surprised.

During the last couple of days Chrissie had had plenty of time to imagine what had gone on after her leaving: Joe in the kitchen with Kate, him begging forgiveness, swearing it had only happened the once, that they were drunk, that it would never happen again, ever. Him crying and pleading, making his peace, blaming Chrissie, or maybe even Kate, for his fall from grace. With Joe anything was possible.

Chrissie, staring into the tired, world-weary eyes of her reflection, was under no illusions, first and foremost Joe was one of life's survivors. Chrissie had one last look in the mirror and then took off her glasses. Her eyes were still way too sore for contacts.

Over the years she had come to realise that despite Joe's cool, sexy man of the world exterior, he needed Kate or someone very like her to get him through the day, to smooth the kinks and the creases out of life for him.

On one particular occasion after they had had a long lazy afternoon in bed Joe had sat on the end of the bed looking all doleful and hangdog. For an instant Chrissie had been overcome by a great wave of compassion, wondering if it had all been a terrible mistake after all; what was this? Love? Regret? Remorse? His conscience finally kicking in?

'What is it?' she'd asked, after a few minutes, gently settling her hand on his shoulder, almost afraid to say anything, and Joe had turned and said, 'I can't find my sock. Have you seen my sock anywhere?' Bloody man.

Chrissie licked her lips, and then huffed into her cupped hand, wondering if her breath smelt or rather how much her breath smelt. Was Joe likely to want to kiss her? Probably, if he thought he could get away with it. She rootled in the hall drawer for a packet of Polos.

Poor Kate. As the name formed again in

Chrissie's mind, briefly, fleetingly, she wondered how she was. Not that she hadn't thought about her since Saturday, it was that her mind refused to stay there for more than an instant, as if it was too painful to stand so close to the white-hot glow of all those emotions.

Chrissie was shattered; the emotional scenery inside her head shifted from hour to hour, sometimes minute to minute, there were just so many things she felt. Guilt, regret, sadness, pain, defensiveness, anger, outrage and disbelief at being caught. A sense of inevitability and unreality were all wrapped up into thoughts so dense and impenetrable that they gave Chrissie a headache and left her exhausted, wishing that she would wake up and find out that none of it had ever happened.

If she was honest, hand on heart, an occasional leg over with Joe really wasn't worth this much aggravation and most certainly wasn't worth losing Kate for, but it was way, way too late to pull it back from the edge now. Chrissie stared hard again at her reflection.

Without her glasses everything was in softer focus, less wrinkled. It was a terrible shame she couldn't find something to play the same trick on her mind. Life at the moment was a complete mess and nothing Joe could possibly say was going to make it any easier or any simpler or any less painful; he wasn't that clever. Chrissie fluffed her hair a bit more. The doorbell rang again, the tone a little more insistent this time.

There was a part of her that still believed there was a chance that the storm would blow over, while another part of her knew the best plan was to go down to the estate agents and put the house on the market. Maybe the whole Joe and Kate thing was a sign, maybe now that her boys had grown up she was ready for a fresh start. A chance, a challenge. Maybe, maybe . . . She ought to answer the door and see what Joe had to say for himself.

Chrissie jerked open the door, defiantly, and peered myopically out into the gloom.

'Hi Chrissie, how are you?' said Bill. 'I spoke to Kate earlier and I thought I'd just nip round and see how you were.'

Chrissie sniffed. 'You'd better come in.'

'When did you say Mum would be back?' Danny asked, helping himself to the last of the 7-Up. He didn't bother with a glass, just tilted the big plastic bottle and sucked it dry with a crackle.

Joe stared at him, taking a moment or two to register the words.

'What?'

Danny backheeled the fridge door shut and stood the empty pop bottle down on the nearest work surface. 'Mum? When is she coming home? Only I can't find my games kit and stuff.'

'End of the week as far as I know. And don't just leave that there,' Joe waved towards the bottle. 'Put it in the rubbish bin. And anyway at your age you should be able to find your own things, keep your room tidy, clear up after yourself. Put stuff away so you know where it is.'

Danny gave him a cutting, patronising look, which Joe realised with a jolt was one of his own and then his son's gaze moved very slowly around the room. On to the sea of plates and bowls and dishes, the chopping board and the splashes of blood-red tomato paste, the discarded pasta sauce jar, the pots and pans, the onion skins, and the empty tins that were strewn around the kitchen, as if to highlight Joe's own shortcomings.

If Kate had been at home order would have been restored by now, everything tidied away and mopped up or stacked in the dishwasher, the empty lasagne dish soaking in the sink under a shroud of healing bubbles, not hardening up on the kitchen table. Danny sniffed to underline his point, picked up the empty plastic bottle like a holy relic, posted it into the swing bin, and made a beeline for the hall

'Whoa,' said Joe. 'Just hang on a minute there, son. I made it, I cooked it, and dished up, you can help clear up and pack the machine.'

Danny groaned. 'What? Ah come off it, Dad, I've got loads of homework to do.'

'You should have done it at Gran's this afternoon.'

'Oh yeh, right, like I could work over there while she was watching the TV at full blast. So many soaps, so little time. You know she records them, don't you?' he said sulkily. 'And anyway I've got stuff that needs handing in tomorrow.'

'Now,' Joe snapped and immediately got to his feet. The gesture wasn't meant to be threatening, Joe just wanted to get out of the kitchen and have a beer in the garden but Danny, all hormones and pecking order, saw it as some sort of alpha male gesture.

'All right, all right, keep your wig on,' he

snapped, looking distinctly rattled. Joe, careful not to change his expression, thought that maybe he should try sounding tough more often.

'What about Jake?' whined Danny as soon as Joe looked away. 'How come he hasn't got to come and help? He ate supper too.'

'He should be in bed.'

Danny snorted.

Joe felt a flare of temper. How come kids couldn't do what they were bloody well told? How come this sulky, petulant, selfish boy-man couldn't see that Joe hurt and was in pieces and needed, for once, for things to just go smoothly? Whatever happened to yes Dad, no Dad, whatever you say Dad? Joe pulled a can of beer out of the fridge; okay so maybe that was only in cartoons.

'Don't you worry about what Jake does. I'll get him to unpack it tomorrow morning.'

'What, before school? You'll be lucky. It's an uphill job getting him out of bed in the morning let alone getting him to do anything.'

'For Christ's sake, just shut up and get on with it, will you?' snapped Joe, resisting the temptation to give Danny a swift backhander as he headed out into the garden.

Danny rolled out a sullen bottom lip.

Once outside Joe settled himself on the patio. The light and heat had almost gone out of the day and the evening wind whispered through the fingers of woodland that backed onto the bottom of their garden.

The idea of woods in the city was one of the things that had drawn Kate, a country girl, to the house in the first place. Joe clearly remembered standing with the estate agent looking out over the overgrown tangle of brambles and conifers and scrub and thinking more along the lines that it was a great place for perverts and burglars to hole up while casing the house or watching Kate undress, but over the years he had been glad she'd talked him into it. On nights like this the woods seemed like an insulating blanket between him and real life; he could be almost anywhere. Through the trees he could hear a vixen calling for a mate.

Joe grinned, wishing he had brought his guitar out for company. He had the sort of ache in his chest that cried out to be transformed into a song. A good song, a song about love and betrayal and moments lost or maybe seized through madness, a song that would finally put his name on the map. The next great song the world had been waiting for. Maybe he'd get

Robbie Williams to cover it, number one single on his next album. Title track. Christ it was about time.

Joe tipped back in his chair, set crossed legs on the table and stared up into the golden grey-black haze that passes for night in the city, letting his mind run free. One thing Joe had never had was any problem with his imagination.

He felt around the edge of the ache. It would make a great video – he'd pick up a cameo role obviously, or maybe he should go a different route, write the hit single for the film soundtrack, or maybe he ought to have a shot at the screenplay, something bittersweet with Minnie Driver playing Kate. Or maybe Nicole Kidman. Yeah, that would be good. Joe let the fantasy roll. He could so easily see himself at the BAFTAs, the Oscars, the Tonys, the Brits, the Palme d'Or – you name it, Joe had already written the acceptance speech for it and decided what to wear.

From somewhere close by he could hear the discordant wails of a police siren which, like the flippers on a pinball table, pitched his mind in another direction; maybe he ought to have a shot at an action-adventure script. Mentally, Joe struck a martial arts pose. Oh yes, that looked good. Joe had always known that he'd got a film in him. Perhaps it was time to concede that music wasn't his final resting place after all; film, that was the way forward, maybe that was what the ache was about.

All that pain, the angst, to work through. Joe could visualise himself stripped to the waist, oiled, nicely sweated up, up on his toes with a belly like a washboard – not as part of the main story obviously but to set the scene, to show what kind of man he was. Maybe now was the time to renew his gym membership, not that it would take a lot of work to get back to his fighting weight, after all the superstructure was sound, like steel. Maybe they'd get him a personal trainer, although Joe thought, running a hand over his belly where it shelved out over his jeans, they'd probably want to use a body double for the early years. He wondered who they'd cast as him, in the lead role in the movie of the same name. This thing with Kate, maybe it was just the kick-start he needed, and out of a crisis came a masterwork. That's what he'd say on *Parkinson*, leaning forward to emphasise his pain and his sincerity.

Joe closed his eyes and eased his way – somewhat reluctantly – past the praise, the plaudits, the interviews and the critical acclaim, searching around for the first few bars of the melody or the opening line of the story. It had to be there somewhere, although at the moment it seemed just beyond his reach.

Irritated by the absence of his guitar but not sufficiently to go back inside and squabble over trivia with Danny, Joe turned to watch his son at work. In the glow of the lamplight Danny was busy banging and clattering around the kitchen, his annoyance transferred into clumsiness and noise.

Joe had no plans to mention anything to Danny about him and Kate. She'd cool down in Norfolk. Chill out, come round. What were the alternatives? Oh yes, they'd sort it out. They were good together.

So he wouldn't say anything, no need to upset the boys if it was going to blow over. Danny could wait until it came out on film or CD to get to the true grip on what his father felt, a legacy, a living letter. Joe nodded to himself contentedly. Whenever he thought about the events of Saturday morning it seemed a long, long while ago now and felt as if he had been watching it rather than taking part in it, a spectator rather than a participant, and, Joe realised, it was something that had happened between him and Kate not between him and Chrissie.

But that was how it was, wasn't it – how it had always been – him and Kate against the world.

And Chrissie? He really ought to go and see her, at least she would understand how he was feeling. Joe hesitated for a few moments, still watching Danny through the window as he moved around the kitchen. Would it be better to ring Chrissie, or just to go round there and drop in, like normal? Just drop by as if what had happened wasn't important? A no sweat, no big deal kind of thing. Talk face to face. Danny looked up as Joe got to his feet as if the movement had caught his eye. Should he tell Danny where he was going?

'Just going next door, Dan, shouldn't be long.' He'd say it casually.

But what if Kate rang while he was gone? What if Kate had already told Danny and he was putting a brave face on it? What if Kate asked casually when she got home, 'So did your dad go and see Chrissie?' Joe froze; this guilt stuff was so damned tricky and sticky and hard to pull away from.

Squaring his shoulders, Joe got up and headed

through the back gate and round to next door. As he got to the alley he could see Bill waiting on Chrissie's doorstep. Talking to her. It seemed that now wasn't the moment after all. He'd go round later, when Bill had left, assuming of course that Bill wasn't there too long. As the door closed behind him Joe wondered for an instant if Chrissie was sleeping with Bill as well.

Chrissie looked Bill up and down, not quite sure whether she was disappointed or relieved to see him there.

'It's a bit late,' she said and sniffed, folding her arms defensively across her chest. 'I was just about to get ready for bed. I've got a busy day tomorrow. We start stocktaking at the shop.'

Bill didn't move and so after a few seconds Chrissie waved him inside. He squeezed past her. Past Robbie's bike in the hall, past the piles of laundry just waiting to be taken upstairs, and the coats and three bags of stuff that Chrissie planned to take to the charity shop when she got a minute, past the stacked newspapers and magazines and a bag of aluminium cans for the recycling run. It crossed her mind, as

Bill picked his way through the detritus of her domestic arrangements, that maybe she ought to have a clear out before the estate agent came round to do a valuation. Until Bill had paused in the hall she hadn't realised that there were still Christmas decorations pinned into the ceiling above the hat stand, wound around the wind chimes and back through the light fitting.

Ahead of her Bill had stopped, obviously uncertain whether to go right into the sitting room or straight on through into the kitchen.

'So,' he said, turning back to face her, looking even more uncomfortable. 'How's it going?'

Chrissie had no intention of making things easy for him, every instinct told her that he had come round to cast judgement. God alone knows what Joe had told him – after all, Joe had had first crack at both of them, Kate and Bill. Probably said he'd taken pity on her. A mercy shagging.

'Fine. You want some coffee?'

'Yes, that would be good.' The relief in his voice was audible.

'Go in and sit down then and I'll make one,' she said, waving him into the sitting room. 'Do you take sugar, I can't remember?'

'No, just white and strong. Please.'

Chrissie left him there on his own while she filled the washing machine, cleared the draining board, waiting for the kettle to boil, all the while gathering her thoughts. When she finally came back in with his coffee, Bill was perched on the edge of one of the armchairs. Chrissie deliberately hadn't made herself a drink – she didn't want Bill to think this was a social occasion or that he had her permission to linger.

They had known each other since Bill had moved in to Windsor Street, back in the good old days when Chrissie still believed that happy ever after, if not probable, was still possible. Even so, she still felt uncomfortable with him and not just for the obvious reasons. Bill didn't often come in to her house – Chrissie couldn't actually remember the last time he'd been there. When they met it was usually at Kate and Joe's or occasionally Bill's for supper or a party or barbecue. It wasn't that Chrissie was ashamed of her place exactly, more that she was aware that over the years what little spare money she'd had had gone into the kids not the house. Things looked a little tired, a little faded, and not in an arty, bohemian way but in a saggy, rough, rescued out a of skip kind of way. Seeing Bill perched there on the edge of the armchair, all dressed up in his trendy and quietly expensive casuals, made her feel even grubbier than if it had been Joe calling. Bill nodded his thanks for the coffee and smiled nervously. Chrissie resisted the temptation to smile back. They both knew that she fancied him and had done for years, and that for some reason it had just never happened, and yes it made for a little added *frisson* that even now hung in the air between them like a wisp of smoke.

'So,' she said, getting up to light a joss stick on the mantlepiece. 'What brings you here then, Bill? Social call? Lecture? Moral outrage? I don't see any tar and feathers. Leave them outside, did you?'

He shook his head. 'I've just been talking to Kate; I was worried about you.'

She feigned shock to cover her genuine surprise. 'Me? Well, I'm impressed and *very* touched, Bill. What about the wronged wife and the contrite tortured husband? Aren't you meant to be on their side?'

Bill sighed. 'For Christ's sake, Chrissie. Stop pretending you're a tough little cookie, all hard arse and attitude and that all this is just water off a duck's back to you. You don't fool me, I've known you way too long to be taken in by all that crap.'

Chrissie felt her bottom lip tremble but turned away, refusing to let Bill see, as he continued, 'I feel such a prat; I'd got no idea about you and Joe – no bloody idea at all. I'm annoyed about not knowing. And Kate – at least you and Joe knew what was going on, she'd got no idea at all.' He stared at Chrissie and shook his head. 'Christ, you've got some balls, Blondie, it must have been like waiting for a time bomb to go off. You've got to be stark staring mad. I only hope he's worth it.'

Chrissie stared back, some sort of knowing stirring in her belly. 'And what about Joe? Aren't you worried about Joe?'

Bill held her gaze without any hesitation. 'If you ask me the man's a complete fucking moron, who deserves everything he gets.'

Chrissie snorted. 'Well, don't hold back will you, Bill? Say what you think while you've got the chance.'

He lifted an eyebrow. 'What? So, you're telling me you're glad Kate caught you pair together, are you? Glad that it's all out in the open and that you and Joe plan to live happily ever after?' Bill paused. The shadow strewn room filled up with silence. When it got uncomfortable, Bill said, 'This is the bit where you're meant to tell me that you're madly in love with Joe.' He took a sip on his coffee and mimed heavy duty waiting.

Chrissie reddened, wishing now that she had made herself a drink after all. Surreptitiously, she pushed the warped lasagne tray under the sofa with her heel.

'It would be better if I was madly in love with him, wouldn't it?' she said, resignedly. 'It would make more sense then. The stupid thing about it is that it isn't anything special, it isn't even a proper affair.' Chrissie's colour deepened further as something way down in her head struggled to define what it was that constituted a proper affair. 'You know what I mean – we didn't go anywhere, we didn't do anything as a couple. We never had plans to run away and start over. When I look at it, it makes no sense at all. For what it's worth I never had any intention of splitting Kate's marriage up or her ever finding out, it wasn't like that at all. Joe was just – just, I don't know – convenient. There were never any promises, no pretending, no happy ever after, just a good old-fashioned uncomplicated screw. At least that was what we both convinced ourselves.'

Bill's face wore a cynical expression, and who could blame him? 'Often?' he said. 'You and

Kate were so close I don't understand how come you could do it at all.'

Chrissie shrugged. Her private life was none of Bill's business, even so she was relieved to finally be able to lay some of the burden down by telling him.

'When me and Joe first got together I didn't know Kate. He told me – well you know what Joe's like. He told me all kinds of crap. And it stuck. It was like there were two different people, the Kate Joe talked about and the woman I knew. And the sex thing kind of happened in bursts, and then one of us would get freaked out, you know, worried about getting caught or getting too involved and we'd agree that it had to finish and that we'd never do it again. Or I'd start dating someone. And then it would fizzle out.'

Chrissie didn't have to add until the next time.

'I didn't want Kate to get hurt. And yes, I know how stupid that sounds now but I fancied Joe for a long time before I realised they were a couple. I'd seen him playing a few times in different pubs – Kate knew that, I told her once, said how good he was, and she laughed and told me not to say anything, Joe's ego was big enough – and then I moved in here and there he was. Next door. I couldn't believe my eyes or my luck when I first saw him. There are no excuses but it sort of happened in some other place, some place away from real life – at least that was the way it's always felt.

'After you'd gone home on Friday night I helped Joe to clear up and tidy away and one thing led to another. We were having a kiss and a cuddle and Joe suggested I stay for another drink. It must have been the first time in – I don't know, a couple of years maybe. The boys had already come round here – Robbie was home, but you already know that, you were there.'

Bill's gaze fixed her and then he nodded. 'I know, trouble is I keep thinking I was at another supper party. I didn't guess, not a bloody clue.'

Chrissie swallowed hard to try and choke down the tears that were blocking her throat. 'Hardly my fault you weren't wearing your X-ray specs, was it, Clark Kent? Oh, I don't know, Bill. Looking at it from this side it was totally bloody stupid, but it has been going on for years. It was just another thing in my life and let's face it my life has never exactly been plain sailing.'

'And what are you planning to do now?'

Chrissie shrugged. 'I don't know. Move probably. I thought I'd drop into the estate agents on the way home from work tomorrow, see what they say. Get someone to come round and do a valuation.'

Bill nodded in agreement; Chrissie was shaken. He didn't argue with her or say it was crazy or a bit drastic or suggest that maybe it might be better to see if things settled down before she did anything, he just nodded and looked around the room as if assessing the house's saleability.

Bill grinned. 'I think you're mad, but if you need a hand, Blondie. Well, you know. The four of us have been friends a long time and friends should stick together.'

Aware of the irony, Chrissie daren't say very much in case she cried. It occurred to her that maybe Bill fancied her more than she thought, maybe he saw this as his way in or maybe he was just genuinely being nice, maybe he felt sorry for her. Chrissie didn't trust her intuition, too confused and too upset to be able to pick the bones out of what she felt about him or sensed from him. So Chrissie smiled a funny wobbly smile and didn't fight when Bill gave her a pointedly non-sexual hug, stood his half-empty mug down in amongst the tangle of stuff on the coffee table and made his way to the front door.

After Bill left, the house suddenly seemed

very empty and very very quiet. After a couple of minutes Chrissie picked up the phone and dialled Kate's mobile. She wasn't altogether certain what it was she wanted to say or where she planned to begin but knew it was important to try.

She took a deep breath as the phone rang once, twice, and then a recorded and terribly efficient voice said, 'You are through to the voice mail service for Kate Harvey. If you'd like to leave your name and number after the tone then I'll get back to you as soon as possible. Thanks for calling.' The anticlimax was almost more than Chrissie could cope with.

Joe stood in the alleyway, watching Chrissie's house in a vague, increasingly abstract way until he began to feel cold. What it was that Bill and Chrissie were doing and saying in there? He was angry that Bill was with Chrissie when he wanted to talk to her, angry and frustrated and very slightly envious. Just when it got to the point when he felt he ought to do something and he was beginning to get wound up, the front door swung open and Bill reappeared, no post-orgasmic glow apparent, zipped up his leather jacket, and sauntered off down the road back towards his house.

Joe waited for a moment, feeling a bit non-plussed. In his imagination he'd just burst in through Chrissie's front door, found the pair of them rolling round on the hall floor, all knickers and shirt-tails, fumbling frantically to cover their tracks and now, with Bill gone, there was nothing. He sighed, feeling cheated. Maybe he wouldn't go and see Chrissie after all, it was getting late and he wasn't altogether certain what it was he planned to say to her or where any conversation might lead.

What if she took him by the hand and led him upstairs, glowing with anticipation, relieved that they didn't have to hide any more? What if she had plans for the two of them? What if she asked him to leave Kate? What if she didn't?

Turning slowly, Joe wandered back up the alley and into the house. The boys were nowhere in sight and suddenly everywhere and everything seemed very empty. After a couple of minutes Joe picked up the phone and dialled Kate's mobile. She had to be home by now. He wasn't altogether certain what it was he wanted to say or where he planned to begin but he knew it was important to try.

He took a deep breath as the phone rang once, twice, and then a recorded and terribly efficient voice said, 'You are through to the voice mail service for Kate Harvey. If you'd like to leave your name and number after the tone then I'll get back to you as soon as possible. Thanks for calling.' The anticlimax was almost more than Joe could cope with.

Chapter 8

'It's no good. I've got to pull over,' said Kate desperately, flicking on the indicator and swinging the car into a lay-by. The A47 was still busy even though it was getting late.

Maggie looked anxiously across at Kate, her pallor accentuated by the halogen glare of oncoming headlights. 'Are you all right?' asked Maggie. 'I did wonder about that curry. I think there's a garage up here. On the right. It can't be that far now. Or there are some bushes over there.' She pointed across the road towards dense dark hedgerows picked out by the headlights of the passing cars. 'I've got some tissues.'

Kate smiled. 'No, no, it's not that. I'm all right, I just need to listen to my messages.'

Maggie stared at her. 'Your messages?' she said flatly.

Kate nodded, reaching over into the back, dragging her handbag off the seat and switching on the interior light. After a few seconds she gave up rootling through the contents and tipped everything out into her lap.

'It won't take a minute. I should have picked them up while we were outside Liz's but I wanted to get away and thought I could wait until we got back home, except that I can't.' Kate puffed out a long breath and dialled her voice mail.

Maggie's gaze did not falter. 'Right. Okay. Just tell me one thing, Kate, are you having an affair?'

'No.'

'Are one of the boys in trouble?'

'No.'

'Is anyone terminally ill?'

'No.'

'I suppose I ought to feel relieved but it's very hard not to ask what the hell is going on, and believe me I am trying, I really am,' said Maggie grumpily staring out of the windscreen.

Kate's attention had already moved on, she had pressed the buttons to activate the voice mail service and was listening intently with a finger in her other ear to cut out the traffic noise – and Maggie.

'Hi, it's me,' said Chrissie in a voice that sounded very far away and totally disconnected. 'I've wanted to ring you for days. I need to talk, Kate. I don't know any other way to say it. I feel terrible. I can't sleep, I can't think straight.' There was a deep sigh and then Chrissie continued, 'I was going to ask you to call me back when you get a minute, but I suppose it ought to be me who rings you, really, didn't it? I'll try again tomorrow.' There was another weighty pause and then she said, 'I miss you.'

Kate felt an odd pain in the middle of her chest, a hot unhappy pain, which if she dwelt on she knew would turn to tears.

It was a relief to press delete. Kate retrieved the next message. It was Joe, who in a brisk no nonsense tone said, 'Hi, Kate, I must admit I wasn't expecting to get your machine. I rang your mum's as well but no one's answering there either. So where the hell are you? I thought you were supposed to be looking after Maggie. You and I ought to talk. Try and sort this thing out. I'll ring tomorrow unless you want to ring me in the meantime. I'm assuming you've had an early night, long drive and that – okay, well if you get this message and want to ring you know where I am. I'll talk to you tomorrow.' It was brisk and controlled, skirting the edge of frustration and anger. He was annoyed that she wasn't there to take his call.

And finally there was the message from Bill. 'Hi Kate, I just wondered how you were. I'll be up late if you want to talk.' There was a pause and then he added, 'Don't think you've got to go through this on your own. I'm here if you need someone. We've been friends a long time, Kate. You may be in Norfolk but all you've got to do is pick up the phone, doesn't matter what the time is.'

Kate shook her head, amazed that of the three of them it was only Bill who appeared to be the slightest bit concerned about her welfare.

From the passenger seat Maggie was watching her with interest. 'Well?'

Kate smiled apologetically as she snapped the phone shut. 'It's all right,' she said, easing the things in her lap back into her handbag. 'Nothing important.'

'Really.' Maggie raised one perfectly plucked eyebrow. It was her trademark gesture, one that

Kate recognised from her childhood. 'Nothing important?'

Kate switched off the car's interior light and turned the key in the ignition. 'That's right,' she said, with no conviction whatsoever. As they pulled back into the stream of traffic Kate, eager to change the subject, said, 'I thought you told me that Liz had been on some sort of cookery course.'

'She has,' Maggie replied with a heavy sigh.

They drove the rest of the way home in silence, Kate trying hard to keep her mind on the road and not let it slip into overdrive. From the passenger seat she could almost feel Maggie trying to compose the one question that would give her all the answers she needed.

Kate just hoped Maggie didn't find it, because she didn't feel ready to say all those things out loud.

Back home, Kate helped her out of the car, across the gravel and inside and then made them both coffee.

'You okay?' asked Maggie as Kate finished comfying her up with cushions and folding the duvet over her.

'Uhuh, I'm fine, I'm just going check my email and then I'm off to bed. Is there anything you want before I go?'

Maggie beaded her. 'Well, you could start with an explanation. More clues. Some little piece of the puzzle that will stop me fretting.'

Kate managed a thin smile and blew her a kiss goodnight. 'You've got enough to worry about just getting better. It's nothing, honestly. I don't want to talk about it.'

Maggie didn't look convinced. 'And I'm not convinced I want to listen but I'm worried about you. You look absolutely awful.'

'It's nothing.'

'Then tell me.'

Kate bit her lip. 'Not now, Mum.'

As she got to the door Maggie said, 'Sweet dreams, darling.'

'You too.'

In the dining room Kate switched on the computer and pulled up the last of the day's email. It was a habit she'd had for years. In her office at home it was always the last thing she did before the day ended, whatever time that might be.

She glanced up at the clock on the sideboard, ticking away the minutes. It was coming up for midnight although it wasn't unusual for her to be working late. It hadn't mattered so much when Joe was gigging regularly. When they first got together he'd had a tour in a support band, and then he'd had a couple of summer seasons chasing the big break. Once they were married Joe had managed to work from home, although that often meant he'd be out half the night at some pub or a club or church hall, creeping home in the wee small hours, reeking of beer and fags.

When the boys were born Kate more or less stopped going with him, having long since got over the novelty of being married to a muso. While he had been packing the van, unpacking the gear, doing the sound checks, she'd be at home with the kids and then, once they were safely tucked in bed, would carry on with work.

At first there was a big space left by Joe's irregular absences in her life. Stepping back from the social life surrounding the bands he'd been in had felt very lonely and isolating at first, as if she was edging out and it took no time at all to lose your step and not know who people were or what the latest gossip was. But they could hardly drag the boys around with them and she'd never quite felt comfortable on the girls and wives and lovers' table at gigs; the band was like a club with an exclusive membership in which she never quite fitted.

So in lots of ways, over the years her job had grown to fill the gap Joe's career left in Kate's life. It offered her some odd kind of comfort too. A sense of doing something worthwhile. But these days it was – more often than not – that she went into her office in the evening to escape from him.

Kate started at the screen, the realisation stopping her in her tracks; she was deliberating trying to get away from him.

Used to her working, the boys just got on with it, since he'd stopped playing regularly it was Joe who was at a loose end now, all alone in the sitting room flicking through the channels, picking at his guitar. Maybe that was it, maybe since the last band broke up and he only got the odd gig here and there, she *had* been neglecting him, hiding behind an unspoken accusation that one of them needed to earn a regular living. Was that the reason he'd slept with Chrissie?

Caught in the middle distance, waiting for the modem to connect, Kate tried to work out what she could have done differently? The mortgage needed to be paid whether Joe had a gig or not; they had to eat.

Kate had a vision of Joe – exaggerated by her growing sense of guilt – huddled in the darkened sitting room, glazed over, watching the TV without seeing the pictures, depressed, lost and lonely with just a can of beer for company, while in the office she and the boys roared with laughter, a whole happy family without him. Was it any wonder he had gone next door for comfort? Kate tried to rework her thoughts, trying to fathom out what was right and which way was up, what was true and what was just her brain firing buckshot at any moving target, her conscience finally wrestling itself into exhaustion.

Meanwhile on the screen a flurry of post appeared in the in-box.

Glancing back at the computer Kate was astonished to discover that there were thirty-eight new emails. What the hell was going on? Four at the end of the day that weren't ads or mailshots would have been about average. Kate looked more closely at the addresses and then the penny suddenly dropped. What with work and the phone messages and dinner at Liz's she'd completely forgotten about Vulnerable Venus and the ad on RomanticSouls.com. It seemed that Venus was a very popular lady.

As Kate stared at the unfolding list of mail, her first instinct was to ignore them, but then again what the hell, who was it going to hurt if she picked them up? It was certainly better than sitting here all alone with her thoughts.

She clicked onto the personals site and began to read the replies and the profiles that went with them. It was like another world. Tall, thin, short and plump – some were quite obviously no hopers, emails misspelt, brusque, too brief, too long, too young, too old, too ugly. In fact out of all the ones she read there was only one that really stood out:

'Hi Venus, you sound really nice. I'm certain that you've been inundated with hundreds of replies so I won't be at all offended if you decide to ignore mine. I'm 39, not bad-looking, all my own everything, that is to say nothing comes off, straps on or sits in a glass by my bed at night. I'm solvent and sane with my own home and a good job that I really enjoy. I like all sorts of music, good foods, wine, the cinema, theatre. How about you?

You sound as if you've been through a

rough time just recently. I'm a good listener if you need to talk. I know what it feels like to be alone and let down by people who say they love you. Maybe you're in need of a little bit of tender loving care – a pair of strong arms to hold you tight, or just a shoulder to cry on when the going gets rough, either in real life or just in cyberspace? You never know I might just be that good man you say you're looking for. So, no pressure, and no rush. It would be nice to hear from you if you've got time. But whatever you decide I hope things work out for you – you sound like a good woman. With all best wishes, Sam57.'

Kate stared at the email. How could this man, lurking behind a pseudonym, possibly know *how* she felt? And then it occurred to Kate that of course he didn't know, that he was just fishing with the right bait. Chrissie's profile had mentioned nursing a broken heart and that she was looking for a good man to help her heal, rather than a record-breaking 100 metres dash down the aisle.

Kate grinned. This guy was a natural, he should be working in PR, and then she laughed aloud; maybe he did. On the bottom left-hand corner of the message, underlined in red, was an on-screen button, a link, that if she pressed it, would take her straight to Sam57's personal profile. It was impossible not to and anyway, reading it wouldn't hurt anybody, would it?

Kate leant back and scanned what he'd written about himself. God, this man was good; he sounded perfect.

> 'Tall, blond, late 30s, businessman, solvent sane and sensitive seeks a good woman to share good times with. I'm not bad-looking in a craggy, lived-in sort of way. I'm not looking to rush you into something you're not ready for, just wine, dine and woo you with low lights, soft music, good company and long walks in the park with a bottle of wine and a picnic. Are you equally at home on a deserted beach as on a plane to New York? I'm not looking for a commitment for life, just a commitment to live. Maybe you'd like to talk . . . Why don't you mail me?'

Kate, still smiling, looked at the ad and then clicked back to the email Sam57 had sent her, and then back to the ad. In the box asking what he expected to get from a relationship the only one he had ticked was 'friendship first and then let's see what happens' which was pretty restrained out of a list that began with casual sex and ran all the way through to marriage and happy ever after.

He certainly had an easy way with words; Kate found it impossible not to let her mind wander. Wouldn't it be wonderful once in a while to be with a man who knew exactly what to say and when to say it? A man who didn't lean, who led? A man who knew what he was doing, who planned, organised and then took responsibility for his own actions and decisions? A man who would whisk Kate away to wonderful places? Who surprised her? Who took her out to dinner or away for the weekend? A man who – Kate stopped dead in her tracks and blushed scarlet, looking over her shoulder to check that Maggie hadn't come in when she wasn't looking.

This was total and utter madness. What the hell was she thinking about? This was ridiculous.

Kate knew nothing at all about Sam57 other than that he was very good when it came to self-promotion. Although even so, said a mischievous little voice in her head, it would be such a shame and maybe even downright rude not to thank him for his interest, for his concern.

Kate re-read his email. She didn't owe him anything but what harm would it do to drop him a few words of thanks, say that he had cheered her up, made her feel better? Her reply would be as anonymous as his was. And so, after a moment's hesitation Kate began to type:

> 'Dear Sam57, thanks for your email. What a perceptive man you are . . . although I've got to come clean, I didn't write the Venus ad for myself. I have this very good friend, or maybe it would be better to say I *had* this very good friend until this weekend. Let me explain – I'm married and my friend Venus was so lonely after this guy did the dirty on her, so we decided to advertise . . .'

Head down, mind fixed on the screen, Kate continued to type.

It all came out, every last word of it. Chrissie and Joe, the whole thing. It felt a bit like putting a message in a bottle or one of those time capsules buried under a public building, something that wouldn't be seen or read or discovered except by accident. Somehow, by laying it all out, the weight on Kate's chest shifted and left her feeling lighter and clearer.

When she was finished she glanced down at the keyboard, wondering if there was some extra keystroke, some extra letter or symbol she could add to the end of the final sentence that would indicate her pain or somehow reflect or record the terrible sense of world-weary exhaustion that she felt about it all.

'Kate?'

Instinctively she swung round. Maggie was standing in the doorway behind her, resting heavily on her crutches; she looked pale and pained.

'I thought you were in bed,' Kate said, turning so that her body hid the computer screen.

'I was on my way to the loo, I thought I'd come in to see if you were still working. It's late, sweetheart. You should be in bed. Do I have to say that I'm worried about you?'

Kate laughed, 'No, and it's supposed to be the other way round. You should be snuggled up sound asleep not gallivanting about the place. Is there anything you need? More coffee, more painkillers, someone to tell you a story and tuck you in tight?'

'I was going to ask you the very same thing.'

Kate shook her head. 'No, I'm more or less finished here.' And with that she turned and pressed send, watching as the email to Sam57 vanished off into the ether.

In Windsor Street, Chrissie was still awake too, sitting hunched on the ottoman in the bay window of her bedroom, draped in a blanket, staring out at the corona of street lamps outside her window. When she first moved in the lights had been a real comfort, like some sort of celestial nightlight that kept away the darkness and the monsters, both in reality and in an emotional sense.

Dressed in a faded baggy tee-shirt, Chrissie looked down at the familiar lines of the street, painted in half tones, the trees, the sepia-coloured pavements, the deep folds of inky black shadow draped under the hedges and around the bins.

The house seemed horribly quiet and still. She craned to pick out some noise to get some sense that she wasn't alone, although of course she was.

Robbie had rung to say he was crashing at a mate's house and might not be home till the weekend. Simon hadn't even bothered to ring. It was nearly two in the morning and Chrissie was caught in that hellish place where she was tired but couldn't find the pathway that led to sleep and wasn't awake enough to read or watch TV. Her mind had raced and run and twisted itself into knots since Bill left. She had had a mug of tea, a glass of warm milk and a couple of shots of Scotch – not that any of it seemed to have taken her any closer to unconsciousness.

This was the third night in a row that she had sat here in the window watching the night turn into day. On Saturday and Sunday night, exhausted, too tired to cry, too tired to fight, she had finally drifted off to sleep, curled up under the rug and woken up a few minutes before the alarm, cold and stiff and full of pains.

Oddly enough, despite it being so late, she wasn't altogether surprised to hear the doorbell ring again. Climbing stiffly off her perch, Chrissie crept downstairs and padded barefoot across the hall. She didn't even hesitate or call out before undoing the lock.

Joe was standing on the doorstep, dressed in tee-shirt and shorts, a towelling bathrobe pulled over his shoulders. 'I couldn't sleep,' he said.

'You'd better come in.'

He shook his head and for a few moments they stood there, him on the doorstep, her on the mat, in the gloom not quite able to look at each other, not quite able to speak and then all of a sudden Joe said, 'So what did Bill want then?'

If Chrissie was expecting a few words of comfort or concern she was out of luck.

'Spying on me now as well, are you?' she snapped.

'No,' Joe protested, 'I just asked. He came round to see me too. Have you spoken to Kate?'

Chrissie flinched. 'No, I tried earlier to ring but her machine was on. I assumed that she didn't want to speak to me – to any of us. Look, are you coming in or staying out there only I'm getting cold and I'm so knackered I can't think straight.'

'So what *did* Bill want?' Joe's tone was slightly more aggressive.

'Oh for Christ's sake, Joe, what's this? The little green monster surfacing at long last? He came round to offer me a shoulder to cry on, to talk. Which is a lot more than some people did.' Joe didn't catch on to the rope being thrown to him. Chrissie started to shiver. 'He said Kate rang him earlier. Anyway what is this, Joe? It's two o'clock in the morning, for God's sake.'

He sighed. 'I'm sorry,' he said, although Chrissie wasn't altogether sure what he was apologising for, but before she could ask, he stepped inside and grabbed hold of her.

'Joe!' she protested. 'What the –' but it was pointless. He held her close and, catching hold of her head with both of his hands, kissed her hard. He was cold and she could sense how hungry. Without a word he kicked the door shut and then practically dragged her upstairs; they barely made it to the bedroom. His kisses were insistent and ferocious, though Chrissie knew even as he was dragging her tee-shirt off over her head that what Joe really wanted was reassurance and comfort. Not that it worried Chrissie all that much, because at that moment she needed exactly the same thing.

She wondered fleetingly, as he guided her down amongst the tangle of sheets, whether this was the last bite of the cherry. As his hands worked eagerly up over her breasts, his lips just a fraction behind, she considered whether this was one final fling before Joe waved goodbye forever? A farewell fuck. Or was it that he saw this as the first time in a real, out in the open relationship that would change shape and grow and become . . . become what?

Chrissie looked up into his lust-glazed eyes; however it might appear Joe Harvey hadn't changed his spots. He was still the man that he had always been. He had leant on Kate and he would lean on Chrissie too if she let him, even if it was just long enough to fish him out of his current dilemma. She knew all this and more and yet didn't, couldn't resist him.

'I love you,' he purred, coming up for air, nuzzling her neck and shoulders with warm hungry kisses.

'No, you don't,' she said, but he didn't hear her.

Kate lay alone under the duvet staring up into the darkness feeling more alone than she could ever remember. Maggie had Guy. Liz had Peter. And Joe? Well, part of her assumed that, left to his own devices, that Joe probably had Chrissie. For an instant, reading Sam 57's profile, she had had a clear uninterrupted view of all those things she had chosen not to see about Joe. Those things that were missing, those things she longed for but had convinced herself didn't matter. It would be naïve to assume that it wasn't the same for him. Familiarity breeds resignation.

Somewhere on the edge of her consciousness Kate heard the phone ringing downstairs and without thinking leapt out of bed to answer it. Out on the landing, cold and feeling even more alone, it took her a minute or two to realise that the call wasn't for her at all. From the sitting room she could hear the subdued giggling and low warm tones of late night welcome and then intimate eager conversation; Guy was obviously missing her mum.

Close to tears, Kate sloped off back to bed. Curling up into a foetal huddle she remembered how her dad used to make Maggie laugh like that too. Even when she was quite little Kate had always had some sense of the gentle secure intimacy between her parents, and now that she had the vocabulary to express it, she realised that their closeness made her feel excluded and yes, okay, maybe even a little jealous.

She remembered her mum standing in the kitchen washing up, her dad coming home from work and snuggling up to her, slipping his arms around her waist, kissing her on the neck, her craning round to kiss him back.

How had they managed to do that for so many years? If there was one thing Kate remembered about her parents, it was the unselfconscious, unforced way that they had genuinely loved each other. There was passion and fun and sometimes huge rows and door slamming, but on balance as a child Kate had always had the sense that they were on the same side, fighting the same battles, and that the bad things, the monsters and the hurt, and all the really bad stuff, was outside beyond the walls. Despite her being an adult her dad's death had somehow seemed like a violation of that magic safe space.

Maybe that was why she felt so bad about Joe. And now there was Guy, giggling and talking.

How was it that one woman could have two men who so patently adored her? What was it that endeared them to her? What was it Maggie had that she didn't? For an instant Kate was furious and full of envy; it simply wasn't fair. Why didn't she have a man who rang up and comforted her, who supported and loved her in real ways?

Kate pulled the blankets up over her head. As she closed her eyes for a moment Kate imagined Sam57 sitting at his computer composing an email to her. He had his back towards her but Kate sensed that he was smiling.

Chapter 9

Unless aliens had stolen Joe, he had to have left Chrissie's house while she was still asleep. In fact, for a few moments on waking, Chrissie wondered if perhaps Joe's late night visit had been a dream. But in a Cinderella-like gesture, Joe had left a single navy sock in the middle of her sheepskin rug. There was a large hole in the toe.

Although Chrissie and Joe had talked for a while in the warm intimate period between making love and falling asleep, she was none the wiser about whether it was an end or a beginning and any sense of comfort Chrissie had found lying in Joe's arms had evaporated on waking.

* * *

Kate was glad when morning came too; at least she didn't have to pretend to be trying to sleep any more. Tuesday's schedule appeared to involve getting Maggie up, washed, dressed and then . . . and then after making them both breakfast, staring idly out of the kitchen window into the garden. There used to be a swing and a climbing frame, just over there. Her dad had built a shed under the hedge as a playhouse for her and Liz – it had a little veranda edged with fretwork to match the main house. They had camped out there on summer evenings under makeshift tents, and had had bonfires and barbecues and birthday parties under the watchful eye of the big old house.

Kate smiled; the events of childhood ran into each other. No sooner had you blown out one set of candles than it was time to light the bonfire, turn round and drop the last of the glowing sparklers just in time to hang up your pillowcase, pull on your mittens, and build a snowman before stepping out of the front door into high summer.

Now there was a very grown up terrace where the sandpit had been, with a hanging water feature and elegant square trellis, trimmed with honeysuckle and clematis and heavily scented climbing roses, against the wall that they'd hung their first dartboard on.

'Penny for them?' said Maggie, from the other side of the table.

Kate jumped, whipped back into the present. 'I should keep your money, Mum, I was on a whistle-stop tour down memory lane.' She got to her feet and began clearing the table. 'Is there anything you'd like to do today?'

Maggie sighed ruefully. 'I'd like to know what's going on.'

There was a little pause while Kate ran hot water into the sink and started tidying things away, so Maggie continued, 'And I had been planning a trip to Cambridge before this,' she nodded towards the unwieldy plaster cast, with its five pink piglets poking out of the end, which was currently resting on a chair. 'Go round the market, indulge myself at the Monsoon sale shop, find somewhere trendy for lunch that does extraordinary things with goats' cheese, treat myself to a glass of champagne, and then wander home, tired but happy.'

'We could still do that if you wanted to,' said Kate, although she couldn't quite keep the reluctance out of her voice.

Maggie stared at her and then laughed. 'You always were a lousy liar, Kate. It'll keep and anyway I'd only spend too much money. I want to nip in and out of places not be wheeled about like some grand old dowager on her rounds. I'll be fine here, I thought I'd take a book out into the garden if it stays as nice as this. It's so frustrating not being able to get on with anything. Guy said he'd ring me this morning if he gets time so that I can moan at him.'

There was a moment of stillness and then Maggie said, 'I hope the phone didn't disturb you last night.'

Kate sensed the ongoing invitation to talk and wondered, if she opened her mouth, exactly what words might come out. One thing was for sure, Maggie was right about her finding it very hard to lie.

'He's totally besotted with you, isn't he?' Kate said, wiping crumbs off the pine table with a damp cloth.

Maggie nodded. 'And then some, and if I'm honest I suppose I am too. He's a lovely man. Kind, funny. I've known him for about eighteen months now and the shine still doesn't seem to have worn off. I'd expected to resurface by now – you know, the three month madness rule?'

'You don't have to justify yourself to me.' It sounded harsher than Kate intended.

'I wasn't.'

Kate took a deep breath, wondering where to start but her mouth was already well ahead of her, 'Taz told me that he'd asked you to marry him.' The words came out like an accusation, petulant and affronted.

Maggie calmly nodded. 'Uhuh, that's right, he did. And?'

Kate shifted her weight feeling uncomfortable. 'Didn't it occur to you that maybe Liz and I ought to know about it?'

'Probably – I suppose I don't see you often enough to find the way into those kinds of conversations, Kate. You know what it's like when we talk on the phone. It's all football teams and exam results. It's hard to just launch into those conversations about doubts and considerations, weighing up the pros and cons, the ones about not knowing.'

Kate felt her colour deepen a shade or two as Maggie continued, 'I suppose that when it comes to relationships I'm not comfortable about discussing my deliberations or my hopes and fears with you. At my age those are my mistakes to make. However much we love each other there are just some conversations that parents and children find it hard to have.

'If I was worried about it then, trust me, I'd tell you. With Guy I needed time to think about what I felt before I said anything.' And as she spoke Maggie met Kate's eye without hesitation. For an instant Kate was thrown. Wasn't she keeping secrets just as close to her chest, closing Maggie out because she was afraid too? Did she fear Maggie's pity? Was it that she felt sordid, as if Joe and Chrissie's adultery had tainted her too? Or was it that Joe's affair made her feel as if she had failed?

'And besides which,' Maggie said, taking a bite out of the toast crusts piled up on her plate. 'I said no.'

'Oh, right. And did you mean it?' asked Kate, struggling to regain her composure.

Maggie nodded, speaking through a mouthful of crumbs. 'For the moment.'

Kate felt a wave of heat roll through her. 'Then you might say yes?'

'I might do. Eventually. The thing is I genuinely haven't made up my mind. I'm enjoying my freedom.' She looked across at Kate and laughed, 'Oh come on, Kate, lighten up for God's sake. It's a big decision to make at any age, and I've certainly got no plans to rush into it. But trust me, if I ever decide to get married again you will be one of the first to know.' Her tone was patient but had a real no nonsense edge to it.

Kate knew she ought to back off. There was no way, as an adult, that she wanted Maggie nosing in her affairs – hadn't she just spent the last twenty-four hours batting her off? But even so Kate couldn't quite hold her feelings in, they bubbled out between her lips unbidden. 'But what about Dad? What about me and Liz? Doesn't how we feel count too? Don't we have a say in what you do?' It sounded preposterous when said aloud.

Maggie's gaze didn't falter. 'Certainly you can have a say, love. But I'm not spending my life sitting home waiting for you to call or to tell me what you think I should be doing, Kate. You are entitled to an opinion but not the final word. Surely you know me well enough to know that I wouldn't deliberately do anything to upset either you or Liz but this is my life. Your dad loved me far too much to want me to spend the rest of my life alone.'

'I understand that, I can see that you need company, but the thing is, Mum, it's just that

Guy is so, so . . .' Kate reached around for some polite euphemism, some softening words but there were none, '. . . so young.'

There it was, it was out now. There was no going back.

To her total amazement, Maggie laughed. 'You don't say,' she said without missing a beat.

Kate blushed furiously as the tension that had been steadily growing between them broke into dozens of pieces.

'I suppose you're going to tell me that he is incredibly mature?' Kate said grumpily.

Maggie still laughing, said, 'No, not at all, quite the reverse in fact and I'm glad. I don't want to be with someone who makes me feel old and responsible, Kate. I've done all that. What I want is to be with someone who loves me as I am, someone to have fun with, who sees *me* not my age. When I was young and maybe should have been doing silly, exciting, romantic things I was married and had you two. Don't get me wrong, I don't regret it for an instant and I loved your dad, and being a mum; you and Liz gave me more joy than I can possibly say. I wouldn't have wished him gone for the world, but he *is* gone and in that space – that second chance –

I'm going to do some of the things I didn't get chance to do first time around.

'I've been on my own five years now and I've been out with quite a few men, most of them around your dad's age, but I think that to appreciate their finer qualities you really have to have grown older with them. So many of them are incredibly boring and set in their ways, pompous, overweight, under-sexed . . .'

Kate looked away, reddening furiously, but Maggie wasn't done yet.

'. . . with hernias and haemorrhoids and heartburn – it's absolutely terrifying. Middle-aged men don't seem to wear well. I just kept thinking that all they really wanted was someone to look after them in their old age and almost anyone would do, someone to cook and clean and take care of them. I don't want that. I want someone who wants me, not a substitute, not a nurse, not a mother, but me. And yes, I do know exactly how old I am and how old Guy is, Kate. But I also want and deserve a companion and a friend and a lover, someone to share with and travel with and plan things with, someone who has got as much zest for life as I have.'

Kate nodded, feeling a wave of tears that took her by surprise. 'But what about if he goes, what if he gets tired of you? He's so young, and so bloody pretty. He could have anyone –' It sounded dreadful but Kate couldn't stop now. 'What if he up and leaves you for some sexy little twenty-eight-year-old? Some dolly bird. How the hell are you going to feel then?' It was cruel but the words were all out before Kate had any time to soften them.

Maggie shrugged philosophically, although Kate sensed the flash of pain. The ideas could hardly have come as a surprise to her.

'Who knows?' she said after a few seconds. 'I haven't lied to him about my age, Kate – he knows who and what I am. Let's face it he could run off with somebody else even if he was sixty – age is no guarantee of fidelity. I have given it a lot of thought, but realistically I'm just as likely to be the one who gets bored and ditches him. All right, from where you're sitting logic and natural paranoia would suggest that Guy will eventually leave and probably find someone younger. But what if he doesn't? What if he really, truly, wants to spend the rest of his life with me or even just a few years of it? Am I going to pass up the chance of being happy with him because of what might happen? I'd rather have a little bit of something wonderful than a lifetime of mediocrity. Whatever happens I know I'll survive, Kate; losing your dad taught me that. Life doesn't come with guarantees.'

'But what about getting hurt?' said Kate desperately.

Maggie sighed. 'Even if I get hurt or end up hurting him, it's worth the risk. I love him, Kate, and I know that he loves me. It might not be forever but it is for now. He wasn't what I had expected at all but fate can be so odd. I like being in a relationship. I like being in *this* relationship. Don't get me wrong, I don't mind being alone or having my own space – in some ways I really enjoy it, but I'm just happier as part of something bigger.'

Kate stared at her. What else was there to say? For a moment, the two women looked at each other and then Kate looked away, conceding defeat without rancour.

But before either of them could think of the next thing to say, Kate's mobile rang. She glanced down at the screen: it was Joe. Without a backward glance, Kate got to her feet and headed out into the garden. The sun was already warm, creeping in through the trellis, its shadow cutting the patio into bite-sized, sunlit pieces. She pressed the button to take the call and at the same time took a breath.

'Where the hell have you been? I thought you said that you'd ring me,' Joe barked abruptly without any preamble before Kate had chance to speak.

Taken aback, she spluttered, 'Hang on a minute, Joe, you told me to ring you; I was going to call you later.' She was already on the defensive with no clear idea of why.

'You got my message then?'

'Yes. I took Mum over to Liz's for supper last night, we didn't get back until late. I didn't want to disturb you.' As she spoke Kate was aware of her mind carefully forming each word and as it did examining every one for anything that might be inflammatory or that could be misinterpreted. It made her feel sad. Things had changed between them forever.

'Right. And so? What? You didn't turn your phone on? Or you didn't take it with you?'

Why did he want to know that? The conversation was so stiff that it felt as if the words might snap off and break.

'No, I just told you. I thought it was too late to ring. The thing is, Joe, I –' The words were hard to find, even harder to say. How could Kate tell him that she hadn't wanted to speak to him? As it was, Kate didn't have to because Joe jumped in before she had time to finish the sentence.

'You know Bill came round here last night, don't you?' he snapped. 'He told me he'd already spoken to you, said that you'd rung him. To be perfectly honest, Kate, I'm surprised that you said anything to Bill and I'm angry that you didn't ring me first. I'm your husband, for Christ's sake.'

Kate was surprised too. Part of her at least had hoped, maybe even assumed, that Joe might be apologetic, conciliatory, although in her mind's eye she could see him now, standing there in the hall, and as she did, caught a glimpse of the way he looked. She imagined his stance, his face, the way he twisted the coiled flex between supple guitar player's fingers and she knew without a doubt that Joe was furious and affronted by her calling Bill.

'I rang him yesterday,' Kate said in a neutral voice. 'I just wanted someone to talk to.'

He snorted. 'Right. So you talked to Golden Boy? Poured your heart out, did you? Very cosy. Couldn't wait to tell him your side of the story. What, wasn't I good enough?'

The venom in his voice stunned Kate. 'Sorry?'

Joe's reply came back in an instant. 'You know what I mean, Kate. Washing your dirty linen in public. Why did you have to tell anyone anyway? Couldn't you just keep it to yourself? Why couldn't you talk to me? What were you trying to do, get the sympathy vote? I know that we can work this out, if we keep it quiet, just between ourselves, but now Bill knows and I suppose you've told Maggie as well and what about your precious bloody sister and Peter? You telling people changes everything, Kate. We need to put it behind us and you're making it very difficult. You're not the only one in this, you know, and you're certainly not the only one who's been hurt.'

Reeling, Kate had to fight to catch her breath. It was such a strange thing to say and then Kate had a revelation. 'Oh my God, I get it. You've been to see Chrissie, haven't you?' she whispered. It wasn't a question it was a statement.

For a moment Joe said nothing and then he said, 'I was worried about her, that's all. You know what she's like. She's in a really bad way at the moment.'

Kate shook her head in disbelief, amazed at the depth of concern in his voice. 'And whose fault it that, Joe? You're the one who is always going on about how she brings it on herself. Well, she certainly did this time, didn't she? What am I supposed to do? Rush back home to comfort her? Ring her up and offer her a shoulder to cry on or my sympathies? You didn't want me to tell Bill so as to protect Chrissie, that's it, isn't it?'

There was a brief pause. 'She wants to talk to you.' Joe didn't even bother to deny it.

'She told you that, did she?' Kate snapped. 'What was it you just said, "Very cosy?"'

Joe's voice froze over. 'Jesus, Kate. You can be such a hardfaced bitch at times.'

Kate flinched. In all the years they had been together Joe had never resorted to insults.

'I can't understand why you had to tell Bill of all people,' he continued.

'You're worried about what Bill will think of you, aren't you?'

Again Joe chose not to bite and instead said, 'We can put this right but not if you go around making it public knowledge.'

Kate shook her head in disbelief. Joe was afraid of what people might think, afraid that whatever justification he had come up with would not stand up to scrutiny once it was out in the daylight. She took a deep breath and said the thing that was right up in the front of her mind. The thing that had been haunting her for days. 'I'm not sure that I want to put it right, Joe.'

There was a deep dark silence on the end of the line and then Joe said, 'Our relationship means so little to you, does it?'

Kate was incredulous. 'How the hell can you say that? You were the one who went off and fucked somebody else.'

'I was deeply unhappy. You know that. It was a symptom, Kate, surely you can see that – it was no more than that, a symptom.' He sounded deeply wounded.

'A symptom? A symptom? Of what, for God's sake?'

'Depression, disillusion and all those things that aren't right between us. You don't understand me, I don't think you ever have. It's always been me, me, me with you, Kate.'

Kate nearly choked with hurt and outrage. 'Which marriage have you been in? How dare you, Joe? I don't think I want to talk to you. When things weren't right I worked harder, listened more, and tried to support you while ignoring your bloody mood swings and excuses for not getting off your arse and getting a job. I didn't go off and get myself laid. How would you feel now if this was the other way around?'

'Oh right, that's it turn it around, why don't you? You're always such a goodie fucking two shoes, aren't you,' he snapped and hung up a second before Kate had the chance to.

'You bastard,' she roared, full to the brim with fury and tears. 'Bastard, bastard, bastard.' And without thinking, slung the phone across the garden as hard as she could. It bounced once, twice, narrowly missing the water feature, the battery pack flew out and buried itself in amongst the hostas while the handset landed plum in the middle of the herb bed.

As she walked across to retrieve it Kate realised Maggie was sitting watching her from the kitchen window. She was still nibbling the last of the soft buttery crumbs of the toast crusts.

'Anything you want to tell me?' Maggie asked, as Kate pushed the kitchen door to.

'No, thank you,' Kate shook her head, laid the phone on the kitchen unit alongside her, and with her back to Maggie, plugged in the kettle. She didn't trust herself to say anything else without resorting to the kind of language that you wouldn't normally use in front of your mother.

Wisely, Maggie said nothing.

Once she had helped Maggie out onto the terrace Kate headed for the dining-room, dropped her re-assembled mobile phone in her briefcase and settled down to the day's work.

As she got to the table, Kate straightened her shirt, picked up her glasses – like the wardrobe into Narnia there was a place in her head where she could step, a gateway through into the businesslike frame of mind that was her saving grace.

In the diary were a couple of advertorials that needed to get sorted and sent off, some admin, accounts. It was a relief to open the folders on the computer up and see that some things hadn't changed at all. Within half an hour, Kate's brain was firmly in work mode, her mind swiftly – and gratefully – locking down onto the task in hand.

When, a little later, she heard the house phone ringing Kate ignored it. If it was Joe she didn't want to talk to him and if it was Guy she didn't want to know. Anyway Maggie had the walkabout phone outside with her; she could answer it.

'Kate?'

With the best will in the world she couldn't ignore her invalid mother. Kate went outside to see what she wanted.

'Yes?'

'That was Julie Hicks on the phone, just to remind us about her house-warming party tonight.'

Kate pulled a face.

Maggie wasn't in the least bit fazed. 'We don't have to go if you don't want to, but I think I ought to ring her and let her know one way or the other.'

Kate considered the options for a few seconds. Joe was bound to ring back later when he had time to compose himself. And what if Chrissie rang? Kate thought about the phone tucked down in her briefcase. Because of work she couldn't keep her mobile off forever and if she did Joe and/or Chrissie would probably, eventually, catch her on Maggie's phone anyway. And then what was she going to do? Or say?

Kate made a decision; what she needed was more time to think.

'What time does Julie's party start?'

'Seven apparently, because of the children, but we don't have to go until later.'

'Seven is just fine. It would be a real shame to let Julie down.'

Maggie didn't bother to ask what it was that

had changed Kate's mind. Instead she smiled. 'I'll ring back and tell her we're coming then, shall I?' Although there was something in her tone that still offered Kate a way out if she should need it.

'Yes, fine,' Kate nodded and headed back inside, hoping that Chrissie, Joe and Bill would have the good grace to hold off until she was out.

Just before lunch Kate picked up her email. There in the in-box was a message from Sam57. It was odd how much it felt like a nice surprise.

> 'Dear Venus, Hi, it was great to hear from you so soon. I thought you'd be snowed under – to be honest I hadn't actually expected a reply, so I'm doubly pleased. Sounds like things are pretty complicated for you at the moment, but the offer still stands – maybe at the moment you are more in need of a friend than ever.'

Kate began to type her reply, hers written between the lines of his so that it looked as if they were having a real conversation.

> 'You don't know how complicated.'

'Is there any way that I can help?'

'I'm not sure; it felt good yesterday to just be able to dump it all on you. Pretty self-indulgent though. And then this morning I had a stand up row with my husband on the phone – it's like I don't know him anymore.'

'And don't worry about offloading. Having someone outside of your situation can be helpful, someone who's got no vested interest in the outcome.'

Kate sighed.

'Yes, but I don't want to string you along, Sam. I just wanted to explain, I suppose – you sounded so nice – but the thing is I'm really not looking to be rescued by a knight in shining armour. Maybe you ought to look elsewhere? Realistically I'm not looking for a relationship at all at the moment. I've got enough problems with the one I've got. I'll understand if you're not interested in carrying on with this – being a full-time shoulder to cry on isn't exactly the most glamorous or rewarding role I could think of. It's been nice to know you, though,

however briefly. With thanks and best
wishes, Venus.'

This time Kate didn't hesitate pressing send and watched her mail vanish from the out-box into cyberspace.

As they were eating lunch, the phone rang again. Maggie still had the walkabout handset tucked in her jacket pocket so there was no way Kate could escape. She just hoped it wasn't Joe, although she did wonder whether she was too old to invent one of those urgent calls of nature the boys conveniently came up with.

Maggie, hand over the receiver, mouthed, 'It's Liz.'

Kate sighed with relief; odd how times change. A week earlier a phone call from Liz certainly wouldn't have been something that gave her relief, more something to avoid, like cholera.

'Hi Liz,' Kate called loudly in Maggie's general direction, hoping that it might spare her any real conversation.

'She'd like to talk to you,' Maggie said, after the basic pleasantries, how-are-yous and thanks had been exchanged.

'Hi, I was going to ring and thank you for last night,' said Kate as Maggie handed her the phone.

'You know you're always welcome. It was nice to see you.' Liz sounded almost gracious. 'Nice to have the chance to cook something special.'

'Absolutely, Mum and I were talking about the food all the way home, weren't we?' said Kate, miming finger down the throat vomiting to Maggie who smiled indulgently, while wearing her keep-me-out-of-this face.

'I was just wondering if you'd had chance to talk to Mum about you know what.'

'You know what?'

'Yes, you know. The house. Have you had any chance to talk about her fall and the idea of moving into somewhere smaller? I've got some nice brochures and I've been talking to a woman from Age Concern. I wasn't sure whether to bring the details up last night over dinner or whether it might be a bit too soon. What do you think? I was thinking of taking Mum on a visit – they do a tour at this place – the warden place sounds terribly nice. Not that I've made any definite arrangements or anything, it's just that they're now building the second phase,' adding defensively, 'although this woman did suggest it might be a good idea to get the house valued. What do you think?'

Kate looked at Maggie. Liz was like a terrier once she got her teeth into something. 'Actually we've already talked about it, briefly.'

'Really, well done. So what did she say?' Liz whispered as if there was some possibility that Maggie might be able to overhear her.

It wasn't comfortable having this kind of conversation with Maggie sitting within spitting distance. 'Actually Mum was the one who said that maybe this place was too big for – for her current circumstances,' Kate said, carefully enunciating every word in case Liz planned to take it down and use it in evidence against her later.

Across the kitchen Maggie rolled her eyes heavenwards.

Liz made approving noises. 'Good, that's wonderful. It's obviously beginning to sink in – you know, a sense of her own limitations and vulnerabilities. Her frailties. Which is wonderful. I don't mean wonderful exactly but you know what I mean. What I'm trying to say is that this way we won't be going against the flow.'

If only she knew. As Liz began to wax lyrical about alarm bells and ramps, Kate glanced across the kitchen.

'And they get a little pull cord over the bed and one in the loo, just in case they fall over,' Liz was busy saying. 'It's all added into the rent so the care costs are spread over the year. It seems very reasonable.'

For a moment Kate wondered – for the millionth time – if Liz had been born into the right family. She was going to have a hell of a shock when she finally realised that Maggie was a long way away from hanging up her high heels.

In the corner of the kitchen Maggie had got her good foot up on the edge of the scrub table and was busy painting her toenails and smoking a roll-up. There was a telltale pungency in the air that suggested maybe it wasn't just Old Holborn.

When she hung up, Maggie looked up expectantly, waiting for a resumé of the conversation. 'And?' she asked, as Kate came over to where she was sitting.

'Liz thinks it's high time that you went into a home. Nice colour by the way.'

Maggie nodded, wriggling first her fingers and then her toes. 'I think so too,' and then added almost as an afterthought, 'Just promise me, Kate, that you won't die young and leave me to Liz in your will.'

Kate smiled. 'I'll do my best', at which point Maggie, busily holding her breath held the roll-up out towards Kate.

Kate shook her head. 'No thanks, Mum. I've got to think of my health – and yours, obviously.'

'Right,' said Maggie taking another toke on the joint. 'I'm glad someone is.'

After lunch Kate finished off two batches of invoices and then logged on to pick up her email, telling herself as she did that it was just one of those things, routine. No sweat, no big thing. After all she could hardly expect a reply yet from – Kate stopped short, just shy of actually thinking of Sam57 by name. She clicked the button to send and receive mail and felt her heart give a little lurch when she saw that his name was there in the in-box amongst at least a dozen new replies to the Vulnerable Venus ad. Kate opened up his message. He must be writing from the office, stealing a few minutes to reply to her.

'It was great to hear from you so soon, Venus. Actually friendship is fine by me. I'm not sure that I'm looking for anything serious at the moment either. I suppose I did harbour this fantasy plan of riding up on a white steed and rescuing Venus Mark One from the clutches of Mr Wrong, but this sounds – well, if not better, then at least something more possible. I have always valued friendship – let's see what happens, shall we? Maybe I'll hang on in here and you'll change your mind. One thing, though, before we go on – and something which may make you change your mind about me. This is hard to write but I think I have to come clean about it. I'm married too or at least that's what it says on the licence . . .

Are you still there or have you deleted this in disgust?'

Kate stared at the screen in disbelief. 'Oh my God,' she whispered under her breath but couldn't stop herself from reading on.

'I've only just put the ad on RomanticSouls and yours is the only one I've replied to so far. Thing is I'm really lonely and I've discovered over the years that there is nowhere more lonely than inside an unhappy relationship. I know it sounds like a cliché but my wife doesn't understand me. At the moment I'm trying to convince myself that I'm only staying here for the sake of the kids, that and the fact I've got nowhere to go and don't want to be on my own. This must sound totally crazy to you but it feels good to get it off my chest. You sound so straight – I didn't want to carry on writing a lie . . .'

Kate shivered.

'. . . My wife is a good woman but we are just poles apart. I still love her dearly which sounds mad too, huh? The thing is that I can't seem to reach her anymore. You've been so honest about where you're at that I thought I ought to confess – and offer you the same get out clause. If you don't want to carry on writing – well – under the circumstances I can completely understand. In which case, so long and thanks for all the fish. It's been nice to meet you, Venus, and I really hope it all works itself out. But if you'd like to carry on mailing then I'd be happy to hear from you again.'

Kate re-read the mail and then very slowly started to type.

'Odd isn't it, that I'm on the other side of this equation. Here, I was the one that couldn't be reached.'

She paused for a few seconds, composing her thoughts, marshalling her emotions, wondering whether she dare go on, but what was the harm? After all, if Sam didn't like what he read there was no need for him to reply, was there?

'I need to understand why you are looking for someone else. You say you still love your wife but surely love is about faithfulness and being with someone, tolerating those things that drive you mad and celebrating those things you love? I realise that no one person is everything we need but surely if you make a commitment, if you make a promise then you shouldn't go looking elsewhere until you've told that person, talked to them, said it's over? Or is that you feel the need for another person to lever you out of where you are? To give you the courage to go? I know it might sound like it but this isn't about criticism – I suppose I'm asking you to help me, Sam; help me to understand what the hell is going on in my life. I'm lost and so angry and so hurt –'

Pressing send gave Kate no problem at all.

Chapter 10

'Taramasalata anyone?' Julie Hicks piped up, shouldering her way through the dozen or so people already grouped around the plastic outdoor tables, which were set up under a large green-striped awning by the patio doors. There were other people dotted in small groups around the well manicured lawns, sipping drinks and chatting in the warmth of the early evening sun.

It was a good turn out for midweek, thought Kate murderously as she ploughed Maggie and the wheelchair across the grass from the back gate. Julie had requested that everyone park 'around the back' so as not to cause a problem for any of the other residents. There were a lot of cars and guests out there, shame none of them seemed to think helping her would be a good idea.

Julie was heading their way bearing a large circular tray the centre of which was dominated by a forest of crudités: slivers of carrot, celery and something indefinable and white – possibly raw potato – sticking out of it. Beneath the forest were vast puddles of what looked like pink semolina.

'Hello Kate, Mrs Sutherland,' Julie nodded and smiled in welcome. She was wearing a vivid turquoise halter-neck sundress and had obviously spent the last couple of days out in the sun. The dip and her shoulders clashed violently.

'How lovely to see you both. I'm so glad that you could make it. I thought perhaps you'd be too busy. I'll rally some of the troops to get you up on the terrace, Mrs Sutherland,' said Julie, as Kate struggled to bump the wheelchair up onto the paving slabs that passed for a terrace.

'I knew I should have brought my crutches,' Maggie hissed uncomfortably. Meanwhile, Julie waved over a couple of men, tall thin things with sloping shoulders and circlets of sparse red and grey hair wrapped around conical skulls. Looking them up and down Kate decided they would probably snap something if they had to lift Maggie *and* the chair, but they managed after a fashion, finally getting her up off the lawn with much 'One, two, three'-ing and 'heave-ho'-ing,' and even more huffing and puffing.

Maggie pulled a stricken face as they bore her at knee height towards the buffet.

'Do you want me to nip back to the car and get your crutches?' called Kate anxiously.

But before she could answer Julie jumped in, 'No, we'll be just fine, won't we, Mrs Sutherland? Now where would you like to be, shade or sun? Have you met my husband Malcolm?'

Maggie nodded politely in the direction of one of the tall, thin, gingery struggling men, while Julie continued, 'And this is my toy boy, Keith,' smiling towards the other tall, thin, gingery man, who looked as if he might be about to have some kind of seizure.

Kate smiled in a small private way; Julie obviously hadn't heard about Maggie and Guy on the grapevine or she would be busy wishing the ground would swallow her whole by now.

'Actually he's Malcolm's younger brother, he helped us move, didn't you Keith, love? He's been such an angel, I really don't know what we would have done without him, I really don't.'

Julie leant forward and ruffled his balding pate.

Kate looked Julie up and down; there was no way that this could be the same person who used to drink Jack Daniels and Coke like it was going out of fashion, the same person who was reputed to have slept with the whole of the senior school football team, including both reserves and the linesman, and smoked so much dope that some days in the sixth form common room she could barely stand up, let alone form a coherent sentence.

It seemed so unfair. Julie used to be a bad influence, for Christ's sake, one of those people who, when you mentioned their name, adults exchanged uneasy glances. Julie Hicks used to be the kind of person that parents like Kate's had tolerated only because they thought the novelty would wear off and if they stopped Kate seeing Julie it would just make her lifestyle seem all the more glamorous. Kate knew this because it was the same kind of tack she was currently using on Danny, and his little drug dealing *compadres*. Maybe a few Polaroids of what had happened to Julie might do more good.

Kate bet Malcolm had no idea about the football team either.

'Well, here we are then,' Julie was saying,

patting Kate's arm affectionately. 'I daren't even think about how many years it is since we last saw each other. How are you?' On the periphery of her hearing Kate could pick out the strains of something by Enya.

Kate smiled inanely wondering how long she would have to stay. How long could she bear to stay? Dying of boredom and social pleasantries was a high price to pay for any temporary sanctuary, although at least Maggie offered her the perfect get out of jail free card.

'What do you do? I'm sure that I ought to know this,' said Julie warmly, speaking in the universal patois of the perfect hostess.

'I'm in PR. Freelance mostly,' said Kate. It was the start of one of those terrible, forgettable party conversations, where you don't care what you say and the other person cares even less.

Julie nodded. 'Right.' Kate might as well have said vivisection for all the reaction it got, although then again maybe that was what Malcolm was into. He certainly looked the type.

'And what are you up to these days?' asked Kate hopefully. 'Still the good girl gone bad that we all knew and loved?'

A few yards away under the awning, pinned like a butterfly to a board, and helpless in the face of an enormous amount of solicitous attention and good humour, Maggie was being introduced to everyone by Malcolm and his evil sidekick, Keith.

'Who, me? Oh goodness me, no.' Julie was laughing. 'No, I'm still working in hospital administration. Part-time obviously since we had the girls but I was very lucky. I managed to get a transfer when we moved back here, same grade, same hours and everything, but no, I'm just plodding along. It's Malcolm who's the high-flyer in this family.'

Kate looked at him; it didn't seem likely. Having moved on from Maggie, Malcolm was currently substituting for Julie in the nibbles department, manfully shouldering his way through the throng, wielding a dish of Pringles, closely marked by Keith who appeared to be in charge of the dip and paper plates.

'Really, and what does Malcolm do?' Kate said, wondering if the sarcasm she could hear inside her head was as obvious on the outside.

'Laser microscopy, he's involved in a government research project, it's all very hush-hush. Near Cambridge. Although he's been spending a lot of time in London recently, lecturing.'

Kate looked again across the patio at their

host. Seems that she hadn't been far out after all. Malcolm looked like just the kind of little boy who used to set fire to ants with a magnifying glass.

'I think I'd better go and give him a hand. We really must catch up some time,' said Julie.' How long are you home for?'

'Just until the end of the week.'

'Right, I'll try and pop in before you go then. Can I get you anything to drink? A little white wine? Or how about a nice cup of tea if you're driving? We've set up the bar in the utility room – through the back of the garage and turn left.'

Kate waved her away. 'It's okay, I'm sure I can find it. You go and help Malcolm, I'll be fine, honestly. I've got to go and get Mum's crutches. I'll get a drink when I come back.'

'If you're certain.'

It was one of the few things in life Kate *was* certain about. She smiled. 'Honestly.'

Julie, beaming with gratitude, hurried back into the fray while Kate took a long hard look around before heading back towards the gate, wondering again why it was she had come.

Julie's new home was large, rectangular, built in the mid seventies in the pale yellow brick pre-feature era. There wasn't a plastic Doric column, a fake beam or a fibreglass coping stone anywhere in sight, just a rather bleak utilitarian box faced with UPV windows and an air of expensive practicality. The estate they were on, Church Pines, consisted of ten or so large individually designed houses and about the same number of big sprawling bungalows, which now would have been called executive dwellings, and had been built when Kate was a kid.

She remembered being invited to a birthday party in the house across from Julie's that belonged to her dad's bank manager and it was still those kind of people that were attracted to Church Pines, although it wasn't a place that was naturally attractive to children. Arranged around a neatly winding cul-de-sac two sides of estate abutted the churchyard at the back and to the right, with an old people's home across the road in front of it, Victorian carrstone town houses were strung out along the remaining side.

The people who lived there then and now were quietly, discreetly wealthy professionals who had got keeping themselves to themselves down to a fine art. The planners had managed to retain all the mature trees which for some reason added to the air of genteel exclusivity. Just the place for a laser expert, thought Kate, picking her way towards the back gate across the grass and sunken stepping stones. High heels hadn't been such a good idea either.

She nodded and smiled her way through Julie's guests but didn't hold eye contact for more than a few seconds, which seemed to work, certainly nobody came over to ask her how she was or who she was or try to engage her in conversation. It wasn't that Kate didn't recognise any of the faces, more that she couldn't be bothered to talk to them and play join the dots to connect up the last eighteen or so years of their different lives.

'So what *did* you do at uni? Did you get married to What's-his-face in spite of that thing at the leavers' ball? Oh, you were that thing at the leavers, ball,' all seemed a bit superfluous bearing in mind her whole life was hanging in shreds.

When she got back a few minutes later, Maggie was still enthroned beneath the awning and seemed happy enough. Painkillers or no painkillers, she was hitting the Cab Sav like there was no tomorrow and was talking to some tall, good-looking man, who was managing to look distinguished and important while wearing a baggy grey tee-shirt and jeans.

Despite his white hair it certainly didn't *look* as if they were talking about hernias and haemorrhoids and heartburn. He was laughing at something she'd just said. Maggie too. Maybe the exchange of medical notes came later.

Kate sighed, slipped her the crutches and went inside. Ten minutes into the party and already her mother was flirting outrageously and partying like she was born to it; there was just no stopping some people.

Kate took a long pull on the drink she had found in the utility room being ladled out by someone's elderly aunt and looked long and hard at Maggie. Maybe maturity wasn't such a bad deal after all. As Mr Tall and Distinguished topped up Maggie's glass Kate glanced down at her own, half full of a lurid pink non-alcoholic punch. It would be really good to go out and get totally and utterly wasted. Kate couldn't remember the last time she'd done anything even mildly outrageous.

'Are you all right?' Maggie mouthed as their eyes met.

Kate mimed a gesture that implied she was choking.

Maggie raised a single eyebrow and for the millionth time in her life Kate wished she could do that. It was the perfect comment, the perfect exclamation point, for so many social situations.

The garden – or at least the paved terrace around the house – was slowly filling up with guests. Kate recognised Julie's parents, who probably still couldn't believe their luck that their tearaway teenager had finally grown up, got a job in the NHS, and married a man who zapped things with sharp pointy lights and was quite obviously earning a mint.

Beyond the strings of lights slung under the awning, the rest of the garden was very gently slipping into soft golds of early evening. Kate headed back down the garden to where she and Maggie had come in, making out that she was exploring what passed for the grounds. The garden was large and had been professionally landscaped at some stage; no one but a pro would build raised beds like that, all swoops and banks and French curves, full of cleverly arranged multi-colour toning and/or contrasting scrubs.

There were a couple of rustic benches at the bottom tucked out of the way in carefully contrived arbours. As Kate headed towards them, she noticed, tucked away amongst bushes and creepers, that there was a gate in a much older side wall on the boundary. It just had to lead into the churchyard.

It was too good a chance to miss. Kate glanced back over her shoulder; the evening breeze carried a low babble of voices towards her like a bank of fog. It would be bliss to slip away, and let's face it, she thought, easing the gate open, no one other than Maggie would give a shit where she was.

It was a bit of a struggle to get the gate to run over the grass behind it, although presumably there had to be a right of way, as someone in the not too distant past had mowed a path right up to the door into the garden. Kate couldn't quite close the gate but surely that didn't matter either.

Beyond the garden the burial ground, surrounded by ancient yews and Scots pine and the overhanging branches of trees that Kate couldn't name, was totally silent, the air heavy with the smell of pine resin and the accumulated heat of the long hot day. Here the graves were so old that someone had decided to give up the fight and let the area run wild.

Grave markers and tombs weathered down to standing stones sprang up between rills of tall swaying grass, dog roses clambered up over fallen trees and tombs alike. Here and there groups of stones had vanished entirely beneath a carpet of green, parcelled together by great plaits of pale pink convolvulus, morning glory, its eyes already closing against the fading light.

It was exquisite. Kate walked for a while until she found a place that suited her mood. Off the mown path, under the spread of an ageing conifer, she sat down on a low tomb, dappled with patches of lichen, and tipped her face up to catch the last rays of the sun. She took a deep breath, feeling the tension ebb out of her body. No phones, no old friends, no Joe, no Maggie, and as the heat and stillness of the day brought her to the very edge of sleep, no thoughts. Remarkable. Peace at last, just the sound of her breath rising and falling. Bliss.

Kate had no idea how long she had been sitting there like a lizard on a hot rock, when she heard a noise, a rustling close by, and then a male voice. 'Whoops. I'm so sorry, I didn't mean to disturb you.'

Kate opened one eye, very slowly.

There was a man standing directly in her sunlight. He was tall and, back-lit, had taken on a celestial corona, although one thing Kate was pretty certain of was that this wasn't the angel Gabriel unless he had taken to wearing Bermudas and trainers on his days off.

'Are you okay?' he said pleasantly.

Kate opened the other eye. 'I was until you came along.'

His face looked familiar in that terrible been-to-school-together, old friend of the family sort of way.

He grinned; it seemed that he recognised her too. 'Hi, how're you doing?'

Kate looked him up and down. 'Have we met before?' she said, the effort of remembering making her frown.

The grin broadened out a notch or two. 'You could say that we ran into each other earlier in the week.'

Oh God, oh yes, she had it now. Had her memory got that bad? 'Andrew Taylor, the crazy vet,' Kate groaned, without thinking.

'Kate Sutherland, the mad angry woman,' he retorted. It was a brave thing to say and just the right thing because it made Kate laugh.

He indicated the tomb next to her own. 'May I?'

'Help yourself, although I'm not sure that it's me you should be asking,' she said, rubbing the weathered letters on one of the side panels. But the vet sat down anyway.

'I didn't expect to see you here. Have you kept in touch with Julie since you left school?' he asked, nodding back towards the house.

'Me? No, good God no, I ran into her yesterday while I was in town.'

'Driving were you?' he laughed.

'No,' Kate growled.

'Joke,' he said, holding his hands up in surrender.

'How about you?'

'No, I barely knew her at school,' he said. 'Julie came down to register her pets for inoculations and to buy some worm tablets and stuff a few weeks ago. She's been down to the surgery a couple of times since then. To be honest, I didn't recognise her until she told me who she was. She remembered me though and one or two things about me that I'd prefer to forget.'

'And she invited you to her house-warming?' asked Kate incredulously. Maybe Julie hadn't changed her spots after all. Andrew was good-looking in a James Herriott-ish way and despite the quickfire replies there was something slightly self-conscious about the way he spoke and moved, a kind of endearing boyishness that

Kate could see was very attractive, if you liked that sort of thing.

Kate resisted the temptation to ask him if he played any team games.

Andrew reddened. 'No, well not exactly. It turns out by pure coincidence that I was at college at the same time, same place as . . . as . . . What's-his-name.' He screwed up his nose. Seeing that moment's hesitation told Kate everything she needed to know. He and Malcolm were far from bosom buddies, which oddly gave Kate a real sense of relief. In fact, from the expression on Andrew's face, he could barely remember Malcolm at all or better still perhaps had loathed him. Presumably Julie had put two and two and a veterinary certificate on the wall together and come up with some warm fuzzy connection.

'Malcolm,' Kate offered.

He nodded. 'That's it, Malcolm. I'm not very good with names.'

There was a few moments' silence and then he said, 'Sorry, I'm not very good at social chitchat either really – better with hamsters. Do you want to talk? Did we catch up the other day? Did you tell me if you were married or what you did or anything?'

Kate shook her head. 'God no, I was way too angry to exchange any of the social pleasantries.'

'Right, I thought so,' he said and extended the hand that didn't have a glass in it. She noticed that he too was drinking lurid pink pop. 'Hello, my name is Andrew Taylor. I'm a local vet.'

'Pleased to meet you, Andrew. I'm Kate, Kate Harvey. I'm in PR, freelance, two kids, a large mortgage and a black Golf.'

His grip was as warm and strong as it had been before. He smiled pleasantly, obviously waiting for her to say something else. Kate took a sip of punch, playing for time. Did she go for the nice weather we've been having, isn't it a beautiful evening conversation or . . .

'You look absolutely knackered,' he said.

Kate glared at him. Bloody hell and after all the time she'd spent in the bathroom with the concealer stick and light-reflective foundation. 'Well, how very kind of you to notice,' she snapped.

'No, I didn't mean it like that.' He reddened again. 'What I meant to say was are you okay? I wondered if you weren't feeling well or something.'

Kate's expression held. 'What – were you

planning to rub my belly and look to see if my nose was cold?'

He shrugged. 'It works on most of my patients,' and then added, 'No, it's just that you're sitting out here all on your own, not at the party. I just wondered,' his voice tailed off, 'you know.'

'You aren't at the party either.'

'I don't really know anybody,' he said lamely, sipping the lurid pink punch.

'Me neither.' Kate paused for an instant. 'Actually, that's not strictly true. We both know a lot of the people here or at least I used to know a lot of them, a long time ago when life was simple, when the days were long and sunny and the winters short sharp and snowy, but I'm not really in the mood for small talk tonight. I brought my mum. I thought it would do her good to get out of the house for a while.' Kate didn't add she was running away from the phone.

'The woman on the patio in the wheelchair?'

'You were introduced?'

'Yes, by Julie, but I would have guessed anyway. You look very much alike, you know.' He looked Kate up and down as if ticking off the similarities. 'She's an interesting woman.'

Kate snorted. 'She most certainly is. When I

left, she was flirting outrageously with some grey-haired bloke in a tee-shirt –'

'My boss.'

'Julie invited him too? Good God, there's no stopping that woman. What excuse did she use on him? Do they use the same washing powder? Bump into each other at Tesco's?' Kate looked down suspiciously at the punch wondering whether maybe one of the old aunties had spiked it with a bottle of vodka. She wasn't normally this grumpy or sharp.

'No, I think Malcolm knows him. They are on some kind of rural development committee together.'

'Right.' Kate looked back towards the garden wall. There were no other signs of life, although she could just catch the tail end of a tune wafting towards her on the breeze, and just a hint of fried onions that suggested they'd finally got the barbecue fired up. 'Couldn't you persuade your wife to come along? Or is she up there manning the buffet, selflessly doling out the doilies?'

'No. Actually I'm here on my own; I'm widowed. That's one of the reasons I came back to England with the kids.'

It was Kate's turn to blush. 'God, I'm so sorry, I didn't know.'

He waved her embarrassment away. 'No reason at all why you should. She died seven years ago now, I still miss her – we've got two boys – twelve and thirteen. Makes me feel terribly old. How about you?'

'I've got two boys too. Twelve and fifteen going on forty.'

'And a husband?'

Kate looked up at him, knowing that she had hesitated for a split second too long before replying.

'Sorry,' he began. 'If it's painful, I'll shut up – none of my business.'

'No, no you're fine, unfortunately he's forty going on fifteen, all hormones, drink and misplaced lust, you know how it is,' Kate said with a heartiness she couldn't quite sustain and then paused and caught his eye. 'Sorry, you'll have to excuse me. I'm in a weird place at the moment.'

They both looked round the deserted overrun graveyard, aware of the little squirm of awkwardness, and then Kate laughed and said, 'Actually I suppose we're both in a pretty weird place, or do you normally spend your evenings camped out on a tomb drinking liquid nougat?' It was enough to break the tension.

Andrew laughed. 'Not quite so often these

days. How long are you staying in Denham for, a week? A month? The rest of your life? Your mum said you'd come up to give her a hand while her partner was away –'

Kate grinned. Guy was her partner now, was he?

'I'll be here till Friday.' She saw a flicker of disappointment pass over his face which, although it surprised her, for some reason prompted her to add, 'but I'm sure I'll be back pretty soon. Mum's going to have that cast on for a while.'

'Good, I mean, I don't mean good, not really. I was just wondering. I know this might sound a bit forward but . . .' He blushed so hard that Kate leant forward to touch him.

'What is it?'

'I was wondering if you might like to go out to lunch with me sometime?'

Kate stared at him. She felt her jaw drop. 'What?' she snapped. It sounded rude and abrupt, but it was such a surprise. On the other end of the tombstone Andrew flinched as if she'd hit him.

'Sorry,' he blustered, standing up abruptly. 'Bit insensitive of me. It was – just – I really didn't mean to offend you, it was only a thought, you know. Sorry, sorry.' He looked so uncomfortable. Kate was on her feet before she knew quite what she was doing and caught hold of his arm to stop him from scuttling back to the party.

'Please don't apologise, Andrew. That was unbelievably rude of me, I'm so sorry. I don't know what to say. Nobody's asked me out in God knows how long.' Kate blushed furiously in case she had misinterpreted him. 'You *were* asking me out, weren't you? That was a date thing, not just an invitation to a friendly, catch up let's talk about school days lunch, was it?' Kate looked up into his face for clues and saw nothing that was of any help whatsoever, so she pressed on. The words dried up in her throat.

Kate stared up into his big brown hurt eyes, totally bemused. How the hell had *this* happened? One minute she was a happily married woman, the next she'd got an adulterous husband, a best friend who was betraying her, emails from amorous married strangers, and was being hit on by the tastiest man she'd been alone with for a long time. It felt as if her entire life had undergone a polar shift.

'The thing is . . .' Kate began.

'That you don't want to go out to lunch with me?' he said flatly, turning back towards the path.

Kate shook her head and hurried after him. 'If it was only that simple.'

In Windsor Street it was a beautiful evening, barbecue weather, not that Joe was thinking about barbecues, more like hell fire and damnation. He was seething with pure undiluted frustration; Kate's voice mail was still on and no one was picking up the phone at Maggie's house either.

He'd left ringing her all day, waiting for them both to cool down. It was nearly ten o'clock, he'd been ringing on and off since eight; surely to God either Maggie or Kate had to be about somewhere. Was it that they were out again or had the pair of them gone to bed already? No one went to bed at eight. It had crossed his mind that Maggie might have a caller display unit and once Kate saw who was ringing she was choosing not to pick it up.

Joe punched Maggie's number into the handset and caught the message one more time, '. . . if you'd like to leave your name and number after the tone then I'll get back to you as soon as possible. Thanks for calling.'

Bloody sodding woman! He slammed the

phone back down into its cradle. Kate could have at least had the decency to call up and see if the boys were all right. Joe took a pull on the beer he'd just got out of the fridge. It wasn't his first of the evening.

How much had Kate told her family? Was that why Maggie wasn't answering either? Just like Kate, she couldn't keep anything to herself, she had to go and tell someone. Fancy telling bloody Bill, and him coming round with that holier than thou expression was the final straw, arrogant smug bastard, as if his relationships ever ran smooth.

'Dad, do you think you can give us a hand with my science homework?' asked Danny from the kitchen door. 'I just want someone to help test me on this stuff we've got to do tomorrow.'

'You have got to be joking,' he growled. 'Ask Jake.'

Danny looked hurt and sounded indignant. 'No, he can't pronounce the words. I've got to hand this in first thing tomorrow and then we've got a test.'

'You should have thought about that over the weekend instead of gallivanting out with your mates and playing on the bloody internet,' Joe growled. He knew he was taking his anger out on Danny but couldn't work out how to stop himself. Danny met his gaze for a few seconds, just long enough to register his disgust, and then turned and swore under his breath.

'What did you say?' Joe snapped, aware he was ready to fly at the least provocation.

Danny turned back, face set to match Joe's own. 'You're the one who's always going on about how much this bloody school costs, always going on about doing my friggin' best.'

It was all Joe could do not to punch him.

'If I don't do well in science this year I stand to lose my bursary and Mum's already said I can't stay there without it because she can't afford full fees.'

Danny had said *she* not *you* or *we*, Joe noticed. Although Kate was always careful to say *we* in conversations the kids knew the real state of play. Kate was the one who really made things tick, who oiled the machine, who made it all come right, who made sure the money went around and no one suffered because of Joe's . . . Joe's . . . Momentarily, Joe stiffened, not wanting to think those thoughts, refusing to admit that any of those things might be his responsibility.

He squared his shoulders; Kate had known the

kind of man he was when she married him. He was a free spirit, a creative, most certainly not your average nine to five man. Joe had always thought, always hoped, that one of the reasons Kate had fancied him was because he was dangerous, a little bit wild, outside the system. Someone who would take her outside her experience. It was just like a woman to marry a maverick and then want to house-train him.

Across the hall, Danny was still watching him, waiting for a reaction. Realistically Joe knew that Kate didn't see him as dangerous, nor did Danny, not at all. Danny saw him as a pain in the arse. School was a sore spot and one that Joe had no wish to pick at.

Kate had sorted out assisted places for both of the boys at local private schools, partly on some sort of bursary and partly by offering them hands on help with PR. It was a coup, a masterstroke really, and one of which she was justifiably proud. Jake had already been promised a place at the school on the same terms as Danny if he could pass the entrance exam. So this was sacred ground.

Joe took a breath, not quite sure what he was planning to say, when the door bell rang. They both looked relieved and Danny hurried down the corridor to answer it. ‘It’s Bill,’ he said, stating the obvious.

As Bill and Joe’s eyes met, Joe sighed, ‘You’d better come in.’

But Danny wasn’t going to let Joe off the hook that easily. ‘Bill, is there any chance you could help me with my science homework, only Dad’s busy at the moment?’

Bill glanced at Joe who waved a hand towards him. ‘Carte blanche, mate, liberty hall, here. I haven’t got a fucking clue about what he’s doing anyway. I was an arts man, not sciences.’

Bill’s focus sharpened. ‘Have you been drinking?’

‘And what’s it to you if I have, Claire-bloody-Rayner? What are you now, the voice of my conscience?’

Meanwhile, in the house at Church Pines the barbecue was in full swing by the time Kate and Andrew got back to the party. While Andrew went inside to refresh their drinks Julie sidled up to her. ‘I’m very impressed,’ she said in a stage whisper.

‘Impressed?’

‘Don’t come the dark horse with me, Kate

Sutherland, I know you, remember. Andrew Taylor is a real catch – apparently he's terribly standoffish, keeps himself very much to himself. Shy, I've always thought. You and your mother have got sort of some special knack. It has got be genetic.'

Kate smiled noncommittally, glad she had inherited her mum's charisma and not her dad's hairy ears.

Julie had obviously been at the real punch, and some residual shade of the schoolgirl formerly known as Easy whom Kate had known and loved, was slowly resurfacing.

Although Kate could feel her colour rising; it had been a long time since she had unashamedly flirted with someone, even longer since it had been reciprocated so enthusiastically.

'Well?' demanded Julie. 'What have you got to say for yourself?'

Kate took a breath, composing her thoughts but fortunately it seemed that fate was on her side.

'Julie?' She swung round at the sound of her name being called from the house, at which point Kate made off into the shadows saved by a catering emergency involving paper napkins, a box of matches and two small boys.

If Andrew wanted her company he would have to come and sniff her out. Kate was hoping that he wouldn't interpret her lurking behind the ornamental bay as a desire to get away from him.

Maggie, by contrast, was sitting talking to a group of women although holding court would be a better description; she sat centre stage and they were all giggling, drinking, and quite obviously having a whale of a time.

Kate grinned at her on her way to the shadows. 'So where's his nibs gone then? I can't take you anywhere, can I? Even Julie wanted to know what you'd sprayed yourself with.'

Maggie lifted that magic eyebrow. 'You mean Charles? I think he's gone off to get me something special from the barbecue.'

Kate laughed.

At which point Andrew reappeared carrying two drinks and this time Maggie was the one to do a double take. Kate introduced them and then made her way back down the garden with Andrew, well aware that every eye in the place – or at least those of the women under the awning – was on her.

Away from the circle of lights and the hardcore of party goers, Andrew settled down on one of the low walls round the flowerbeds. 'So what are you going to do about Joe?' he asked picking up the conversation they'd been having earlier exactly where they'd left it.

She shook her head. 'At the moment it's like looking into a snowstorm. The good wife in me says I ought to go home and salvage what I can – I've always been someone who does the right thing and sticks at things. And yet there is this other part of me that is kind of pleased, relieved. Does that sound crazy?'

Andrew shook his head.

'There's no peace anywhere at the moment, nowhere to escape from my thoughts, from Joe, from Chrissie, even when I'm working on my computer.' Kate started to tell him about RomanticSouls, Sam57, Vulnerable Venus and then realised with a start that he was staring at her in a way that suggested he hadn't heard a word she'd said. He moved closer and for one amazing unbelievable unexpected moment Kate thought he was going to kiss her.

'Do you want something to eat?' he said, pointing towards the barbecue. 'I've just realised that I'm absolutely famished.'

Kate laughed, relieved, and yet at the same time oddly disappointed that he hadn't made a move. 'Yes, I would,' she said, trying to recall her cool. 'I thought you were about to share some pearls of wisdom about the nature of life, love and the universe.'

'I was thinking more of a beefburger and a big bowl of salad,' he said offering his hand, helping her to her feet.

As their hands touched, Kate felt an odd, excited little kick in the bottom of her belly. For a vet in Bermudas, Andrew Taylor had a lovely hutchside manner.

Chapter 11

It was eleven by the time Kate and Maggie finally rolled home to the house in Church Hill. It was still warm. For a few moments as Kate stood by the back door, her heart ached for all those nights already spent, the nights she had stood here as a child, as a teenager and a young woman, looking up at this view, the moon glowing down, framed by the house, the magnolia and the ever-murderous laburnums. The night's canvas was as black as Indian ink. Clear and fine, the sky was littered with a million stars and Kate realised that here with Maggie was the first time she had truly felt safe and at peace for a long time. Nothing had fundamentally changed, Kate was aware of that. There was no magical solution to the things that haunted her, but for the first time since she had arrived in Denham, Kate had a sense of sanctuary, a real sense of coming home.

'Well, that went a lot better than I'd thought it was going to,' said Maggie, sounding tired, manoeuvring herself across the hall and into the kitchen with the aid of crutches.

Kate looked at her and grinned. 'It's quite remarkable that you can do that after so much red wine.'

Maggie snorted and lowered herself very gingerly onto one of the chairs at the kitchen table. 'My arms and shoulders ache and my leg is throbbing like crazy. I think maybe I've overdone it,' she spoke through gritted teeth and then, once she had lifted the cast up onto a chair, added, 'Julie Hicks has changed, hasn't she?'

Kate handed her a mug of coffee and a bottle of painkillers. 'I almost heard the total disbelief in your voice then, Mum. Mind you, the same thought kept going through my mind. She's so straight now that it's scary. I kept thinking that this couldn't be the same girl who used to roll up here first thing in the morning for the walk to school with a fag on, purple hair and eyeliner so thick she could barely see.'

‘Remember when she came round in a black leather miniskirt, basque, black stockings and suspenders? I thought your dad was going to explode,’ said Maggie with a grin.

Kate giggled. ‘And you asked her where she was going and she said Girl Guides.’

Both women burst into a peal of easy unself-conscious laughter.

Across the table Maggie stretched and then yawned dramatically. Her colour was rapidly fading away as if tiredness was stealing her resistance to the pain. Despite a lot of make-up the bruises and stitches still looked deeply painful.

‘I’m going to bed now; I’m totally shattered. Would you take my coffee through, please? I can hardly keep my eyes open. I just want to nip to the bathroom. Although,’ she said, the grinned fixed, ‘maybe nip isn’t the word I’m looking for.’

Kate nodded and as she reached the doorway said, casually, over one shoulder, ‘Would you mind if I popped out for a little while tomorrow? I’ve been invited out to lunch.’

Maggie didn’t miss a beat. ‘Of course I don’t mind Who are you going with then? Julie Hicks or the good-looking vet?’

Kate opened her mouth to speak but no words came out.

'Not that it's any of my business, of course,' Maggie continued, bobbing off towards the loo, 'but I think it's getting to the point where I ought to know what's going on. I checked the phone when we came in; there are eleven calls from Joe on the caller display and God knows how many messages. I can't imagine he's that desperate to find out how I'm getting on.'

As she got to the door Maggie looked back, beading Kate with knowing eyes. Kate, still looking for words, wasn't sure whether she wanted to protest or apologise but Maggie shook her head.

'Don't panic, I haven't listened to any of them but I think that it's time we talked whether you want to or not. I said this morning when we were discussing Guy that however much we love each other there are just some conversations that parents and children aren't meant to have, that I wouldn't dream of meddling in your affairs without your asking me. But if I were worried about something then I'd tell you. Well, Kate, I have to say I'm worried and nothing that you've said or done or any of the evidence so far have eased my concerns.'

Kate stood very still. Unable to find any words that sounded even vaguely appropriate.

'And another thing.'

'Yes.' Kate braced herself for whatever was about to come next.

'Tomorrow morning can we put one of those plastic garden chairs in the shower cubicle and wrap my plaster up in a bin liner? I could really do with a shower, I'm sure that I stink.'

Kate laughed with a heady combination of amusement and relief. 'Of course you don't stink, don't be ridiculous – you had a wash before we went to Julie's.'

'I don't care, a wash doesn't count, I feel dirty.'

Kate nodded. 'Okay. We'll do the shower thing tomorrow then.'

'Good. Good night and sweet dreams, darling.'

And with that she was gone, swinging and hopping off towards the downstairs loo.

Kate set one coffee alongside the sofa bed that was made up in the sitting room and then took her own mug through into the dining room. Switching on the lamps it was looked as if she was creeping back into a nest or a den that she'd built earlier. Her papers and things were still there, all arranged in a neat arc around the laptop, flanked by pens and Post-it notes and the detritus of her working life. Late or not, Kate turned on the computer and checked her email. The modem kicked in, burring and whizzing, and then the mail retrieval system announced that she had no new messages.

Kate sat for a few moments staring at the empty in box with an odd but very real sense of regret and loss. Maybe honesty, both hers and Sam's, had driven him away. Maybe he didn't want to sort his life out or hear how she felt about being betrayed by someone just like him.

Kate sighed. It was a risk she had had to take although it felt as if somewhere she had lost the key to all sorts of knowing and understanding. There was nothing much else to do other than close the computer down. Feeling tired and heavy, Kate picked up the phone. She ought to check on the messages Maggie had told her about. In her current mood they felt like splashes of icy cold water.

Joe: 'Kate, I'm surprised that you haven't rung. The boys are okay. Missing you obviously and there are all sorts of odds and ends that they need sorting out – sports kits, some form or other that Jake needs for a trip, where things are generally. I just wanted to talk, you know – see how things are going. I'll ring you later.'

And then, 'Where the hell are you? It's nine o'clock.'

And then later still: 'Kate, I can't believe you, this is really beginning to piss me off, pick up the bloody phone, will you?'

They got worse, much worse, the last one just a string of furious expletives.

Feeling sick and shaky, Kate looked up at the clock. It was too late to ring Joe now. Maybe it had been a mistake to try and avoid talking to him but there was no way Kate could or wanted to put it right tonight. She'd ring him first thing tomorrow, although even as the thought formed Kate wondered what on earth she would say to him, what she wanted to say – after all the reason she'd gone to Julie's had been to avoid talking to Joe in the first place.

Picking her mobile out of her bag Kate switched it on, bracing herself for more of the same but here at least it was as quiet as the grave – there had been two calls from Joe but he hadn't even bothered to leave a message, perhaps he had finally run out of ammunition. The only one was from Bill.

'Hi Kate, I appreciate that maybe you don't

want to talk to anybody at the moment but the offer's still open if you need me. You know where I am. The boys are fine. I popped round tonight.' He laughed. 'Danny collared me to help with his homework. It's amazing – I don't think we did that stuff in science until we were at uni.' And then his tone dropped to something more serious, 'Kate, Joe's not coping with this very well at all. I don't suppose that comes as any great surprise but I thought you ought to know. If you get this message and want to talk . . . I don't have to tell you this, do I? Night, night, sweet dreams, hon.'

Kate's eyes filled up with tears. How could it be that the world appeared to be filled with so many men who would happily listen to her when her own seemed deaf? And then it struck her that of course Joe wasn't deaf at all. He was just deaf to her.

No doubt Chrissie could confide in him, tell him her secrets and her fears, and no doubt he listened or at least pretended to, as convincingly as Bill or Andrew or even Sam57. Kate shivered. It was too dark a thought to contemplate for more than a few seconds.

She glanced back at the computer screen and then re-read the emails she had sent to Sam. She could feel a headache coming on. Such a shame that truth was such a difficult and poisonous pill to swallow. But she couldn't have knowingly written to man who was married without saying something, it made her no better than Chrissie. Kate rubbed her eyes telling herself it was tiredness, not tension, her moods at the moment seemed to be as tidal as any ocean. Switching off the machine and heading upstairs to bed, Kate's mouth was as full of a bitter taste as her head was full of bitter angry thoughts.

'Why don't you go home, Joe?' Chrissie said briskly. 'Come on,' while trying to encourage him to his feet by getting to hers. 'It's getting late and I've got to be up early for work. Up you get.'

It was ridiculous. She had wanted to see him so much over the weekend, wanted to talk to him to make sure everything was okay, longed for some comfort, and now she would be bloody glad to see the back of him. Without Kate to balance Joe out he was a complete mess.

'Do you want a hand, Mum?' asked Robbie, appearing in the sitting room door. He had been home about half an hour but far from looking as if he was about to go to bed, he had showered and was dressed up like a dog's dinner.

She shook her head, 'No, you're all right I can manage, love. He's going home now, aren't you, Joe?'

Robbie looked at Joe in disgust and then headed towards the hall.

'Robbie?'

He reappeared at the door. 'Yeh?'

'You're not going out again, are you?'

'I'm just going to the club with some of the lads from work.'

'Any idea what time you'll be back?'

He grinned. 'No need to wait up, I'll probably crash round at Paul's tonight.' He lifted the holdall he was carrying. 'But don't worry I've got me toothbrush and a clean pair of pants in case I'm run over. I'll see you tomorrow.' He brushed her cheek with his lips. He smelt wonderful and she envied him so many things that it made the breath catch in her throat.

'What is he doing here anyway?'

Chrissie shrugged. 'I don't know really,' she lied. 'He and Kate had a row, I think he's just looking for a shoulder to cry on.'

Robbie tutted. 'You want to get her to come round and fetch him then. He looks as if he's going to throw up. He's such a loser.' And then when Robbie saw how upset Chrissie was, he continued more gently, 'Are you sure you don't want any help with him before I go? I could take him back next door. I'm used to dealing with drunks.'

Oblivious to the two of them, Joe took another pull on the can in his hand and belched dramatically. 'She won't talk to me you know. Won't ring, Christ alone knows how many messages I've left on the bloody answer machine for her. She said she wasn't sure that she wanted to put it right. What the fuck does that mean, eh? What am I going to do? She even won't talk to me.' He looked up expectantly at Chrissie and Robbie.

'I love you,' he spluttered, eyes filling up with tears.

Robbie glanced heavenwards as Chrissie waved him away. 'Go on, off you go. Be careful.'

'You too,' said Robbie, casting one more glance at Joe.

'Why won't she talk to me?' said Joe, turning his attention back to Chrissie. 'We need to talk.'

Chrissie didn't know what to say other than, 'Kate's not talking to me either, Joe. But she'll be back on Friday, you can talk to her then. Come on, let's get you home. It'll be fine, don't worry, you'll sort it out. You need to give her a little more time, that's all.'

A little more time? In her heart Chrissie doubted that Kate would ever speak to her again. A century wouldn't be enough to heal the look of hurt and disbelief she had seen on Kate's face when she walked into that kitchen. It was an image Chrissie was trying hard to forget but it kept resurfacing and now was so close that she could almost feel Kate's breath on her face.

Slouched in an armchair, Joe shook his head, the gesture over-large thanks to God alone knows how many cans of lager. 'It's not right you know.'

Chrissie was thinking much the same thing, there was no way she wanted to end up with Joe by default. It wasn't fair, she wanted a man of her own, a man who she had chosen, who would love her and look after her and hold her in the night and tell her that everything would be all right and mean it. With Joe almost exactly the reverse was true; he was not so much an equal as a high maintenance hobby.

Joe hadn't made any effort to move, a little gobbet of spit clung to his chin. He hadn't shaved for days and looked as if he might have slept in his clothes.

'Come on, you have to go home now, Joe,' she said, more forcefully this time, grabbing hold of his free hand and attempting to pull him to his feet. It was like trying to move a sack of damp pebbles.

Joe looked up at her and blinked, once, twice, his big eyes filling up again as he pulled her down on to his lap. He stank of beer and worse and crushed her to him so that she could barely breathe, let alone move.

'You know that I love you really, don't you, Chrissie?' he slurred, as she tried to extricate herself. Chrissie grimaced levering herself back onto to her feet. Men could be so naïve – they had no idea that sometimes love alone was nowhere near enough.

For the first few moments when Kate woke on Wednesday morning she had absolutely no idea where she was, just a blissful sense of free fall; sunlight flooded in through cream nets, the air was still with just a distant soporific hum of traffic. Far from panicking, Kate had a sense of peace and calm and being totally at ease, which lasted for as long as it took for her head to fill up with thoughts about Joe and Chrissie, Sam57, and Andrew the vet. Odd how overnight he'd turned into another source of pressure.

It felt almost as if she had been robbed. Getting out of bed, Kate wondered if there was any way to make the cacophony of voices in her head shut up.

It was early – before seven – but despite there being no hurry Kate showered and went downstairs, not wanting to be alone with her thoughts.

In the sitting room, Maggie was already awake and flicking through the channels on early morning TV. She looked exhausted and Kate wondered how much sleep she'd had.

The only comforting thing, Kate noticed, was that she had the walkabout phone tucked alongside her. Kate hoped that once she had picked up her messages Maggie had rung Guy and wished him goodnight and snuggled down with him. She suppressed a smile. Odd how quickly things change.

Odd, too, how quickly life settled down into a routine; she made tea, helped Maggie to get up and dressed, sorted out breakfast for the two of them, while Maggie hopped off to the bathroom

– they had tried the shower trick and it worked a treat – and then Kate opened up the French windows to let the day in before settling down in the dining room to get on with her work.

Along with everything else, Kate had a peculiar sense of unreality; being back at home with Maggie felt as if she was playing house. This couldn't be real life, this was the de-stressed, uncomplicated version of living that didn't have Joe or Chrissie or the boys or running a house in it.

Kate glanced up at the clock; thinking of pressure and responsibility, she ought to ring Joe before it got late and even more awkward. Time to open the door and let real life back in. She let the clock register in her mind so she could work out if he would be too busy with breakfast and sports kit and getting the boys off to school, or on his way to the office, to talk to her. *If* he was going in to the office, that is – Kate couldn't remember what he was doing this week or whether he had any work booked or not. Glancing down at the dining table, Kate realised that for the first time in God knows how many years she was no longer custodian of Joe's diary.

Her own was open on today's date and on the

page was a neat list of work things waiting to be worked through, ticked off, mailed out. She had a deadline for an advertorial on a coach tour to Biarritz, a couple of recruitment ads, and half a dozen telephone interviews to do for the in-house catering magazine that her agency handled.

'Jake swimming club @ lunch time,' was all it said in the top right hand corner of the page, the piece of the page she allocated to domestic arrangements. If Joe was away or had something on, Kate usually duplicated the information here but it appeared that she hadn't written anything down for him at all this week. Nothing, as if he had never existed. Gone. Kate stared at the page.

No Joe; it was a scary possibility. What would she do if they really couldn't go back, couldn't fix it? What would life be like if they couldn't find a way home from this? It was almost impossible to imagine. They had been together so long. Kate had grown up with Joe, so many of the big milestones in her life had been marked in his company.

They'd met when she was eighteen, doing a job at a recruitment agency in the long summer before she went to uni. Staying with her aunt in London had seemed like a huge adventure. She'd even got a buzz hopping on the bus into work every morning. It was like Kate had finally grown up, finally arrived. Meeting Joe had been the icing on the cake. Compared to the guys in Denham, he had seemed so worldly and so knowing. Kate allowed herself a wry smile; hard to believe it was the same man really. They had known each other for nearly twenty years now. Jesus, could it really be that long?

She'd gone out with Joe all the time she was at uni. Him driving up to see her in a battered Mini van, her travelling down by train until they could afford to get a place together. They'd got married a month after she graduated. Kate sighed; all those years ago it had seemed like they were on the edge of a huge adventure. What could she possibly ever put in their place? Worse still, what if Chrissie hadn't been the first? What if there had been others? In her imagination one became a dozen and then a dozen more. How long had Joe been playing her for a mug? For a moment Kate had a glimpse of life without him.

She closed her eyes, making the effort to still her mind.

At around twenty past nine, when the rush and panic ought to be over, Kate picked up the phone, tapped in her home number and waited. Someone picked it up on the ring before the machine cut in.

'Uhuh,' said a familiar voice.

'Danny?'

'Mum?'

It would be very difficult to work out who was the more surprised.

'What on earth are you doing there?' she said. 'You ought to be at school.'

There was a peculiar little pause; Kate could almost see him scrabbling round for a half-decent excuse. 'Overslept,' was the best he could come up with at short notice. 'But I'm going now. Well, in a few more minutes, I'm just waiting for my toast to do.'

'What about Jake? Where's Jake?'

'He's still here too but I've got him up. He's just doing his teeth and looking for his kit.'

'What on earth is going on –' she began, and then decided annoyance probably wouldn't do any good at all. 'You'll need to ring the school and tell them that you're on your way. This is not on, Danny, what happened? Did you forget to set your alarm? Where's Dad?' demanded Kate, meaning will you please pass the phone to him.

There was pause and then Danny said, almost

as a throwaway remark, 'I dunno. He's not here.'

'What? What do you mean he's not there?' Kate was genuinely stunned, her mind instantly galloping around looking for an excuse and explanation, almost as desperate to defend Joe as to condemn him.

'Dunno. He wasn't here when I got up this morning.'

'What do you mean wasn't there, when did you last see him?' Kate asked, trying hard not to let the panic drown her voice.

'Last night, 'bout half ten. After Bill went home I went upstairs to finish my homework off, and Dad was down here watching the box.'

'Right, okay, well, maybe he had an early meeting and forgot to say anything, probably thought you should be able to get yourself sorted out,' Kate said, taking a deep breath. 'Get yourself ready for school and I'll – I'll . . .' what could she do? She was two hours' drive away. 'I'll sort it out.' It sounded good.

While Kate was trying to think, her brain was mawkishly shifting through the possible permutations. In an instant she had Joe swinging from a beam in their bike shed, his face crimson, tongue hanging out like a kipper tie. Or maybe he had been squashed under a night bus like a beetle – this despite her rational mind telling her that the most likely explanation was that he was round at Chrissie's or possibly Bill's. Although Joe being at Bill's did come as an afterthought.

Or maybe he was still in bed sleeping it off? Had Bill's comment about Joe not coping well been a polite euphemism for pissed out of his skull? That was also highly possible. Joe's way of coping with stress almost inevitably involved running away and hoping a grown-up would come along and sort it out for him.

'You okay, Mum?' asked Danny cheerily. 'How's Granny Maggie?'

Kate coughed to fill the silence, 'Yes, I'm fine, love, just fine, and Granny's fine – a bit tired and very sore but she's okay. Go and get you and Jake sorted out and I'll ring you later.'

'Okay, see ya,' said Danny.

'Give my love to Jake, and love you too.'

There was a little pause and then Danny said, 'Miss you.'

Kate wanted to cry. 'Me too. Can you just check Dad's not still in bed and then I want you to get yourself off to school. I'll ring and let them know you're on your way and if Dad turns up in the meantime tell him to call me.' Kate didn't like to add, 'So that I can ask him what the hell he thinks he's playing at,' although she was certain Danny could fill the gaps in for himself.

'What, before they start dredging the Thames?' he added as a final shot.

Kate smiled wryly. Danny might have his father's looks but he most definitely shared her sense of the macabre.

'What do you mean, he's not there?' said Bill incredulously. 'Of course he's not here; I wouldn't have let him leave the boys on their own.' Now Bill sounded affronted and indignant as well as concerned.

Kate wasn't altogether sure why she rang Bill first – maybe it was because she could use the sympathy, maybe it was because she held out a frail hope that at the last minute Joe had come good and not scuttled next door to Chrissie's.

'Do you want me to see if I can find him?'

They both knew exactly what Bill meant.

'No, but I'd be grateful if you could check up to make sure the kids have gone to school.'

'Sure, no problem, anything else?'

Kate wondered whether to ask him to check in the bike shed just in case, but realistically Joe wasn't the hanging kind. 'No. Oh yes, wait, Bill. How much had Joe had to drink last night?'

The silence told Kate everything she needed to know. 'And how drunk was he when you left?'

'He wasn't really drunk, Kate, he was just a couple over, you know how he gets. I told him to get himself off to bed.'

'Thanks, Bill,' she said.

'Let me know if he's at Chrissie's, if not, I mean if there's a problem, I can have the boys tonight if you like.' Momentarily Kate reconsidered the bike shed, wondering if Bill knew something that she didn't.

'Thanks, I'll let you know how it goes,' was all she could manage before hanging up.

Kate rang the school, and Joe's mobile, which was switched off, leaving the most obvious number until last.

Chrissie didn't answer the phone, not that Kate had really expected her to.

Kate let it ring and ring until the machine cut in and then said, 'Hello, Chrissie, this is Kate. I need to know if Joe is there. Joe, if you're there and you get this message, call me.'

Once she had hung up, work went very slowly.

Bill rang to say that as he was going round

to her house he'd met the boys on their way to school and that Chrissie's house looked all shut up. He'd knocked on the door but there were no signs of life.

No sooner had Kate put the phone down than it rang.

'Kate?'

'Joe, where the fuck have you been? The kids have only just gone to school.' Kate couldn't help herself, it wasn't the most useful way of starting a meaningful dialogue but she was furious. 'Anything could have happened to them.'

'Don't take that tone with me. Why didn't you ring? Why didn't you answer my messages? I was worried.'

'So worried that you got completely hammered.'

'Who told you that, oh let me guess. Bill, the boy wonder. For your information I wasn't drunk.'

'Really, so what was it then? Malaria?'

'Stress. I only had a couple of cans. Where were you when I rang?'

'Out.'

'Yeh? Out where?'

How come she was defending herself? Wasn't the shoe supposed to be on the other foot?

'I took Mum out to a house-warming party in town. But it doesn't matter what I was doing.' A vivid image of sitting side by side with Andrew flashed unbidden through her mind and made her blush furiously. 'Where were you?'

'You care?'

Kate felt the fury rising up, ice cold and unstoppable 'You want the truth, Joe? At this moment I couldn't give a tin shit where you were or who you were with, but I do care about what happens to the boys. You're supposed to be at home looking after them.'

'I was, I just nipped out for a little while and anyway, they're old enough to look after themselves for a few hours; it's you mollycoddling them that's the problem, that and you up there gadding around with your mother.' He sounded petulant and peevish and thuggish.

What else was there to say? Presumably Joe had decided that this was not the moment to talk about all the things that he'd had on his mind the night before because he said, 'I've got to go,' and slammed the phone down, leaving Kate listening to the uninspiring burr of the open line.

Shaking, Kate went back to her laptop and re-read the holiday itinerary she was supposed to be waxing lyrical about. Tempting people off to explore Europe seemed pretty irrelevant by contrast to the other things that were going through her mind, but those were the things that kept the baby in shoes. Kate read the brief and then read it again, longing for it to catch hold of her mind and carry her away but today the magic door just wouldn't budge.

She stared unfocused out into the garden. Maybe she should just give up and go home. It was ridiculous that Joe couldn't even get it together to look after the kids for a week. Kate was hurt and angry and eventually, cramming the chaos back down, she started to type. It was like pulling teeth and by mid-morning Kate gave up and opened up her email.

> 'Morning,' said Sam57. It seemed that he had written to her at around the same time that she had been speaking to Joe.
>
> 'Thanks for your email – the things you asked knocked me back a bit but I suppose I should have expected as much. I've been thinking about you a lot since then and given a lot of thought to the things that you said.'

Kate cleaned her glasses so as to see his message more clearly.

'The problem is I can't find the words to tell my wife I've moved on, not without hurting her. It's like saying that the life we have together isn't good enough, that she isn't good enough any more. But it isn't like that, or that simple. It's like we've both changed and she hasn't noticed or maybe it's that she refuses to notice. I don't know who she sees when she looks at me but it isn't who I am any more.'

Kate shuddered. Was that what had happened to her and Joe?

Had they lost sight of each other too, somewhere in amongst building a family and paying the bills and trying to make it through the day?

'But I will tell you, Venus, because in an odd way it helped me to get a clear picture of what's going on here. How's your day going?'

Kate looked at the screen, touch-typing the letters so they appeared almost as if by magic.

'Dreadful so far. I've been trying to work – work's usually a great way to take my mind off the rest of the madness but it isn't doing it today. Last night I went to a party and got myself chatted up, which is amazing, those sort of things never happen to me. It's as if I've got this sign above my head that says married, unavailable – but not last night. This guy's asked me out to lunch today and I've said yes. Not that it means anything, in fact sitting here writing to you I'm not altogether sure why I agreed to go at all. I suppose it was flattering; I don't know, maybe it felt a bit dangerous – sauce for the goose and all that kind of thing. But now I'm going because I can't think of a good enough reason not to.'

Kate looked up at the clock; she ought to be getting ready.

'Got to go now, Sam, talk soon,'

Kate typed and then pressed send and switched off the machine, feeling as if she was going to an execution. What on earth had made her accept Andrew's invitation in the first place? It was cruel as well as being totally mad.

'Hi Kate, how are you? You look absolutely terrific,' said Andrew, getting to his feet as Kate walked into the cool dim interior of the riverside pub. For a moment they stood facing each other, just a fraction too close, not sure whether to shake hands, embrace or just sit down. Kate felt a little flutter in her belly but wasn't altogether sure whether it was nerves or – unexpectedly – lust.

Andrew looked gorgeous. Kate made a mental note to get her libido checked; was this the same woman who had driven all the way down here thinking of good reasons to drive straight back home? Lust wasn't meant to play any part in this. Andrew ran his fingers back through his hair. He was wearing a cream and blue narrow-striped granddad shirt and jeans. He looked kind and craggy and outdoorsy and she realised with a horrible surety that she fancied him. This was not how it was meant to go at all.

Moments passed. They both looked at each other as if they were waiting to be rescued. In the end it was Andrew who leaned in closer and, catching hold of her by her elbows, kissed Kate on both cheeks. It was an odd gesture, a little coy, a little self-conscious, and yet far more familiar than Kate had expected.

'I wondered if you were going to show up. Not that I thought you'd stand me up or anything, I didn't, I mean um – er, what do I mean?' The uncomfortable silence hovered, waiting. 'What would you like to drink?' he asked suddenly.

'Something long and cool and non-alcoholic would be good,' she said, glancing towards the counter. 'Orange juice and lemonade?'

Kate was unintentionally a few minutes late. It had taken longer than she remembered to drive to the river, and as she had driven down long forgotten lanes she had wondered by turns whether Andrew would wait and what the hell she was doing. In some ways it might be better if he thought he had been stood up and left. But, as Kate pulled into the car park, there was his jeep parked up under the trees, so she hadn't missed him and he hadn't run home.

He nodded. 'Right – okay. Shall we go and sit down?'

There was a handful of people in the bar, more out in the conservatory eating lunch. Kate realised with a start that she was seeking out familiar faces.

'You look good enough to eat,' Andrew said, still holding her elbow, blushing almost as much as Kate as he turned to guide her towards a table overlooking the locks and the Great Ouse. Before she could reply Andrew winced for her, and said, 'Sorry, that was awful, straight out of the oily creep's book of smart lines. I'm hoping it's just nerves and that it'll pass.'

'It's all right,' she said, 'I was about to giggle and blush furiously. This is ridiculous. I feel about fifteen,' she said, wondering if they had really got this far the night before? Kate had been stone cold sober all evening. There was no denying the chemistry between them, but maybe Andrew was reading too much into it . . . wasn't he? Or was it her?

'Which was about how old you were when I first noticed you,' he said. If he got much redder he would explode, Kate thought.

'You noticed me when I was fifteen?'

'Oh yes.'

'And are you saying you fancied me when I was fifteen?'

'I think I probably am.'

Kate nodded. 'Okay then, in that case maybe it would be better if I did giggle and blush. God, this is hard. How about if we pretend that we're not out on a date at all?'

Andrew laughed. 'What and spoil the fun? I'd forgotten how weird this feels. When you walked in I got that funny little kick in the bottom of my belly.'

She pulled a face. 'Probably just hungry.'

As they turned towards the dining room, Kate caught sight of her reflection in one of the mirrors behind the bar; Andrew was right, the prospect of seeing him had done something to her face. She looked light and full and sunny, quite stunning, despite being dressed casually in a white tee-shirt tucked into jeans, with a little sleeveless grey fleece over the top, her long red brown hair rolled up into a wispy top knot.

As they walked, his hand rested easily in the small of her back, lighting a tiny fire that she had no idea was ready and kindled. Once they were settled at a table Andrew handed her a menu and moved slightly closer.

'I've been thinking about you all night. It's bloody ridiculous. I couldn't help it. I don't know whether to offer you lunch or just take you home and make mad passionate love to you. What do you think?'

He said it in a way that could easily be taken as a joke but for an instant Kate saw the little glint in his eye – not of desperation but of a real earthy desire – and laughed to try and defuse the tension. 'Just as long as you don't get the two mixed up; I'm sure it would put the punters off their pasta, and anyway, Andrew, I'm hungry, not easy,' Kate continued more firmly, scanning the starters, smiling still, trying to hold tight to her composure. The idea of making love over the equivalent of the kitchen table with Andrew telegraphed itself through her body like a rush of silver sparks.

'Sorry, I wasn't saying – that was a stupid thing to say – God, I'm so nervous. I haven't been out with a woman other than my mother in God knows how long. I was up at seven this morning trying to decide what to wear. It's ridiculous, isn't it? I'm better with cows –' He paused and then said, 'God no, that isn't what I mean either.'

Kate laughed. His discomfort was incredibly endearing.

'Just relax,' she said, patting his hand. She didn't tell him that she thought his nerves were sweet or that he looked mouthwateringly gorgeous, instead she slowly turned the pages of the menu and tried to focus on the food, conscious of her wedding ring.

Kate had considered, while upstairs getting ready, whether to take it off, well aware that whatever she did with it, it said something very loud and inescapable about the state of play, if not to Andrew, then to herself.

'So,' Andrew said, catching her eye, 'what

will it be then?' And they both knew he wasn't just talking about the shrimp pâté served with crisp slivers of French toast and baby leaves in a raspberry vinaigrette.

For an instant Kate looked up into his face and felt that odd little thrill of stars track down her spine again.

'Why don't you ask me again after we've eaten?' she heard herself say with a lighthearted laugh.

God, this wasn't just bad or mad it was getting very, very dangerous.

Looking relieved, Andrew smiled and indicated the menu. 'And how about for lunch? The fish here is great, mind you, so are the steaks.'

'I really don't know what I want.'

Andrew's eyes didn't leave hers. 'Maybe I can help you with that,' he said, all nervousness gone, and then he leaned across the table and kissed her. Gently, soft lips exploring hers, tentatively as if expecting to be rebuked.

Kate was stunned, almost too stunned to make herself pull away. She gasped, struggling to breathe. This was way too much, much too soon. Her heart upped its pace and she jerked back, blushing, and totally unsettled.

'Oh my God,' she whispered, looking down at

the menu again, struggling to compose herself, 'which page of the oily creep's book of smart lines did that come from?'

'It didn't,' he said. 'That was all me.'

'Bloody hell,' said Kate. She'd have to be dead to miss the intensity in his voice, but before either of them had a chance to say anything else, Kate's mobile rang. Without thinking, and in part to defuse the electrical storm that arced between them, Kate snatched it out of her handbag and pressed answer.

'Kate?'

It was such a stupid thing to do. A great wave of something hot and fluttery and uncomfortable rolled through her.

'Chrissie?' she said, feeling her stomach instantly tighten into a clenched fist.

Chapter 12

'We need to talk,' said Chrissie. 'Is now okay? Or would you rather I called you back later?'

'No, no, it's fine,' said Kate, quickly getting to her feet, aware that her manner was extremely businesslike and crisp, although it was more for Andrew's benefit than Chrissie's.

Chrissie caught the tone and said with less confidence, 'Kate, this is hard enough, please don't shut me out. I wanted to say that I'm sorry. I don't know what else to say to you.'

Kate moved away from the table, holding the phone tight against her body, and then to Andrew said, 'I won't be a minute.'

'Sure. You want me to order you something?' he half said and half mouthed, indicating the menu, and Kate nodded, wanting nothing more than to be away from him or, more honestly, to be away from the things that he made her feel. What the hell was happening to her? This was ridiculous.

'You okay?' he added.

Kate stared back at him as she put the phone back to her ear. How could she possibly answer that one?

Doubly wrong-footed, Kate headed outside, aware that she was running away from one problem slap bang into another.

'Before I rang I'd got it all worked out,' Chrissie was saying. 'All the things I wanted to tell you, even how I wanted to say them. How to start –'

Kate didn't say a word, instead she moved rapidly out onto the lawn that ran down to the river, past the diners on the terrace and the ducks and kids playing, trying hard to get away from something that she couldn't put a name to.

At another time, Kate would have laughed and told Chrissie to cut to the chase before they both went grey, but today she didn't know what she wanted to say or hear any more than Chrissie did.

'I want you to know that despite appearances this thing with Joe isn't important, Kate. You have to believe me. I know how crazy that sounds but it never was important. You know what I'm like. I want happy ever after, not him – not Joe – of all people. I'm not trying to get away with what I've done or trivialise something that must seem so hurtful to you, but you have to know that I don't want this to ruin everything for you; for any of us. Kate, are you listening to me? I don't love Joe, I've never loved Joe – but I do love you and so does he. He needs you, Kate; he's hanging on the wire at the moment. Don't blow your lives apart over this, it's not worth it.'

The words twisted like a knife blade deep beneath her ribs, ripping so hard into her heart that it made her cry out in panic and fear and pain.

'Kate, please you have to listen to me. Joe loves you. Kate, please talk to me. Please.' Chrissie's voice was heavy with emotion.

Kate stared at the phone. Under different circumstances she would be telling Chrissie about flirting with Andrew and Chrissie would – if it hadn't been Joe – be telling her all about the red-hot man she had just met. But it *was* Joe, it was Joe, Kate's mind screamed furiously. This wasn't her friend; this was the enemy.

Kate struggled to find something to say, the right thing to say – she was good at finding the right thing to say – but it felt as if Chrissie had somehow drained her of every last breath. There wasn't even enough air to speak, and when the words finally came out it was as if Kate had to fight to make herself heard before some great pain-driven gale tore the sounds out of her lungs.

'Go away,' Kate whispered, the threat of tears ripping through her on the teeth of the same gale.

'No, no, please listen. Please, Kate, please don't hang up –' Chrissie began, her voice full of appeal and regret and discomfort. 'We have to talk, we need to talk. Joe was here last night, he was –'

Kate took another breath, a deeper breath, wrestling with the flow of emotion, wanting to find something to make Chrissie stop talking but it was too late. To her horror, instead of speaking, Kate burst into tears, there by the water, watched by a bemused man on a narrow boat.

'How can you do this? How can you?' she sobbed, tears flooding down her face, talking even though the phone was down by her side, even though Chrissie couldn't hear her, even though she had no idea whether she was talking about Chrissie or Joe or maybe just fate.

It felt as if her heart might burst. The tears came in big raw snotty waves. Kate glanced over her shoulder, hurrying further along the river bank; she couldn't do this here, not now, not where people could see her.

An instant later and to her total amazement, Kate felt first a hand on her arm and then arms around her shoulders, holding her tight, holding her close, taking the phone away, making comforting noises. She looked up in disbelief into Andrew's big brown eyes.

'Don't look at me,' she snorted furiously, pushing him away. 'I look bloody terrible.'

He nodded and brushed the hair back out of her eyes. 'You're right, you do,' he said, 'but trust me, compared to a goat in labour you're a picture.'

Kate snorted, and with no fight left to resist, she curled up against him, her head on his broad shoulders and cried until she thought she would probably die of pain or grief or exhaustion or all three, weeping until each breath felt red-hot and raw, burning through her chest.

It was a relief to finally let some of the pain out.

After a few minutes the sobbing eased off. Her head ached, her nose was running. There was no way Kate could go back into the pub now.

Andrew guided her to a quiet corner of the pub garden, sat her down on a bench under the lee of a weeping willow, and handed her a brandy. Kate blinked and looked down into the bull's-eye shot glass; she had no idea where the drink came from, whether he had brought it with him or gone off at some stage to fetch it from the bar.

'Here,' he pressed it into her hand. 'Drink this.'

'I can't, I'm driving,' she began, but Andrew insisted.

'Drink it, you're not in any fit state to drive home anyway.'

He was right. She was trembling so much that he had to steady the glass for her. The booze trickled and rippled and warmed her right through to the core. She didn't resist or object when he put his arm around her again and pulled her close, glad of the warmth and the comfort, nor did she argue when he left her and came back with another shot of brandy.

'I haven't eaten anything since this morning,' Kate said, aware of the alcohol careering through her bloodstream like a runaway train.

'Don't worry,' he said, helping her to her feet, 'we can go back to my place, I'll fix you something there. It's not far from here. I've got loads of food in.' The way he said it, so self-assured, so certain that she would agree, somehow made it all right.

In the car park he helped her into the jeep and to belt herself in, her fingers having seemed to have lost any sense of control.

'Want to talk about it?' Andrew said, as they were reversing out of the car park.

Kate shook her head, dropped the sun visor, and stared miserably at her reflection. It looked as if she had had a run-in with a baseball bat – both eyes had swollen up like ringed doughnuts, rimmed by what remained of her eye make-up, her nose was bright red. She looked awful and felt drunk.

'Can you just drop me off at my house?'

He nodded. 'Sure, not a problem. But are you certain you don't want something to eat first, or at least have a cup of coffee? Get yourself together.' He grinned; there was no hint of pressure in his voice. 'Wash your face, fix your make-up? Girl stuff, you know, those things that men don't know about?'

Kate scowled at him. Of course he was right, if she went straight home looking like this Maggie would be even more worried than she was now.

'You're way too clever for your own good. I'm sorry about this,' she began, avoiding an answer until her sluggish brain had had time to work its way through the possibilities. 'I don't normally behave like some mad woman let out of the attic on a day trip.'

He waved the words away. 'Don't worry, it's quite exciting really.'

She glared at him but he didn't seem to mind in the least.

'My house is just up here on the left.' They couldn't have driven more than a mile or so. Andrew pointed through the windscreen to a large detached flint faced house set back off the strip of common land that edged the narrow road down to the river.

'So which is it to be? Lunch, coffee, or would you prefer to go straight home?' He leant back to survey her.

Kate reddened as his eyes picked their way through the wreckage. She hesitated for a few seconds longer and then said with a confidence that she didn't really feel, 'Actually a coffee might be a good idea.'

'And a sandwich?'

Kate smiled; there was something quite attractive about his gentle persistence. 'Okay, fine, and a sandwich.'

She needed something to soak up the alcohol. 'But I can't stay very long and don't ask me any difficult questions.'

'Goes without saying,' he said, jumping down out of the jeep.

'So how was the drive up?' Maggie asked Joe.

'Fine.'

'And how was the traffic?'

'Fine.'

Maggie looked her son-in-law up and down. Joe didn't look or sound very fine at all. They were in the kitchen drinking tea, it was almost three o'clock, and they had just about run out of things to say and niceties to exchange. The air was so thick you'd have needed a chainsaw to cut it.

Maggie surreptitiously glanced up at the clock above the cooker, wondering where the hell Kate had got to, whilst trying not to let the thought or her growing anxiety show on her face. What if Kate had invited the vet back for coffee? Kate hadn't actually told Maggie she was going out with Andrew but it had to be him she'd gone out with because, surely to God, no one in their right mind would volunteer to have lunch with Julie Hicks?

Kate would see Joe's car in the drive, wouldn't she? Or would she? What if he had parked somewhere else, out on the road, and she didn't see it and just sailed straight in.

Maggie blushed in anticipation. She was almost certain she had already asked Joe about the journey as he came in. He had been there the best part of an hour and this was their second pot of tea, although Maggie was taking it steady. It took her way too long to get to the loo these days to risk drinking gallons.

'Did you park in the yard?' she tried.

He grunted in a disinterested way, leaving Maggie none the wiser.

'Did I tell you I was planning to redesign the garden later this year?' she said cheerily, nodding towards the terrace. 'I've been giving it a lot of thought, I've been sitting out there to try and get an idea of what might work.'

'Right,' said Joe, who was staring out through

the French windows although it was quite obvious his thoughts were focused elsewhere.

Maggie's too. It was like pushing water uphill. She glanced back at the clock, willing the hands to stop. When she had heard the back door opening earlier Maggie had assumed it was Kate coming home, or possibly Liz or someone from the bookshop had dropped in. Joe hadn't even entered her mind. She had been so stunned when he stuck his head round the door that she had let out a little shriek, which she had hastily tried to disguise as a cough.

'Well, hello. How are you? Come in,' she'd managed. 'Nice to see you, this is a surprise –'

'Where's Kate?' he asked. It seemed that Joe had decided to dispense with the social graces.

'She's nipped out to lunch with a friend, but she shouldn't be very long. I didn't expect to see you Joe. How are things going?'

Joe wasn't telling.

'I suppose Kate's told you all about it?' he said. It was impossible to miss the intense emotion in his voice.

At that point Maggie had been tempted to pretend that she did know, to pull a face, lift that eyebrow implying that of course she had heard it all, knew it all and held an open opinion. But in fact, faced with Joe, who was quite obviously in a foul mood, Maggie had shaken her head and said, 'Actually, Joe, Kate hasn't said a word to me about anything. I know that she's very upset about something but that's as far as we've got. You know what she's like, she's always played her cards close to her chest. Kate likes to sort things out for herself.'

Joe looked at her squarely as if trying to decide whether Maggie was telling the truth or not and then grunted. 'Right, so have you got any idea where she is or how long she's going to be?'

Maggie had made a noncommittal noise, and then, looking at her cast, Joe had asked, almost grudgingly, 'So how are you?'

'Fine.'

Which was as big a lie as Joe's answers. Maggie's foot throbbed so much that the pulse echoed in her ears and was making her feel sick. Her other hip and leg ached from bearing the load when she was on crutches, and lying down with her foot up on a pile of cushions was beginning to drive her totally and utterly bats. She felt sore and sad and sorry for herself. She needed Joe there like she needed a hole in the head. That and the fact she missed Guy and was worried about Kate didn't help one little bit.

‘Would you like some tea?’ she enquired, pleasantly.

Joe nodded, and they had gone into the kitchen where Joe had made it, but only after he had watched Maggie struggling with the potentially dangerous combination of kettle, teapot and crutches.

Although that seemed an awfully long while ago now.

Maggie eased her leg up into a marginally more comfortable position. It wasn’t that she didn’t like Joe. She had always seen what it was that attracted Kate to him. When Kate first brought Joe home he had been a good-looking, sexy, moody boy with a mop of floppy brown hair, pushed casually back off his face. Gone now of course, the hair, and his mood had hardened up to into something less attractive, sullen, the corners of his thin lips turned down making him look sulky and hard done by and permanently disappointed.

‘So Joe,’ Maggie said, ‘are you going to tell me what’s going on?’ She made a real effort to ensure her tone was reasonable rather than confrontational. ‘I’m worried about both of you.’ She was also tired of repeating herself and trying to come up with cunning questions.

He reddened a little and after a few seconds' deliberation waved the words away. 'It's just one of those things, Maggie, just a bit of a hiccup. Kate's – well, Kate's being Kate, overreacting, getting herself in a state about nothing. We've got things that we need to sort out. Nothing that can't be worked out with a bit of time, but she won't talk to me about it. How the hell are you supposed to sort things out if you won't talk about them? You know how it is.'

Frustrated, Maggie didn't let her gaze drop and despite the fact that Joe still looked and sounded annoyed, he wriggled uncomfortably. Maggie hoped that if she held her nerve and pushed just a little bit more then Joe would crack and spill the beans. 'No, Joe, I don't know how it is or I wouldn't be asking,' she said, ensuring her tone stayed even and measured. No point startling him. 'And I feel I ought to know. Kate is my daughter and you are my son-in-law – I'm interested and I care about you both.'

'Well,' Joe said, after an uneasy pause, 'the thing is –'

Maggie leant closer and then they both heard the front door open and footsteps tip-tapping across the hall. Both of them froze. Maggie sighed, foiled again, and when she was so close as well. She and Joe looked up as the kitchen door swung open to reveal Kate.

'Hello, Joe, what are you doing here? Did you bring the boys with you?' She sounded brisk and businesslike as if she had been preparing her speech outside. She pulled off her fleece gilet and dropped it on to one of the chairs, apparently unconcerned and totally at ease; she didn't fool Maggie for an instant.

Joe glared at her. 'Where the hell have you been? I thought you were meant to be here looking after Maggie.'

'And I thought you were meant to be home nights looking after the boys,' Kate snapped straight back, dropping her bag alongside her jacket. Despite the fighting talk, Maggie thought Kate looked extremely uneasy as if she had been caught with her hand in the biscuit tin, but Joe appeared oblivious. 'And anyway, I have been looking after her, but Mum's not bedridden, Joe. She doesn't need me to be sitting within arms' reach all day. It would drive us both mad. I just popped out to lunch. Mum didn't mind, did you?'

So far she had managed to avoid Joe's eyes and answering his question. Not bad, thought Maggie, finishing off the dregs of her Earl Grey.

'How's it been?' she asked, grazing Maggie's cheek with a kiss. She smelt of booze and panic. 'Is there any tea left in that pot or would you like me to make a fresh one?'

'It's gone three o'clock,' snapped Joe, as if Maggie wasn't there. Kate swung round to face him. 'I can tell the time, Joe.' She felt sick, the brandy chopping back and forth, diluted by two cups of very strong coffee and two rounds of cheese and tomato sandwiches.

'Maggie's been here all on her own.'

'So you just said. What are you doing here anyway? I thought you were supposed to be working.'

'This seems to be the only way to get you on your own long enough to have a conversation. I've tried ringing and talking to you since you got here,' he added darkly.

'I've already told you, Joe, I've got nothing to say to you. I need time. I need to think.'

'What do you need to think about for God's sake?'

Kate stared at him; how could he not know that she had done nothing but think since she had found him in the kitchen with Chrissie.

'It was nothing,' he continued, red with frustration. 'I've already told you that. I don't know why you're making such a big thing about it, Kate. It's done, over, finished.'

Kate couldn't believe what she was hearing, and she certainly wasn't going to let Joe off the hook that easily. 'Really? So where were you last night and what's happening to the boys while you're up here? Chrissie keeping an eye on them, is she?'

Joe's expression hardened up. 'No. I've asked my Mum to have them tonight.'

'What, all night?'

He nodded.

'So you can spend another night out on the tiles once you've left here? I don't assume that you were planning to stay, were you?' Kate's tone was icy cold and venomous.

'What if I was?'

'I wouldn't have you staying here even you asked me, Joe.'

Maggie looked from face to face and, as their eyes met, Kate decided that there was nothing left but the truth. Having watched the fallout, Maggie deserved to know what was going on. With her eyes firmly fixed on Joe's, Kate said very slowly, as if it was important to enunciate every syllable, 'Joe and Chrissie are having an affair.'

Maggie gasped in genuine disbelief. It wasn't at all what she had expected. An affair maybe, by either one of them, but not this. Chrissie and Kate were best friends; it was like spilling blood on sacred ground.

'Chrissie? I don't believe it,' she said incredulously, understanding now why Kate couldn't bear to talk about it. Even once removed, the weight of betrayal felt like a rock pressing down on her chest.

On the other side of the kitchen, Joe went from red to ashen with sheer fury. '*Was* having an affair – no, no not even was. I told you, Kate, it was never an affair. But that's half the trouble, isn't it? We always have to have your side of things, don't we? Always your version of the truth. I screwed her a few times, that's all.' He swung round to face Maggie, as if appealing to the umpire. 'Chrissie and I are not having an affair.'

'What would you call it then?' Kate snapped. 'You keep waving it away, the pair of you, trivialising something that isn't trivial. Making out as if it was nothing. You don't even respect Chrissie or yourself enough to call it what it is. You slept with her in my bed, for God's sake, and you've been doing it for years, haven't you?'

Maggie gasped again.

Joe was on his feet now. 'I thought we could talk this through like adults.'

'Really,' said Kate.

'I thought we could sort it out.'

Kate turned very slowly towards him. 'Well, we can't. Not at the moment. Maybe not at all. Go home, Joe,' she said in a low voice, a voice that bubbled with a dark deep ice cold rage.

'Look, let's not have a scene,' he pleaded. 'I've driven miles to have this conversation, the very least you can do is hear me out.'

Kate glared at him. 'You could have saved yourself the trip. I've got nothing to say to you that I haven't already and I don't want to hear any of the things you've got to say.'

For a moment Maggie wondered if Kate had pushed him too far. Joe tensed, his fists clenched, and then shook his head and turned away.

'For Christ's sake. I thought you were bigger than this, Kate.'

Kate stared at him in amazement. 'Bigger? What do you mean bigger? Big enough to just turn the other cheek and pretend nothing's happened? Did you expect me to do that thing that politicians' wives do when their husband's been caught under some red-hot blonde? Make some excuse for the way you've behaved, draw a veil over it? Stand by you? I've always stood by you, Joe, always, and look where it's got me.'

'Oh that's it, here we go again,' he said, throwing his hands up in the air. 'St Katherine the bloody Martyr, the one who worked while those around her squandered away their time and talent.'

Kate stepped back as if Joe had slapped her. 'You bastard. I've always been there for you –'

'Not this week,' Joe bawled, heading out towards the door.

'But this week it's not about you or me, it's about my mum.'

'Oh really,' said Joe. 'It doesn't look like it from where I'm standing. You're so concerned about her welfare that you sod off out for lunch with somebody else and leave her here to manage all on her own.'

Maggie watched powerless as Kate and Joe headed out into the hall, the surprise and disbelief lingering around her like a wraith.

* * *

Kate stood for a second or two in the cool shadows of the hall trying hard to regain her composure, her heart pounding out a rock and roll rhythm in her chest. She felt sick and dizzy. Joe was the last person on earth she had expected to see at Maggie's. As Andrew had dropped her off she had seen his car parked in the driveway and broken out into a cold sweat.

'About your car –' Andrew was saying, as Kate scrambled to collect her jacket and handbag. She began to tremble.

'I'll sort it out later, it's not important,' she said, feeling her colour rising furiously, while all the time her mind was working overtime. What if Joe was sitting over there watching her, what if he happened to be looking out of the window right now? What if, what if . . . In the driver's seat, Andrew was still talking.

'Sorry?' she said.

'I said I'll nip back later if you like and drive you down to the pub to collect it.'

'Right. No, it's all right – I'll, I'll call a cab once I get in.'

'Don't be ridiculous.' Andrew caught hold of her arm. 'Are you okay? You seem really upset. What's the matter? Do you want me to come in with you?'

Kate tried to focus on his face. She thought for a moment that he was going to kiss her goodbye and then knew with ice cold certainty, as Andrew leaned closer, that that was exactly what he had in mind. Kate sprang out of the car like a cat out of an airing cupboard.

'I'm fine, I'm fine,' she said, and scurried across the road, aware that he was watching her and aware too that he might not be the only one.

God, what on earth had she done? What was she going to do?

'I'll ring you later,' Andrew called after her.

'I'll ring you later,' Joe said, as Kate reached the front door a footstep or two behind him. He looked exhausted and in the uneasy silence Kate was torn between sadness, exasperation and anger.

'Joe?' she said miserably, feeling her eyes fill up with tears, but instead of turning towards her or replying, Joe's attention shifted out through the open doorway towards something in the yard.

'Hi, is Kate there?'

Kate stiffened as she recognised Andrew's voice.

Joe stepped out into the sunshine. 'She might be, it depends who wants to know.'

Kate was after him in a whisper.

'Ah, there you are,' Andrew said brightly.

'Who the fuck is this?' hissed Joe to Kate, as he looked Andrew up and down.

It was hardly the most appropriate moment for cocktail party introductions. Kate toyed with the idea of telling Joe that it wasn't important except that would probably only make things worse and also of telling Andrew to run away while he still could. As she glanced back inside Kate caught a glimpse of Maggie hopping towards the door and felt a sudden rush of panic. She needed to get whatever it was over quickly before Maggie got involved.

'Andrew, this is my husband, Joe; Joe, this is, this is – Andrew, Andrew Taylor, he's a vet.'

'What the fuck do you want a vet for?'

Andrew's open and warm expression closed down to something more guarded and formal.

'Hi, Joe. Kate and I are old friends,' he lied, extending a hand pleasantly. 'If this is a bad time?' He held Kate's gaze. 'I was a bit concerned about you. Would you like me to go? I can always come back later if it's more convenient?'

Beside her, Joe's expression had gone from angry to something far out the other side of rational. 'What do you mean, you can come back later? Who the fuck *is* this, Kate?' he repeated furiously.

Andrew misguidedly began to try and explain. 'I'm a friend of Kate's, we've just been out to lunch and she –'

Kate looked heavenwards and prayed for a miracle.

Joe rounded on Kate, his face a mask of fury. 'Oh you have, have you?' he snapped. 'Your mother didn't say anything about you having lunch with a man.'

'We went to the Boatman's Arms, do you know it?' asked Andrew.

Kate willed Andrew to shut up, but it seemed that being nervous made him talk all the more – and then talk some more. 'Kate and I were at school together, so I'm an old friend –' Andrew repeated pleasantly. It was totally the wrong thing to say, not that there were any right things to say under the circumstances.

'Really?' Joe growled. 'Just an old friend, eh?'

‘We’re all allowed a friend, aren’t we?’ Andrew joked.

Kate closed her eyes; it was like Ghandi going up against Genghis Khan.

‘Seems we’re all allowed friends,’ Joe said, turning towards Kate with something that pretended to be a smile on his face.

Kate shook her head, trying to distance herself from the two of them.

‘You know,’ Joe said rounding on her, ‘that Chrissie was my friend too.’

‘Yes, but we’re not just talking friendship here are we, Joe?’ she snapped right back before she could help herself.

‘Oh yes, you’re so bloody smug, aren’t you? So quick to point the finger. What have you been up to with laughing boy here? Nice cosy lunch, the two of you? You telling him about how cruelly hard done by you are? What a bastard I am –’ And then he poked her. It was an odd gesture and one that took Kate by complete surprise. In all the years they had been together she had never felt threatened by Joe but for an instant she realised that in the mood he was in he was capable of anything and she was suddenly nervous of him.

‘Joe,’ she said in a very low and very reasonable

voice. 'Please go home now before you do or say something you'll regret. I don't want it to be like this.'

'Oh, and how do you want it to be? Me grovelling on my knees? Begging you to forgive me?'

'No, of course not,' she began, although the thought had crossed her mind once or twice.

And then for some reason that wasn't altogether clear Joe took a step closer and Kate closed her eyes and flinched. It was Joe's turn to look surprised but Andrew had seen her reaction and said, 'I think you really ought to go.'

It was the moment when the tinder finally caught alight. Joe had been itching to let rip at something. 'Oh you do, do you, and what exactly has it got to do with you?' he growled and swung round to face Andrew. 'Why don't you just bugger off out of it and go play with your precious bloody animals? This is between me and my wife.'

Andrew stepped closer, opening his mouth as if to speak when Joe took a swing at him. It was such a wild and unlikely punch that Kate couldn't quite believe what she was seeing.

Even so, instinctively she shrieked, which was

enough to distract Joe, so that instead of pulling back from the swing – he was well wide of any potential target – his whole body followed through, and he tumbled forwards, losing his footing on the gravel.

Pulling a face, Joe swayed for an instant and then tottered and fell headfirst into the flower-bed. If it wasn't so humiliating it would have been funny. Kate made an effort to swallow back the laughter and – along with Andrew – helped Joe to his feet and brushed him down. Joe was livid, more than livid. He'd caught his face on something on the way down and grazed his cheek. His shirt was covered in compost and bark chippings. Angrily, he pushed them away, straightened himself up, rubbing the green off his knees, cradling his face, all the while looking around for what remained of his dignity.

After a few seconds Joe squared his shoulders as if to speak but before he could someone called out.

'Cooeee. Hello everyone,' said the cheery voice behind them. 'Not interrupting anything, am I? Only I thought your mum might like some of last night's party food. It seems such a terrible shame to let it go to waste.'

Everyone turned to watch Julie Hicks picking

her way across the gravel in white high-heeled sandals. Today her sundress was yellow. She smiled, looking ruefully from face to face. It was obvious that she had been there at the gate watching for some time.

'Hello, Andrew, how are you?' she said, and then nodded first towards Joe and then to Kate before winking theatrically. 'Shall I take these inside?' She waved the Tupperware box she was carrying. As she passed Kate, Julie whispered, 'Two of them fighting in the street over you, eh?' and then grinned. 'I'm *so* jealous.'

Chapter 13

'So let's have a little look. What have we got so far? Edwardian family house. Two receptions, cloakroom. Downstairs WC – always handy. Decent-sized kitchen. Hallway with under stairs cupboard. In need of some renovation.'

The estate agent glanced up from his clipboard but didn't quite look at Chrissie. He might as well have been talking to himself, in fact it occurred to Chrissie that quite possibly he was. He had one of those faces that smiled all the time, like a ventriloquist's dummy, and was just as disturbing. His tone was cultured although occasionally he lapsed into something distinctly more Norf' London; Chrissie couldn't work out whether this was deliberate, to add a little street cred and savvy to his otherwise faultless middle-class accent, or whether he was a wide boy with pretensions.

'Needs a bit of work but there are some very nice period features – just needs a little bit of TLC – but then again don't we all, eh? Live here on your own, do you?' As he spoke he looked at her out of the corner of his eye. Chrissie was so thrown that she couldn't work out whether it was patter or pity or whether he was actually flirting with her. Whichever it was, it was repulsive. Chrissie reddened, taking it as a personal insult.

Chrissie had mentioned at work that she was thinking about selling her house and one of the girls upstairs in Human Resources had said her brother-in-law might be able to help. A phone call later and here he was, Bob Sleight. She'd had to have the afternoon off work to let him in. Before Mr B. Sleight arrived she had been convincing herself that it was a positive move, a step in the right direction, but now she wasn't so sure. It felt sordid, almost as if she was doing a moonlight flit, the sensation not helped by the arrival of a man in a mac and trilby, who was a dead ringer for Terry Thomas. North London or Oxbridge, Bob

Sleight was slime whichever way you looked at it.

'But don't you worry, my dear,' he was saying. 'Good area like this, always lots and lots of interest. We've got a waiting list a yard long back at the office of people looking for houses round here. Or maybe I should say metre these days?' He laughed to himself. 'Anything that comes up give them a ring.' He looked around as if seeing the house for the first time. 'Should be no trouble shifting it; nothing structural by the looks of it, just a lick of paint and a bit of work here and there, which often means we get a quick sale, you know. People think they're getting a bargain. Won't fetch top dollar obviously but don't you worry, my hunch is that we'll shift it in no time at all. I'll ring round as soon as I get back, lots of times we get an offer in before the board even goes up.' And then his patter slowed. 'So where are you moving to then?' And when Chrissie didn't bite, pressed, 'Got something lined up, have you? Or maybe someone?' He grinned salaciously.

The man was a total dinosaur and at any other time Chrissie would have taken him on and won hands down but at that precise moment she was too tired and too vulnerable.

When she had talked to Robbie and Simon about selling up they had made a noise or two but basically seemed indifferent.

'No, I haven't even started to look yet. I really want somewhere smaller, my boys are growing up, things change,' she blustered. 'You know how it is.'

He nodded sympathetically. 'Oh, yes. Tell me about it. Always a wrench but trust me once you get shot of this place there'll be no looking back. World's your oyster. When did you say you bought it?' Not waiting for her answer, he glanced down at his oracle, the clipboard. 'You should make a tidy profit, particularly if you're down-sizing. I might be able to help you there, actually – we've just got the sole agency for a great little conversion, four flats, two beds, terrace, lovely area off Becks Row, just up beyond the traffic lights, on your left? Balconies, terrace on the mezzanine floor. Very stylish, very you. Shared garden; you've got my card. It'll be a new lease of life. Now, let's go and have a little shufty around upstairs, shall we? I've got the measurements for down here – real boon these little laser dooberries, tape measures are a thing of the past, you know.' He paused for a few seconds in the hall, sucking on his ballpoint.

Chrissie was exhausted by the sound of his voice but it appeared that he had barely started.

'Word to the wise, and don't take this as a criticism, but I'd have a little tidy up if I were you before any likely purchasers come round. I know it may sound obvious. Pack up what you're going to take on your move and skip the rest. Leave out a few tasteful knick-knacks, couple of nice pictures, fresh flowers. Quick coat of magnolia over anywhere that looks a bit grubby, maybe a coat of gloss on the front door. Makes the world of difference and brings the offers up much closer to your asking price.' Bob spoke as if he couldn't see the hall full of junk, the bike, the coats, the shoes, the recycling boxes stacked by the bundles of newspapers. But as he looked away she caught a glimpse of his unguarded expression, his booze-berried nose wrinkled up in disgust, those thick, slack, indulgent lips pursed, although his conciliatory tone didn't change. 'I'm sure you get my drift, dear. Three bedrooms, was it?'

Chrissie nodded as he made his way upstairs and pushed open each door in turn. It was as invasive as a strip-search. 'Bed 1, large well appointed room with ample scope for improvement, elegant bay overlooking the main road.

Large bathroom. Bed 2, Bed 3 . . .' He intoned the details into the little Dictaphone he was carrying, each phrase heavy with the lingua franca of house sales. In the back bedroom, Bed 3, he stopped for a moment to twitch aside the net curtains and admire the view out over the back gardens. 'Nice out there with the woods at the back. A real feature.'

'Yes, it's lovely this time of the year. Lovely any time of the year really,' Chrissie said sadly; she'd miss the woods.

'Nice garden. Always goes down well does a decent garden.' He ticked something on his clipboard and then pointed the little laser gismo at the far wall, before noting down the measurement. 'Back-up – can't be too careful, technology is wonderful stuff, when it works,' he said in answer to some unspoken question. And then, 'Good area, respectable – I wouldn't be surprised if we haven't got a couple of offers in by the end of the week.' He tucked the curtain back into place. 'Very nice. Get on well with your neighbours, do you?'

'Are you sure you're going to be all right?' asked Andrew anxiously.

Kate nodded, willing him to leave. 'I'll be fine, thank you. It would probably be better if you went now.'

'Ring me, won't you?'

Kate made a face that she hoped would satisfy him. He left reluctantly, looking back at the gate and then again as he reached his jeep.

She turned her attentions back to Joe. 'You'd better come back inside and get cleaned up.' She made the effort to sound brisk and well meaning. 'I don't think that's going to bruise.' Unlike his pride.

Joe snorted but nevertheless followed her inside as if the wild punch and the even wilder fall had finally earthed out his temper and frustration and drained him of every last shred of energy.

Inside, Maggie didn't say a word, while Julie, following up the rear and still carrying her plastic offering, chittered away like a demented monkey about the weather, the party, and Maggie's accident, as if she was afraid that if she stopped talking they might throw her out. She didn't know just how close to the truth she was.

In the hall Kate smiled and took the box out of her hands. 'Thanks for these, Julie. It was a kind thought. I'd ask you to stay but it's time for Mum to have her nap. I hope you don't mind?'

In the sitting room doorway, Maggie lifted an outraged eyebrow but at least had the decency to look wan and limp when Julie looked round.

'Oh right, yes, well, of course,' Julie said, quite obviously playing for time, looking hopefully towards the kitchen where Joe was hunching over the sink bathing his face. In a gesture of gruff masculinity he had taken his shirt off.

'I just thought I'd pop round and catch up on the gossip. You know, old times, new times.' Julie's attention was still very firmly fixed on Joe's nicely toned torso. She looked back at Kate. 'See what you'd been up to.' Julie left the invitation to confess all hanging in the air like a tripwire.

Kate wasn't that stupid, although she had to admire Julie's gall. 'Sounds like a lovely idea. I'll give you a ring or pop round later in the week, shall I?' she said, catching hold of Julie's elbow and guiding her firmly across the hall and back out into the sunlight. 'It was a lovely party last night but now is not a good time.' How blatant did the notice to quit have to be?

Julie beaded her. 'Is that your husband?' She motioned back towards the kitchen.

Kate nodded.

'Wow. Very nice-looking. Always that fiery,

is he?' Kate couldn't help but notice that there was a real hint of envy in Julie's voice.

'Sometimes.'

Julie smiled knowingly and then winked. 'Lucky girl. How about if I drop round tomorrow?'

'So how did it go then?' said Chrissie, in a cheerful, bluff voice that she hoped might fool them both.

'It didn't,' said Joe sounding weary. 'I'm just on my way back to town now. I wondered if maybe you fancied going out somewhere tonight?'

Chrissie, phone tucked under her chin, looked out of the window. It had just started to rain. Bob Sleight hadn't been gone long. He said he'd send a lad round the next day with the For Sale board, as long as she was happy with the terms. He'd left her a carbon of the agreement she'd signed.

'Do you really think that's a good idea, Joe?'

Joe laughed, the sound echoing and crackling as the signal on his mobile shifted. 'Might as well get hung for a sheep as a lamb, eh? Why not, Chrissie? I could do with a night out to be honest. My mum's got the boys. So, the world's our oyster, babe.'

Odd, that was exactly what Bob Sleight had said not more than an hour ago; he hadn't convinced her either.

Joe was still talking. 'So, what do you fancy? Chinese? Indian? What would you *really* like to do?'

Chrissie pressed her forehead against the cold glass; life to be back to normal, time to run backwards? Press restart and have four new lives? 'I don't know, Joe. I don't mind really.' She had never been out with Joe as a couple.

'How about Thai? We could go to the Golden Lotus if you like? Walk if it's a nice night – means that we can both have a beer.' She sensed his eagerness, his need to please.

'Sure, okay. Yes, that would be, be . . . fine,' she said, searching around for a fairly noncommittal adjective.

Outside, the garden looked wonderful in the rain, the leaves glittering like jade and emeralds, the flowers like bright tropical birds fluttering in the light breeze. What would it feel like to wake up somewhere else? Without this house? Without the woods? She'd miss the woods and Kate and the boys next door, and the bus stop at the end of the road, and Bill, and the sense of being part of something bigger. Leaving Windsor Street would be like leaving her family, like cutting away her history.

Last time they had gone to the Thai restaurant it had been Kate and Joe's wedding anniversary although that fact seemed to have slipped Joe's mind.

They had staggered home, giggling madly, Kate and Chrissie arm in arm singing a medley of Andrew Lloyd Webber hits and horrors, while the kids tried hard to pretend that they weren't with them, and then, making up the rear, Bill and Joe had been working hard on the harmonies. It seemed like a lifetime ago now.

'Do you want to ring up and book a table?' Joe's voice splintered her thoughts.

'If you're sure?'

'What's to be sure of? I want to take you out.'

Since when, Chrissie thought, but was too tired to argue. 'What time?'

'I thought that maybe we could eat early. What do you reckon? Eat early, that way we've got the whole evening ahead of us,' he purred.

Chrissie caught every last implication.

* * *

Once she was sure that Joe had gone, Kate went back to tidy up the kitchen, which now looked more like a field hospital. Bearing in mind Joe had only had a few minor scratches he had managed to generate a huge amount of blood and mud-stained cotton wool, not to mention two bowls of antiseptic wash and the half a tube of Savlon squeezed out all over the top of the cooker.

'And?' asked Maggie, from somewhere behind her.

'And you're supposed to be out back taking a nap.'

Maggie laughed wryly. 'I think it can probably wait. Why don't you come in here, sit down and talk to me.'

'What, so that you can make me spill the rest of the beans?'

'Uhuh.'

Kate sighed. 'I'm sorry but I'm tired of talking. Tired of thinking. Do you want a coffee?'

'No, not really, I thought I might join you in whatever it was you'd had with the vet.'

If Kate could have done the eyebrow trick she would have done it right then. 'Brandy?'

'That will do very nicely.'

'It's a bit early.'

Maggie shrugged and then puffed out her lips in a gesture of dismissal. 'The afternoon we've had? I don't really think so, do you?'

'I'll get the glasses,' said Kate.

'Is your husband feeling unwell, Madam?' said the manageress of the Golden Lotus. She couldn't have been more than five foot tall in her high heels, beautifully dressed in Thai costume, and was a woman who possessed an innate air of authority.

Chrissie wriggled uncomfortably under the woman's unflinching gaze. Unwell was a polite euphemism for rolling drunk. Chrissie's discomfort was accentuated by the fact it was so early and that Joe's face was scratched and bruised and his knuckles were cut too. Not to put too fine a point on it he looked like trouble.

'He's not my husband. He's just a friend,' Chrissie protested. It sounded ridiculous. He was draped around her like a cheap coat.

The woman shrugged. 'Would you like me to call you a cab for your friend?'

Chrissie nodded, not meeting her eyes. It was barely nine o'clock.

* * *

Andrew rang Kate at nine. 'I've been thinking about you all afternoon. Are you sure you don't want me to run you down to pick your car up?'

'No, and for God's sake, stop fussing. I've already said I'll be fine. Thank you. I'll get a cab tomorrow.'

'I could drop by if you like. I'm looking for an excuse. Got any stray cats you need neutering? Goldfish looking a bit peaky? Do you want me to come and look at your mum's ankle and tut sympathetically?'

'You didn't mention you were a stalker when you introduced yourself,' Kate growled.

There was a little silence and then Andrew said, 'About this lunch-time. I didn't want you to think that it was a one-off.'

Kate shivered; she had been trying to put the whole thing clear out of her mind.

'I'm not normally like that, and – well – the thing is, Kate, I'd really like to see you again.'

'Andrew, this is ridiculous. I barely know you. Did you happen to notice the mess I'm slap bang in the middle of when you dropped by this afternoon? I need another man in my life like I need a stuffed canary on a stick.'

'Please Kate, I don't want you to think badly of me –'

'I don't think badly of you, Andrew, actually at the moment I don't want to think about you at all.' Kate stared at the phone, wondering whether it would be too cruel just to hang up, and as she did remembered the press of his lips against her skin as her mind replayed a single moment when they had been standing in his kitchen admiring his garden. He had been standing behind her, pointing out a wren in a tree. He was a little too close, in that space reserved for family and lovers and small children, and just when it got the point of being uncomfortable, just when she planned to say something or move away, she felt him move closer still, felt his breath on her neck. It was delicious. Dangerously delicious.

Kate had felt almost relieved when his arms had slid around her waist. An instant later he had kissed the delicate flesh where her neck and shoulder met, and then almost without thinking she had turned in his arms and he had kissed her with a hunger that took her breath away. But worse – much worse – she had felt her whole body fire up in response to his and kissed him back. It had been all she could do to disentangle herself from his arms and step away.

'No,' Kate had said firmly, holding up her hands to keep him back. Not that Andrew had moved forward but the gesture seemed really important. 'I don't do this. I don't want to do this. I can't do this. I'm not like this at all, Andrew. This is a dangerous game. I'm married.'

So why had it felt so good and why had she wanted to do it again? Kate groaned inwardly. It seemed that her body and her mind had different management policies.

'So you are,' he'd said. 'I'm sorry. I shouldn't have, but it was so tempting. Don't worry, I'll make a sandwich. Is cheese okay? Do you want salad or just a tomato?'

The banal conversation was totally at odds with the energy and desire that ricocheted between them. Kate took a breath, trying to still the thump, thump, thump in her chest and the white-hot ache that growled low down in her belly.

'Joe did this with my best friend, but that doesn't make it right for me to do it. I couldn't cope with the guilt.'

'It's okay,' he said, busy taking things out of the fridge. 'I'm not going to push you into anything you're not ready for, but I want you to know that I can wait. And I do understand, Kate.'

Kate wasn't altogether sure that she did though. Did that mean that guilt was the only thing stopping her from kissing him? From kissing and touching and ending up in bed with him? Was it only a sense of guilt that held her marriage together? Kate shivered at the thought, trying to convince herself that her reaction to Andrew had been purely physiological. A knee jerk, a reflex.

Now, sitting at the table in Maggie's house, hearing his voice on the phone every one of the contradictory feelings was back. He turned her on in a way that she hadn't experienced for years.

Kate shivered. 'I'm sorry. Look, I don't want to do this; I'm much too vulnerable and far too confused to talk to you, Andrew.'

'Okay –' He sounded hurt. 'Well, hang up then.'

She didn't like to say that had been her plan, because he said it in a needy tone that compelled Kate to say something conciliatory, something to make him feel better. She could feel herself about to agree to him taking her down to the pub to pick the car up, or arranging to see her again, but Kate stopped herself. Maybe that was part of the problem, maybe she was too eager to make things better for other people. With Joe she almost always tried to sort things out or throw herself into the breech before he got too angry or exasperated or hurt. It was one of those moments of revelation.

'Thanks, Andrew, good advice. Goodnight,' Kate said and hung up before he had chance to reply or she had a chance to feel sorry for him.

'He's not going to be sick, is he?' asked the mini-cab driver suspiciously, eyeing up Joe as Chrissie clambered in and hauled him into the cab outside the Golden Lotus.

'I don't think so,' she said breathlessly, trying to settle him and find the seat belt. Joe groaned and then spluttered miserably.

'That's it,' said the mini-cab driver. 'Sorry, darling. Get him out. I can't abide clearing up after other people.' He climbed out of the front seat and started to pull Joe out through the other door. 'It's always curry. These velour seats with loops and lots of piping – have you got any idea how hard it is to get vomit out of that? You have to use a toothbrush.'

It wasn't an image Chrissie particularly wanted to linger over, and anyway on the far side of the car Joe was staggering round and swaying into the middle of road. Chrissie hurried round to guide him back onto the path while appealing to the driver.

'Please don't leave me here with him. What am I supposed to do if he passes out?'

The driver shrugged. 'Not my problem.'

'I'll double your fare,' she offered.

He snorted. 'Doesn't matter how much disinfectant you use, the smell never goes, put the heater on and phhuh – there it is,' he said, as he got back into his car and drove off.

It was a good walk home on a normal night – tonight it was a long slow spiralling drunken hike; a hundred yards from the restaurant it started to rain. Joe staggering added a lot of extra steps to the journey and as he was leaning heavily on Chrissie she had no choice but to go with him. Fortunately, he didn't pass out and he wasn't sick until he got right outside his house.

And so finally here they were back in Windsor Street with the whole night to themselves. Joe sighed; through the drunken fug things were oddly clear.

Maybe Kate finding out about him and Chrissie wasn't such a terrible thing after all, maybe it was going to work out okay. Today had given him a real sense of clarity. It was obvious that Kate didn't want him and equally obvious that Chrissie did. It was all blindingly simple really. Maybe Chrissie had always secretly wanted him. Maybe they could actually make a go of it. Maybe this was what was meant to happen all along. He could feel the tension that had hung around in his shoulders and back slowly ebbing away. It was going to be all right after all.

Once inside and he'd been to the bathroom for a wash and – with Chrissie's help – brushed his teeth, had a pee and a cup of coffee, things seemed to fall into place.

'You know that I love you, don't you?' he murmured thickly into Chrissie's shoulder, fumbling with her jacket, peeling off her blouse. 'God, you're beautiful.'

'Oh Joe,' Chrissie said and laughed.

Jesus. What a fool he had been, she'd been waiting all this time and he just hadn't realised it until now.

Joe pushed open the bedroom door, switched

on the bedside light. Nice to admire the view. In bed with a willing woman. Joe grinned and stretched before turning his attention back to the job in hand. It was just like the good old days when he'd been on the road with the band before he got hooked up with Kate.

'What if Dad's not home when we get there?' whined Jake. It had just started to rain again. Big heavy street-lit jewels of summer rain that was both welcome and the same time seemed misplaced and out of sync with the dusty heat. Jake hadn't brought a coat with him.

Danny sighed. 'Look, for the last time, it doesn't matter, Jake. I've got my keys and anyway he said that he's going to be late back, not that he's not coming home at all. If he's not there when we get in then you can go to bed and I'll wait up for him. I've left a message on the answer machine.'

Jake pulled a face. It was a long walk home from the tube.

Danny rounded on him. 'Give me a break, will you? It was you who said you'd left your homework at home. You who wanted to stay and watch the film at Gran's. Now stow it or

I'll give you something to moan about.'

'You said you needed your tennis stuff,' Jake whinged.

Danny looked heavenwards. 'All right, stop, quits, pax – exesis,' and then he slipped the key into the lock. It was late, about twenty to ten, but it felt really good to be home.

Chrissie stared up at the ceiling, watching the darkness creep into the room little by little. She could hear the rain on the windows, scribbling through the dust on the panes.

'Oh Chrissie,' Joe grunted. 'I love you. I want you so much.' She winced as he rolled over onto her arm. She would have liked to have believed him, but it was only a line and not a very good line at that. It wasn't for her or even about her, just one of those universal lines like how are you or some throwaway comment about the weather. Chrissie was under no illusions and it made her feel icy cold inside.

Tonight was the confirmation – had she needed it – that she was second best. Worse than second best. If Kate had welcomed Joe in, forgiven him, said that they could work it out, there was no way he and Chrissie would be there now, thrashing around under the duvet like teenagers. Odd how your mind could wander while your body was so busy. Outside the rain was getting harder. Joe grunted enthusiastically. The walk and being sick had really sobered him up.

Ironic, too, how many times there had been over the years when she had dreamed about being here in this room. Dreamed of hearing those words, of wanting him to want her. She had fantasised about curling up in Kate's big double sleigh bed, curling up under Kate's pristine white duvet with its delicate embroidery, curling up here with Kate's husband.

Beside her, Joe was making lustful eager little noises but she felt totally removed as if it was happening to someone else. Actually she wished it was happening to someone else.

'You do know that I love you, don't you?' he murmured into her shoulder, while fumbling with her clothes. Forty-two and the man still had no idea how a woman's clothes came off. 'God, you're beautiful.'

'Oh Joe,' Chrissie said and laughed as two buttons off her best blouse pinged across the bedroom floor.

* * *

In the hallway Joe's good leather jacket was slung over the newel post at the bottom of the stairs. His shoes were there too, levered off and left by the coatstand, and the downstairs lights were on. Living-in, being-at-home lights, not out for the evening lights, left on to fool the burglars.

Danny sighed with relief. At least he wouldn't have to wait for his dad to roll in at God knows what time and then try and explain why they had come back. He was about to call out when they heard a noise. It was a giggle or maybe it was a sigh. Hard to tell from the hall.

'Mum?' called Jake, and before Danny could stop him Jake belted upstairs.

'You ought to go to bed, honey. It's been a long day.'

Kate nodded. 'Seems like a week ago since I got up. I'll just check my email.' Maggie and Kate were sitting side by side on the sofa in the sitting room watching some old film on Channel 4 that was good background noise to the conversation that kept resurfacing.

Maggie shrugged and then leant closer to

touch Kate's face. 'I'm so sorry, about all this, sweetheart. Whatever you need –'

'Please don't be kind to me, Mum, I'll only cry. It's hardly your fault, is it?' Kate said, although she made no attempt to move.

'What are you going to do?'

Kate shrugged. 'I still don't know. I can't see a way back from here, but then I keep thinking about the boys. How much they mean to Joe, how much Joe means to them. Do I make a decision based on damage limitation? Is that the grown up thing to do? Do I stay with him for their sake – go back, try and make a go of it?'

Maggie shook her head. 'I don't know, and I can't make your mind up for you, it's you who'll have to live with the decision. But just don't rush into anything. You can stay here as long as you want, you know that. I'm not defending Joe for an instant; what he's done goes beyond words but even so don't rush into something you might regret.'

'You mean like Andrew Taylor?'

Maggie's expression didn't flicker. 'I didn't say that – I just mean don't rush.'

Kate closed her eyes and for a few seconds held Maggie's hand close against her cheek, enjoying the uncomplicated comfort of it. 'It's all right, he's not anything anyway, just a nice man who fancies me. It's been years since anyone fancied me, Mum. Why now? It's an added complication. I must have been totally crazy to go to lunch with him. Another time I'd have been flattered and gently brushed him off, but it was like Joe has broken all the rules so why shouldn't I do something silly? I wanted to snatch something back.'

'And did you?'

Kate laughed and shook her head. 'No. All I could think about was how I wasn't ready for any of this kind of stuff. Besides being flattered there was a part of me that was indignant that Andrew was giving me the come on. Oh I don't know, what the hell am I going to do, Mum? It some ways it seems such a waste to throw so many years away. And then in the next breath I can't get past the fact that Chrissie and Joe have been carrying on behind my back for all of those years too. All those same years that I'm so anxious not to lose.

'It's too cruel, like all my memories are wrong and kind of muddied and muddled. I keep looking back over all the things we've done and wondering after which of those things they were scurrying back to go to bed together. When were they planning it, when did they talk about it? They must have talked about it, mustn't they? It's like there are these big grey rocks in my mind that I keep lifting up to see if there's something nasty hiding under them. Everything I've got, everything I've done since Chrissie moved in next door is tainted now. If I think too hard about it, it feels as if I'm going to go mad.'

Maggie sighed, 'You need to talk to Joe about all this stuff.'

Kate pulled away as if Maggie had slapped her. 'What? What could he possibly say that would make it any better?' She knew the words came out sounding childlike and petulant but that was exactly how she felt.

'There isn't anything he can say but maybe he can give you some of the answers.'

Kate shook her head. 'I don't want Joe to twist it all round and make me give in, Mum. I'm afraid of what he'll say. I'm afraid he'll try and make me believe it was all my fault all along. If it weren't for the boys I don't think I'd go back at all. It hurts so much. I hurt so much.'

Maggie stroked Kate's cheek. '*You* know

what's true and what's not; the problem is we all have a different version of events.'

'Are you saying Joe's right? That it was my fault he went off with Chrissie?'

Maggie shook her head. 'No, that isn't what I meant at all, but you do need to talk to him or to Chrissie. Don't be long before you go to bed,' she said, getting to her feet slowly.

Kate laughed through a voice brittle with tears. 'I'm supposed to be taking care of you.'

'Don't worry, there'll be plenty of time for that.'

The phone rang twice before Kate had time to log on. The first call was from Liz: 'I know it's late but just wondered if you'd had another chance to talk to Mum about sheltered accommodation? I think it's very important that we keep it at the forefront. Keep it fresh in her mind. I was wondering whether to pop over tomorrow and bring those brochures I was telling you about. There are some super places out this way. We're all well – the girls have been to ballet and tap this evening so they were all tucked up early. Peter's still busy working, upstairs in the office at the moment. I keep telling him to slow down but he just won't listen.'

Kate sighed; the implication was of course that compared to Joe, Peter was a living saint. Liz was about as sensitive as a pile of buttered toast when it came to other people's feelings; there was no way she would have picked up the tension or the pain in Kate's voice any more than she would think driving Maggie into a home was anything other than an ideal solution to a potentially sticky problem.

'I really don't know what that company would do without Peter. He's been video-conferencing with someone in Thailand this evening, Mind you, at least with modern technology he doesn't have to travel quite so much. So what do you think? Shall I pop over tomorrow?'

Kate barely had chance to get a word in.

And when Liz was done, the phone rang again; this time it was Guy calling to speak to Maggie.

Kate struggled to read through her to-do list for work, while waiting for Guy to hang up and wasn't altogether surprised when her mobile rang – although this time she checked who was calling before answering.

'Hi Kate, this is Bill.'

'Hello, I was planning to phone you,' Kate began, trying to think up a reasonable excuse why she hadn't.

'There's no need to apologise.' He paused as if composing himself, and then said quickly, 'I've got the boys here with me.'

'What? What do you mean you've got them there? I don't understand; they're supposed to be with Joe's mum tonight.' Kate tried to keep the indignation out of her voice.

'They were and then Jake realised he'd left stuff at home that he needed for school tomorrow.'

'So what happened? They came back? Isn't Joe home yet? He left here around three –'

A ripple of panic shimmied through her. What if Joe had had an accident on the way home? Would she have to nurse him? What if he was crippled? What hideous twist of fate would do that to her? Kate struggled to keep her mind from backflipping away and listening to Bill instead; it was an uphill struggle.

'He was at home.' Kate could hear the internal voice in her head sigh with relief as the horribly maimed, having-to-nurse-Joe-for-the-rest-of-her-life scenario slipped through her fingers and melted without a trace.

'I don't understand, Bill. In that case why didn't –' Her brain was back, busy offering all manner of macabre solutions. 'Oh my God, he wasn't blind drunk, was he? Or stoned?'

'Whoa, just slow down a minute, Kate, and listen. Joe wasn't on his own when the boys got there.'

In the background Kate could hear Danny's muffled voice and then more clearly. 'Can I speak to her? Mum, Mum, is that you?'

'Hi Dan – ' She barely had chance to ask if he was all right or really take in the implications of what Bill had said.

'Did you know about Dad and Chrissie?' he snapped.

Kate felt something tightening in her belly as comprehension dawned. 'Oh my God,' she said in an undertone.

'So you did know?'

'Yes, but –'

'Christ – yes, but nothing, Mum! How come nobody said anything to us? How could you?'

'Danny, wait, please,' Kate jumped in, desperate that he shouldn't be angry with her, it would be more than she could bear. 'I've only just found out myself. Last weekend, when I came back from Gran's –'

'Oh, so that that makes it all right does it?' He was outraged and then said more softly, 'Jake is totally gutted. He thought it was you up there.'

Kate felt icy fingers track down her spine. 'Up where?'

'They were in bed together when we got back here. Dad and Chrissie. Jake is beside himself.'

The room spun and Kate, impotent with a cocktail of emotions, didn't know whether to scream or swear and cry.

'Kate?' Bill came back on the line. 'Look, don't panic.'

'What do you mean, don't panic? What the hell am I supposed to do?'

'The boys are going to stay here for the night. I'll get them to school tomorrow morning. They didn't want to stay at your place with Joe.'

'Where *is* Joe? What did Joe do? What did he say?' Kate said, glancing up at the clock. If the traffic wasn't too bad she could be back in town before midnight, not that she wanted to run into either Joe or Chrissie but the boys needed her. Her mind raced. Maybe she could stay at Bill's too. It took an instant longer for her to remember that her car was still parked down at the Boatman's Arms.

'Damn, I haven't got my car here. I can't get back tonight,' she said quickly.

'Look, take a deep breath. There is nothing you can do here tonight even if you could get home. And how's your mum going to manage without you? If you like I can bring the boys up to Denham tomorrow.'

As he spoke, Kate felt the first wave of tears catch in the back of her throat, threatening to knock her over and drag her down. She wrapped a hand over her mouth to hold the noise in. After a few seconds Kate said in a strangled tone, 'I'll ring you first thing. I'll be home tomorrow. Can I speak to the boys now?'

'Sure, and Kate? Try and keep a handle on this. I know you don't believe it but it's going to be all right. The boys will be fine here until you can sort things out.'

Of course they wouldn't, Kate thought angrily, but how grateful did that sound under the circumstances?

'I can't believe Dad,' Danny began. 'How could he, with Chrissie of all people? He's always going on about what a cow she is. How could he? I don't understand it.'

The pain in Danny's voice ripped and roared through her as anger and outrage and plain blind fury; how come no one thought to tell him what was going on?

Kate listened on and on and said nothing until his fury was finally exhausted.

'What did Dad say?'

'What the hell could he say?' growled Danny.

She couldn't have put it better herself.

'I told him I was going to go round Bill's and taking Jake with me and then he said I was running away, just like you always did.'

Kate winced and then said, 'Okay, don't worry. I want you to keep an eye on Jake, and I'll be home as soon as I can.'

And then she spoke to Jake.

'Mum?' He sounded so uncertain, so blitzed, that as he spoke she started to tremble, feeling her eyes refill – this time with tears of compassion. Poor little sod.

'Bill said he could drive us up to Grandma's if you want. Because she's broken her leg and that.'

She let him talk. He talked about everything and nothing, while all Kate wanted to do was to take him in her arms and cuddle him. Finally the monologue ground to a halt and Kate launched into the yawning silence. 'Do you want to talk about what happened with Dad?'

She heard a long low whine of pain from the far end of the line. 'It was disgusting,' Jake yelped. 'You two are married, aren't you? It's totally gross. I don't even want to think about it. He isn't supposed to do that stuff with other people.'

'No, love, he isn't,' said Kate, wishing she had the benefit of the uncompromising black and white vision of youth, rather than the one that came with the critical soundtrack making it her fault. 'Can you get Bill for me?'

In the other room she could hear Maggie wishing Guy sweet dreams. It was too cruel.

Kate sat in the darkness and stared unseeing at the computer screen, listening to her brain replay Danny's and then Jake's anguish. As soon as Maggie hung up on the house phone, Kate's modem on the laptop kicked in and sought out a connection to the internet. It seemed that she had a night time caller too.

Chapter 14

'Are you asleep? Chrissie? Chrissie, wake up. I know you're in there. Let me in. Come on, Chrissie. Get up.' A peculiar brittle, cracking, rattling sound followed the words.

Chrissie yawned and rolled over onto her back, eyes snapping open as she was dragged out of a dream. She was being shot by a firing squad, Bob Sleight was in charge of the riflemen although she was quite certain that Joe was tucked away there somewhere in the crowd, egging them on.

Bemused and confused, it took Chrissie a few seconds to get her bearings. She looked round. She was in her own bedroom, all alone – so where the hell was the voice coming from?

'Chrissssssie!!'

The voice was louder now and much more insistent. It was Joe. Her name was followed by the same odd, cracking, splattering sound. Oh, God, not again. This was getting beyond a joke. What was it they said? Be careful what you wish for, you might just get it. Hadn't Joe Harvey once upon a time been top of her wish list? Chrissie groaned. It had been a long time ago, presumably fate had a waiting list and she had only just floated to the top of the heap.

'Chrisssieeeeeeee.'

She rolled over, burying her head in the pillow. And then it occurred to her that Joe was in the front garden outside the bedroom window and what had woken her was the sound of gravel hitting the glass.

She scuttled across the bed and, wrapping a sheet around herself, wrestled to lift the sash.

'What the hell do you think you're playing at? What do you want?' It's, it's . . .' she glanced back at the clock, 'Jesus, Joe, it's half past three. Go home. Go back to bed. I've got to go to work in the morning. This morning. I'm sick of this.'

'I can't sleep.' The words came out as a loud

whine. He was standing in the flower bed peering up, moonfaced and wan.

Chrissie sighed. This had been the first night since Saturday that, against all the odds, totally exhausted, she had dropped off to sleep almost as soon as her head had hit the pillow.

'Bugger off,' she snapped.

'No, you have to let me in,' he wailed. Now that he knew she was listening the volume rose by a decibel or two. Loud enough for lights to go on across the street.

'No, I don't, Joe,' she hissed. 'Go away before someone calls the police.'

'You have to let me in,' he said, louder still.

'No, I don't, now piss off before you wake the whole bloody street up.'

Not that it was likely, but it was her only weapon.

'I love you,' he bawled at the top of his voice. 'You must know that. I want to talk to you. LET ME IN!' In the arms race he won hands down.

Chrissie looked heavenwards and headed downstairs.

When she opened the door Joe was pressed up against it so hard that he practically fell in.

'What do you want?' she snapped.

'You.'

'Don't be ridiculous.'

'Did anyone ever tell you how beautiful you look when you're angry?'

'Oh for Christ's sake, Joe, at least try and come up with something original. You can have a cup of coffee and then go home. Do you understand?' She was so angry the words zipped out like bullets.

'Did anyone ever tell you how sexy you look in a sheet?'

Chrissie swung round and glared at him. 'That's enough, Joe. Haven't we already done enough damage tonight between us? You go and put the kettle on while I go and get a dressing gown.'

'No need to bother on my account.' He moved closer, arms extended, eyes glazed over with a combination of booze, tiredness and lust. 'I'm cold and lonely.'

Chrissie pulled away. 'Jesus, have you got no shame at all? Stop it.'

But he didn't, which made her even angrier.

'No, I'm serious, Joe,' she said, pushing him away. 'I thought we'd agreed after tonight's fiasco that this is not on. It's over. We can't do it – it is a recipe for total and utter disaster. We'll just end up hurting everybody. No more, the end, finito.' Chrissie paused to make sure that Joe had kept up; he looked as pale as she felt and much in need of a good night's sleep.

'But I'm all alone in that great big bed,' he said in a little boy lost voice.

'And whose fault is that?' she growled. 'I don't want you here and I don't want to be there, Joe. Go home,' she indicated the door.

'You don't really mean that,' he said.

Chrissie sighed. 'I do Joe. I really truly do.'

'But I love you.'

The universal panacea. Chrissie groaned, manoeuvring him into the kitchen while she pulled a robe off the back of the downstairs loo door. The tiles on the kitchen floor were cold and slightly sticky under her bare feet. She had always meant to put carpet down and now would never have the chance. The thought made her shiver more than the cold.

'Did you go round and see the boys?' she asked, plugging in the kettle and fishing two mugs out of the sink. The water in the bowl was grey and greasy; Chrissie couldn't remember the last time she'd washed up. There was a smell around the sink, a smell of stale water and neglect.

Joe pulled a face, the kind of face that children pull when they are made to go and tidy their rooms. 'No, but I rang them.'

'You rang them?' Chrissie said incredulously. 'What the hell do you mean, you rang them?' There wasn't any milk.

She had heard the noise when they were upstairs in Kate's bed and wondered what it was, heard it again, turned to look over her shoulder and seen Jake standing at the end of the bed with his mouth open. There had been a moment of total stillness and then he and she had gasped in unison as comprehension dawned. The expression on Jake's face would stay with her for a very long time.

And then, a moment later Danny had been behind him in the doorway, ignoring Chrissie completely, saying, 'How could you? You bastard – how could you?'

Joe hadn't moved as Danny swung round to leave. It had been Chrissie who had called him back, Chrissie who had scuttled across the bed dragging on a bathrobe to try and stop him from running away, attempting to find some words to excuse and soften the inexcusable.

'Danny,' she had called after him as he gathered Jake up like a lost sheep. 'Danny,' she had repeated as he had glared back at her with total loathing.

Looking up at her from the bottom of the stairs, pointing a finger, he had said, 'I'm going over to Bill's house and when I get back I want you out of here, do you understand?' There was such disdain and disgust in Danny's voice that Chrissie had flinched.

Across her kitchen now, palms up in defence of himself, Joe was still talking. 'I thought it would be better to ring first and see how things were. Check the lie of the land.'

'And how were they? How *did* the land lie?' He didn't pick up on the bitterness or sarcasm in her voice.

'Danny didn't really want to talk to me, you know what kids are like, but he said that Kate would sort it out when she came home.'

'And you said?'

'Okay. I mean what else was there to say? What could I say? I'm sorry you caught me in bed with your mum's best friend, son, it won't happen again?'

'It might have been a good idea.'

'Oh come off it, Chrissie, you don't mean

that.' Joe shook his head and sighed. 'What a bloody mess. This isn't how I wanted the kids to find out about us.'

Chrissie was about to make some flippant remark and then stopped herself when she realised what Joe had said. 'Sorry? What do you mean *find out about us*? They weren't supposed to find out about us at all. It was meant to be a secret, Joe. We were having a bit on the side. Do you know what you're saying?'

Joe looked up at her and nodded. 'Yes, I do. I've been thinking about it over the last few days. Maybe we ought to bring it out into the open, what if it's time? Maybe we've been fooling ourselves all these years. What if we were meant to be together all along.'

Chrissie stared at him, panic and amusement mingling with surprise and disbelief. 'Oh, come on,' she laughed, expecting the joke to crack and break. 'Don't do this to me, Joe. Maybe you've been fooling yourself all these years but I certainly haven't. It's complete bollocks and you know it is. We've always said that it doesn't mean anything – friends that screw that's all, that's what we said right from the start. No false promises, no lies, no bullshit, don't let's start now, for God's sake.'

He looked so hurt that she thought he might cry. 'Are you saying that you don't care? That that's how you want to keep it? That you don't want the real thing?'

Chrissie shook her head. How could she possibly tell Joe that she had waited all her life for the real thing but not with him?

'Things change,' he said, in what she could only assume was meant to be a seductive serious tone.

'For the worse as well as the better, Joe. Don't you understand that this situation is not a recipe for happy ever after? This is not hearts and roses. This is an earthquake. This is disembowelling, shit and bullets.'

He stared at her; she might as well having been talking in Serbo-Croat.

'I'm certain that given a bit of time everyone would get used the idea,' he said with a kind of bluff, heavy-handed confidence.

Chrissie shook her head, knowing that even if they did, she most certainly wouldn't.

The kettle clicked off the boil, she unscrewed the Nescafé. It seemed there was no coffee left either.

* * *

Sam57 was waiting for Kate, there in the in-box. It was odd how the sight of his name on the address bar made Kate's spirits lift. Sitting there in the lamplight she began to read:

'I've been thinking about writing to you all day. I'm still working but it's not so bad knowing that you're here for company. It's been a long day and I've still got God knows how much work to shift.

Please be careful with this lunchtime date thing. No, it's not because I'm feeling jealous – well, okay so maybe just a little! I just think it's a mistake to fight fire with fire. You were frank with me, Venus, so it's my turn to return the compliment.

I know you're feeling vulnerable and angry now but just go carefully – you have to live with the consequences of your actions and at the moment you're possibly too close to the fire to be able to make rational decisions. In a nutshell, what I'm saying is don't do something daft that you'll regret later.'

Kate smiled and then started to type slowly, gathering her thoughts:

'Don't worry, Sam, I managed to behave

myself. Trouble is, I hadn't realised how lonely I am or how needy. I'm not sure if I should be telling you this really, but I did manage to resist temptation. It wasn't so much resisting my lunch date as resisting myself. All these little lights in my head flashing when he looked at me.'

Kate hesitated – she couldn't bring herself to write when Andrew touched me, when he kissed me, the way my body had warmed and wanted – Kate closed her eyes thinking about the great surge of desire that had taken her by complete surprise. It had stunned her and at the same time it was a kind of relief to know that it all still worked.

She fancied Andrew, her body fancied Andrew, it was just a simple physiological reaction, not that she wrote that either. Instead Kate said,

'I've been married for so long and up until recently have always thought no, assumed, that we were happy. Well, at least most of the time and on balance – you know how these things go, more ups than downs more good than bad – but now I'm beginning to wonder. This thing with my husband has made me peer over the ramparts, and the view's not so bad on the other side.

Have I been kidding myself all this time? Is it just that you learn to live with the things that aren't right? Was I too busy to really look at what was going on? Is that why my husband slept with somebody else, Sam? Did he realise that we were living in a mirage sooner that I did?

So in answer to your question, lunch went just fine, although it seems like a lifetime ago now, so much has happened since then. It's like somebody detonated a bomb under my life. First of all, my husband's lover rang me at the pub during my lunch date, a mixed blessing as I was just beginning to go all gooey around the edges – so in some ways she saved me from myself – and then as I was getting back home from lunch my husband turned up, followed by the guy I'd just been out to lunch with and then, when I just getting over the shock of that, my neighbour rang to say that the kids found my husband and my best friend in our bed tonight, so to say life's a bit messy at the moment is something of an understatement.'

Oddly enough it was a relief to see everything written down in well-ordered paragraphs. Putting the things that had happened up on the screen somehow relieved Kate of the burden of them, contained them, and helped to make some kind of sense or shape of what was going on.

'Tomorrow I'm going to ask my neighbour to put the kids on the train. It's straight through from London to here with no changes so they should be okay. I'll pick them up at the station. I can hardly ask him to drive all this way and don't feel I'm ready to go home yet – the thought of facing my husband and his lover is almost unbearable. To hurt me is one thing but to do that to the kids is unforgivable – okay, so you could probably argue that he didn't know they were coming back tonight. But the two of them were in our bed – they must have been in there before, but somehow it seems much worse that the kids found them there. I bought that bed as a wedding present to the two of us. To my husband and me. *My husband* – even that seems wrong now, I mean he's hardly mine, is he? He hasn't been mine for years. Maybe I ought to think of something else, something less possessive to call him.

We can't go back to how we were. I don't know if I'm even able to go into the house again. Everything is tainted. You probably think that I'm mad, or over-reacting. The problem is that the house is the very least of it. I can't imagine going to bed with him again – how can I do that knowing that the last time he slept in our bed was with her? The last body he touched was hers? It makes me feel physically sick thinking about it. Please, whatever you do, Sam, don't let it get to this point in your marriage. Go home and sort it out while there is still a clear way back or forward.'

Kate re-read his mail. It was odd talking about such personal things to a complete stranger, but there was real relief too, a bit like pouring your heart out to a stranger you meet on a train.

'So how's your day been? I won't mind at all if you tell me it's been dull – I'd really like to read something sane and ordinary – something about shuffling bits of paper from one side of the desk to the other. Meeting clients, doing business . . .'

She read through her page and then scrolled down his:

'Venus, I know this might sound crazy but how about if we met up some time for a coffee? Or a meal maybe? No strings, no pressure, cross my heart. In many ways you and I have got a lot in common, or at least a lot we could talk about. I'm based in London a lot of the time – or would you like to call me, maybe? I'd be happy to give you my mobile number? It would be such a help to talk to someone who understands – from the outside I've got a good marriage, I've really got no one else I can confide in without letting the light in.'

Kate reddened slightly. The last thing she wanted at the moment was to talk to anyone else but it sounded churlish and ungrateful, after all hadn't he spent most of the week listening to her?

Kate considered it for a few moments and then wrote,

'I don't think meeting up at the moment

would be a good idea, Sam. My life is so bloody complicated I can't work out which way is up and which down, so I'm not sure if face to face I'd be any help at all. Can we just carry on mailing for the time being? It isn't that I don't want to meet up at some stage. It might be nice. I kind of feel as if we are both survivors from some terrible disaster, dragged from a sinking ship. So maybe later when things have settled a bit – for both of us? I hope that's okay. Thanks for being there, Sam. Night, night. With all best wishes, Venus.'

Kate pressed send and stretched before switching the machine off and heading up to bed. Across the hallway Maggie's lamp was still on. For a few seconds Kate hesitated outside the sitting-room door wondering if she ought to go in and say goodnight. Eventually she turned and headed for bed; there would be lots more time to talk in the morning.

'Will you stop snoring,' Chrissie snapped in frustration, furiously digging Joe in the ribs.

'Uh-mth-tun-m,' snorted Joe, rolling over onto his side. Blessedly, it was enough to shut him up, but for how long? Waiting for him to start again was almost as bad as listening to him rumbling and snorting and growling.

Chrissie was cold and tired and on the edge of tears as well as the edge of the bed. The light outside the bedroom window was already changing from streetlight-orange to grey. The alarm would be going off soon although Chrissie didn't dare look at the clock to check; she was depressed enough already. Beside her, Joe shifted position again, farted triumphantly, and then rolled back onto his back, dragging the duvet with him. She waited with baited breath for the snoring to resume.

How the hell had this happened? She'd traced the cracks that crossed and re-crossed the ceiling, tracing them to the lighting rose, and then back again to the edge of the room. Chrissie would have liked to close the curtains but couldn't risk disturbing him. If she woke Joe he might want to talk some more or make love some more, or possibly eat some more, as he had pointed out at least half a dozen times that he'd had nothing but the Thai meal all day and he'd been sick since then.

Although it was late, Chrissie had fixed him beans on toast, hoping it would soak up any residual traces of alcohol – it was all she had

had in the house – but it was maybe not such a wise choice for one who enjoyed his flatulence with such boyish gusto.

The bedside clock ticked. There was a long silent tense hiatus and then all of a sudden Joe made an odd wet noise in the back of his throat as finally he breathed in and then out. A one-man orchestra tuning up for his next performance, and then, sure enough, he fired up again with a great bubbling sonorous bellow.

Chrissie groaned and covered her ears, not that it was much help, the vibrations were almost as ghastly as the noise itself. Surely to God Kate hadn't spent sixteen years listening to this?

It was too much. Careful not to wake him, Chrissie slithered out of her side of the bed, dropped onto all fours, and crawled silently across the bedroom, pulling her dressing gown after her as she went. Robbie hadn't come home; his bed at the far end of the landing was empty. She could set his alarm, maybe get a couple of hours sleep before it was time to get up. As she got to the door Chrissie glanced back at Joe.

Rolled up in the duvet he looked like some enormous bull elephant seal beached up there amongst the pillows, lying diagonally across the bed, but more than that, worse than that, the whole room seemed to be suffused with him, his smell, his clothes and something less tangible that, if she was still a practising hippie, Chrissie would have sworn was his aura. Joe filled her space with self-centred gusto, squeezing her to the margins.

Kate stared at the bedside clock. The numerals were as red as her eyes felt. She felt as if she hadn't been to sleep yet. Every time she closed her eyes her brain dropped down a gear and raced away into the distance finding new and terrible things to torment her with.

Finally, admitting defeat, Kate crept downstairs and went to the kitchen to get herself a glass of brandy. Maybe that would help. A shot of liquid anaesthetic to soothe away the residual pain. In passing she glanced up at the hall clock, annoyed by its smug tick-tick-tick cutting through the gloom. She felt horribly disturbed and unsettled and tired right through to the core. When the boys were little Kate used to think it was purely a matter of time before she died from lack of sleep.

Joe had been gigging a lot back then and would roll in, in the wee small hours, high as a kite on a combination of lager and adrenaline, banging and singing and – once he had got past the pretending to be quiet phase – desperate to talk, to share the evening with her. On those nights, as he had sprung onto the bed reeking of booze and fags, Kate had wished him dead. Or worse than dead, as one or other or both of the boys woke up at the sound of his voice, unnaturally loud in the otherwise quiet house.

At noon Joe would still be sound asleep. Lying in, unwakeable, while she sat in front of the TV trying to juggle a grizzling toddler with a pile of ads to write. Kate sighed and unscrewed the brandy bottle. Was that the smell of martyr burning? she thought grimly, pouring herself a hefty slug. Seemed that the torment hung on in there even when she hadn't got her eyes shut. Maybe the booze would quieten her mind.

Across the hall Maggie's light was still burning; Kate assumed that she'd left it on in case she needed to get out in the night, so it came as a surprise, when, as she tip-toed back to the bottom of the stairs, she heard Maggie's voice call, 'Kate? Is that you?'

Kate went over to the door and eased it open. 'Yes, Mum. Do you want anything? Are you all right?'

'I was about to ask you the same question.'

Maggie was propped up in bed, surrounded by a great nest of pillows, her plaster cast supported by a foam wedge and cushions. Unkindly the light picked out the bruises, the plains of dark and shade pointing out the tired circles under her eyes.

Kate smiled. 'I'm sorry. I hope I didn't disturb you. I can't sleep. I was just getting a drink.' She held out the cut glass tumbler as if proof were needed. The brandy glittered in the lamplight.

Maggie looked as exhausted and pale as Kate felt. 'I'm so angry,' she said. 'I keep snoring and waking myself up. It's absolutely infuriating. God alone knows how Guy puts up with it. Presumably I don't do it when I'm lying on my side or he'd have left me by now. Do you want to talk?'

Kate sighed thoughtfully. 'Actually, I think I've probably done enough talking to last me for the rest of my life. I'm sick of the sound of my own voice, sick of the noise of my own thoughts. And I'm so tired,' her voice was wobbly with emotion. 'I'm tired right through to the core.'

Maggie beckoned Kate closer. 'Come here, honey, it'll be all right,' she said gently.

Kate didn't resist, instead she put the brandy

down on one of the side tables and, like a child, settled down on the outer shores of the makeshift bed. Wriggling her toes under the comforter that hung over the end, she teased it up with bare feet until she was under it.

Maggie watched in amused silence. 'If you're going to stay there you'll have to stop jiggling around.'

Kate giggled; they were words straight out of her childhood.

For a few minutes they lay side by side in companionable silence staring up at the shadows on the ceiling.

It was Kate who spoke first. 'Is it all right if the boys come down here until Guy gets back?'

She felt rather than saw Maggie turn to look at her. 'Well, of course it is, you know it's all right. It doesn't matter whether Guy is here or not. You can stay as long as you want. Want to tell me why now?'

Kate shook her head. 'No, not tonight.'

Maggie stroked the hair back off Kate's face. 'Okay. Snuggle down then.'

Kate curled up onto the bed enjoying the uncomplicated feelings of comfort and within minutes was sound asleep and if Maggie snored, she certainly didn't notice.

Chapter 15

'Look, I'll tell you what Mum, how about if I just leave these brochures with you and then you can take a look through them later, when you're feeling up to it. At your leisure. Kate mentioned that you'd already said the house was getting too big for you.' Liz paused, her mouth fixed in a little moue of concern.

Kate looked heavenwards. 'I didn't put it like that at all, Liz.'

'No, no, it's fine,' Maggie said, waving her embarrassment away. 'It *is* too big. I've been thinking about getting somewhere smaller for a while now.'

They were all sitting out on the terrace the following morning and if Kate had ever doubted

God's warped sense of humour this was the morning to prove her wrong.

Liz had arrived bang on ten.

'Exactly. You see, Kate? I think it's much better to make the move while you're still fit and active and able to enjoy it. And South Acres Park looks absolutely perfect to me, although don't let me influence you. They've got bowls and a little luncheon club, bus trips,' Liz held the brochure out towards Kate and Maggie, 'whist drives, and these wonderful self-contained little bungalows with a warden and meals brought in if you want them.'

Bloody brochures. Kate glared furiously at Liz, forgetting that her sister was totally flame-resistant.

'Sounds like heaven if you ask me,' said Julie Hicks, sipping her coffee. Julie had arrived at ten past ten bearing a Victoria sandwich and an extremely determined expression. Denied access the previous day she was unstoppable this morning. She took the leaflets Liz proffered and began to flick through them as if they were for a holiday cruise.

'Looks so nice, I wouldn't mind living there myself,' Julie continued enthusiastically, reading the words under an artist's impression of the finished development. '"The bungalows are situated around a secure and attractively landscaped environment, complete with extensive gardens, paved seating areas, a pergola, wildlife pool and wrought iron bird table, and yet are just a short walk from local amenities and bus route."'

Liz looked smug. 'There we are –'

Kate didn't like to point out that she'd spent almost all her working life writing stuff like that and that Julie and Liz had taken the maggot, the hook, the line and the sinker whole.

Julie was on a roll now. 'Twenty self-contained luxury flatlets, and twenty-five one-bedroom superior standard bungalows, with a central alarm system.'

'It'll be just like a little village when it's finished – for a nicer class of person, obviously,' Liz said. 'The developers said it had already generated a lot of interest from a wide range of people, mostly retired professionals obviously at those prices. An ex-guards officer, a nice lady from quite high up in the civil service. It would be good to get in quickly on this new phase; they've got a view over the pond.'

'You never know, you might even find yourself a new man, Mrs Sutherland,' Julie interrupted with a wry smile.

Liz looked affronted. 'Don't be silly,' she snapped.

For a moment Kate and Maggie's eyes met conspiratorially, but before either of them could say anything, Liz continued, 'It seems like a reasonable solution whichever way you look at it. I was talking to Peter about it; I thought that maybe we could get you one of those little pendant things that have got an alarm in them. I've seen them in the Sunday papers. We could get it as an early Christmas present.'

'Oh yes,' said Julie, 'I know what you mean, with a red cross on them.'

Kate watched this performance in a kind of awe-struck silence wondering who it was that Liz – and come to that, Julie – saw when they looked at Maggie. Certainly not the woman curled on the beechwood sun lounger sipping apple and mango juice through a straw. It had to be some kind of fictional projection that passed Kate by entirely.

Maggie was wearing a white tee-shirt and a denim skirt that finished just above the knee, one flat sandal, her hair tucked away in a soft knot, the tendrils falling round her face framing her strong jaw, and a pair of pendant drop earrings. Her toe and fingernails were painted dark flame orange. She had a light tan, she was wearing eyeliner, and smoking a roll-up. She could easily pass for someone in her late forties. She certainly wasn't someone who appeared in need of meals on wheels, an alarm pendant and the odd shuffle round beautifully landscaped gardens to put crusts on the bird table to keep her going.

Kate glanced surreptitiously at her watch. It was just after eleven; the boys were due to arrive on the 12.03. It would be a relief to get away from Julie and Liz who had buddied up a treat.

Liz had turned up with a whole stack of catalogues, leaflets and brochures, covering everything from stress incontinence through lightweight surgical stockings to meals on wheels. Some of them had Post-it notes on the cover to flag up pages of interest. From the sun lounger Maggie had been watching Liz conduct her hard sell with a kind of bemused indulgence.

Liz was expecting to stay for lunch and Kate realised that unless she was very careful Julie Hicks might very well flex her gate-crashing muscle one last time and insist on joining them.

Julie and Liz had really hit it off and in an odd way Kate was relieved that they were picking on Maggie; she feared, though, that unless they could come up with another topic of conversation pretty quickly, Julie was planning to steer the conversation around to Joe. And then very possibly Andrew.

Kate was torn. Did she stay and help entertain the gruesome twosome, keeping everyone off the subject of men, marriage and common misconceptions, or leave things to fate and make a start on lunch?

'So, how are things with you?' Liz asked finally, turning to Kate now that her prepared speech had run its course. It felt like the opening wager in what might prove to be a long drawn out and possibly bloody game.

'Yes,' said Julie, with a broad smile that did nothing to hide her enormous curiosity. 'I've been dying to hear all your news, Kate. It was such a shame that we didn't get chance to talk yesterday.'

As Kate was about to make her excuses and a tactical withdrawal to the kitchen, the door bell rang. With a sigh of relief, Kate – in loco hostess – got to her feet and hurried into the hall to answer; it was Andrew. It appeared that fate wanted to up the ante.

She reddened and looked back towards the

garden. Fortunately no one had followed her. Yet.

'Hi,' she said in a pleasant but generally non-committal way. 'I was planning to ring you. Sorry, I – I've been busy. Mum and everything – you know.' Annoyingly her stomach did that excited to see him flipping, fluttery thing.

He nodded, shifting his weight nervously from foot to foot. 'No, it's fine. I just wondered if you'd got your car back yet?'

Kate, feeling hot and nervous, shook her head, 'No, not yet, I was planning to get my sister to run me down there later on. My boys are arriving at lunchtime. Bit of a surprise. And my sister's come over today to see Mum.'

Kate nodded towards the shadowy interior of the house, aware that Andrew was hankering for an invitation to come inside, although the idea of Liz and Julie interrogating him didn't bear thinking about.

'Right, not a good time then. I was in town, just passing,' he said, gazing back towards the garden, waving a hand to encompass something and nothing. 'Got half an hour spare. Thought I'd pop round. See if you were okay.'

'Right.'

'About yesterday –'

Kate blushed furiously. Hadn't they already had this conversation?

'Kate? Are you all right? Who is it?' A familiar voice seared through the gloom. She looked around again and saw Liz heading through from the garden followed a step or two behind by Julie. The woman had no shame.

'Er no one, I'm fine – I'll be back in a minute –' She could feel her panic rising, while in the doorway Andrew appeared to be rooted to the spot.

She shooed him away. Still he didn't move. 'Would you please – please –' There was just no polite way to say this. 'Leave,' she hissed.

He looked uncertain. 'Sorry?'

'Leave – go – vamoose – now.'

Too late.

'Andrew,' said Julie, her tone heavy with recognition. 'How lovely to see you again so soon.'

'Julie.' He reddened now, every molecule of his body looking guilty as if he couldn't wait to own up to any one of her unspoken accusations. 'How are you?'

'Oh, I'm fine. And how about you?'

He smiled gamely at Kate as Julie turned to introduce him to Liz, 'Liz, this is Andrew Taylor, our local vet.' There was a heady little pause during which Kate wondered if she had time to run away and then Julie added, 'Another house call, is it?' looking first at Kate and then back at Andrew.

Good form ensured that Liz shook his hand and murmured a polite greeting but she couldn't quite stifle her surprise. 'I don't understand, Mum hasn't got any pets, has she, Kate?'

As Andrew looked across at Kate she could see the whites of his eyes. He needed rescuing. She needed rescuing. Kate took a deep breath and launched herself into the void. There was no point whatsoever waiting for divine intervention; if God had been on form he'd never have given Kate Liz for a sister, Joe for husband or let any of them run into Julie Hicks in the first place.

'Shan't be long,' she said with bluff good humour, catching hold of Andrew's elbow.

Everyone looked confused now.

'Long?' asked Andrew.

'Long?' repeated Julie and Liz, apparently sharing a single thought and the same breath.

Kate nodded and pencilled in a confident smile. 'Andrew came round to run me down to pick up my car. So, won't be long then.'

'Your car? Where is your car? What's the matter with your car?' Liz pulled a face, her world-famous, little sister, what exactly is going on face, her if you don't tell me I'll tell Mum face, and opened her mouth to add something edgy and unpleasant but before she could load the words into the magazine, Kate, very careful not to say 'we', said, 'I shouldn't be more than half an hour, maybe, Liz, you'd like to put the new potatoes on while I'm gone? Everything else is done. There's lots of salad in the fridge and cold meat. I popped down to Tesco's this morning. Oh, and there's strawberries and cream for pudding.' And with barely a backward glance, Kate pushed Andrew out of the door, picked up her handbag from the hall stand and headed out across the gravel, head up, shoulders back, the very epitome of self-assuredness. Andrew followed a step or two behind. He looked considerably less confident.

'I thought you said your sister was going to take you to get your car,' he hissed, as they reached to the gate. 'Not that I mind.'

'You're right, I did.' Kate, whose heart was thundering in her chest, didn't slow her pace until they got to his jeep. 'Although I hadn't actually asked her.' She paused while he fumbled for the keys. 'What sort of animals do you work with, Andrew?'

He looked up in surprise while his hands were busy unlocking the door. 'Small animals, cats, dogs, livestock, the usual country vet fare. Why do you want to know?'

'Those two in there are predators, they'd rip you to bits, buttons, balls and all. Me, too, if they got half a chance.'

He glanced back over his shoulder looking amused. 'What Julie Hicks? Not Julie, surely, she always seems such a pleasant woman.'

Kate sighed and caught hold of his arm. 'Just get in the car and whatever you do, don't look back or they'll turn you to stone or maybe salt.'

'It rather depends on whether you're talking about Lot's wife or Medusa,' he said, with apparent seriousness.

Kate sighed. 'You've got a lot to learn about women, Andrew. I'm talking spite and curiosity and divine retribution here, not mineralogy.'

'Are you all right?'

Chrissie looked up in surprise as a voice cracked through her thoughts like a spoon through an eggshell.

'Yes, thank you,' she said hastily, recovering her poise. 'May I help you?'

'You don't look well,' said the woman. They were at the cash desk in the department store where Chrissie worked. Another seventeen minutes and thirty seconds and she'd be on her lunch break, she'd been surreptitiously counting down the minutes with the aid of the clock above the escalators.

'No, I'm fine,' said Chrissie, who realised with a start that she had been totally oblivious to everything except the clock, her rushing thoughts, and an almost terminal feeling of tiredness. 'I was just drifting off, you know how it is sometimes.'

The woman peered at her name badge; it had, 'Christine Calvert, Team Leader,' printed on it in discreet gold lettering. Her apparent concern turned quickly to disapproval. 'I'm surprised they don't make you drift off in your own time, once you get to a senior level. What sort of example does it set, the girls in here are surly enough as it is. Or half sharp.'

Chrissie buckled her smile down in case it slid off. 'I'm terribly sorry, madam, would you like to make a complaint? I'd be very happy to take you to see our customer services manager.'

The woman sucked her teeth as if considering

and then said, 'I don't suppose it would do any good and besides I'm in a hurry. Have you got this in a size 16?' She thrust a skimpy black and red cocktail frock towards Chrissie. It had a kind of gathered, ruched arrangement crawling up over one shoulder, curling around the low neckline like a deformed caterpillar, and held in place just above the collarbone by two faux silk roses. One black, one red. It was tasteless, shiny and very, very expensive.

'Is it for you, madam?' asked Chrissie, taking the dress from her, politeness straining at the seams.

The woman nodded and Chrissie wondered how she could tactfully point out that unless the woman planned to have the dress liquidised and sprayed on she would need at least a size 20. Staring at the woman's face – a study in superiority – Chrissie was very tempted not to bother with the tact. Maybe it was time to change careers as well as houses.

'Well, *have* you?' the woman demanded. 'I'm here in my lunch hour.'

Chrissie nodded and, leading the way across the shop floor, encouraged the woman back towards the area where the red and black dress and several other overblown concoctions hung on padded hangers to emphasis their exclusivity.

'Yes, I think we have,' she said. 'Let me see what else we've got.' She pulled out a spiteful floor-length black sheath that wouldn't have looked out of place on Morticia Addams, had it not been for the pod of dolphins picked out in blue and silver lurex swimming purposefully up over one breast.

'There's a matching ecru trimmed jacket with this,' she said, handing it across to the woman. 'With a contrasting silver lining.' Payback would be such sweet revenge. This woman and her tasteless choice in frocks unknowingly would get it all, for her feelings of loss, and hurt and anger and Joe, for Chrissie's frustration and all the other things that weren't right with the world.

The woman sniffed imperiously. 'Fish?'

Chrissie, now smiling for England said, 'They're mammals actually, and ten per cent of the proceeds from this particular evening dress are being donated to the Oceanic Dolphin Research Fund. Why don't you go and try it on – you've got the height to carry it off.'

The woman peered at the dress. 'I was more thinking black and red.'

Chrissie wasn't put off that easily. She nodded as if reflecting on her comments. 'Fine, but why don't you try it anyway while I see what else we have in your size. How do you feel about owls?'

'So how did your move go, Julie?' asked Maggie in a cheery, good hostess voice. 'You seem to have settled in very quickly. It's a lovely spot up there, and a very nice house – ideal for your girls. And so kind of you to bring a cake, I'm sure you've got lots of other things on your mind at the moment besides baking.'

Maggie winced; maybe that was a poor choice of words but she was rapidly running out of steam. It was obvious that Julie's brain was working in overdrive. They were all back out on the terrace, Kate was off God knows where with the vet, and Maggie was sitting between Julie and Liz, sipping her fruit juice, struggling to keep the two of them at bay. It was an uphill struggle.

Liz had put the new potatoes on but it would be a few minutes yet before Maggie could call attention to them and suggest they might need checking or stirring or draining or something;

she'd been thinking all sorts of possibilities. And how long she could reasonably hold out before having to invite Julie for lunch?

'Isn't it glorious today? Although we could do with some rain. For the garden.'

The two younger women both looked at her with an expression that suggested they were expecting an explanation or possibly blood, certainly not an impromptu weather report. Maggie smiled again. It was like casting rose petals before heavy artillery.

Taking a long pull on her drink gave Maggie a few seconds to regroup her thoughts. Did she, assuming natural politeness would dam the great tidal surge of curiosity, steer the conversation towards holidays or shopping, or the price of fish? Or would it be better to launch into some vague résumé of Kate's current situation (despite her not fully understanding the vet connection), offering a scant explanation for Kate's behaviour or just wait for this show of good manners to crumble and for Liz and Julie – like two rabid Jesuits from the Spanish Inquisition – to break out the nasty sharp probing questions.

'Where did Kate say her car was?' asked Liz, gazing unfocused at the house.

'I'm thinking of remodelling this part of the

garden,' Maggie parried, aiming her remark squarely at Julie, well aware that besides sounding extremely evasive her unrelated reply also made her sound slightly demented, which played straight into Liz's ideas about sheltered housing, meals on wheels and bird tables.

'He was here yesterday as well,' said Julie, sipping her coffee.

'Who was?' said Liz, sharp as a ragman's whippet.

'The vet. Andrew Taylor. The chap who came to take Kate down to her car.'

Liz's eyebrow lifted. It was such a shame that she had inherited Maggie's signature expression. 'Really?'

'Oh yes, he was here when Kate's husband was here.'

'Joe was *here*?' said Liz, sounding genuinely surprised. The question was directed at Maggie but before she could answer, Julie jumped in, 'Oh yes, it was terrible. They had the most awful row and then he hit him.'

Liz's eyes widened. 'What do you mean he *hit* him? Who hit who?'

'Kate's husband, Joe, hit the vet.'

'I wouldn't say hit, not really, not exactly,' Maggie interjected hastily. 'It was more of a gesture. And it was hardly a row and then Joe stumbled. It was more of a stumble.'

As she spoke, on the periphery of her hearing, Maggie registered the sound of the front door opening and shutting and sighed with relief; at last the cavalry were on their way. Kate must have driven like the clappers to have got home so quickly.

Maggie took another long pull on her fruit juice, wishing it were something much stronger. She looked round waiting for Kate to call out. Maybe she was hanging back in the kitchen to see if the bush fire had already burnt itself. Or maybe she was checking on the potatoes. Maggie sighed, wishing she would hurry up.

'Yes, but he *was* taking a swing at the vet at the time,' Julie snapped right back. 'If it had hit him it would have broken Andrew's jaw. I thought to myself there's more going on here than meets the eye.' Julie didn't quite tap her nose or heft her bosom up with a well-placed elbow but she might as well have done. 'I had no idea about Andrew and Kate,' continued Julie. 'No idea at all. Took me totally by surprise. He's widowed, you know. Bit stand offish. I didn't even know that he and Kate knew one another.'

Liz's face was a picture as Julie went on.

'I thought Kate might have said something – although obviously she was trying to keep it quiet – though we do go back a long way, Kate and me. I thought she would have told me, of all people.' She sounded quite affronted.

Liz's colour was rising rapidly.

Julie spotted it at once. 'Oh, and you obviously, you being family.'

Liz swung round to face her mother. 'What on earth is going on and how come nobody told me about any of it? Did you know that Kate was having an affair with the vet?'

'No, of course I didn't,' said Maggie, defensively, not sure whether she ought to add that actually it was Joe who was having the affair, realising too late that by denying it she had made it sound as if Kate *was* having an affair. Anxious to claw her way back from the crumbling edge, Maggie said, 'No, that isn't what I mean at all –'

'Hello. Surprise!'

Everyone turned at the sound. It was one of those moments that in the films they would have recorded in slow motion. Maggie looked up to see Guy standing there, framed by the French windows. He was smiling. He looked gorgeous.

'What on earth are you doing here? I didn't think you'd be back until tomorrow,' Maggie said, keeping neither the surprise nor shock out of her voice.

He grinned, running his fingers back through his fringe. 'I was worried about you, darling. I've missed you so much and I felt a total bastard going away when you needed me. I managed to wrap the deal up last night, although I didn't want to say anything in case I couldn't get back and disappointed you.'

Liz's jaw dropped, Julie's eyes widened.

Oblivious to Liz and Julie, he strode across the terrace and kissed Maggie. Hard. Twice. Maggie was so pleased to see him she could have wept.

On the far side of her, Julie Hicks inhaled her fruit juice.

Kate and Andrew drove in silence down to the Boatman's Arms. Her car was parked up under the trees where she had left it. Andrew pulled up alongside, as if taking her as far as he possibly could before letting her out.

'Thank you,' she said, clambering down out of the jeep.

'Kate –' he undid the window as she slipped the key into the lock of her Golf. 'I don't understand what's going on,' he said.

'Me neither. Don't worry about it. Thanks for the lift, I owe you one.'

He frowned. 'I thought yesterday in the kitchen, that – well, that you were attracted to me. Just a bit –' He reddened. 'Was I wrong? Have I made a complete arse of myself?'

She shook her head; if only he had. Moving closer, Kate very gently cupped his face in her palm. 'No, you didn't, Andrew. You read it right. You're a really lovely man, and maybe if I was in a different place, an ideal kind of man, but I'm not in a different place, Andrew, I'm here.

'At the moment I can't work out whether you're a bit thick-skinned or just downright dense, but in case you've not noticed I'm *not* available. I'm standing right in the eye of the hurricane. Chasing me while I'm in this state would be like pulling the wings off flies; I can't pursue this or be pursued. In fact, I can't quite believe we're having this conversation again. I'm emotional mincemeat. It's bad enough that Joe is having an affair without this and and then last night, Bill rang and he said that –'

Andrew leant closer and kissed her. 'Shhhh, don't get so upset.'

Just as her body melted into it, Kate groaned and hastily pushed herself away. 'I've told you about that,' she snapped. 'Don't do it again.'

He grinned. 'Even though you like it?'

Kate moved closer with half a mind to slap his face.

'Particularly because I like it.' It was the kind of thing she had always wanted to do but instead found herself kissing him back.

'I need saving from myself at the moment,' she said, pulling herself away from him. 'Anything I do or say is fuelled by craziness; the idea of having someone on my side is incredibly tempting, someone to cuddle me and tell me it's going to be all right and make it all better, but it isn't all right at all. I've got to sort this out on my own.'

He was watching her with those big eyes of his as she turned towards the car. 'Thank you for the lift but I've really got to go and get my boys now. And Andrew?'

He looked back at her

'I never want to see you again as long as I draw breath.'

'Okay. Ring me when you get home.'

She shook her head.

'I don't mind how long it takes,' he said with a grin. 'I'm not going anywhere.'

Kate let her eyes move slowly over his face, drinking in every last little detail, before getting into the car and firing up the engine. She waited until Andrew had pulled out of the car park before leaving. It might be true for Andrew Taylor but every instinct told Kate that catching Joe with Chrissie had set her on a journey with no clear destination. Andrew might not be going anywhere but she damned well was.

In Church Hill things were tense.

'So what sort of business did you say you're in, Guy?' Julie enquired, sipping a glass of water. The expression on her face implied that she couldn't quite believe her luck. Two birds with one stone. Two rich seams of gossip to mine at a single sitting – the motherlode.

Meanwhile, across in the other garden chair, Liz stared at the two of them, utterly speechless.

Maggie smiled with delight and to mask her discomfort. It was impossible not to. Seeing Guy lifted her spirits and made her heart glow warm and tender. Seeing the look on Liz's face made her cringe.

Love was such wonderfully therapeutic stuff. To say Guy looked gorgeous would be an understatement; he was wearing a beautifully cut navy blue Italian suit, with a white shirt and a red tie and he was tanned, his dark wavy hair shot through with the merest suggestion of grey that just lifted him a degree or two into the mature, mouth-watering category.

He was hunkered up alongside her on the sun lounger, his arm casually draped around her shoulders, the other hand lightly resting on her thigh. His touch was electric. He looked urbane, self-assured and couldn't keep his eyes or his hands off her. He smelt wonderful, although her delight at seeing him was tempered with a sense that between them they had just prised the lid off a huge can of worms.

Liz, on the other hand, looked as if she had just sucked up a mouthful of battery acid. She was hunched and tightly strung, eyes fixed on the two of them as if waiting to pounce.

Guy glanced at the table, his attention wandering easily across the brochures Liz had brought; after all there was nothing there to hold his interest so he moved on. Maggie was immeasureably grateful – but then again why on earth would something like retirement homes figure in his thinking?

'Information technology,' he was saying to Julie. 'Internet, e-commerce. We write bespoke software, mostly security programs.'

Julie made an approving noise. Liz was too stunned to make any noise at all.

'But if you ladies will excuse me for few minutes, I'm going to pop upstairs and get changed out this monkey suit. Can I get any of you anything?'

Julie looked as if she might want something.

'Could you check on the new potatoes while you're up?' asked Maggie.

'Sure.' He looked from face to face apparently unaware of the landmine his arrival had detonated. 'Everyone staying for lunch?'

'Well, if it's not too much trouble,' Julie said, preening furiously.

'Kate should be back at any minute; she's gone to pick the boys up from the station,' Maggie added as Guy headed towards the house. 'I'm not sure how much food we've got – Kate did the shopping this morning –'

He grinned. 'Don't panic, babe, I'll sort it out. One more shouldn't make much difference. Oh, and by the way, I came in off the bypass. You know that new estate up by the swimming pool that we were looking at? They've got a sign up saying the show-houses are opening up next weekend. I thought maybe we could go and take a look if you like?'

Ruefully, Maggie glanced down at her leg.

Guy laughed. 'Okay. Ground floor and blue prints then,' and then even more playfully, 'or I could maybe give you a piggyback.' And then he was gone.

'Well, well, well,' said Julie almost to herself, with a smile so wide it looked as if her face might just split in two.

'Mother,' snapped Liz, coming to with a vengeance. 'Would you like to tell me exactly what is going on here? This can't be right. That man was the lodger last time I saw him.'

Maggie, voice very steady said, 'You assumed Guy was the lodger.'

Liz blushed furiously. 'Well of course I did. What else could he be? I mean this is – is – ridiculous. It's worse than ridiculous, it's disgusting. He's barely out of short trousers. Does Kate know about this?'

Maggie nodded.

Liz made an unpleasant noise in the back of

her throat that was part growl, part snort. 'What does Kate know about this and why did nobody bother telling me?'

'And what about Kate and the vet?' said Julie.

Liz rounded on Julie like an angry Rottweiler. 'What has this got to do with you? This is a family thing. Why the hell are you still here anyway?'

Maggie couldn't have put it better herself.

Julie reddened. 'I've been invited to lunch.'

'Hello,' said Kate. 'I just wondered if before I go and get the lads there is anything you want, Mum?'

Kate had come round the back and slipped in through the side gate. She still looked confident, as if the drive had done her the power of good, and was swinging her keys as if she hadn't got a care in the world.

'There's another car in the drive. I had to park out in the lay-by. I thought maybe someone else had arrived.'

'Oh, they have,' said Julie gleefully, 'they have.'

Chapter 16

They put the For Sale board up outside Chrissie's house at around one o'clock on Thursday afternoon. Joe knew that it was one o'clock because the two guys who were doing it banged on his front door to make sure they'd got the right address at around ten to. They got him out of bed, which was probably a good thing, all things considered. He offered them a beer but they said they'd got to work so he had one anyway. A little heart-starter to get him up and running.

After they'd gone, Joe noticed that there was a note on the doormat. It read:

'Dear Joe – Kate has asked me to put the boys on the train to Denham this morning. She said

> she would ring the school to let them know they would be away until next week. Hope you're okay. Bill.'

Joe sniffed; at least it was brief and to the point and didn't offer any advice or throw any wild accusations. He had a good scratch through his stubble before padding barefoot into the kitchen. The day was too bright to think about opening the blinds. Maybe he should grow a beard. It felt as if he was on holiday. Shame that Chrissie was at work or they could have gone out to lunch together somewhere. Gone up into the city and found somewhere trendy by the river. Or maybe just stayed in.

In their bedroom Kate had hung these really nice heavy voile curtains to help cut out the traffic noise. Sometimes, when the wind was right, they caught the breeze and billowed out like full sails and for some reason it always made Joe think of Provence. Wandering through to the kitchen he imagined that he was in some glorious old stone farmhouse tucked away in a quiet valley, miles off the beaten track, surrounded by olive trees and orange trees and the cheery chirrup of crickets, although Joe wasn't certain if olives or oranges grew in Provence. Maybe it was something he ought to check up on on the internet when he got a spare minute, now that the kids weren't there. But olives or no olives, it was the kind of summer retreat a world famous singer-songwriter and screenwriter really ought to have.

He could imagine the spread in *Hello* now; Joe Harvey and his second wife Chrissie eating out on the terrace. Joe paused briefly, wondering whether he ought to try it out one more time with Kate first, but then again last time he'd tried it, she'd told him he ought to be working and thrown the photographer out – right there in the opening frame of *his* fantasy.

So, Joe Harvey and his second wife Chrissie eating out on the terrace – a light salad, newly baked baguettes with local cheese and olives, maybe even local olives. Posing in front of their big log fire, and then Chrissie standing looking on adoringly as he picked out a tune in the studio he'd had built in the old winery. Joe sucked the suds off the beer; one of these days he'd have a damn sight more than just the voile curtains.

Grinning, he opened the fridge to see what there was to eat. There wasn't an olive in sight.

* * *

'You made quite an impression yesterday.'

Chrissie, who was in no mood for puns, guessing games or cryptic clues, peered at the girl alongside her. They were in the queue for the coffee machine in the staff canteen.

'Sorry? I'm not with you.'

The girl grinned. 'Bob, you know? My brother-in-law? He rang me up last night to find out all about you.'

Chrissie reddened, letting the pieces drop into place. Somehow in amongst everything else she'd forgotten that this was the person who had recommended him. 'Bob? The estate agent.'

'Uhuh, that's right. He told me that he thought you were a very attractive woman. Very nice.' She giggled. 'I put him straight obviously. He wanted to know if I thought you'd mind him ringing you. Said he'd like to ask you out.'

Chrissie's eyes narrowed. 'And you said what exactly?'

Before coming up for lunch Chrissie had sold Ms Superior Size 22 plus a lilac dress with a bodice so tightly ruched that it looked as if her not insubstantial bosom was composed entirely of corrugated cardboard. The toning boa had been for Mr Bob Sleight. Chrissie wondered if she ought to warn the girl from Human Resources that despite appearances she was in fighting form and was currently engaged in a grudge match against fate, men and life in general.

'I told him that he'd have to use his own discretion, very perceptive is our Bob when it suits him.'

Chrissie bit her lip and took a breath to steel herself for the next bit. 'There's really no nice way to put this, but I'm looking for an estate agent who will sell my house with the minimum amount of fuss for the highest possible price, not some ageing old stoat with a laser tape and a wandering eye hitting on me. Could you tell Bob, if he calls again, that I'd rather gnaw my own leg off than go out with him?'

The girl took a step back and for a moment Chrissie wondered exactly what she would do or say and then she grinned again. 'So, I'll take that as a no then, shall I?'

Warily, Chrissie nodded.

The girl laughed. 'He's always been bit of sleaze has our Bob but I had to ask or he'd have crazed me until I did. Mind you, I suppose it's an uphill struggle to find anyone half decent once you get past forty.' Chrissie wasn't sure whether the girl meant for herself or Bob and she most certainly wasn't going to ask.

On the 10.45 out of Kings Cross, Jake and Danny were sitting either side of a small carriage table, which was covered with the remains of the impromptu picnic they'd bought from the buffet trolley. There were crisp packets, sweets wrappers, the dog-ends of rolls and empty Coke cans. The urban landscape had long since given way to the flat bleak monochrome lines of the fen. The soil here was as black as jet under the summer sun, its rich darkness emphasised by the vivid greens of grass and crops and the wind-carved trees on the margins.

'So, do you think Mum and Dad'll get divorced then?' Jake asked, picking a wine gum out of his teeth. His tone was very matter of fact.

Next stop Denham Market. It said so on the rolling electronic notice above the carriage doors and then on the tannoy.

Jake watched Danny intently as if it was possible that the answer might be etched on his features.

'I don't know. How should I know? I know as much as you. Got any chewing gum left?'

Jake shook he head. 'Nah. I was a minority up until yesterday.'

'What?'

'A minority, at school. I was an endangered species. In year six there were only three of us left. The natural children of two parents, still married, still living together under the same roof, two parents of different sexes.'

Danny snorted and picked through the food wrappers to see if there was anything left worth eating but Jake wasn't ready to let it go just yet. 'So what do you think is going to happen now?'

'How the hell should I know? I should think Mum will – I dunno, you know what Mum's like. She'll sort something out. It'll be okay. Well – not okay maybe, at least not straight away, but all right. In the end.'

'Do you think they'll stay together?'

Danny's expression darkened. Jake had asked the same question in various different ways for the last hour and twenty minutes. 'I keep telling you, Jake, I've got no idea. Now get your stuff together, we've got to get off in a minute.'

'You don't think we'll have to come and live down here, will we? Will we get two holidays? Mike Eddy in my class gets two holidays and his dad bought him a new mountain bike, said it was to ease the trauma.'

Danny didn't say anything; Jake was just saying stuff out loud, maybe trying to help his fear fly away with the words. On their feet now, waiting by the electronic doors, Jake stared out at the traffic queuing beyond the closed railways barriers and then said, more seriously, 'Do you think Dad and Chrissie will get married?'

Danny groaned, not sure whether to hit Jake or cry. 'How the hell should I know? I hope not, Chrissie's cooking is almost as bad as Grannie Harvey's.'

'Oh God, we won't have to live with them, will we?'

Danny felt hugely relieved when he saw Kate waiting for them on the platform. He really hoped that she would be able to sort it out. It was the kind of thing she did best, sorting out and smoothing things over.

As the doors opened, Jake practically leapt off the train, bags trailing, straight into Kate's arms. It was so unexpected that he winded her. He didn't give Kate chance to say hello. Behind him

Danny was slower, more deliberate, carrying a holdall, but even so as she lifted an arm to embrace him, he stepped up and snuggled under it without a word of protest.

The three of them stood there for a few minutes on the platform, oblivious to the other travellers flowing around them. The three of them against the world, or that was how it seemed.

Something in Kate's chest tightened as if someone had caught hold of her heart and squeezed hard. For a moment she felt as if they had all been washed up here, dragged from the sea, the survivors of some terrible shipwreck.

The boys smelt of home and the sensation of their warm bodies curled up one against the other made her eyes fill up with tears. How could Joe do this to them? They were his family, for God's sake.

'Hello,' she finally whispered into Jake's hair, with her face pressed hard up against Danny's shoulder. He smelt of aftershave and soap, of boy and man combined.

When Danny looked down at Kate he thought that maybe she might cry too. He wasn't certain whether that him feel better or worse.

* * *

One thing that was certain was that the arrival of the boys and Kate at Church Hill changed the atmosphere no end, or at least on the surface it appeared to. Once they'd dumped their bags in the back bedroom Danny helped Guy set up the big picnic table and parasol on the terrace, turning the tense lunch into an impromptu party, while Jake was roped in to carry out piles of plates, dishes and cutlery. Maggie, pinned to the sun lounger, continued her valiant attempt to keep Julie and Liz at bay. Ever cautious, Liz only spoke between the boys' trips in and out.

'So, are you telling me that you are living together, with this man, Mother?' Liz hissed, waving towards Guy's retreating back. Gone the cordial 'Mum'.

Maggie nodded. Kate, overhearing them, smiled. Her shock had been equal when she found out about Maggie and Guy, but was relatively short-lived, unlike Liz's which seemed to be taking root. Kate's fear – she hoped – had been more about Maggie being hurt than anything else. Kate stopped and made an effort to cull her smugness – that wasn't true, she had been jealous of Maggie and Guy and against all the odds there was a part of her that had a nagging sympathy for Liz.

'Yes, love,' Maggie was saying. 'And I'm

extremely glad you brought up the subject of selling the house because we've both decided that maybe it's time to move on – well, at least out of this house, not out of Denham necessarily. Being so old it takes a lot of maintenance and it's too big for just the two of us.'

'But you were talking about remodelling the garden a few minutes ago,' Liz snapped, lips fixed in narrow angry lines.

'Yes, well, if we don't sell then we'd like to do something out here.'

Liz sniffed. 'I'm worried about all this "we" business, Mother. It seems to me that you're moving far too fast. How long have you known this man? Didn't you think it might be a good idea to consult us about what was going to happen to the family home? Or didn't *we* think it was necessary?'

Maggie squared her shoulders; Kate flinched. This was not going to be pretty unless Liz throttled back and shut up and there wasn't much chance of that.

'Obviously, Liz, if it got to the point where I intended to sell up then I'd have to talk to you and Kate about it, but surely a few minutes ago you were saying you thought it was a good idea. Or did I misunderstand you?'

Liz beaded Maggie with dark angry eyes. 'That was different. Peter and I were thinking about you getting settled in a retirement property. We'd talked about setting up a trust fund, what with Dad's pension and the proceeds from the house and any savings that you've got, so that you could have an income, and safeguard the capital sum. That was the kind of thing I had in mind, not running off with some, some boy. He could be after your money for all you know.'

'Don't pull any punches will you, Liz,' said Kate, setting the cutlery on the table.

'Well, he could be, couldn't he?' protested Liz. 'You hear about these kinds of thing on the TV all the time. All sorts of stories about smooth con men, gold-diggers conning older women,' continued Liz, indignantly, looking at Julie for support.

'He certainly looks very smooth to me,' purred Julie.

On the sun lounger, Maggie's expression had iced over and her voice dropped to something quiet and dangerous. 'I do know what I'm doing and even if I don't it's my right, my choice, to do those things. I've broken my ankle, Liz, not lost my mind.'

Liz sniffed; it seemed that in her opinion, at least, the matter was up for debate.

It was the final straw. Maggie pulled herself up to her full height. It didn't take a genius to work out that she was hurt and angry and had had quite enough. Even Liz couldn't miss the thunderous expression on her face. She said in a steely voice, 'I treat you with great respect, Liz – sometimes when it's the last thing you deserve and I expect the same in return. If I wanted your opinion, trust me, I would ask for it. Contrary to your opinion, I am not a complete fool. I'd also like you to know that Guy has asked me to marry him.'

Despite herself Kate practically skipped back into the kitchen with joy. It looked for a moment as if there was a real possibility Liz might spontaneously combust.

'Oh my God. But that's absolutely ridiculous,' Liz spluttered. 'He's – he's so, so –'

'Young.' Kate, bearing a dish of new potatoes lovingly tossed in butter by the young and oh so lovely Guy, finished Liz's sentence for her. 'I've already said that, but apparently Mum already knows.'

Julie nodded enthusiastically. She was too polite to take notes but it looked as if the thought might have crossed her mind.

'How can you be so bloody flippant? And how come you knew about this and didn't tell me?' Liz growled, rounding on Kate.

Kate winced instantly, wishing that she had kept her mouth shut. 'Well, I've only known this week, Liz and – well, I was surprised and a bit shocked too, but Guy's a lovely man, once you get used to the idea, and I've had a lot of other things on my mind at the moment.'

Julie Hicks nodded enthusiastically, apparently hoping for more from Kate. Instead Kate and Liz both looked at Maggie who sighed and then said, 'With hindsight I probably should have said something earlier, but it's a job to find the right time. I wasn't sure what to say, and I wasn't totally sure about how I felt about Guy –' Maggie didn't get the chance to finish her sentence.

'And are you telling me that you're sure now?' Liz snapped

'Oh, absolutely,' said Maggie with a warm smile.

Liz was ashen. 'So have you said yes then?'

'No, not yet,' said Guy, appearing with a tray of wine glasses. 'But it's just a matter of time. I'm slowly wearing her down, aren't I, honey?'

The boys were out of earshot. Maggie laughed, Julie laughed, Kate laughed, Liz didn't. Three out of four wasn't bad, Kate thought. Maggie looked magnificent. Angry and pale, but magnificent.

Kate and Guy, who was now dressed in jeans and a white tee-shirt, went back into the kitchen where he was putting the finishing touches to a chicken Caesar salad, ably assisted by Jake. Beside them, Danny was struggling with a bottle of wine. He'd got the bottle between his knees, gritted teeth and a look of furious concentration.

'Do you want me to help you with that?' asked Kate, nervously.

'He'll be fine,' said Guy, waving her away. 'My advice would be to stay out there and stop any fist fights breaking out.'

To her surprise, Danny grinned. God knows what Guy had told him but it was obvious they were sharing some boys' joke. Kate almost regretted not being in on it. And then Jake giggled. 'Guy said that Auntie Liz will have to call him Daddy when he and Grandma Maggie get married.'

Kate snorted and then Danny did. Suddenly they were all giggling and laughing and holding their sides because it hurt so very much, even though Kate knew it was stupid and it wasn't that funny, and was probably hysteria brought on by stress and pain and too much sunshine.

'What exactly is going on in here?' Liz demanded, standing in the doorway, all chin and outrage. Which of course made it all the worse. Kate laughed so hard that she thought she might pass out from lack of oxygen.

'I really hope that you're proud of yourself,' Liz snarled. Kate wasn't certain whether she was talking to Guy or her but whichever it was it didn't matter. Jake sobered up first and headed outside, carrying the salads.

Lunch was a trial. Guy flirted shamelessly with Maggie all the way through; you'd have to have been dead not to sense the electricity sparking between them. Liz, torn between walking out in a huff and staying under sufferance, decided to stick it out and look alternately affronted and offended. But if she was waiting for an apology it was going to be a long time coming. Maggie was still seething.

So the wine flowed and the salad was served and across the table Liz, who had a very low tact threshold when she felt under threat, waxed lyrical and long about what she feared might happen to her inheritance. Although Liz didn't actually say that – she talked about some documentary she'd seen on ITV and then talked about how the grandchildren's inheritance had been eaten up by court costs and God knows what else. Although she added quickly, in case anyone accused her of being mercenary, that her main concern over what she referred to as 'the current situation' was what people might think and the effect meeting Guy would have on her girls.

Kate, delighted to have her boys with her and not be the main topic of conversation, got pleasantly drunk, while Julie, eyes alight with the sheer joy of it all, looked from face to face totally unable to believe her good fortune. Kate smiled and took another sip of Chardonnay. She had no doubt whatsoever that come tomorrow morning, she and Maggie would be right up there on the Gossip Top Forty with Pippa the cross-country lesbian.

Meanwhile back in Windsor Street, Joe, half asleep and as naked as the day he was born, lay back on the bed, hands tucked behind his head. Comfortable amongst muddled sheets and crumpled pillows, he stared up at the ceiling, wondering if Kate had Chrissie's work number anywhere and what would he have to say to persuade her to come home? There had to be something.

Joe ran a hand over his belly. He felt much in need of some company. Female company, company that would make him feel good and relaxed. Very relaxed. Joe turned over to squint at the clock beside the bed, trying to work out exactly what time it was. When the phone alongside it rang, it felt as if somehow his looking had startled the phone into life and he wondered for a moment whether it was Chrissie.

Chrissie might be psychic; stranger things had happened particularly between lovers. Maybe that was it, maybe they were twin souls. Perhaps she had sensed him thinking about her. Perhaps she was calling to tell him she was already on her way home. And then, with the phone still ringing, Joe thought some more about who else might be phoning him – most likely it was Bill, calling to tell him what a tosser he was. Not that Bill had ever said it in so many words but you didn't need to be psychic to work out what was going on in his head. Joe had seen that look on his face.

Or maybe it was Kate. Of all the possibilities this one disturbed Joe the most, he wasn't sure if he could cope with it being Kate. Unless of course she had finally had a change of heart, come to her senses and forgiven him, although even then he wasn't sure he was prepared for the long hard journey back to salvation and absolution.

The phone stopped and gratefully he rolled over onto his belly, closed his eyes, relieved of the burden of finding out who it was, and then just when he thought that the coast was clear, it started again, ringing on and on. It was too much.

'Hello?' he said.

'Joe? Where the fuck are you?' growled an angry male voice.

It took Joe a moment or two to sort through the fog. 'Who is this?' he said tentatively. At least it wasn't Kate, he thought with relief.

'What do you need, Joe, fingerprints, for Christ's sake? North London Light and Sound? Ring any bells? We'd got a meeting booked for two o'clock, you said you'd be here. You promised me, Joe. I've got three people waiting in my office, including that uppity bloody Yank you stood up on Saturday morning, all desperate to see the presentations for the launch of their company's new product. All coming back to you now, is it? You know, the one you told me was a piece of piss? I'm fresh out of bullshit, Joe. Any ideas how I can stop the three of them from walking right out of here and taking my bread and butter with them?'

Joe felt something cold and dark shift in the bottom of his belly. 'I thought that was tomorrow,' he stalled. Actually he hadn't got any idea, not a clue, when the meeting was or even that he had one. He'd forgotten all about it. Joe paused for an instant. There had to be a solution, and of course there was: this was Kate's fault, she should have reminded him.

The man at the end of the line was silent but it was one of those heavy messy silences that suggests lack of patience and not being much impressed.

'I can be there in an hour,' Joe offered hopefully.

It didn't do the trick. 'Don't bother, Joe, this is once too many, mate. I'll send you what we owe you.'

'Wai –' Joe began, but it was too late, the phone went dead in his hand.

After a few seconds Joe clicked the button to give him an open line and then rang directory enquiries. They had three numbers for the department store where Chrissie worked.

* * *

'Chrissie?'

'Joe? What do you want? What the hell's the matter, why are you ringing me at work?'

'I've lost my fucking job, Chrissie, I don't know what I'm going to do. You've got to help me.'

Chrissie covered the receiver. It sounded as if he might be crying. 'Joe, can you hear me?' she said, after the worst of it had abated.

'Yes,' he snuffled miserably. 'I didn't know what else to do.'

Chrissie glanced round the office. They had called her up off the shop floor to take the call; told her it was an emergency. Bob's sister-in-law winked at her. Chrissie managed a very convincing brave smile. 'Where are you now?' she asked in an undertone.

Joe, still wrapped up in the duvet, blew his nose. 'I'm at home. I've just come back to bed. To be honest, I don't know what I'm going to do, Chrissie. The bastard bumped me just like that. That's the trouble with being a freelance, if they can undercut you they will, you know. All the work I'd done for that bloody presentation and he just rang me up out of the blue.' At least that bit was true; Joe hadn't been expecting him to ring. 'And then he said he was letting me go.

Not even a sorry. Just like that. I don't know how much more I can take. I wondered if Kate had rung him up and let him know the score – thick as thieves, those two.'

It wasn't true, up until that moment it hadn't even occurred to him, but Chrissie clucked in a comforting way and then said, 'Don't be silly, Kate isn't like that. Just stay where you are, and I'll be there as soon as I can.'

Joe smiled to himself as he dropped the phone back on to the bedside cabinet. It seemed he had found the thing that would persuade Chrissie to come home.

Speculatively, he sniffed an armpit; there was plenty of time to have a quick shower before she arrived. He glanced around the bedroom. It would look more convincing if he hung his good trousers and best leather jacket up on the back of the door, slung a clean shirt and a tie on the chair so that it looked as if he'd ripped them off in disgust and disillusion. Sprayed a bit of aftershave about the place. Mustn't forget the shoes, Joe thought, as he padded naked across the landing towards the bathroom. Women? He could play them like a banjo.

Joe switched on the shower; he'd be good at set designing. It would be a good career for a creative like himself. He turned sideways to admire himself in the bathroom mirror and then turned slowly to get the full effect. He sucked in his belly and put his hands on his hips; not bad, not bad at all for a man his age. Damned good-looking as well. There were a lot of guys who'd give their eyeteeth to be in the kind of shape he was in. Turning the shower on to full blast he stepped into the torrent wondering what the traffic was like and how long Chrissie would be; she preferred the bus to the tube. Or was that Kate?

The first course of lunch had been delicious in all sorts of ways.

Dessert was fine, although a little fraught when Julie – several glasses into the Australian Chardonnay – suggested that the back garden at Church Hill, before remodelling and presuming that Maggie and Guy didn't move beforehand, would be a grand place to hold a family-style wedding reception.

Liz went a very peculiar colour and had to get a drink of water.

Coffee was an altogether calmer and quieter backwater as Liz, exhausted, finally began to run out of steam and Julie lolled contentedly in one of the garden chairs, drunk as a skunk.

Guy, Kate and the boys cleared away the remains of lunch.

'Once we're done here do you fancy a walk?' Kate asked, as they stacked the last of the things into the dishwasher.

Jake nodded. 'Okay.'

'And how about you, Danny?'

'Sure.'

They all had things of their own to talk about that didn't include Maggie and Guy. It felt good to leave the others to it. Beyond the garden Denham was busy basking in the mid-afternoon sunshine. Kate smiled and said hello to at least half a dozen familiar faces as she and the boys walked down through the town, for once relishing the sense of belonging, albeit in reprise, to the community she had grown up in.

So few things had changed; there was a new housing estate here, a change of shop front there, a new supermarket up by the old courthouse, but in essence, fundamentally it was the same place. Denham still had a real sense of itself, and was as slow and warm and tolerant as it had ever been.

There was a part of her that had always longed to come home and regretted that Danny and Jake hadn't had the same kind of safe, roaming, uncomplicated childhood that she had.

City people, Kate knew, made the mistake of equating rural with ignorance or stupidity or bigotry while her experience of it was so very different. Here it was still possible to truly be part of a community, to carve a niche, to know the names of almost everyone you met. Kate sighed, considering what it might feel like to belong all over again. Maybe it would have been better if she and Joe had spent their lives here instead of in London.

When Danny was born they had considered it for a while, but Joe said he'd never make it in the sticks, it was hard enough in the city. No work, no decent gigs or venues. No, the country was the place to retire to when you'd made your money. And then of course there was the little matter of Kate's job which, at that point, was even then paying the lion's share of their bills.

Head full of might-have-beens, Kate glanced at the boys, striding out ahead of her, already showing signs of the men that they would soon become.

'Where to?' asked Danny over one shoulder.

'The Rushpool.'

Danny nodded, Jake, who was closer, grinned. 'We ought to have brought a fishing net.'

Kate shook her head and smiled; the world may crumble around them, but boys will inevitably still be boys. They walked down past the market square and the town hall, buying an ice cream on the way, heading out along the road that eventually led to the river before dipping away into the great rolling expanse of fenland.

A brisk ten minutes' walk away from Church Hill was a piece of parkland at the back of the railway lines, a public space given by some benefactor or other to the people of the town. Parts of it – around uncleared boggy pools – had been allowed to run riot as a nature reserve, while other areas around a big fishing pit, the Rushpool, although barely tame, were mowed so that wild meadow plants could thrive.

Over the years Kate and her mum and dad had regularly brought the boys here when they were on holiday, as babies and toddlers and small boys eager to track down newts and frogspawn and play in the wild flower meadow.

Today the silky green water of the pool was shot through with great stands of yellow iris and citrus water lilies, dragonflies embroidering the surface with their long Persian blue bodies. From time to time, big lazy well-fed fish would break the surface to frighten off the insects.

In the boggy areas, buttercups, hogweed, long tall grasses and rich green reeds filled every available inch of land and mire. Here and there butterflies hung from the flowers, tongues out, wings closed, feasting on the summer harvest.

Nobody spoke and Kate was almost reluctant to begin the conversation that she knew she ought to have with the two of them. She took a deep breath but before Kate could begin Danny said, 'Jake and me talked about all this stuff on the way down here. And last night with Bill.'

'So are you saying you don't want to talk about it any more?' Kate replied slowly, watching their faces.

Danny shrugged. 'Dunno, I feel horrible. Sick. Really sick. I keep thinking that it's a dream.'

Kate looked at Jake; his face was as pale as fresh milk. God, why on earth did they all have to go through this? Wasn't the rest of life tough enough?

'I love Dad,' Jake began. Kate could feel and hear the tears in every word. 'But –' he stopped and sniffed.

‘What, love?’ Kate encouraged after a few seconds.

‘But you can’t go around doing stuff like that if you’re married. It’s gross – and not with Chrissie.’

‘Are you going back to him?’ asked Danny.

Kate sighed. It was the question that had haunted her all week. How on earth did she discuss the pros and cons of going back with an eleven-year-old and a fourteen-year-old who had such a vested interest in the outcome?

‘I’d understand if you didn’t,’ said Danny slowly. Kate saw a flush of shock, crimson and raw, rise and roll across Jake’s face.

‘I don’t know, Danny. Most things in life aren’t as black and white as they might look from the outside. What if something I did made your dad want to be with Chrissie?’ It was a thought that had come back to her again and again and refused to leave.

Danny nodded his head, sage as an old man. ‘Yeh, I know what you’re saying but you and him should have dealt with the stuff that was going wrong. Talked about it, not gone and, well, you know, and like Jake says, not with Chrissie. That doesn’t solve anything, does it?’

Of course he was right.

‘And when you get married,’ said Jake, ‘you make a promise to be with that person. It might not be black and white, Mum, but he’s still broken a promise.’

Worse than that, Kate thought, watching a reed warbler on one of the bulrushes, Joe had broken her trust into a million unfathomable, unfindable pieces and she couldn’t believe – whatever he said or did or promised – that she would ever be able to trust him again. And what sort of life would that be for any of them?

The three of them walked slowly around the fishing pit, in companionable if sombre silence. Kate could sense the grief in all of them but she was also beginning to get a clearer sense of what she could and couldn’t live with, what could be fixed and what couldn’t. Against all the odds she began to feel her spirits lift.

As soon as they got home, Kate went upstairs, ignoring Julie and Maggie and Guy and Liz – who had already rung the au pair to ask her to pick the girls up from school – picked up her mobile and tapped in Joe’s number.

Chapter 17

'Joe, you can't do this, you've got to get a grip. I can't have time off work to come over here and sort your problems out. Why didn't you phone Bill, he's at home all day?'

Hangdog and hunched, Joe sat on the side of the bed, dressed only in his boxer shorts. 'I couldn't ring Bill, Chrissie, he wouldn't understand. What the hell does he know anyway?'

She was about to point out that of all the people they knew, Bill, freelancing less than a hundred yards down the road, seemed like the ideal person to moan to, but Joe had plans to steer the conversation in other directions.

'I can't believe it, them giving me the boot now, just like that. Of all the times for this to happen. I don't know what to do, what to say. It doesn't seem real. That's the thing about being a one-man band; I'm on me own, no one to take up the slack, no system to soften the blow. I haven't got a leg to stand on.' He paused, and turned towards her, eyes glazing over. 'Hold me, Chrissie, please, just hold me,' he mumbled miserably.

It sounded as if Joe might still be on the verge of tears. He looked so very vulnerable.

Unable to resist, Chrissie sighed, sat down alongside Joe and took him in her arms. Instantly, he turned and snuggled up against her, rubbing his face into her breasts, sliding his hands around her waist, while trying to unbalance her so that she fell backwards. She resisted long enough for him to groan softly and kiss her neck.

'I love you,' he purred, making the flesh tingle and vibrate under his lips.

'Oh, Joe,' she murmured. 'Stop it, for God's sake. You are such a bloody idiot.'

What he really meant of course was that he needed her, which was strangely endearing and would have been a lot more honest.

One thing struck Chrissie as odd, though. Joe's hair was wet. When she looked more closely his socks were still bundled up in a tidy pair and tucked neatly into his shoes by the bed. Chrissie stiffened. This certainly wasn't the Joe Harvey she knew. Her eyes, sharpened by suspicion, moved very slowly around the bedroom to weigh the evidence. Oh, it was all there if you knew where to look. Everything all very artfully arranged; his leather jacket there on the hanger, his briefcase standing by the door. The shirt so casually discarded over a chair didn't look as if it had been worn – or at least not for any length of time, the creases on the arm were unbroken. But more than any one thing that she could see Chrissie had an unshakeable, unreasonable knowledge that Joe was trying to take her for a ride.

Concentration focused elsewhere, when Joe pushed a fraction harder Chrissie didn't think fast enough to resist him and they rolled back in amongst the pillows.

'God, you've got no idea how much I want you,' he whispered, eager fingers working on the buttons of her blouse. 'I've been thinking about you all morning. You look bloody gorgeous in that uniform.'

Chrissie wriggled out from under him. 'Not again, Joe, I've already told you, I want you to stop it.' And then more forcefully, 'Stop it!'

He looked confused. 'What do you mean, stop it? What's up with you? You're not usually like this.'

Indignantly, Chrissie struggled back to her feet, straightening her clothes, picking up her bag, preparing to leave. 'You mean sensible? On the ball? Got my act together? You didn't go to that meeting at all, did you?' she snapped.

He made a bluff blustering noise though pursed lips.

'Did you?' she demanded more furiously.

'Look, Chrissie, I've already told you, they booted me off the project. That's the important thing. It doesn't matter where I was, or how they did it. It's my bread and butter. Sacked. Screwed. Shafted.'

'Because you didn't go to the bloody meeting, did you?' she said in a low, even voice. 'You let them down, that's why they bumped you, Joe – you don't fool me. You'd like to but you don't.'

He reddened. She had no proof, but the look on his face told Chrissie everything she needed to know. 'You got me here under false pretences. I bet you've been lying in bed all bloody day, haven't you?'

He didn't bother to deny it. 'I got up to tell the

blokes from the estate agent's which was your house. For the sign.'

'Without Kate to run around after you, clearing up your mess and organising your day, you're a disaster, Joe – what did the light and sound people do, ring and wake you up?' Chrissie growled.

He wriggled uncomfortably. 'I told them I could be there in an hour. No sweat. They overreacted, that's all. It was totally uncalled for. Totally unreasonable.'

'You make me sick, Joe I came home for *this?* For *you*? I must be totally mad. Have I got gullible written across my forehead? Have I?' Chrissie demanded, barely able to speak, she was so angry.

And then the phone rang. They both looked at it for a few seconds and then to her amazement Joe covered his ears. It rang on and on, until the sound seemed to filled the bedroom.

'Joe?' Chrissie said.

He didn't move.

'Joe, for God's sake.'

Unable to bear it any longer, Chrissie snatched the handset off the bedside cabinet and snapped, 'Hello?'

There was a peculiar silence at the far end of

the line and then Kate said very slowly, 'Hello, Chrissie. Fancy you being there. Is there any chance I could speak to Joe?' Her tone was distant and cool.

Chrissie closed her eyes and groaned in pure frustration. Of course, it had to be Kate, didn't it? It couldn't have been some bloke selling double glazing, could it?

'Kate, before you jump to conclusions, it's not what you think,' Chrissie began, knowing as she spoke how lame it sounded. 'Joe rang me from work. The light and sound company have dropped him off the latest contract. He's in a real state. I was worried about him.'

There was a pause as slippery as ball bearings on a skating rink and then Kate said very slowly, 'Well, I'm glad somebody is. Can I please speak to him?'

Wordlessly, Chrissie handed the phone to Joe.

'Joe?'

'Uhuh.' His voice sounded thick and heavy as if he had only just woken up. It occurred to Kate that despite Chrissie being there maybe he had.

'I've been thinking,' she said, which was something of an understatement.

'Me too, babe,' he said, in that laid-back man

of the world voice he had been practising for years in case the *New Musical Express* ever wanted an interview.

Kate shuddered; even now he couldn't stop it. 'Joe, there's no easy way to say this, but I have to say something and I have to say it now. I want you to leave. I want you out of the house.'

'What – but,' he spluttered.

'But nothing, Joe, I'd like you out as soon as possible.'

'What do you mean, out? When?'

'Actually, as far as I'm concerned today wouldn't be soon enough.' Kate spoke quietly and calmly with a surety and composure that she had no idea she possessed.

'What?' protested Joe. 'After all the things we've shared, after all we've been through –'

'That's not a particularly good card to play, Joe, bearing in mind you were sharing it all with someone else as well.'

Cut off at the pass, he tried another route. 'What about the boys?'

'What about the boys?'

'Come on, Kate, you know that what happened last night was a mistake I wouldn't have –'

'You wouldn't have what, Joe?' Kate couldn't

bear to listen to any more of his excuses or justifications. 'Wanted them to catch you with Chrissie? Maybe it's a good thing that they did, because now they'll understand the reasons for all the stuff that happens next. To be honest it doesn't matter what you say, how you say it, or whatever it is you promise, I'll never trust you again. And as for all those things we shared? This thing with Chrissie makes me doubt how real, how true, any of those things ever were. I want you out, Joe. As soon as possible, that's all I've got to say. I'm going to see a solicitor as soon as I get back –'

'Please, Kate, listen to me, please, you have to listen to me –'

She braced herself, holding back the tears. 'No, Joe, that's the whole point. I don't.'

'But I've got nowhere to go. I've just lost my job.'

Kate closed her eyes, fighting the last impulse to cave in, fighting all those old habits and desires to try and make it come right.

Joe was still talking. 'Look, I know you're upset but don't do or say anything you might regret, Kate. Kate?' He paused, waiting for her to say something. Kate kept her eyes shut; he could wait until hell froze over.

'The thing is I missed a meeting – one meeting – and that bastard told me I was off the project. Just like that. Can you believe it?'

Still Kate said nothing and now she sensed Joe's growing anger. 'If you'd been here this wouldn't have happened, you know that don't you? There was nothing written down in the diary, you hadn't put it in – I didn't know. You can't do this to me, Kate. I love you.'

They were altogether the wrong cards to play.

Kate hung up and then lay down on her bed. Oddly enough, in amongst the pain and the terrible ache, she was surprised to find that there was a huge sense of relief.

Maggie looked up inquiringly as she got downstairs. Kate smiled. 'I'm fine, just had a bit of sorting out to do,' she said. 'Where are the boys?'

'I said they could go down town and hire a video. You don't mind, do you?'

'No, not at all.'

Liz got to her feet. 'Right, well now you're back I think I better be off and get home to the girls. Now that *you're* here to keep an eye on Mum.'

Kate suppressed a smile. Obviously Liz didn't trust Guy to be alone with Maggie's mind, her body, or her money.

'I was just wondering,' Liz continued, in a voice too loud to ignore, 'whether while Mother is incapacitated like this it would be a good idea to get a home help in. Or maybe meals on wheels.'

It was her parting shot.

Guy said nothing, instead he got to his feet and helped Liz to find her jacket and keys and opened the front door for her.

Fortunately, Julie took this as her cue to leave too. She smiled, like some hungry animal, and said to Kate as they air-kissed goodbye, 'We really must keep in touch. When did you say you were going back to London?'

'Tomorrow probably.'

'That's such a pity. It would have been nice if we could have had lunch at mine one day. Never mind, I'll take your address.' She scurried around in her handbag for a piece of paper. 'Seems such a terrible shame to lose touch again after all these years, don't you think?'

Still smiling, Kate opened the front door for her. 'Don't worry, Julie. I know where you live,' she said, waving her out.

Julie looked at her as if to check whether or not she was telling the truth. 'No 62, Tall Pines. We're in the book.'

Kate nodded. 'Right.' And then – blessedly – Julie was gone.

But any peace was shortlived. Kate had barely got back into the sitting room when the doorbell rang again. She turned mid-stride and went back to answer it.

'Kate?'

'I thought that you'd gone home, Liz. Are you all right?'

Compared to the angry, outraged cow that had marched out the door a few moments earlier, she looked really shaken. 'I was just backing out of the yard –' her voice cracked into brittle anxious fragments. 'Oh God, Kate, I've knocked over a bloody cat. It must have been under the wheels before I drove off. I was trying to get past Guy's damned car. I didn't see it. It's a grey and white tabby.'

'Small, deaf, incontinent. Tiddles.'

'You know it.'

'Not really; it was just that that was how I met Andrew.'

All Liz's bluster had evaporated. 'What if I've killed it? Oh my God.'

Kate said, 'I'll go and get a towel.'

'Do I move it? What do I do? What if the damned thing dies? What if it's dead already?'

'Don't panic, Andrew gave me his mobile number. I'm sure he'd be only too pleased to come to the rescue.'

Liz looked Kate up and down, and then said, 'Are you having an affair with him?'

Exasperated, Kate shook her head, 'No, I only met him on Monday and strange though it may seem to you, he fancies me. And you can take that look off your face, Liz.'

'What look?'

'The one that disapproves and thinks life is always straight up and down. Black and white. On or off.'

Thoughtfully, Liz looked past her, through the open door of the sitting room to where Guy was handing Maggie a cup of tea. 'I suppose anything is possible,' she murmured without much conviction.

Kate sighed. 'Please give Guy a chance, Liz. I know that it's a shock but he's a nice man and he really does seem to love Mum.'

Liz snorted while Kate picked up a towel from the downstairs loo and handed it to her. 'Will you be all right or do you want me to go and see how the cat is?' Kate asked. Liz, the woman who once fainted over a rare steak.

'Julie's keeping an eye on it.'

'Right, I'll go ring Andrew,' said Kate briskly.

Miraculously, Andrew arrived inside ten minutes, dispensing TLC and pain killing injections like manna from heaven. Kate stood by, watching with a mixture of amusement and gratitude. It was almost as if he had been waiting by the phone for her to call him.

He'd even brought a cat basket to whisk Tiddles off down to the surgery. Reassured that the cat, if not guaranteed survival, was at least in safe hands, Liz left for Norwich. Julie too, although more reluctantly, finally left Kate and Andrew standing side by side on the gravel.

'I've already been next door,' said Kate. 'Mrs Hall's out but I'll nip round and tell her about Tiddles later.'

He nodded. 'Okay. I need to take Tiddles back to the surgery.'

'Stupid name for a cat.' Kate couldn't think of anything else to say.

'Would you like to come with me?' he asked.

What could she say under the circumstances?

'I'll just go and tell Maggie and the boys where I'm going.'

'I can't believe that she wants me out,' said Joe. He was truly, genuinely stunned. 'It's ridiculous. It's unreasonable.'

They were sitting downstairs in Joe's kitchen either side of the table. Chrissie with an uncomfortable sense of *déjà vu*, kept glancing up at the back door.

Handing him another mug of tea, she said, 'It might be good to have a break, Joe. You know, like a trial separation to get your head straight. It will give you both chance to get things sorted out.' Chrissie was rapidly running out of things to say to appease him and knew – from experience – that Joe's next tack would be to pull the sympathy vote and try to get her in to bed. Shame was that once upon a time it would have worked.

Once upon a time she had genuinely believed Joe when he said Kate didn't understand him. Early on, at the beginning, when things were clearer and the edges less blurred, Chrissie thought she had seen those things too, seen the sensitive artist oppressed by the competent cool-hearted businesswoman who demanded he lay down his art for a steady job and a regular income. Wasn't that the yarn Joe pedalled? Maybe not directly but that was certainly what he implied. Truth was, of course, that Kate understood Joe only too well and had a heart as warm as an Aga. Chrissie understood him too now. In this light she could see exactly what Joe was: a good-looking, lazy parasite who thought the world owed him a living and that the people around him – those people he professed to love – should be only too pleased to pick up the pieces he so casually dropped.

'Maybe she needs some more time, Joe. More space to think things through.'

'I don't think so, I know Kate, I know that voice. She's already made up her mind. It's over. I can't believe she's taking this attitude. After all these years.'

'Any idea where you're going to go? I'm sure that Bill would be happy to –' she saw the look of disgust on his face. 'Okay, so maybe not Bill.'

'I was thinking,' said Joe casually, 'maybe I could stay at your place for a few days, after all your boys are out most of the time. It's a big place with just you in it.'

Chrissie shook her head and held up her hands

in protest. 'No way, Joe, I sorry but I can't have you there. It would be crazy. I've just put it up for sale. It's *next door,* for God's sake.' As if he didn't know. 'Kate and the kids will see you coming and going all the time, every day. No, I can't.' He was looking at her with those big soulful eyes of his. 'No –' She could feel the emotional pressure Joe was exerting from four feet away. 'I said no and I mean no, Joe.'

'Oh, come on. It would only be for a little while until I get myself straight and in a way this is partly your fault.'

Chrissie stopped dead in her tracks and stared at him. She couldn't believe Joe had said what he just had. 'What?' she began, but Joe hadn't finished.

'Well, I'm right, aren't I?' he continued, oblivious. 'If it hadn't been for you, Kate would still be here.'

Chrissie was so angry she couldn't speak.

Kate waited in the surgery while Andrew X-rayed the cat.

He appeared after a few minutes, smiling. 'Well at least there's nothing broken. I've given her something to ease the pain and I'll keep her in overnight just to make sure everything's okay. She should be fine but with a cat this age you can never be certain. Better safe than sorry.'

'Thanks for coming out so quickly. I don't know what we'd have done –'

He shrugged. 'Not a problem. My pleasure, bearing in mind that a couple of hours ago you told me never to darken your door again. Have you got time for a coffee before I run you back?'

Kate didn't move.

'So, you want to go back now then?'

Kate nodded. 'I don't want to give you any false encouragement or hope, Andrew. This is just one of those things. Horribly bad timing.'

'Okay.' He indicated the door. 'Bad timing, my particular forte.'

Kate opened her handbag. 'How much do I owe you for rescuing Tiddles?'

He grinned. 'You can have this one on the house. Just don't make a habit of running down or maiming small animals in a bid to get my attention. You can always drop by or phone for a chat without a corpse or a collision being involved.'

'I'll bear that in mind.' Kate turned towards

the door and then something made her turn back. 'Andrew?'

'Yes?'

'I'm serious, this really is the wrong time; I don't want a relationship with you.'

Somewhere close by a phone rang and then a bleeper sounded and Kate could sense that despite shepherding her towards the door, Andrew really wanted to deal with one or both of the noises. 'Never?' he said in a low even voice.

For a moment Kate stared at him. How on earth could she answer? 'I don't know, Andrew. I can get myself home.'

'Sorry?'

'What I mean is that there's no need to run me back. It's no more than ten minutes' walk back to my house from here. I know, I used to bring my rabbits to one of your predecessors when I was a kid. Go on, go see to business.'

He hesitated but she waved him away. 'Go on. I'll be fine.'

Andrew did as he was told and as he got to the door that divided the public space from the clinical said, 'Can I ring you?'

'As long as you're not expecting me to fall head over heels into your arms or your bed.'

He grinned. 'Damn,' and then as she stepped

back out into the sunshine, added, 'Don't forget me, will you?'

'Of course I will,' said Kate with a grin.

They watched TV in the evening, Jake sprawled on the floor, Danny curled up beside Kate on one of the sofas. Across the room Guy and Maggie snuggled up side by side on the other sofa. Kate felt still and relaxed and oddly calm.

When the boys went up, she retired to the dining room to give Maggie and Guy some time to themselves, and logged on.

It was no surprise to find that Sam was already there.

'Hi Kate, how's life been today?'

As Kate picked up her glasses, she felt a sense of relief and lightness that had eluded her for days.

'Funnily enough, it's fine. Today I told my husband that I wanted him to leave. I've realised that I can't live a lie and I don't trust him anymore. The things I'm going to say aren't meant to hurt you but you need to think about what you're doing. It's weird but I care about you, Sam – I feel as if we know each other. You're out here fishing on the net. But unless you are a completely heartless sod either you need to make your marriage work or let her go. Doing this isn't fair.

Living together without any truth or hope is impossible and soul-destroying for both of you. She deserves better and so do you. It might not be easy to broach the subject but surely she must know that things aren't right between you? And if she doesn't then you have to tell her. If there is anything worth saving and changes that you can make to make it work then you owe it to her and to your kids to give it one last shot and if not, then go. Give yourself and her the chance to be happy. Alone or apart.

I keep looking back at the past and of all the things that hurt it's the lie the hurts the most – more than the adultery. People I've trusted and loved for most of my adult life have been lying to me every single day. If you genuinely want to talk and meet up then once you've got this sorted out then sure, but not until then, Sam – even if just to say

goodbye. Talking to you has helped me no end, but I'm going home tomorrow to get on with my life and you should do the same. It's been nice to know you, Sam.
With love and best wishes
Venus.'

And then Kate rang Bill, and without even saying hello, for fear if she did she might lose the impetus, said, 'I've asked Joe to leave.'

It took him a few seconds and then he said, 'I can't say I'm altogether surprised. Anything you need me to do?'

Kate laughed. 'Well for a start, help me to stay strong when the shit hits the fan. Things are probably going to get a lot worse before they get any better. Don't let me feel sorry for him and let him back in and remind me what he's really like when he's not charming and doing that puppy abandoned in the pound face.'

'Okay. And?'

'No, that just about covers it.'

'When are you coming home?'

'Tomorrow. Afternoon or early evening probably.'

'Okay, I'll see you then. Do you want me to be waiting to lend a helping hand or are you planning to do the first bit on your own without the aid of a safety net?'

'I think I can manage. I just want you to be around in case I waver.'

She could hear the warmth in his voice when he said, 'Whatever you need.'

Kate smiled. 'Thanks, Bill. I owe you.'

He laughed warmly and wished her goodnight.

And that's exactly what she had; for the first time in days Kate fell straight to sleep, a sweet dreamless sleep that – almost as soon as she closed her eyes – carried her away into the soft velvety black.

Joe had felt a kind of pre-apocalypse euphoria when he climbed the stairs, and oddly enough, a deep sense of relief, too, as if knowing what fate awaited him somehow set him free.

So here he was, his last night in the marital bed, and, said some dark wild maniacal voice deep inside his head, he might as well make the most of it.

Joe couldn't understand for the life of him why Chrissie had declined his invitation to stay, after all they had been outed now, everyone knew about them. They were a couple, an item.

It was way, way too late to pull back from the edge, but for some reason she had refused point blank and scurried off home. Women, eh? You offer them what they've always wanted and what do you get? A big solid, concrete No. Ah well, she'd come round and they'd have plenty of time to indulge themselves while he was staying there. Not that Chrissie had actually agreed to him staying with her but Joe couldn't believe that she was the kind of woman who'd see him homeless.

He'd have to take Chrissie's boys out for a drink, man to man, and explain how things were and how things were going to be. After all, they were almost family now.

Joe grinned and scratched his belly while pondering all manner of possible futures. The way things were going he'd soon be father to four boys, well, stepfather to two. Maybe they could form a group and he could manage then – a Jackson thing or maybe the Osmonds. He sniffed; maybe not.

In Chrissie's absence he drank the last of the Jack Daniels and ate all the chocolate digestives while re-running a few old favourite fantasies. He settled, after a few false starts, on the one featuring a Page Three model, a family-sized tub of plain yoghurt and a children's slide, which up until now Joe had always saved for lonely nights out on the road in hotel rooms. It seemed appropriate to re-run this particular one now, just before he hit the road again.

Joe closed his eyes; on the road again, Jack Kerouac revisited – a contemporary odyssey for a new age. Maybe it was time to start writing the book he'd always known he had inside him. After all, he hadn't got a lot of work to worry about now, other than the poxy margarine commercial, and he could do that anywhere.

The idea made Joe nod to himself while wondering where he had put that nicely scuffed-up flying jacket he used to wear all the time. It had to be somewhere, maybe the loft or in one of the kids' bedrooms tucked away in the back of the wardrobe. He ought to find it before he left. It would make a great picture for the front cover of his first bestselling travelogue – part diary, part modern philosophy, part social commentary, a handbook for twenty-first century hip, him leaning against the side of some wonderful sleek new car – perhaps a Jag like the one he'd seen on the hoardings or maybe something sexy and classic from across the pond, a Pontiac or a big black Buick, Raybans – obviously – and the flying jacket slung on a curled finger over one shoulder, faded jeans and his favourite cream cotton shirt, rolled up to elbows to show off a healthy tan.

'Yes,' he smiled. Maybe things weren't going to be so bad after all. Joe closed his eyes to work out some of the finer details and was momentarily put out by the arrival of a statuesque blonde with large pneumatic breasts and a tub of Greek's finest, but he soon got over it. A few minutes later Joe was sleeping like a baby, all curled up in the cosy little nest he'd made himself in the big sleigh bed.

Chrissie, meanwhile, lay wide awake still staring up at the cracks in her ceiling; not that they would be her cracks or her responsibility for much longer.

'Just a few days, just till I get myself sorted out, after all if it hadn't been for you Kate would still be here,' Joe's voice seemed to be on a loop tape linked directly to her conscience.

This wasn't how Chrissie had imagined her life going at all. None of her recent wish lists had ever included Joe.

Outside the For Sale sign caught the tail of the evening breeze and whistled and flapped. It was going to be another long night.

Chapter 18

There was a holdall on the floor in the hall of Kate's house in Windsor Street. Standing alongside it were one of Joe's precious guitars, a pair of shoes, a briefcase and his old leather flying jacket. It looked as if Joe planned to go away for the weekend rather than move out.

Kate eyed the pile without a word.

Joe said flatly, in response to the unspoken comment, 'This isn't fair, Kate, or reasonable.' As he spoke he fidgeted with his keys. 'Asking me to leave and move out in the space of a day. It's crazy. You know that I've got nowhere to go, don't you? What am I supposed to do; sleep in the bloody car?'

'There's always your mum's,' Kate said,

dropping her own bag onto the bottom of the stairs.

One in, one out, and astonishing, she thought, how even now Joe was expecting her to problem solve for him. Or was she being unreasonable?

'Oh right, of course, my mum's, I'd forgotten,' Joe snapped sarcastically. 'You have got to be bloody joking. I'm not going to tell her that you've thrown me out, how does it sound, for God's sake?'

Kate's expression didn't falter but her mind did. Wouldn't it be better, kinder, to let him stay until he found a place to go? How long would it take to find a flat or a room? Kate squared her shoulders to strengthen her resolve. Wouldn't it be nice to be able to snuff out that renegade voice in her head, the one that always saw the other point of view, the one that always pointed out her mistakes with such snippy accuracy? Kate had no idea when she would have this much strength again; maybe it was a one-shot deal. Maybe it was now or never.

Kate shrugged. 'To be honest, Joe, I don't care how it sounds. What about going to your sister's in Welwyn Garden City?'

'Yeh,' he said without enthusiasm. 'And tell her what?'

Kate said nothing, so Joe continued, 'It's not right in this day and age, we could have gone to counselling, worked it through. We still could. Maybe you should go to see the doctor.'

Still Kate said nothing. Working it through, to her mind, meant being persuaded by Joe that what he had done was perfectly reasonable and that she was the one with the problem. Even if that was true, Kate had no wish to hear it from some intense well-spoken neurotic who said 'we' all the time and tried to look totally involved while surreptitiously glancing at his or her watch. Kate paused, wondering where on earth that image came from and then realised with a start that it was the way Chrissie had described a counselling session she and her ex had had with a woman from Relate. Kate closed her eyes for an instant; God what was she ever going to do without Chrissie?

Meanwhile Joe looked past her towards the door. 'So where are the boys now, then?'

Kate hesitated before framing her reply. Was everything she ever said or did going be considered and reconsidered to gauge the effects? It would've been a cheap shot to say if Joe was that bothered about the boys he wouldn't have shagged Chrissie in the family bed while there was any chance they might catch him in the act, but she didn't use it. 'They're still up at Mum's. She said they could stay there for a couple more days. Guy'll put them on the train on Sunday morning.'

Joe didn't ask her who Guy was, instead he said, 'Kate, about the boys –' and took a step towards her.

Kate leapt back.

'What? What?' he demanded furiously, throwing up his hands up in the air. 'What do you think I'm going to do? Bite? Hit you? What?' He looked totally shocked by her behaviour.

Kate shook her head; it had been an instinctive reaction, certainly not something she was able to rationalise. 'I don't know what you're capable of any more, Joe, in fact I don't think I've known you at all for years.'

'Oh that's it, here we go again, you're always so bloody melodramatic. What is it you don't know about me, Kate? Eh? What? Tell me? You know everything, you always have, all except for that one thing.'

She couldn't believe what he was saying. 'Can't you see that it was that one thing that made everything else a lie?'

Kate had already seen the For Sale board up in the garden next door. Had felt the dull ripping pain, had acknowledged it as the confirmation that all this hadn't been a bad dream after all. Chrissie was going. Joe was going. Everything was changing even though it was still hard to believe it was real. Kate had braced herself for whatever she was going to find as she unlocked the front door. It had come as a surprise that inside everywhere looked so remarkably normal. How was that possible when everything had changed?

'I don't want to have this conversation,' said Kate, 'I just want you to go, Joe.'

For a moment, Kate thought he might protest, or plead or, worse still, just stand there with that lost, sad, puppy dog look on his face. But no, Joe sighed, picked up his belongings and walked out of the front door as if it was the most normal thing in the world.

'I'll call you about my stuff as soon as I've got myself sorted out. All right?'

The way he said it, Kate guessed he was hoping that she would change her mind and call him back. He seemed genuinely surprised when she let him go.

Closing the door behind him, Kate dropped the catch on the Yale; surely to God it couldn't be this easy?

* * *

'So how did it go? Shoot him, did you?'

Kate had been dozing in an armchair in front of the television and picked the phone up as a reflex as she resurfaced from sleep. 'Sorry?' she mumbled thickly. 'What? Who is this?' Her mouth felt – and tasted – as if a family of pigeons had been nesting in it.

'I saw your light on and wondered if you were all right or whether I needed to ring the armed response team – talk you into putting the gun down, giving yourself up?'

'Piss off, Bill,' Kate groaned, 'I was asleep.'

'And there was me thinking I was being a conscientious member of the community.'

Kate grunted, while her mind busied itself replaying the last few hours.

There had been the long slow trawl through the house a room at a time, cleaning and washing and opening windows, throwing away all kinds of things that had lingered on the shoreline of shall we keep it for months, in some cases years. It seemed as if somehow Kate could exorcise some of the pain by clearing out, cleaning and scrubbing it away. The terrace outside their back door was now stacked with refuse sacks and boxes and bags.

The pain had receded a little but, despite the

sleep, Kate felt tired and hungry.

'Have you eaten yet?'

'Christ,' said Bill. 'Don't tell me that you whacked him and cooked him and you want me to help eat the evidence? Phuh, no way, I'm very conservative when it comes to diet.'

Kate sighed; bloody creatives. 'Stop trying to come up with something clever,' she snapped. 'It's beginning to annoy me. I was thinking more along the lines of a Chinese takeaway rather than a foray into cannibalism. Besides, there's no way I could haul him into the bath and dismember him all on my own.'

'And me without a chainsaw.'

Kate glanced around the sitting room. Despite the big clear-up she hadn't touched any of Joe's things, afraid that somehow in the touch, or the smell, or the feel of a jumper or the shiny rub of a CD case she might unleash some genie, some memory long forgotten, that would leap out and undo her resolve. So in amongst the cleaning frenzy there remained peculiar outcrops of Joe's possessions, islets and archipelagos, all around the house left for stronger, more resolute times. Kate was worried that if she touched them she might discover that secretly she still wanted Joe back, an emotional connection rekindled by contagion.

Therefore, on an otherwise spotless kitchen floor, were a pair of his trainers, one upright, one on its side, untouched, caged within a neat circle of grime. On the landing were a jacket and a single sock, hoovered round but left for dead where they had fallen or more likely where Joe had dropped them. And here in the sitting room three guitars stood sentinel like small guardsmen by the bookcase that was crammed with shared CDs, shared books, and things chosen with the both of them in mind. Kate shuddered. Maybe tomorrow she'd be able to begin clearing his things away, put everything in the spare room, but today it seemed impossible. What she needed was one of those snake handling sticks, long enough so that no part of him touched her.

'Actually now you come to mention it, I'm famished. Do you want me to order?' Bill was saying.

'If you want to. What are you doing at home on a Friday evening anyway?' Friday? Kate shivered. Was that all it was? Was it only a week since her supper party? It felt like a year ago.

'Work, I've just filed a load of negs, got my accounts up to date. I've been a really good boy –

got it all done tonight so's I could give myself the whole of the weekend off as a reward. And –' he stopped.

'And?'

'And are the boys home with you?'

Kate wasn't convinced that was what Bill planned to say but decided not to chase him to ground. 'No, they're still in Norfolk with my mum.'

'Right, well in that case I won't need to order up a lorryload. How did it go with Joe?'

For a man it was a nicely sneaked in question. 'I don't think I've got enough words to describe it. I've been with Joe so long. I've lost –' Kate stopped herself from following through with the rest of the sentence. She had lost a whole life and two of the people she loved most in the world in one foul swoop. People who she had truly believed cared for her and had her best interests at heart. A friend and lover all gone, just like that. That pain, that great raw gaping hole, would be a very long time healing.

'He left,' she said, 'what else is there to say?'

'Any idea where he went?'

'Don't hold back will you, Bill? I had no idea you were so nosy.'

He made a peculiar little noise that might or might not have been an apology but Kate carried on. 'At the moment, to be honest, I really don't care where he is. I've got his mobile number if I need to get hold of him.' She glanced round the sitting room. 'Always assuming he's remembered to take it with him.'

'And you?'

Kate stretched, trying to gauge how her mind and body responded. 'I'm completely knackered, mixed up. Angry. Shaky, shell-shocked, ragged around the edges. How specific do you need this to be, Bill? I've cleaned the house from top to bottom, worked myself to a standstill. Oh, and I had a man round to change the locks.'

'Jesus. Bit drastic, isn't it?'

'It seemed like the right thing to do. It's a gesture; Joe's got a key, Chrissie's got a key –' The words ground to a halt.

'So Chinese food then?'

'Uhuh –'

'Is that uhuh yes or uhuh no?'

'Uhuh yes.' Kate snapped. 'It was me who suggested it, remember?'

'Don't be so picky. Fancy anything in particular?'

Kate groaned indecisively. 'Something with

noodles. Chicken? Prawns? Cashew nuts? Duck, beansprouts – I don't know.'

'Leave it with me.'

Three quarters of an hour later Bill turned up on the doorstep carrying two brown paper bags, two cans of Diet Coke and a bottle of wine.

'I've put plates in the oven and got the soy sauce out of the cupboard,' she said, taking the bags from him.

'Whoever said the art of entertaining was dead?'

'Certainly not me,' Kate said, 'I'm totally ravenous.'

Later, as the night pulled in, they sat in the kitchen, dipping cold greasy prawn crackers into the last of the sweet and sour sauce while Kate told him all about Guy and Maggie and Liz and Andrew and Julie and Joe showing up and well, everything really.

'So did you sort the email thing out?' he asked, shuffling a sliver of cracker into his waiting mouth.

It took Kate a minute or two to cotton on. 'Vulnerable Venus, you mean?'

'If you say so.'

'Sort of, although I have to confess I've been emailing one of them.'

Bill snorted. 'Oh bloody hell, Kate. I thought you were going to cancel the membership. Why, for God's sake? Don't tell me. It's got to be long tall Larry with the gift-wrapped willy, right?'

'Oh, you guessed,' Kate teased and then more seriously, 'No, it's another guy. He's married actually, which might strike you – and me – as ironic under the circumstances but it's helped me to sort out how I feel about Joe. This man is so nice, so easy to talk to, a good man, but he's really lonely inside his marriage. It made me understand that it was important to let Joe go.'

'What, because Joe's such a good man and so easy to talk to? It's hardly the same, Kate. Joe wasn't lonely in his marriage. He was just –' Bill looked across at her and Kate guessed that her expression stopped whatever he had planned to say next.

'I don't know, Bill, it all made perfect sense yesterday. Staying with Joe when he thinks that hopping into bed with Chrissie can solve the things that are wrong between us isn't right either. We should have both seen that there was another way to sort this out. But no matter how hard he tries and let's face it – knowing Joe, it isn't likely to be much of a sustained effort – and how much I want it, I'll never be able to trust him again. Even so, there is still a piece of me that believes we're both equally to blame.'

Bill lifted an eyebrow. 'Shit. That's incredibly magnanimous of you.'

Kate sucked the sauce off another prawn cracker, letting it pop and crackle and melt on her tongue. 'I said a piece of me, not all of me. At the moment I'm so hurt and so bloody angry and scared, I want to hit Joe as hard I can and keep on hitting him. But there is also another bit that knows that the boys and I will be fine. We'll survive. And so will Joe.'

Bill topped up their glasses. 'As long as he can find someone else to take care of him and pay the bills and sort his clothes? Oh, and make sure he turns up for work on time?'

'You heard about that?'

'Bad news spreads fast as flu 'round these parts,' he said in a broad country brogue. Not that Kate was fooled for an instant.

'Chrissie rang you, huh?'

'Yep, just to let me know that what Joe really needs is someone else to take care of him and pay the bills, sort his clothes out – oh, and make sure he turns up for work on time.'

'If that's what it takes, that's what he'll find.'

'I think he may have already found it.'

Kate felt her jaw drop open as comprehension dawned. 'Chrissie? Not Chrissie. Please tell me that you don't mean it. You can't mean it. He hasn't gone round there, has he?'

Bill shrugged. 'She rang to try and persuade me to persuade you to give it another go, patch it up and after that just to let rip, I think. Apparently Joe told her that it was her fault that he was in this mess in the first place.'

'Oh, for fuck's sake,' said Kate angrily. 'She's got to be mad. She heard me moaning all these years about Joe and she's fallen for it? I don't believe it. She deserves everything she gets.'

'She said she felt sorry for him.'

'Oh please,' snapped Kate. 'He does that so well.'

'Are you angry?'

'Angry? Of course I'm angry but only with her. Daft cow. I thought she had more sense.'

'Apparently he told her that he loves her.'

Kate sighed. '*Really*? Well, in that case it makes it all right then, doesn't it?' Kate looked up at Bill and lifted her wine glass 'Here's a toast then, to true love and happy ever after.' And then Kate started to laugh and laughed until tears ran down her face, until her stomach hurt, until she couldn't breathe, until Bill handed her a box of tissues and made coffee while she cried her heart out.

'It'll just be until I can get myself sorted out,' Joe was saying, for what must have been the fiftieth time. He and Chrissie were eating great wedges of pizza, ham and pineapple deep pan, which Joe had insisted on having delivered from the trendy place up by the traffic lights.

Chrissie sighed. 'I keep telling you, Joe. You can stay here until the end of next week and then,' she used her thumb to indicate vamoose, 'out.'

He looked confused.

'What?' she snapped. 'Which bit of "out" don't you understand?'

'Well, all of it really,' he said pitifully. 'I thought that you and me were friends. I'm not going to be able to find somewhere just like that, certainly not in a week, and what about all my stuff? I need somewhere to put my stuff. To store it until I can find a place.'

Chrissie was angry and so frustrated that she said nothing, so Joe ploughed on. 'How about Simon's room, you said yourself he's barely here now that his girlfriend's got her own place. I could use that, couldn't I?' Despite the words, there was barely a question in Joe's voice.

She stared at him. 'He's my son, Joe, this is his home. I can't go giving his room away. Oh, and while we're on the subject, Robbie left a message on the machine to say he'll be home tonight.'

'Right,' Joe said and then looking puzzled, continued, 'meaning what exactly?'

'Meaning that you'll have to sleep down here on the couch tonight. The spare duvet's in the airing cupboard.'

'Oh come off it, Chrissie. They'll have to know sooner or later.'

'Who'll have to know what, Joe?'

'That you and me are together. An item. I thought maybe I'd take Si and Robbie up the pub, talk to them man to man.'

'I thought we'd already agreed that we aren't an item, Joe, and that this had no future. Or is it me telling myself this stuff?'

'No, you definitely said those things – but things change.'

'So you keep saying.'

'We could make a go of it. I know we could. We're alike, you and me.'

Chrissie shook her head. 'I seriously hope that we're not, Joe, for both our sakes.'

* * *

In Denham, Guy and Maggie were sitting outside on the terrace, curled up side by side on the swing watching the stars twinkling in the magenta and Persian blue late evening sky. The last of the light was losing its grip on the approaching dark. Although it was quite warm, Guy had wrapped Maggie in a rug and she was drinking hot chocolate laced with crème de menthe. Danny and Jake had a telescope set up in one corner of the garden and were busy chasing down the moon. They had hot chocolate, too, but without the added ingredients.

'I love you,' Guy murmured in an undertone, catching hold of her hand and pressing it to his lips.

Maggie grinned and, leaning forward very gently, kissed the end of his nose. 'I know.'

'Marry me.'

Maggie stared into his eyes just as Jake yelled, 'Granny Maggie, Guy, look! Look! A shooting star. Over there, over there.'

They both looked up and sure enough there in the sky, as bright as a firework, was a brief but beautiful flare of scuttering sparks.

'They're meteors,' Jake said knowledgeably.

'Most of them burn up as they enter the earth's atmosphere. The bits that don't and come down are meteorites. We did it in science.'

'Well done,' said Maggie, proudly.

'Well,' said Guy. 'Don't you think that maybe that was a sign? An omen?'

Maggie shook her head and laughed. 'Nice try. What happens if I say yes? You know all the things I'm frightened of, Guy. They haven't changed.'

He stroked her face. 'I love you and want to be with you whether we're married or not. It would nice just to be able to tell everyone, make it official. Get lots of presents.'

Maggie smiled. 'Now Liz knows, trust me, it is official. No going back to being Guy the lodger. Oh, and I wouldn't mention the lots of presents thing in front of her or Peter, even in jest, it'll just prove her gold-digger theory.'

He laughed. 'I'm going to keep asking you, you know.'

Maggie touched his cheek. 'I'm glad, but you know that I'm going to keep turning you down, don't you?'

He nodded as she continued, 'It wouldn't make any difference or make me love you any more or less you know. I'm giving this relationship all that I can. You wouldn't get any more of me just because of a piece of paper.'

He kissed her. 'Stop panicking, I'm not going to force you. I'll catch you off guard one day.'

'There's another, over there, over there,' Jake shrieked in delight and they all looked up to see the white-hot lights flare and die against the ever darkening sky. Maggie felt Guy's hand tighten on hers and smiled, relishing the warm and very real sense of connection and contentment. They might not be married or ever get married, but this – and moments like it – were worth more than any promise.

As soon as Bill had left, Kate packed the dishwasher and then logged on to find a message from Sam57.

'You keep doing this to me. It's like getting email from my conscience! I've been thinking about the things you wrote. I have to have to say, Venus, that my first instinct was to tell you to stuff it – it's none of your business. But, on reflection, you're right. I've been kidding myself that it's all right to do this, that no one was getting hurt this way because there is a slight sense of unreality about it. I suppose if I'm truthful I was hoping to find someone on-line who would be *The One* – you know, the one to give me the courage or the support to call it a day. The one who will love me forever and make it all right? Not the best idea in the world, eh? But it seemed like the best option I'd got.

And then you came along. So – plan b) although this might sound like bullshit, my plan is to talk to my wife. Soon. You're right, we can't go on like this. I'm not sure what the outcome is likely to be. I love her, I really do – I know it sounds crazy bearing in mind I'm on the net looking for women. What I'm saying is that I love her enough to want to sort it out – one way or the other.

I wonder if we could still meet up? No hidden agenda, no strings. I'd really like to talk to you about this before I make the move. You sound like a decent person and probably I'm not so decent, but I do need something, courage, a helping hand, a listening ear. I don't know what it is exactly, but anyway, as I said, I work in London all week. We could meet up somewhere public for lunch, go for a coffee. Please, Venus. I promise that I'll sort it out but I'd really like to see you first.'

Kate began to type and was surprised to find the first word was, 'Okay.'

Just as she got to the end, her mobile rang, once, twice. Kate glanced down at the name. It was Andrew. Smiling, she picked up. 'I thought I told you never to call me again?'

He laughed. 'Long time never. It's not too late, is it?'

'For what?'

'I just wondered how things were going.' She looked at the computer screen. 'Fine. I'm just arranging a blind date with an axe-wielding psychopath.'

'Sam57?'

'Yeh, he's promised me he's going to talk to his wife.'

'And you believe him?'

'Maybe I'm just gullible.'

'Do I need to tell you to be careful?'

'No.'

'Where are you going to meet him?'

Although it was getting late, Julie Hicks was still on the phone to her mother. She had already rung her sister who was two years younger than Kate and Julie but who remembered Kate very well.

The girls were in bed asleep. Malcolm was still upstairs in his office working. Julie glanced resentfully towards the stairs. It was such a shame Keith had had to go home, she missed the company and the attention and the way he insisted on fixing her a drink once the children were tucked up in bed at night.

Most of all, though, she missed the way Keith had watched her cleavage as though it was some sort of profound pagan mystery and the way that once Malcolm had gone off to work in the morning, he had very quietly tip-toed across the landing and slipped into bed beside her.

In the her house in Norwich Liz checked on the girls, and then checked that Maria, the au pair, who should be off any minute for her language class, had cleaned the kitchen, and then finally checked her phone messages. She would have liked to have checked on Peter too, but the door to his office was firmly closed and he always got terribly annoyed if she disturbed him while he was working.

Liz did feel that tonight the things she wanted to discuss with him were important, perhaps not an emergency, not life or death as such, but it was still very important. Normally they had dinner together but tonight he said he'd have his on a tray in the study as he had to get some work out of the way before Tokyo closed or was it opened? It might have been New York actually.

Liz couldn't settle. She flicked through the TV stations and then through the cable channels looking for something to take her mind off her mother and Guy. What sort of name was that for a man?

She had always assumed that when Maggie died she and Kate would have half the house each and half of the estate, but what would happen if Maggie really did get married? What if Guy was a philanthropist and decided to adopt half a dozen Rumanian orphans? What if he already had family; Liz instantly imagined four small handsome Guy lookalikes, standing shoulder to shoulder in descending height in a neat row in the hall at Church Hill. They were all dressed in designer casuals and wearing black armbands. Where would she and Kate stand then?

Worse still, what if Guy really was a philanderer, what if he had spun Maggie some yarn, and took her for every penny she had and more besides, what if he made her borrow money she hadn't got to pay for operations on children that didn't exist?

Liz stood up, face screwed tight with anxiety, full to the brim with righteous indignation. This had to stop and it had to stop right now.

She hammered on Peter's office door.

'What it is?'

'Let me in, I have to talk to you,' snapped Liz.

'I'll be out in a little while,' said the disembodied voice. 'I'm just finishing up here.'

Liz sighed and under her breath murmured, 'Those bloody children are stealing my birthright.'

Peter opened the door and smiled. 'That was good timing, Lizzie. I've just finished, now what did you want? I was about to have a coffee.'

She peered at him. 'I told you about the article I read in the doctor's. It's not good for your prostate, you'll be awake all night, and what have I said to you about calling me Lizzie?'

Peter sighed. 'What is it?'

'I need to talk to you.' She looked him up and down. 'I wish you wouldn't wear tee-shirts about the house, Peter. What sort of message does it give to people? I had Marie put out a lovely polo shirt on your bed. Kingfisher blue.

Now, I need to talk to you about my mother and this man she's been seeing.'

Peter followed her wordlessly downstairs.

As they got to the hall, Liz glanced at the phone and wondered fleetingly whether it was too late to ring Julie.

Chapter 19

'What do you think you're doing Kate? This is absolutely crazy. You've got no idea at *all* who this bloke is. You don't know anything about him. He could be spinning you any sort of yarn; you know that, don't you? He could be anybody. He could be a serial killer, an axe murderer . . . He could be Joe –'

Kate swung round and glared at Bill. 'Okay, that's enough. You've made your point. You know, you're beginning to sound just like Andrew.'

'Oh, so you've told the bloody vet as well, have you? At least we won't have any problem getting people to come forward and identify the body. I thought you weren't going to have anything to do with him?'

'Andrew? I'm not. He just can't take a hint. He rang me last night. If it's any consolation, he thinks I'm crazy too.'

'I like that man more and more with every passing day,' said Bill dryly.

'I told him that I never wanted to speak to him again.'

Bill pulled out a stool and sat down. 'I thought that's what you told him last week.'

'I did. And the week before that. He's very thick-skinned.' Kate shimmied the summer dress down that she was wearing, pulling it straight over her thighs.

'Very nice, it'll look wonderful on the police reconstruction. Where'd you buy it? They like to know the little details.'

'That's enough, Bill,' Kate growled. 'I've already told you I'm going to meet Sam, and nothing you say or do is going to put me off, so you might as well save your breath and make the coffee while I paint on a face. I promised, so I'm going. So there.'

Bill snorted 'You promised? Oh very grown-up, and that makes it all right, does it?'

'Yes. And you can stop looking at me like that,' Kate said, rootling through her handbag for her make-up bag. Behind her, Bill took two cups off the rack and poured them both a coffee from the machine on the counter.

'Like what?' he protested.

'You know, all indignant and disapproving. You'll get crow's-feet and one of those nasty sulky snap-shut mouths and thin lips like a ventriloquist's dummy.'

Bill sighed. 'I can't help it, Kate. I think you're nuts.'

She grinned and, taking the cup out off his fingers, kissed him on the top of the head. 'I'm so glad that someone appreciates my finer qualities.'

He gave her a sarky look.

It was all arranged. Kate had confirmed the time and place the night before by email: Kings Cross at high noon. Kate and Sam57 had agreed that they would both be carrying a single yellow rose. Kate's rose, snipped off a bush in the back garden, was waiting in a jam jar on the draining board; maybe she ought to take a couple of spares in case it got mashed on the bus. Almost in spite of herself Kate was excited about meeting Sam, even though it marked an end rather than a beginning. Getting ready, Kate had experienced an odd sense of both expectation and adventure. It felt like the closing of a circle.

It was hard not to try and imagine what he might look like. Would he look hangdog and hard done by? A gentle man trapped inside a loveless marriage? Or would he be a flirty Jack the lad stringing her along, seeing what he could get? Would he fancy her? Worse still would she fancy him? It would be good to find out one way or the other.

The boys were both at school and despite everything that was going on, they seemed okay. More than okay. Certainly much better than Kate had expected. Without Joe about the place life was altogether quieter and calmer. Although it was only the beginning of their life without him, Kate had a feeling that they were going to be fine. Better than fine. Danny appeared to have matured as a result of Joe's going, almost immediately growing to fill the space his dad had left.

In the few weeks since Joe had been gone, Danny had been clearing up and tidying his things away without being nagged, even chivvying Jake into doing his homework, unpacking the dish-washer and taking out the bins. Kate was aware that it would most probably pass once the novelty wore off but still, she was touched by their gesture of support.

Even though there was still a terribly bitter taste in her mouth and a real keening of betrayal, Kate also had a sense of having escaped from something that she couldn't quite define. A thing that was haunted by decay and a long slow lingering decline. In its place was a flicker of hope and optimism and those feelings gleamed and glittered like one pristine cut crystal glass in amongst a heap of broken shards.

Outside in Windsor Street it was a beautiful warm July day. Through the kitchen window, summer was announcing its presence, overblown and noisy, filling the garden with big dusty roses and a mass of curling unfurling reckless green, the cornflower blue sky peering enthusiastically between the trees and bushes at the bottom of the garden.

Another week or so and the boys would be breaking up for the summer holidays. Kate planned to spend part of it with Guy and Maggie in Denham. One thing Kate had realised in those few days she'd been staying there was that she wanted to be closer to her mum, at least close enough to have the kind of conversations that they both needed to have.

'So, what if he turns out to a be total weirdo?' Bill was saying.

He had dropped by for a coffee on his way back from seeing a client and caught Kate in the final throes of getting ready. Now he was leaning back on a stool against the kitchen units, hands wrapped around a big red mug of steaming Java.

'At Kings Cross?' said Kate, most of her concentration focused on tugging her hair into shape. 'He'll blend right in then, won't he? I'll buy a copy of the *Big Issue*, pat his dog and come straight home.'

Bill wasn't amused. 'I'm serious, Kate. It's not funny. He could drug you – you know, the whole date rape thing? He could slip something in your drink, and you'd never know.'

Kate beaded him. 'I'll get the drinks then,' and then more gently, 'Bill, I'm truly touched that you're so concerned about my welfare and I promise that I'll be careful.'

'What if he's got a knife?'

Enough was enough.

'Then he won't have a spare hand to carry the tray, and drop the dope in my coffee, will he?' she snapped. 'For God's sake, Bill. Back off, I'm going; you've been watching too much telly. I may sound flippant but I do appreciate what you're saying. I've got my mobile with me. I plan to meet him in the open where there are lots of people about, not get too close, not get into a car with him, or go back to his lair. I'll watch my drink and generally promise to keep my wits about me. If he seems in the slightest bit dodgy you won't see my arse for dust. Scout's honour.' She held three fingers up against her ear in some approximation of a salute.

'And aren't you meant to tell someone where you're going?'

'I'm telling you now, aren't I?' Kate said, exasperated.

'Only by accident.'

'I was going to leave a message on your answering machine before I left. And anyway Andrew knows as well.'

'What good's that? He's the other side of bloody England and you knew I was going to be out this morning.'

It was true. Kate knew a lot more about Bill and about his working week now than she'd known in all the years they'd been neighbours. He'd been round two or three times a week since Joe left to see if she was okay, move stuff, listen to her and to Danny and Jake. It was good to know he was there – even if he was a total old woman, she thought spitefully.

Kate reddened. 'I was hoping to avoid this sort of thing.' She waved a hand around to encompass their conversation. 'I'm a grown-up now, Bill. I can look after myself.'

It was his turn to raise his eyebrows. 'So you say. Are you planning to go on anywhere from Kings Cross? Presumably the pair of you are not going trainspotting?'

Kate's patience was rapidly growing thin. 'I've got no idea at the moment, but trust me, Bill, I'm not going to do anything stupid. You can ring me if you like. Sam and I have arranged to meet up for a coffee and then if it goes well and I feel all right about him then we'll probably go somewhere for lunch, maybe Charlotte Street, somewhere trendy, somewhere nice and public.'

Bill slapped his head with his open palm. 'I don't get this at all. Joe's been gone what? Two weeks, three? And already you're out on a date with another crazy guy. I don't believe you, Kate.'

Kate's expression hardened up. 'Sam isn't crazy and Joe wasn't either. Crazy implies that you don't know what you're doing and you and I both know that with Joe that's not the case. Chrissie, on the other hand, in my opinion, has to be certifiable.'

Peering into the mirror Kate added a nice tight oval of dark coral lipstick to her lips and then stopped to admire the effect. Over the last couple of weeks she'd lost a bit of weight and generally was looking pretty good for a recently betrayed woman. 'Besides I've already told you, this isn't a date.'

Bill sniffed. 'So why are you dressed up to the nines?'

'I want to look good.'

'He's still staying round at Chrissie's you know.'

Kate couldn't bring herself to answer him; next door the For Sale board had been covered up with a big red 'under offer' sticker. It was just a matter of time before Chrissie and Joe were both gone, all she had to do was hang on in there a little bit longer.

As if reading her mind, Bill said, 'Chrissie rang last night to see how you were, said she'd really like to talk to you.'

In the spare room, all neatly stacked and packed in labelled cartons, bags and boxes were Joe's things. Bill had helped her make a start one long weepy day when the kids were out; she had been too afraid and too overwhelmed to tackle it alone. So now his clothes were all folded, books stacked. CDs, vinyl, guitars. All the obvious things. Packing Joe's possessions had been like trying to unravel the threads from a complex tapestry, or cutting away a vine that had twisted and curled and teased its way through the whole landscape of her life. And those were just the tangible solid things, lots of tendrils remained that were far, far harder to see.

Since packing Kate had left half a dozen messages on Joe's mobile and had been to see a solicitor. So far she hadn't heard a word from Joe and most certainly wasn't planning to go round next door to have it.

'Divorce, in this day and age,' the solicitor had said pleasantly, while sitting behind his large well-polished desk, 'is really no more than a formality. There's absolutely no need to worry. We can sort the whole thing out with the minimum of fuss, it's no more than a piece a paper.'

In some ways Kate had been glad of his calm warm matter of fact manner – he had reminded her of her father – but in another she wanted to leap up and scream, 'But it isn't like that, this isn't just another piece of paper to me. Can't you see that this is much more important than that? This is about me and my kids and years and years of our lives.' But of course Kate hadn't said anything like that at all. She had just sat there and nodded and smiled intelligently while he explained in his oh-so-calm voice about decrees nisi and absolute and fees and grounds and all shades of legalese in between.

It felt to Kate as if she was in a film and she wouldn't have been at all surprised if, as she got to her feet to shake his hand, someone had shouted 'Cut'.

Across the kitchen, Bill was still waiting for an answer. 'I don't want to speak to her,' Kate said crisply. 'And I don't have to.'

'It might help.'

'Help who?'

He shrugged. 'You've told me over and over again that you want answers, you want to know the whys and when and hows. Joe's never going to tell you because he's probably forgotten but you know that Chrissie won't have.'

Kate let the tension drop out of her shoulders. 'You're right, there are so many things I want to know, Bill. But not yet. Not now. I'm really not up to it.'

He smiled and very gently kissed her on the top of the head. 'Be careful.'

* * *

‘The 12.00 for Edinburgh will be departing from platform four in ten minutes.’ The voice of the announcer echoed over the tannoy around the huge hanger-like building barely making a ripple amongst the people and pigeons.

Kate pressed her lips together, very aware of her lipstick and her hair and the noise her sandals made as they tap-tap-tapped across the marble floors. She looked over her shoulder, wondering if there was time to nip downstairs to the loo and take another quick look at herself.

Against the odds, Kate had butterflies. Shoals of them or was that flights? Was there a collective noun for nervous tension?

Kate glanced around at the sea of unknown faces wishing that she’d had the savvy to bring a book or a magazine. Smiths were open – should she nip in and get one? What if Sam was already there, what if he was watching her even now, picking her way between the travellers, clutching the yellow rose so hard that she was in danger of strangling the life out of it.

Kate took another surreptitious look around, wishing she’d been canny enough to wear sunglasses. Okay, she hadn’t lied to Bill; this wasn’t a date but even so she wanted to look good. She wanted to say to Sam that out beyond the pain there was hope and life and the promise of better things, that it didn't all have to be grief and greyness. Whether his decision was to leave his wife or to stay, the outcome had to be better than living a lie. Kate tried to catch a glimpse of her reflection in Smiths' window wondering if two coats of lipstick and a pair of high heels were really that articulate.

The main hall was incredibly busy. Kate glanced down at her watch and then at the streams of passengers making their way down the platforms, scurrying, bustling, dawdling, striding out and all shades in between. Under the main noticeboard in the huge entrance hall the people were queued and pooled around outcrops of luggage waiting for calls and information. Kate stared into the sea of faces, surprised that it was so busy. She had expected that outside the rush hour it would be relatively quiet.

Rose in hand, Kate made her way slowly towards the old analogue clock that divided the two arrival halls – under the tunnel and across a road were the platforms where she had picked Jake and Danny up from the King's Lynn train.

Staring at the constant flow of people Kate wondered if perhaps Bill was right; maybe this was a mistake after all. What if Sam was awful, what if in the flesh he was ugly, rude aggressive – what if –

And then she saw him, striding towards her through the crowd with a big grin on his face and a bunch of flowers, although not, she noticed, yellow roses.

'Hello,' Kate said, uncertain whether she was annoyed or relieved.

'Hello yourself,' he said and handed her the bouquet.

'I don't know what to say; is this a joke? What exactly are you doing here?'

'Meeting you, taking you for coffee and then if it works out, lunch in Charlotte Street. Somewhere trendy,' and then he paused and said in a voice heavy with delight and desire and expectation, 'Hello, Venus.'

Kate looked down at the flowers, a mixture of big orange daisies, sunflowers and irises; the combination was near perfect.

'Where's your yellow rose?' she asked.

He shrugged. 'I didn't think that we needed a rose to recognise each other.'

Kate grinned as he slipped his arm through hers. 'So was it you all along? Were you pretending to be Sam57? All that stuff about being married? Saving me from the vet – was that you?'

Bill shook his head, 'No, I'm afraid not, I'm just the bloke from down the road,' and as he spoke he wheeled her round to face him. 'I came to save you from making a terrible mistake, Kate, and to tell you that I love you, and that I loved you from the first day I saw you.'

Kate shook her head. 'Don't be silly.' Her voice was full of emotion.

'It's true. In some ways I really wish it wasn't, but it is. Don't worry. I know this is too soon and I don't want to rush you into anything. But I can wait – and you will heal – and I want you to know I'll be happy to help in any way I can. Joe is a fool – I can't believe the way he's treated you. And I do think he was mad. Now shall we have coffee here or grab a cab and go find some lunch? Isn't that what you've got planned?'

'I'm not ready for this,' Kate laughed, clutching her bouquet and the yellow rose.

'I know, but I had to play my hand now before you met Sam, or worse still went haring off back to Norfolk to team up with James Herriot.'

Kate stared up at Bill in astonishment. 'You really mean it, don't you?'

He pulled her closer and very gently kissed her, 'Of course I do.'

'We ought to wait for Sam.'

Bill looked down at her. 'We did?'

'I promised, Bill.'

'If you say so.'

Kate looked up at the clock overhead; it was bang on twelve.

'He's late,' said Bill. 'We'll give him until five past.'

'That isn't much of a chance,' Kate said.

Bill laughed. 'Who said anything about wanting to give this guy a chance?' At four minutes past, Bill caught hold of her arm and guided her back towards the main hall.

As they walked back towards the entrance, Kate caught sight of another familiar figure striding towards them down the platform. He looked as if he was in a hurry too.

'Peter?'

Her brother-in-law looked up at the sound of his name, recognising her a split second later, his expression immediately changing from preoccupation to one of total surprise.

'Kate?'

Kate waved her yellow rose at him. 'How are you?' she called across a dense thread of travellers.

'I'm fine,' he said after a second or two's consideration. 'And how about you?'

Kate hurried towards him. 'I'm really well, it's nice to see you. This is Bill, my neighbour.'

Peter nodded and extended a hand. 'Pleased to meet you,' and then to Kate, 'fancy seeing you here. I'm going home early today to surprise Liz, thought I might take her and the girls out later. Bit of a treat. You know.'

Kate smiled and looked out into the bright blue sky above the shops and buses. 'You've certainly got a lovely day for it.'

He smiled. 'And you?'

Kate giggled and then blushed furiously quite unable to find the words to explain.

'Blind date,' said Bill mischievously.

'Oh,' said Peter. 'Very nice. Got to go, train, you know,' and then he was gone. Kate blushed furiously and slapped Bill with the bouquet.

'Eh ouch, what was that for?'

'God alone knows what he'll tell Liz,' hissed Kate.

Bill grinned. 'That you've finally come to your senses and have fallen head over heels in love with your sexy, solvent, almost sane neighbour.'

Kate looked Bill up and down, struggling to find a punchline to top him, and then smiled; maybe it wasn't such a crazy idea after all.

* * *

It didn't strike her as odd until much, much later that Peter was catching a train from Kings Cross rather than Liverpool Street where the trains run directly to Norwich, but then again Kate hadn't see him dropping the single yellow rose he'd been carrying, or kick it away as he walked towards her either.

Epilogue

'Kate?'

She was coming out of the post office on Muswell Hill Broadway and turned without thinking; this was the call, the voice she had been dreading for weeks.

As the bus pulled away Chrissie was standing on the other side of the road dressed in the uniform she wore for work; it was lunchtime. Rooted to the spot, Kate waited for Chrissie to catch her up.

'You're home early,' Kate said, instinctively hiding behind conversations that they used to have.

'Half day. I've got some stuff to sort out with the house.'

Kate nodded, and then made as if to turn and head for home, hoping that Chrissie would have more sense than to fall into step beside her.

'Do you want a coffee?' Chrissie said.

Kate glanced down without conviction at her watch, wondering what her best excuse might be. Work, the boys, almost anything rather than this. 'I'm not sure –' she began.

'I know that,' said Chrissie, 'me neither, but we have to talk some time.'

Kate looked up, 'Do we, Chrissie, what law's that then?'

Chrissie moved uneasily under her gaze. 'Please, Kate, just ten minutes – we could nip into the café,' Chrissie said, reddening furiously. 'This is hard enough.'

Hard enough? Hard enough for who? Kate thought as she felt herself wavering, felt the heat gathering in her veins, her stomach packed full of something that fluttered furiously.

'Please,' Chrissie repeated before Kate could think of anything to say. Kate looked her up and down. Chrissie looked thin and pale and had dark circles under her eyes as if she had been unwell. Surely the victor was supposed to look better than this?

'All right', Kate said after a few seconds. 'But I can't stay long.'

After all, what else had she got to lose?

'So how have you been?' said Chrissie, once they had settled in at one of the tables.

'Actually,' said Kate, slipping her bag alongside her. 'I'm fine. Really well.'

Chrissie nodded.

'And you?'

At once Chrissie's composure began to crumble. She bit her bottom lip, eyes instantly up filling with tears. 'I miss you,' she said. Kate felt her heart lurch. How was it possible to feel compassion after what Chrissie had done?

'I'm so sorry,' Chrissie began, hunting round for a tissue, although Kate wasn't sure whether she was apologising for being so emotional or for stealing Joe. Whichever it was, the words seemed completely inadequate.

The waitress brought over two cappuccinos. Chrissie blew her nose.

'So, are you happy?' said Kate, taking a sip of chocolate-topped froth.

'What do you think?' Chrissie said, her voice quavering as she poured brown sugar in through the foam. 'I never wanted it to be like this; you have to believe me.' And oddly enough Kate did.

Across the table Chrissie's gaze dropped as if she needed every shred of concentration to ensure that not a grain of sugar was spilt. Kate stared at the top of Chrissie's head, she noticed how her hands trembled as she lifted the spoon. What should she say? What did Chrissie expect? Sympathy? Comfort? Absolution? Or Kate's permission to carry on? Did she want Kate to say that it didn't matter, that it was all right, that she really didn't mind?

There was still part of Kate that wanted answers, she just wasn't sure that Chrissie had them any more.

'Actually, I don't think this is a very good idea,' she said and got to her feet.

Chrissie caught hold of her wrist. 'Please don't go. I didn't want this to happen, Kate. I'm really sorry.'

Kate nodded. 'I'm sure you are,' she said without a hint of malice, and pulling some money from her purse dropped it onto the table alongside her cup.

Outside in the street the sun was bright and warm. Kate sighed, let the tension slip from her shoulders, and headed home.